I do see that there is an argument against suicide:
the grief of the worshipers left behind,
the awful famine in their hearts,
these are too costly terms for the release.

– Mark Twain

CHASING THE LAST WHALE

by Thomas Wictor

Cover by Tim Wictor.

ISBN: 0615819141
ISBN 13: 9780615819143
Library of Congress Control Number: 2013911670
La Puente, California

For Nick, unflagging whale chaser.

ACKNOWLEDGMENTS

Thanks to Tim for his cover (See what I did there?), support, and fists.

Thanks to my proofreader Tom Pickel. Brain fog? Hah! I've got Tom Pickel, so shove it, brain fog!

Thanks to Mark McCann for his hideously painful backhanded compliments.

Thanks to Carmen and Scott for allowing me let go of the past.

Thanks to Stacey for inspiring me to give this a try. Without your input, this book would not have been published.

CHAPTER ONE

"How far do you go?" asked the man in the wheelchair as I lengthened my stride, intending to pass him in an intimidating whirl of arms and legs.

He half blocked the sidewalk about fifteen feet ahead. I could tell by his squinty cowboy face that he was one of the third-generation Okie hell-raisers infesting this part of Southern California. He'd have some dustbowl name like Norland or Coyt, and he got paralyzed screwing around with his buddies. A joust with dirt bikes and iron pipes, or some harebrained commingling of beer, an engine block, and a chain fall.

And now he made the world pay for what he'd done to himself. That lean face scared me. It burned with a merciless challenge. If I pretended I hadn't heard him, he'd ram me with his chair.

"Two miles," I said, the distance between us closing fast.

"Do you do it because you like it or because you have to?"

I gave up and stopped beside him. My heart raced in an unpleasant, bubbly way; a few minutes of rest wouldn't hurt. "Because I have to. The plan is to make it up to the hotel at the top of the hill. That'll put me at five miles a day."

"How long have you been coming out here?"

"This is only my third day."

He nodded. "Yeah, I thought you were new. I never seen you before."

But I'd seen him. I'd driven past him for years. A local fixture, he was always on the other side of the street, sunning himself on the sidewalk next to the high school. He was there almost every day in his electric wheelchair, his head thrown back and his eyes closed. His silvery blond flattop made his purple-brown skin look even darker. Every time I saw him, a chain reaction went off in my head: squamous cell carcinoma to the evil medicine man Misquamacus in Graham Masterson's terrifying novel *The Manitou* to summoning the Great Old One to Cthulhu to the end of the world. A ruminative loop, it's called.

"My doctor told me I had to start exercising and lose about forty pounds," I said.

He looked me up and down. "More like fifty or sixty."

And with that, I hated him. The next thing he'd say in his slight twang was that I looked just like a hog. He'd call me "boy" and order me to squeal.

Instead, he asked, "Are you taking time off from work today?"

"No, I work at home." I rubbed my hands so I could sneak a glance at my watch.

He noticed and said, "Didn't mean to hold you up, man. I'm just nosy. I like to meet new people and find out about them."

"Well, I have to be somewhere soon."

"Cool. You tell me when you wanna leave. So whatta you do?"

"I'm a writer."

"A *writer?*" He looked like a confused dog. "You mean books?"

"No, I'm a copywriter. I work for a marketing corporation."

He lifted a length of clear tubing and sucked on it, sipping water from a white bicycle-racer's bottle attached to the side of his chair. His clenched hands were sheathed in cream-colored plastic wrist braces with elastic straps, the kind typists used for carpal tunnel syndrome.

"What does a copywriter at a marketing corporation do, exactly?" he asked.

I willed myself to not sigh.

"Yeah, I know," he said. "I'm a dumb-ass." His smile was mocking.

"It's just that people fall asleep when I try to explain what I do," I mumbled. I was so angry, it was hard to speak.

"Now you got me interested," he said. "Tell me."

"Okay. I work in the creative department of the frequency marketing division of Soledad Marketing Group."

"Yeah? And what the hell does all that mean?"

Can't a car hit us? Or a bolt of lightning?

"Frequency marketing is how companies boost customer loyalty and increase repeat business," I said. "Uh, you know when you buy a carton of cigarettes and they give you a baseball cap with the company logo on it?"

"Yeah."

"That's a 'continuity-premium program.' If you use a certain long-distance service, and they award you frequent-flyer miles and discounts at a DVD-rental service? That's an 'external-group program.'" I counted on my fingers. "Clubs, sweepstakes, coupons, escalating rebate offers, mail-in rebates, membership programs, time-release programs, points, stamps, contests, scratch-off games, collect-and-win games, gift cards, punch cards—they all lure customers back. My company is hired by other companies to come up with repeat-business programs like that, and in the creative department, our job is to supply all the words and images."

"So if I get a coupon or a scratch-off game, you're the guy who wrote the words on it?"

"One of the guys and gals, yes." Now he could make fun of me some more.

He laughed. "Far out! You got a great job. That's something I never even *thought* of. I was just gonna be a machinist."

His response floored me. My hate turned to intense love, and I almost started crying. "You're the first person I've met who didn't think my job was stupid."

"Yeah, well, that's because *I'm* not stupid. I'm not just some blue-collar asshole." In the blink of an eye, he'd become furious. "You wanna guess how I broke my fuckin' neck?"

My love changed back to fear. "Um…no, that's okay."

He changed back to affable. "Aw hey, it's cool, man. I didn't mean to snap at you. I get carried away." He smiled as he sipped water from his tube.

Sunny-cloudy-sunny-cloudy; he was like a time-lapse video of the sky.

"When I was eighteen," he said, sunny again, "I was helping my dad hang curtains. He made me climb up on this rickety, piece-of-shit stool, and the leg snapped off, and I fell and hit my head on the edge of the dining-room table. There was a big, white flash, and my whole body went pins and needles, and I knew right away I was jacked up. I been in this chair twenty-two years, five months, two weeks, and six days."

I rubbed my beard, took off my sunglasses, put them on again. "I'm sorry that happened to you," I finally said.

He twiddled the joystick on the right-hand armrest of his chair, spinning himself in an aimless half circle. "Yeah. Pretty ridiculous way to break your neck, huh? I don't even have an exciting story to go with it." He nodded. "I know; I'm really bitter. Let's change the subject. You said you gotta get exercise. You got health problems?"

"I…wow. I'm sorry, I'm kind of…having trouble keeping up."

"Yeah," he said, "I'm too abrupt and ask too many personal questions. Just tell me to fuck off. I won't mind."

"Well…no. I'm not going to do that. Uh, I don't think I have any major health problems, except for my weight and my borderline high blood pressure. I just had my physical a few days ago, and my doctor told me I was at the age where I'd start having problems if I didn't get into shape." I laughed. "I can't believe I'm saying all this."

"Yeah? Why?"

"Well, I…I'm sorry, but I don't know you, and I'm, well, I'm a very private person."

"Trey Gillespie." He held out his right hand, palm down. I touched his knuckles with mine, the way I'd seen hip-hop stars do on TV.

"Elliot Finell," I said.

"Nice to meet you. So do you ever run when you come out here?"

"No, I never run if I can help it."

"Don't like running, huh? That'd help you lose weight faster, you know."

"Yeah, but I broke my legs pretty badly when I was a kid."

"Yeah? How'd you do that?"

"Fell out of a tree house. When I run, my legs hurt. They hurt most of the time, actually, but worse when I run." I never spoke about my legs. Trey had bewitched me. He *was* a medicine man!

And now he was an angry, evil medicine man again. "Don't tell *me* about pain! I live with total pain twenty-four hours a day!"

"Oh. Well, I'm sorry to hear that." The spell he'd cast rooted me to the spot, preventing me from shutting up and walking away.

"Yeah, my whole body hurts from the neck down, all the time. You ever burned your finger? My whole body feels like that, like I been burned. Burned and smashed, like when you hit your thumb with a hammer. My whole body throbs. I can't sleep, I can't lie down, I can't sit up, I can't do anything. I couldn't even leave my house for four years after my accident except to go to the doctor. I seen a hundred doctors, easy. I had twenty-five operations. They tried everything. I had a morphine pump implanted. I had electrical therapy. I had my nerves severed. I've tried every painkiller, every single one. I been to every single pain clinic in Southern California. Nothing works."

"That's really terrible," I said, picturing my hands over my ears. Or over his mouth.

"In half a second, I lost everything. I lost my health, my girlfriend, my ability to work. I lost my ability just to have a life. All because I was too chicken to tell my father to cram it. Well, I had enough of this shit."

I didn't respond.

"Yeah, I had enough of this shit," he said again.

"Um. I'm sure you have."

"My father croaked ten years ago. Car accident. Drunk. I made his life miserable. Every chance I got, I reminded him what he did to me. Finally, he couldn't take it anymore and moved out, and about a week after that, he was dead. Too bad. I wish he was here now, so he could see what I'm gonna do."

"That sounds…pretty ominous."

He sipped water, shook his head. "Nah, nothing ominous about it. I'm just gonna...well, let's just say I'm gonna write the last chapter of this stupid story. Pretty soon now. Time to take care of business once and for all."

"Ah." I had to get away from him. Immediately.

"Shit," he said, "I *know* I'm bumming you out with this. I can see it in your face."

"No, it's, I...it's just that I have to *go!* I have an *appointment!*" I didn't know if I was screaming or not.

"Okay. Are you going to come out here some more, or have I scared you off?"

I was an open book to him. "No, I'll be coming out every day," I said.

"Well, if you want, why don't you stop by on my side of the street sometime? I was over on this side today to say hi to someone, but I'm always on the other side. I wanna hear more about frequency marketing."

"Sure." My armpits and belly ran with sweat, and my knees were about to fold.

"Great. Take it easy, man."

* * *

On the way home, I pondered the fact that I'd have to pass Trey every afternoon. No other street led to the hotel at the top of the hill. I'd have to talk to him again and listen to some hideous explanation of what he meant by taking care of business once and for all. It couldn't be any worse than what I was about to do.

Though I'd covered less than two miles, I was exhausted. The handful of berry-flavored antacids I gobbled in my kitchen had no effect on the bubbling sensation in my chest, and an ice-cold shower didn't stop the sweat from rolling off my face and down my sides. As I dressed in jeans and a black T-shirt, I rehearsed the speech I'd give in about half an hour. My sense of fair play nagged at me; I should've chosen a suit and tie or a pink tutu, an outfit that served as an inoculative pre-shock. To walk in on her as my everyday self and then unload was to perpetrate an ambush. But I was too fat for my suits, and I didn't know where to buy a tutu with a forty-six-inch waist.

I got in my ancient Toyota and found that I was unable to begin the drive out to Valley Village. My hand refused to turn the ignition key. Starting the car would set in motion a sequence of events that would culminate in the end of everything. My Toyota was a bomb; the explosion would be slow and gentle, I knew, but it'd kill us anyway.

The bomb didn't have to be detonated. Nothing had to change. It wasn't my responsibility. Everything could stay as it was. I could get out of the car, retreat to my back porch with my laptop, and write, gazing at the cactus and aloe in my garden, watching the hummingbirds until the sun set.

For a few rapturous seconds, I believed my own lies. Then I started the engine.

I had to kill us or let her die.

*   *   *

We were in the living room of her condo; she sat at her desk with her arms folded, and I was on the leather sofa, where I'd given her three orgasms the previous evening. While I delivered my speech, she stared out the sliding glass door that opened to the balcony. On clear nights we'd go out there and take turns gazing at the moon with her telescope. Hers was much more powerful than mine.

"And I wouldn't have done it if I hadn't been really concerned," I finished.

She didn't say anything or look at me; the gentle explosion was in progress. I rubbed my left shoulder, which had begun aching in the past few minutes. Under stress I often became so rigid, I actually pulled muscles. The tension of waiting for her to acknowledge my crime also made me light-headed and nauseated.

Finally, she cleared her throat. "Well, I don't know how you expect me to react to this. I really don't. You've totally blindsided me. All of a sudden, I don't even know who you are. You were the last person I ever would've expected to go behind my back."

...Ah evuh woulda 'spected to go b'hind mah back. When she was upset, her North Carolina accent thickened until it was like a rich, golden batter. She also talked that way when she was very happy. After her third orgasm the night before, she'd smiled sleepily, put her lips on my ear, and rumbled, "Whatcha been snackin' on, man, oh-sters? Hoo-*ee.*" I loved listening to her. It didn't matter what she said; even now, expressing her shock and betrayal, she gave me an erection that I hid under a throw pillow. Her smooth timbre and indestructible Southern graciousness were more potent than any little blue pill.

"I can't believe you'd actually go so far as to spy on me," she went on, calm as ever. "In my own home. After I basically let you move in with me. For once I open the door to someone, and look what happens. That's what hurts so much."

I felt her pain in a bolt that shot from my jaw all the way through my left arm and down to my fingertips. My hands tingled and I couldn't catch my breath. I was about to faint from shame.

"Tell me again, how long have you been doing this?" she asked, still not looking at me.

"About two months," I said, massaging my chest.

"About two months. Let's see…that's almost sixty nights, give or take, that you went through my cupboards and my garbage. How did that make you feel, doing that?"

"Awful." A sensation of prickly cold spread across my forehead and cheeks, down my neck, and over my thorax. Oily pearls of sweat popped out of my skin. A jagged rock formed under my sternum, and my left arm was squeezed in an invisible vise.

"You felt awful," she said with what sounded like genuine sympathy. "I should think you would. All that sneakin' around while I was asleep in bed, totally unsuspecting, after we'd made love and I'd told you again how happy I was that we'd found each other."

I wanted her to shriek at me, to turn purple with rage and sock me in the nose, but she seemed only mildly regretful, as if she'd missed a TV show that she'd kind of wanted to see. It chilled me to my core, made me look for a wastebasket to vomit into.

"Well, you're *concerned* about me, so I presume the next step is that you want me to get help, right?" she said.

"Ow," I said.

She turned and frowned. It was the first change in her face since I gave the opening statement of my speech. "You're all gray and sweaty," she said. "Are you all right?"

"No. I'm pretty sure I'm having a heart attack." I laughed.

For an instant she registered a kind of guilty horror, the look of someone whose dark wish had been unexpectedly granted.

She leaped to her feet. "Oh my God! Are you serious?"

"As serious as a heart attack. Ha. *Owww.*"

"Elliot, after what you just pulled, if you're messin' with me, man, so help me God, I'll slap your face off!"

I wrapped my arms around my swelling, tightening, airless chest. "I'm not kidding. I'm having a heart attack. My left arm and my chest hurt, and I can't breathe. I think I'm going to die."

"Godawmighty. Don't move. Just sit there." She snatched up the phone next to her computer. "My boyfriend's having a heart attack. We need an ambulance. Yes, I'm positive. His skin's all gray and he's having chest pains and he can't breathe."

After she gave her address, it happened for at least the eight-hundredth time that I'd known her. "Gary Pruett. No, not Carrie. *Gary.* G-A-R-Y. Yes, like the man's name. *Yes,* I'm a woman!"

I laughed again as tears of terror flowed into my beard. Gary scowled at me, clawing at her hair.

"Why do you care how weird my name is?" she snapped into the receiver. "What's wrong with you? Just send the ambulance. Okay. Okay."

She raced out. I heard her crash around in the bathroom, dropping things into the sink and running the water. She burst back in and thrust two white tablets at me.

"Aspirin. Open your mouth." She shoved them past my lips. "Chew 'em up real good, now. Come on." I chewed, and she gave me a sip of water to wash down the dry bitterness. She set the glass on the coffee table and vaulted onto the sofa next to me. "Hold on, sugar. The ambulance is coming." I leaned against her; she pulled me into her chest, her powerful arms wrapped around me like metal straps.

"I'm sorry, Gary," I wailed. "I'm sorry. Oh my God, I'm going to die. I'm sorry about everything. I'm sorry about spying on you. I didn't mean to hurt you. Owwwww-wow, *Christ.*"

I put my head in her lap and curled up like a fetus. She rocked me, shushed me, told me to relax. I wasn't going to die. Everything was going to be all right.

"I wet my pants!" I blubbered. "God, I wet my pants!"

"Don't worry about it," she soothed. "It doesn't matter. Shhh. You're gonna be fine, Elliot. Shhh." I cried and apologized, waiting for the sudden plunge into blackness or the fiery pit, while Gary stroked my head and whispered something long and rhythmic, like a chant.

"I can't make out what you're saying," I said into her crotch. I could smell her through her sweatpants. In my wet jeans, another insane erection stirred.

"I'm just praying," she said.

"That won't work. I haven't been to church in twenty years. God hates me."

"Well, then how about some of my gramma's Irish blessings?"

"Sure."

"Uh…um…okay. May the blessing of light be upon you, light without and light within."

"Nice. More, please," I gasped.

"May the blessing of the great rains be upon you, that they beat upon your spirit and wash it fair and clean, and leave there many a shining pool and sometimes a star."

"Pretty. Another."

"May the blessed sunlight shine upon you and warm your heart until it glows, like a great peat fire, so that the stranger as well as the friend may come and warm himself at it."

A clamor of pounding, doorbell ringing, and muffled shouts, as though a jealous husband had found us. Gary gently slid out from under me and ran into the foyer. Two obese paramedics sailed into the living room with a collapsible wheeled stretcher.

"How you doin', pal?" one of them asked.

"Never better," I said.

They both laughed and piled equipment around me.

"Okay, we're gonna ask you a buncha questions and do a lotta poking and prodding to see what's going on," the heavier man said. His name tag read "Salazar."

The other paramedic slipped an oxygen mask over my mouth and nose and took my pulse. "Any nausea?" he asked. His tag said he was Lee-Burnett.

"Yes."

"Pain in your upper arms, shoulders, neck, or jaws?"

"All of the above, especially on the left side."

Salazar cut off my shirt with scissors. Next to him was a device that looked like a combination laptop and fax machine, with a dozen or so cables leading out of it. He stuck paper disks to my chest and attached the cables to them. "This is an electrocardiogram," he said as he listened to my heart with a stethoscope.

"Feeling of anxiety or impending doom?" Lee-Burnett asked.

"You're kidding."

"No, they're possible symptoms of myocardial infarction. Answer the question, please."

"Yes, I do have a feeling of anxiety and a feeling of impending doom."

The electrocardiogram spat out a piece of paper with jagged mountain peaks sketched in black ink. Salazar studied it.

"Yup," he said. "You're having a heart attack."

"Marvelous," I whimpered.

"We're gonna give you some medication and take you to the hospital. You need more treatment than we can give you here."

"I already gave him two aspirin," Gary said from behind him.

Lee-Burnett smiled at her. "Good thinking. Do you have medical training?"

"I'm a copywriter," she answered.

*   *   *

It was my second ride in an ambulance. The first was when I broke my legs nearly thirty years earlier, but it could've been yesterday. Everything was exactly the same, a bright and noisy compartment full of chrome, and a plastic bag of clear liquid sloshing over my face, like a jellyfish with a long stinger poking into my arm. Instead of my mother holding my hand and leaning over me, it was Gary, her wild blonde hair backlit into a corona of flame and her face in deep shadow.

"I can't see your face," I moaned.

She moved out from under the ceiling light and dipped her head down next to mine.

"Is that better?"

"Yes. I'm going to die, aren't I?"

"*No!* Stop *sayin'* that. You ain't gonna die." She turned to Salazar, who sat beside her. "Tell him he ain't gonna die."

"Yew ain't goh-nuh dah," he said, mimicking her drawl. He laughed; she gave him a look that froze *my* innards. Unruffled, he patted my shoulder. "Just trying to lighten the mood. Hang in there. You'll be fine, Gary."

"I'm Elliot. She's Gary."

"What!" Salazar jerked as if I'd pinched his scrotum. He examined her. "*Your* name's Gary? Man, how'd *that* happen? Is that one a those red-state deals, like Billie Jo or Jimmie Sue?"

Her words were like blackstrap molasses oozing down all over him. "Bless your heart. Ah doan mean to be *rude,* now, but Ah jus' went through this on the *phone* fifteen minutes ago. Ah git asked about mah name ever' day, and *normally* Ah doan care, but Ah'm *really* not in the mood to tell the story right this second, *if* you doan mind."

"Sure. No problem." He listened to my heart with his stethoscope. I felt bad for him, even though he was unscathed. He was the type of magnificent, impervious blockhead I'd always wanted to be.

"Why does the other paramedic have a hyphenated name?" I asked. "I never understood why some men did that. Is it a stepfamily, birth-family thing? He wants to honor them both?"

"Beats the shit outta me, buddy."

His indifference infuriated me. "How come *I'm* the one having a heart attack, huh? Both you guys outweigh me by at least a hundred pounds!"

"I'm a Pima Indian. We don't get heart disease."

"That's neat. So what? Every Pima gets diabetes."

Gary squeezed my hand, hard enough to hurt. "I think we'll all stop talking now and just ride along and think real nice thoughts, like about misty mountains and cool ocean breezes and the taste of orange sherbet on a sunny day."

"Okay, we're at the hospital," Salazar said. "You're gonna be fine, I promise. Let's get you inside."

He and Lee-Burnett wheeled me through several double doors that swung open automatically, into a large open emergency room with curtains hanging from curved rails to create separate spaces for individual patients. A clutch of doctors and nurses helped me scoot off the stretcher onto a bed.

"We're going to take some blood and do a quick test, oo-*kee?*" a nurse said. She opened her eyes as wide as they'd go, like a panicky madwoman.

"Where's Gary?" I asked her.

"Haven't seen him, sir."

"I'm right here," she said at my side.

A needle slipped into my arm, and my vision darkened around the edges. The room was a photo someone had thrown on a fire, a snapshot burning inward toward the center.

"Here I go!" I shouted. "Good-bye, Gary! I love you!"

Everything went black, except for a tiny dot of light that lingered, flickered, and finally winked out.

CHAPTER TWO

I woke up in an adjustable bed, propped almost upright with pillows. A hospital room. I thought I was nine again, but my legs had no splints or pins, no wires, weights, or pulleys.

"Elliot?"

Gary looked thin and haggard, as if she'd just been released from a long captivity. She cradled my hand in both of hers.

"What happened?" I croaked.

She picked up a glass of ice water and maneuvered the bendable straw into my mouth. "You don't remember?"

I drained the glass. "No. Someone mentioned a blood test, then I passed out. What happened after that?"

She grasped my hand again. "The blood test showed that you were having a mild heart attack. It's called a 'non-ST-segment myocardial infarction' or 'en-stemee' for short. N-S-T-E-M-I. You had a blood clot in one of your coronary arteries, so they had to run a catheter up the femoral artery in your groin and go into the coronary artery and open it up with a balloon."

"A catheter in my artery? That's *disgusting!*" My stomach pitched and rolled. "I'm going to throw up."

She produced a stainless-steel bedpan from under the bed.

Was she insane? "I'm not going to put my *mouth* in that!"

"Oh, for—Look, it's clean as a whistle," she said, running her fingers around the inside. "Besides, there's nothing else handy. Let 'er rip, man. Bring it on."

"No!"

She turned it over and put it on her head like a tricornered hat. "Look, it's totally disinfected. You could eat your lunch out of it." She took it off her head, tucked her face into it, and shouted, "Hello!" It made her voice clangy and robotic. She straightened. "See?"

"All right! All right! Hurry!" She held it out; I leaned over and retched into it. When I was finished, Gary gave me a tissue and said, "I'll take it out to the nurses' station. Be back in a second."

"I'm sorry," I said. "This is such a nightmare."

"Just hush up, now," she said as she went out the door.

While she was gone, I probed the bandage on my thigh, where the catheter incision was. My chest felt gloriously expanded, light and clean. Gary returned and sat in her chair.

"The good news is that if there was heart damage, it's so slight that it couldn't be detected. They also put a stent in your artery to keep it open."

"A stent?"

"A little wire mesh. The balloon on the end of the catheter expands and pushes the stent into the artery wall, and that keeps the artery from narrowing or closing again."

"I have a wire mesh in my artery, right next to my heart? Won't it come loose?"

"No. The cells in the artery are going to grow through the mesh and anchor it. And the stent will keep the plaque from breaking loose and causing another heart attack."

"Plaque. *Plaque.* God."

She squeezed my hand. "They gave you an anticoagulant and a platelet blocker. You're going to be fine. You were really lucky. They said you'll make a full recovery."

We sat for a while. "Listen," I said, "I'm sorry I went behind your back that way. I shouldn't have done that."

"Forget it."

"I was so worried about you, I didn't know what else—"

Her face tightened. "Stop. Put it out of your mind."

It wasn't a request. "All right. I'm also really embarrassed at the way I went off my rocker. I never knew I was so afraid to die."

"Nobody knows how he'll react to that situation until it happens. The only thing that matters is that you're alive and you're going to be fine."

"It's incredible to be alive. I'll never take it for granted again. From now on I'll spend an hour every day being grateful I'm still here. Boy, I'm really babbling, aren't I? Like a little brook. Have you ever come close to dying?"

"No."

"You were so calm. Have you ever seen somebody die?"

"Uh, no."

"Well, I'm just glad one of us didn't lose it."

She gave me a tired smile. "You didn't see me in the waiting room. That reminds me: Your family's here."

"Oh no. How'd they find out?"

"I called David. I got his number from your wallet."

"You called David?" I tried to take it in. "So you met the family? All of them?"

"Yup."

"How did it go? Did you say who you were?"

She shook her head. "I told them I was one of your coworkers and a good friend, and that we were working on a project together at my condo when you had a heart attack. That's all."

"Good. So what'd you think of them?"

"I don't know. It wasn't the best time to meet them. They seem nice."

"Did you feel weird about not telling them about us?"

"No. Yes." She flapped a hand. "*I* don't know."

"Well, it's not like you were lying to them," I said. "I just think it's none of their business."

"I know."

"I mean, *you* never wanted to tell anybody at work, and I don't tell my family anything that matters because—"

"Because it's not the kind of relationship you have," she finished with me. "I know."

"And if they find out we've been together for over a year and I haven't told them, their feelings'll be hurt, and they'll make everything even more stressful."

"Okay."

"It's just really none of their business," I said.

"I *know.* I'll send them in and wait outside."

*   *   *

Mom and Dad entered with my brother David and my sister Emily. I was glad to see that they hadn't brought my nieces and nephews. My worst childhood memories revolved around hospitals. When I wasn't in one myself, I was visiting elderly relatives who were more dead than alive. I couldn't count the times I was led into a murky room, pushed toward a dais, and forced to kiss the skull of some motionless, genderless mummy that smelled like three-bean salad, its mouth gaping in a silent scream.

"Oh, sweetie," Mom said as she stooped to briefly, lightly hug me.

David inspected me over her shoulder. "Whoa! You look like shit." He laughed. "Just kidding. You look great."

Dad and Emily stood at the foot of my bed, their hands going crazy: jingling coins in pockets; twiddling chins, earlobes, and noses; tapping out complicated drumbeats on the cantilevered tray that held my ice water.

"How're you feeling, tiger?" Dad asked.

"I'm okay. Did they tell you what happened?"

"Yeah. You had a mild heart attack. They don't think there was any permanent damage, thank God."

"They gave me a catheterization and a stent. Just what I always wanted."

David made a face. "A catheterization? *Eww.* Did it hurt?"

"Probably, but I don't know. I passed out."

"Before they catheterize you," Emily said, "they give you a sedative that makes you forget the procedure, like when you get a colonoscopy. It affects everyone differently. Some people forget everything before it too."

"So they may also have given me a colonoscopy, and I wouldn't know it?"

"You may not remember anything that happened in the previous hour or so."

"Amazing. I need about fifty gallons of that sedative for my job."

David laughed. "Your job is getting colonoscopies? Are you a professional colon?"

Ignoring him, Mom said, "They told us you'll have to stay here for about four days and then take two weeks off work."

"Well, since I mostly work at home, what does that mean? I can't reach out of bed and pick up the laptop?"

"It means you have to start taking care of yourself, goddammit," Dad said.

Mom elbowed him. "Can we talk about this later?"

"Well, he had a goddamn heart attack! He's only thirty-six years old! Who has a heart attack at thirty-six? I'm sixty-five and *I* haven't had a heart attack!"

"Glenn, can't we just tell Elliot how glad we are that he's going to be all right?"

"I *am* glad. But I just want to point out that this wasn't completely unexpected. He was a fat kid with high blood pressure, and the doctors told us back then that he had to lose weight and get into shape or he'd be sorry later, and they were right."

"Boy, were they ever!" I said. "When I had my heart attack, I thought, 'You know, this isn't completely unexpected.'"

"Look, maybe you think this is funny, but—"

"All right, enough!" Mom nearly yelled. "Both of you! *Stop* it."

"But I was just asking for it, and now I got it," I said. "I hope I'm happy."

"Chill," David said. "We didn't come here to fight with you."

"No, you came here to tell me I brought all this on myself. I appreciate that. I need a lot of criticism right now to help me recover."

"Nobody's criticizing you," Emily said. "We were just scared. I mean, you've had a heart attack! That's not something to gloss over. We're worried about you. We're all sort of out of our gourds right now. We don't even know what we're saying." I didn't respond.

Mom said, "We met your friend Carrie. She seems very nice."

"She *is* very nice, but her name's Gary, not Carrie."

David hooted like a klaxon. "*Gary?* That's a man's name!"

"Correct."

"What kind of nut-job parents name their girl Gary? Are they actors or something? Did they name her after Gary Cooper? She looks kinda like him. Sounds like him too. 'Yup. Nope.'"

"Her parents were college professors in North Carolina. Next time you see her, make sure to tell her how stupid her name is and how she looks like a man."

"She doesn't look like a man. She's just tall and lanky. She's hot, actually. We were wondering if you two were like, you know." Half his face scrunched up in a depraved wink.

I winked back. "Yeah! We were you-knowing right before you came in."

Mom rolled her eyes. "Nice."

"Just because your brother can't control his mouth in front of your mother doesn't mean you have to talk that way too," Dad said.

"I apologize," I said. "Gary is the other copywriter on my team at work. We have a professional relationship and a platonic friendship. As you can see, she's completely out of my league anyway."

"I see no such thing," Mom said. "Maybe *you're* out of *her* league."

I laughed. "Thank you, Mother. It's not an issue that ever came up. We have a good working relationship and a good friendship. I was at her condo when it happened."

"You were at her *condo?*" David asked. He grinned, waggling his eyebrows. "Being platonic together?"

"We were working on our current project together."

"*Were* you, now? How come you couldn't work on it by e-mail, hmm?"

"I was there because I like being with her! I enjoy her company!"

"Well, she seems very nice," Mom said. She turned to David. "And I think it's childish to tease Elliot about her."

"Aw, I'm just giving you a hard time," David said. He tweaked my foot through the blanket. "Gary's a peach."

"She is, and I'm really tired now," I said. "Thanks for coming by. Everybody says I'll be fine, so you don't have to stay. Tell Gary I need to talk to her about the project we're working on. The deadline's Friday."

"Do you need anything?" Mom asked.

"Maybe a book, if you don't mind."

"What kind of book?"

"Something impenetrable."

"I just finished one on European cathedrals. It's five hundred pages long, with only twenty photos."

"Excellent. And could you please bring me some clothes too? I'm pretty sure they cut up my pants and underwear along with my shirt."

"Of course."

"Were you afraid?" Emily asked. "When it was happening?"

They all peered at me.

"Yes," I said. "I was sure I was going to die."

She seemed to shudder. "But you're not going to die. You're going to be fine."

"That's what they tell me."

Emily leaned down to kiss my forehead, something she'd never done in our lives. It was so embarrassing that my family immediately fled, to my indescribable relief.

* * *

Gary returned and stood next to my bed.

"What's with your brother? He was leering at me like he's never seen a woman before."

"He's retarded."

"Huh. I didn't know that a retarded person could run a chain of sporting-goods stores."

"Well, okay. He isn't really retarded. He's an idiot savant."

She sat down. "So how was it with them?"

"Horrible."

"That's a shame."

"Yes. We just had another fight."

She lifted my hand, kissed the knuckles. "I'm sorry. Did they ask about me?"

"Yeah. They said you seem nice, and they wanted to know if we're an item."

"Yikes. What'd you say?"

"I said we were just pals. I also said you were out of my league, and my mother got mad. She said maybe *I* was out of *your* league."

"You said I was out of your league?" she asked in a wondering, little-girl voice, peeking out from behind my hand.

I nodded. She made a mournful cooing sound as she kissed my knuckles again. The blanket tented over my groin. She eyed it and slowly shook her head, her smile turning down at the corners. "Doctor says not for two weeks."

"Crap. Guy's a jerk."

She rubbed my hand against her cheek. "What about your car?" she murmured.

"Well, you'd have to ask it."

"*That* tore-up ol' heap a junk? Puh-*leeze*. What I mean is, what should we do about it? It's parked on the street by my condo, and you're going to be here for four days. Do you want me to drive it back to your house?"

"How would you get home?"

"I'll get Margaret to follow me."

I grimaced. Gary gently stroked and tugged at the hairs on the back of my hand. "I know, I know. But I really had to talk to somebody. I called her while you were asleep."

"Oh boy. She's not going to visit me, is she?"

She didn't answer.

"Gary, she's not going to visit me, is she?"

"She and Julian are in the waiting room." She hid her face behind my hand. "I'm sorry! What could I say? They're worried about you. Do you want me to tell them to go away?"

I sighed, thrashing my feet. "No. But tell them they can only see me for a couple of minutes. Tell them I keep going into a coma. God, this is so humiliating."

"You have no reason to be humiliated. I'll fetch 'em." She stood, leaned down, and kissed me firmly. "Be right back."

Margaret Alvarez was our team graphic designer, and Julian Buckley was our British traffic controller, who joined us after Soledad was bought by a conglomerate in the UK. We'd last spoken a week earlier, at the Friday meeting. It was not possible that they were about to see me in the hospital after I'd had a heart attack. And had been stripped naked.

The door to my room swished open. Margaret swaggered in. Her broad smile displayed the narrow gap between her front teeth, and her orange T-shirt and stonewashed skinny jeans set off her olive skin perfectly. The silver stud in her nose twinkled. Julian towered behind her, his stubbly head appearing to scrape the ceiling. Gary brought up the rear.

"Holy shit, dude," Margaret rasped. "What the fuck?" She was twenty-four but sounded like a chain-smoking, sixty-year-old barfly, mystifying in a vegan who loathed tobacco.

I cupped an ear. "Is that the voice of an angel?"

Julian said, "Good Lord, Elliot. I mean, really. Was this absolutely necessary?"

"It seemed like a good idea at the time."

Margaret lifted a corner of the blanket, her many bracelets rattling. "What're you wearing under this lovely, snot-colored blankie? You wouldn't happen to be *nuuuude,* wouldja?"

I kicked at her hand. "Stop that!"

"But I wanna *see!*"

Julian stepped around her. "Margaret's aroused by illness. We're visiting the oncology ward next. So how are you, Elliot? Are you in pain?"

"No, I feel fine. Just a little tired."

"Well, we won't stay long. Is there anything I can get you?"

"Thanks, but my parents are handling everything. They'll be back tomorrow with a bunch of stuff."

Margaret shouldered Julian aside and sat on the bed, her taut bottom nestling against my thigh. It felt as hot as a grill. I rolled onto my side, facing her and drawing up my knees to hide the instant return of the blanket tent. An apparent side effect of balloon angioplasty and stenting was priapism. My erection was only an inch from Margaret's perfect haunch.

"Sucks, huh, Elliot," she said, brushing back her blonde-streaked raven hair. "I'm sorry this happened to you. Seriously. Are you going to be okay?"

"Yes." I found it impossible to look into her dark eyes. Her concern was as disturbing as my sister's kiss. "I'm going to be absolutely fine, so you need to cut this out. Insult me. Tell me what a bozo I am."

"Dude, don't worry. You're still a fuckin' bozo. I just don't like kicking people when they're down."

"Rubbish," Julian said. "He's just not down *enough* for you yet. If he'd had half his head lopped off, you'd be kicking him across the room."

"Yeah, you're probably right." She leaned in with a sardonic, duck-lip pout, her eyes tightly shut.

I covered her mouth. "Please. Don't. I implore you."

She knocked away my hand. "Pussy."

When she hoisted her rump off the bed, her heat lingered on the mattress and in the air itself, like a ghost with a fever.

"Thanks, everybody, for coming," I said. "You can all go now. I'm totally wiped out."

"Right," Julian said. "Going now. Get some rest and we'll see you soon."

"Later," Margaret cawed, fluttering her fingers at me.

"Take care," Gary said. "I'll call you tomorrow. Good night." We couldn't say anything else or even really look at each other. Julian wasn't aware of our relationship, but I wondered about Margaret. I'd always felt that Gary—despite her butch, Southern self-reliance—would inevitably seek out female input. My heart attack was a perfect impetus for her unburdening. The problem was that Margaret had the biggest, foulest mouth on the West Coast. Whatever Gary told her would go viral; in twenty-four hours the whole creative department would know.

*   *   *

I checked the TV but found that everything disturbed me. The most frightening broadcast was the school-board channel, a parade of mental patients at microphones doing battle with a long table of droning bureaucrats. I turned off the TV and closed my eyes. A few minutes later, I heard a slithering noise beside me.

"Elliot," a woman's voice whispered.

I opened my eyes. Nothing. Rising on one elbow, I peered over the edge of the bed. Gary crouched there on all fours like a spider, her chin almost on the floor. She stared up at me as if from the bottom of a well.

"Why didn't you die?" she hissed.

My heart slammed against my breastbone with the force of a sledgehammer; I snapped awake, clutching my chest. Another look confirmed there was nobody in the room. I waited for my heart to either settle down or conk out.

Soon I heard the door to my room swing open, followed by heavy footsteps. My personal physician Dr. Larkin bulked out of the darkness. With his lab coat and fluffy white hair, he looked like a polar bear, the most vicious and unpredictable of the ursine family.

"See?" he said. "Did I call it or not?"

"You called it. You certainly did. What're you doing here?"

"Would you like me to leave?"

"Yes."

Instead, he came closer. "I spoke to the resident who performed your PCI. He said there was no detectable damage to your heart."

"That's right. How'd you find out I had a heart attack?"

He thrust his fists into his pockets. "I have several patients here. I saw the paramedics bring you in, but you didn't notice me."

"No, I was distracted. I hope you enjoyed being proven right."

"One of the reasons you had an infarction—apart from your weight and blood pressure—is because you're a very angry person, and you refuse to admit it. It comes out on occasion, as it did just now with that comment, but for the most part, you simply swallow it and let it eat at you. It's going to kill you."

I closed my eyes. "You know, I'm really not up to being psychoanalyzed right now. I'm tired and depressed, so I'd appreciate it if you'd just go away."

"I came up here to tell you that you're a very lucky man," he said as if he hadn't heard me.

"Yes, I know. We went over that already. No permanent damage to my heart."

"*No!*" he shouted.

When I first went to him, he scared me to death with that. A big, sullen man, he was just another cold-fish general practitioner until I took off my shirt.

"*You're overweight!*" he'd suddenly yelled. "*By thirty pounds at least!*"

He took my fatness as a personal attack. But after five years, I'd almost gotten used to him. I barely flinched at his "No!" even though it was as loud as a gunshot.

"I'm not talking about that," he grated. "*Look at me.*"

I obeyed.

"You're lucky because your girlfriend gave you aspirin when your infarction began. The term 'mild heart attack' is a misnomer. Your heart attack was mild only in terms of the damage it caused, and that damage was limited by your girlfriend's quick thinking. She saved your life. I hope you thanked her. That thought never occurred to you, I see."

"No," I said, "it didn't." I rubbed my face.

He crashed down into the chair next to my bed. "All right. Now you're going to listen to me. You apparently don't have actual coronary disease, and that's another reason to thank whatever higher power you believe in, because heart disease is a chronic, progressive condition. Once you have it, all you can do is slow its pace. There is no cure. Angioplasty and bypass surgery only address the symptoms. The disease itself will recur and progress. Are you hearing me?"

"Yes."

"When you've recovered sufficiently, you're going to come to my office, and I'm going to show you how to keep from having another heart attack, one that will either incapacitate or kill you. Because you *will* have another heart attack. With your risk factors, there's no question that you will have another heart attack unless you completely change your lifestyle. Do I make myself clear?"

"As a bell."

"Good." He slapped his muscular thighs and stood. "I'll see you in about two weeks, then."

* * *

I lay in my bed, counting my heartbeats. I could feel them in my neck and my ankles. When I lay on my side, I could hear them in my pillow. At some point a nurse brought a meal, which I skipped. An intern came in, told me how lucky I was, and assured me I'd be fine, but I didn't care.

After I planted the knife between Gary's shoulder blades, she saved me, and I didn't thank her. Larkin was right; the thought hadn't even occurred to me.

34

CHAPTER THREE

I spent my four days and three nights in the hospital, and then Mom and Dad took me home. They lived in Pasadena, about half an hour from my tiny city. The morning after my heart attack, Dad drove out to remove the mail from the box on my porch and put it inside on the dining-room table. He was convinced that a full mailbox would signal an open house for burglars or kids looking for somewhere to have a rave.

"The second I lift the lid on your box," he told me, "this muscle-bound guy appears beside me. It was like he shot up out of the ground. He says he's your neighbor, and he's holding a baseball bat sort of discreetly tucked out of sight down by his leg. I had to show him my driver's license to prove I was your father and not some geriatric housebreaker. He said, 'Oh yeah, I remember you. You haven't been out here for years. You used to drive a tan Oldsmobile.'"

"Yup, that's Carlos Garza," I said. "He's very protective of our street."

"Christ, he's like a stalker. He knew everything about our whole family! I told him you had a heart attack, and he said he'd collect your mail. He pretty much ordered me off the property. I didn't argue with him."

My parents and I didn't say much in the car on the way to my house. Before my heart attack, we had their grandchildren, the weather, TV shows, and the wars to talk about. But almost dying was like performing a grotesquely inappropriate act in front of them, worse than exposing myself or defecating. It robbed us of our ability to make even the smallest of talk. Adding to the weirdness, I was now totally back to normal. There were no signs whatsoever of my near death. I came out of the hospital with some stitches in my thigh and two bottles of pills; that was all.

The first thing Dad did when we got home was open my cupboards and refrigerator to make an inventory.

"I have enough food," I said. "You don't have to go shopping for me."

"It's not the quantity I'm concerned about. Look at this shit." He held up a can of soup in each hand. "Steak and potato? Beef and cheese? Have you looked at the calories, sodium, and amount of saturated fat in these?"

"Sweetie, maybe you should let your father and me buy you something a little healthier," Mom said.

I smiled. "Sure, why not? Like when I was in the second grade. Remember? While you and Dad and David and Emily were gorging on steak and French fries, I had to eat skinless chicken breasts and grilled vegetables. And that special no-salt canned food that tasted like water."

My parents exchanged glances of pure revulsion, it seemed.

"And why did we put you on a diet?" Dad asked. "Was it because we just felt like being mean to you?"

"No, it was because I was overweight and had borderline high blood pressure."

"And did the dieting bring down your blood pressure?"

"Yes."

"So what's the problem?"

"There's no problem." I sat down in the breakfast nook. "Why don't we just recreate that whole era? You can prop two-by-fours on empty paint cans and have me spend an hour every day doing track-and-field exercises again. You can also draw up those charts."

"What charts? I don't remember any charts."

"You stuck them to the fridge. Two columns per chart. The left column had the foods I could eat, and the right had the caloric content of each. The total number of calories allowed per day was written at the bottom of each chart in red ink, underlined twice and circled once."

"Still don't remember." He thought, shook his head. "Nope. Sorry."

Mom beamed at me, a warning to leave her out of it.

When Dad had declared that I would consult the charts before every meal, I said I didn't want to.

He'd shrugged. "*I* don't want to go to work every morning, but I do. And I don't whine about it either."

Nearly thirty years later, here we were in another kitchen, having the same conversation. For a moment I forgot how old I was, because my parents hadn't changed much. Like David and Emily, they were ectomorphs, people with lean, muscular physiques. I was the family endomorph, someone with a soft, fat physique. To me, the word sounded like a variety of moist cake with thick, greasy icing.

I firmly anchored myself in the present and said, "Sorry about my whining. I just think it's better if I take care of this myself."

Mom sighed as she sat across from me. "Nobody's accusing you of whining, Elliot. But you have to take it easy for a couple of weeks. You're not supposed to go shopping, so if we don't replace what you have, you'll end up eating it."

"And eating that shit is what got you into trouble in the first place," Dad said.

"Actually, eating shit didn't get me into trouble; I was in trouble from the day I was born. Eleven pounds, twelve ounces. How the heck did I put on weight in the *womb?* Maybe I had a twin, and I *ate* him!"

Dad let out a long, incredulous whistle as though watching someone run headfirst into a brick wall.

"Elliot, please." Mom reached for my hand and stopped before she made contact. "We're just trying to help."

"I have a lot of food that isn't oozing with fat and salt. If you and Dad want to police my cupboards and fridge, go ahead. But you don't have to go shopping for me."

"Fine," Dad said. "You heard him, Bev. We're just making things worse. If he needs anything, he'll call. Come on."

I walked them to their car, and they drove off without hugging me or shaking my hand. As a family, we weren't much for touching.

*   *   *

Back in my kitchen, I checked my cupboards, my refrigerator, and my freezer. I imagined my parents doing that to me while I slept, shining penlights on my failings, cataloging my pain, pawing through my *garbage can.*

And then, after they told me what they'd done, after they'd let me know it was all for my own good, if they both had heart attacks and fell down in front of me, crying and begging me to save them, would I spring into action without a second thought? Or would I stand over them in their helplessness and laugh? Would I kneel close and ask, "What's that? You want me to do *what?* Help you? Let me get this straight: You want *me* to help *you?*"

Could I find the strength to feed them aspirin and call an ambulance instead of reaching for the baseball bat I kept next to the front door?

*   *   *

Two days after I got back from the hospital, I heard car doors slam in my driveway; through the curtains I saw that it was Emily and her children Alex and Terri. They hadn't been to my house in ages. I ran into my bedroom to change out of my bathrobe and put on a T-shirt and jeans.

As I opened the door, it hit me that this was the first time Emily and I had ever met as adults without David or our parents at hand. Emily seemed to realize it too. We didn't look at each other.

Alex was four and Terri was two. They hugged me without fear, which meant that Emily hadn't given them the sort of lecture she and I got when we were little and had to face some perennially ailing ancient: "Now kids, your Auntie Myra-Uncle Roy is very weak, so no running around, no screaming, and no horseplay. You need to be quiet little mice, because your auntie-uncle can't take any kind of shock." It terrified me; I was sure the second we opened our mouths, Auntie Myra or Uncle Roy would topple like a tree. I had nightmares about killing old people with my selfish chatter and hijinks.

"Are you sick, Elliot?" Alex asked.

"No, not anymore. I was sick a few days ago, but I'm all better now."

"Bew," Terri said, her hand on my chest.

"That's right. Better."

She and Alex examined the glass-fronted cabinets where I kept my toys. Before I became a marketing copywriter, I was a freelance toy copywriter. Toys come in boxes, bags, or blister packs, all of which have writing on them. I owned an unopened example of every toy graced by my copy—dolls, action figures, electronic gizmos, animals, weapons.

"Can we play with those toys?" Alex asked.

"Well, those are special toys that aren't really for playing with," I said. "People gave me those toys as presents. I'd be sad if they got broken, so I keep them in the cabinets to make sure they're safe."

"They're for looking at, not touching," Emily said.

"Okay," Alex said. "We shouldn't play with them." He and Terri made a tour of the cabinets, clasping their hands behind them like solemn little museum patrons.

Emily leaned against the doorway to the breakfast nook and twirled her bundle of keys. She examined the wood grain of the jamb, ran her fingers over it.

"So how are you doing?" she asked a knothole.

"Everything seems to be in working order," I said.

"Going on your walk again?"

"Not yet."

"Well, start slowly. Don't go out and try to take up where you left off."

"Actually, I was going to start running tomorrow. Sprinting flat out. And lifting weights while I ran. I mean, what could go wrong?"

She sighed, her head drooping. "Look, I'm not criticizing you. I'm just concerned, that's all."

"I know. You're concerned that I'm an idiot."

"I never *said* that!"

"Oh, but you're thinking it."

We made eye contact just as this final straw took its toll. I caught the precise moment she gave in to utter detestation. She snarled, "You're such a—" but covered her mouth with her hand before she finished. She appeared to fall asleep for a moment, then woke up as herself again. "Come on, kids," she said in her normal voice. "Time to go. Take care, Elliot. Call me if you need anything."

I hugged Alex and Terri and sent them off with a promise to see them again soon. Emily and I ignored each other.

* * *

When David dropped by, we didn't talk about my heart attack, my weight, or exercise programs, even though he was the regional manager of a chain that sold sporting equipment. David wanted to discuss only one topic.

"So tell me about this Gary chick, Elliot. What's she like?"

"She's quiet and a great writer. She's nice to be around because she's low-key. She's smart and really funny."

"Yeah, yeah, yeah. Is she seeing someone?"

"I don't know. We don't talk about our private lives."

"Man, I can't get her out of my mind! She's got the widest shoulders I've ever seen on a woman, and I love her ass. I love skinny women with curvy, substantial asses and perky boobs like that. You know, about the size of grapefruits. I don't like fake tits or floppy cow tits. Great camel toe too. You could see right through her sweatpants that she's got nice, big, juicy lips. I'll bet she shaves. It looked like it, anyway."

"What does Andrea think about her?" Andrea was David's wife.

He deflated. All the air whooshed right out of him. "Christ, Elliot, we only do it five or six times a year. We've got the two kids, the wine, the Mercedes and the minivan, the insane mortgage, we hardly ever screw, and it's boring as hell when we do. How'd we turn into characters in some shitty movie?"

We stared at each other, speechless. David never confided in me about anything. It was even more stunning than Emily letting herself hate me for a few seconds. My aborted trip to the cemetery had opened lots of doors for my siblings. David shook himself like a wet dog.

"Don't know where *that* came from. Jesus. Let's get back to Gary. It's just guy talk, that's all. Why can't I slobber over my brother's hot coworker a little? It doesn't mean anything. I'm not gonna *do* anything about it. Unless you think I got a chance, I mean." He punched me on the arm and laughed.

"Well," I said, "she's got your number. I'll tell her you're interested. Maybe she'll call you."

His mouth fell open and his eyes squeezed shut as if he were about to sneeze. "Uhhhhh…no."

"Well, okay. But you never know."

"Are you seriously telling me you never thought about what she'd be like in the sack? That big pussy jammed in your face? Wouldn't you just like to climb up there and munch out?"

"You're an incurable romantic, aren't you?"

"Yeah, well, you'll be just as blue-balled as me if you ever get married. When was the last time you got laid anyway?"

"By another person, you mean?"

"Oh, so it's been years. Okay. You need to go out more, drain the nut sack once in a while. It's good for you."

"David…" I bent forward in my chair and put my face flat on the table.

"Yeah, okay. So how old is Gary? Mid-thirties?"

* * *

I asked Gary to come in the evenings to avoid my family. She hated where I lived, calling it the 'hood. The last time she'd driven out was almost a year earlier. A carload of young men with shaved heads had pulled up next to her at a stoplight.

"I thought they were flippin' me off, but it was gang signs. *Gang* signs! What, do y'all have blonde women gangsters drivin' around in Saabs out here? Forget it. I ain't goin' to your place anymore. You're comin' home with me from now on."

But she insisted on visiting me after my heart attack. It was unbelievably awkward, as though we were a divorced couple meeting accidentally after years. The first night she arrived with cartons of low-fat vegetarian Thai food. She let me kiss her, but it didn't do either of us any good. We ate on the sofa in front of the TV, the silence like a concrete wall between us.

When I couldn't stand it anymore, I said, "The day my parents brought me home from the hospital, they went through my cupboards and refrigerator to see what I was eating."

Gary froze, her eyes locked on the screen. Her neck seemed as long as a swan's.

"It made me want to kill them," I said.

She put her plate on the coffee table, keeping her eyes on the TV. "I don't want to talk about this."

"I know, but maybe we should."

"No."

I took off my glasses so I couldn't see her face. "It's just that I feel awful about the whole thing, and I—"

"Elliot, please." She held up a hand to stop me. "I can't talk about this. Please don't push it. It's in the past. Let's just get beyond it. Please."

"Okay, but—"

"*Please,* Elliot! I'm asking you to *stop!*"

"I...I...I need to know if you forgive me. Or not."

She slid across the cushions and touched my thigh. "Put your glasses on."

I complied.

"Of course I forgive you. I love you. So please stop talking about it."

"Okay."

She slipped an arm around my neck and rested her chin on my shoulder. When she left the room, she held on to me until the last possible instant, stretching her arm out and maintaining that touch until her forward movement pulled her fingers away. We didn't discuss the fight again. In the year we'd been together, it was the only one we'd had. I'd never been so free of conflict with anyone in my life.

The only other disharmony during my convalescence arose one night when she asked if we could watch something else on TV besides the wars. I had a set-top wireless device that let me stream content from the Internet—firefights, ambushes, drive-by shootings, IEDs, car bombs, suicide bombers, blurry footage of orange fireballs erupting in crowds, all with the soundtrack of male voices singing *a capella*.

"It's so depressing," Gary said. "It just makes me so sad."

"Me too," I said. But I found it impossible to turn off. I'd been watching for years. Gary didn't know why I did it. I didn't either.

So I surfed until I found a movie starring a guy who'd had a hit Mafia series on cable. I'd never watched it.

"You know, you always reminded me of him, except younger, better looking, and with a lot more hair," Gary said. "And a beard, of course."

"I remind you of *him?*" I sputtered. "Really?"

A timid nod. "Is that bad?"

He was a tall, broad-shouldered, absurdly charismatic bulldozer of a man who stole every scene he was in. His paunch was hardly apparent. Like me, he had an oddly light voice that was a surprise coming out of that mass.

"No, it's not bad," I said. "But nobody cares how fat *he* is. I should start talking in a New Jersey accent."

She gasped. "Would you, please? Say 'Youse guys.' Say 'Frankie da Blowfish.' 'Whatchoo cryin' about, ay? Ay?' 'Why, I oughtta—'"

On her visits we ate dinner, watched TV, talked about work, took short walks around the block, and made out a little on the sofa, nothing past first base. She went home at night so we wouldn't be tempted to do more than smooch.

"My brother is madly in lust with you," I told her.

Classic Gary snort. "Yeah, well, he ain't my type."

"What's your type?"

"Unmarried, for one." She put her finger over my lips. "No. No more. Hush up. We ain't gonna get into one of those dumb yackfests about what we want and don't want in someone. You're already with someone, and if I ain't what you want, you can always hie your butt outta here, hon."

"But I *live* here," I said.

Her laughter let us back away from it. Even so, there was no doubt now: My betrayal had made her question her judgment.

* * *

When I went to see Dr. Larkin, he immediately strapped a sphygmomanometer to my arm. The tightening cuff reminded me that I was nothing but meat and juice. My plumbing was *soft*. Squeezing it in one place would expand it somewhere else, in an area with a thin spot I didn't know about. I'd never heard of people dying while their blood pressure was being taken, but that didn't mean it couldn't happen. Maybe the stent in my coronary artery would be blown out by the surge of fluid. That little steel mesh could be swept straight into my heart, where it would bash and clatter around like a hammer in a clothes dryer.

"*Borderline!*" Larkin yelled and pushed away from me with his powerful legs, scooting backward like a squid until his wheeled stool banged into the examining table where my file lay. He slashed at my records with his pen, his massive head propped up by one fist jammed against his mouth. For one full minute, he didn't look at me or say a word. I tensed; these silences usually preceded an explosion, after which he'd go back to being a machine.

44

Instead, he looked up and quietly said, "Mr. Finell, I'm done lecturing you about your weight and blood pressure. You've had your heart attack. You'll have another unless you radically alter your lifestyle. The choice is yours."

"So tell me what to do," I said.

"I *have* told you. Many times. Eat a low-fat diet. Cut out the salt. Cut down on the carbs. Get more exercise."

"I didn't have a heart attack until I started exercising."

"There's that rage again. It's always there, right below the surface. You mask it with glib sarcasm, but it's very real, and it's going to kill you."

"Your bedside manner could use a little work."

"Mr. Finnell, if you don't like my approach, there's the door."

I laughed. "I can hie my butt outta here?"

"I beg your pardon?"

"Everybody seems to be telling me the same thing these days."

"Maybe you should start listening."

He told me to take off my shirt, then he listened to my heart with a stethoscope.

"How are you sleeping?" he asked.

"Not very well."

"That's not good. There's a correlation between sleep deprivation and heart disease. Are you having trouble drifting off?"

"Yes." He'd described it exactly. I couldn't fall asleep because I was terrified of "drifting off," dying in the night, alone in my bed.

He wrote in my chart. "Would you like me to prescribe a sleep aid?"

"Not yet. Maybe later. I'll try other things first."

"Fine. Rest another week before you start your walking program again. How are your legs? Any pain?"

I'd forgotten all about my legs. The last time I was aware of them was when I was talking to that Okie medicine man, that mind-reading quadriplegic, the day of my heart attack. What was his name? Trey. Trey Gillespie.

Oh, don't tell me about pain. I know all about it. I live with total pain twenty-four hours a day.

45

How about the pain of thinking you're living your last seconds on earth, lying in the arms of the only person who ever loved you, right after you'd utterly betrayed and humiliated her? How about *that* pain, Trey?

"No more pain than usual," I told Larkin.

He slammed my file closed and slipped his pen into the breast pocket of his white coat. "Good. Stick with walking instead of jogging. It's low impact, and there's less of a danger of arterial plaque breaking off and causing another infarction."

"Again with the plaque. Why does everybody keep telling me things like that? It's driving me crazy."

"What's the matter? Are you afraid of dying?"

"Of course I am. Aren't you?"

"Not in the least," he said.

"Groovy. Aren't *you* the enlightened one."

"But if *you're* afraid of death," he plowed ahead, "you'll have an incentive to get into shape. A healthy weight-loss rate is no more than one pound a week. And don't try any of those stupid diuretic diets, because you'll die. As I said before your heart attack, I expect you to lose forty pounds this coming year. If you don't, you may still manage to avoid another infarction, but I won't have you as a patient anymore. My time is too valuable to waste on people who refuse to take care of themselves. Good luck."

* * *

In my car I consoled myself with the fact that Larkin hadn't found another birth defect. The first time I went to him, he peered into my ears with an otoscope and said, "Interesting."

"What?" I asked.

"You have the longest ear canals I've ever seen. In twenty-five years of practicing medicine, I've never seen longer."

"Does that mean my brain is smaller than normal? Because there's less room for it between the canals?"

"Possibly. When there's one deformity, there are usually others."

He was right: I was riddled with birth defects. I concealed them all from my family and Gary. About a third of the gastrocnemius muscle on my right calf was nowhere to be found.

"It may not be missing," Larkin explained, "just withered. We can't tell unless we dissect it. With the other injuries to your legs, I'm surprised you walk as well as you do."

In addition to the absent or withered calf muscle and my freakishly long ear canals, I had three cowlicks and lacked the first bicuspid on the left side of my lower jaw. The cowlicks forced me to keep my hair very short or let it grow very long; anything in between, and my hair stood up in back like a rooster tail. There was no problem with the missing bicuspid because the baby tooth was still there, a flat knob with no replacement under it. Since I couldn't do anything about my ear canals or the gastrocnemius muscle, I didn't worry about them.

We hit the deformity mother lode while investigating the chronic pain in my lower back. Larkin sent me to a specialist, who gave me a powder to mix with a gallon of water, chill in the fridge, and drink the day before I had my torso X-rayed. That refreshing, pineapple-flavored liquid turned out to be the most supremely evacuant laxative ever invented. Although the specialist didn't tell me, I found out that I should've slept as close to the bathroom as I could. Actually, it would've been better to sleep *in* the bathroom, in the bathtub. And I was forbidden to eat or drink anything for twenty-four hours before the test. On the gurney, I shook from hypoglycemia and dehydration.

A dye was injected, flooding my mouth with the taste of rubbing alcohol and copper. This was followed by a terrible dropping sensation; closing my eyes made me feel as though I were somersaulting in midair, something else that nobody warned me about. After the technicians slowly rolled a humming X-ray machine down my body, the vertigo and bad taste went away, and I was released to get something to eat and drink. It took a week for the results to come in.

"*You've got three kidneys!*" Larkin screamed at me over the phone. "Three! I've never seen it before. You've got one on the right and two on the left. What a birth defect!"

"Is that the source of the pain?" I asked.

"Your head is the source of the pain. You're an anxious, neurotic hypochondriac who suffers from psychosomatic pain *and* happens to have three kidneys."

"Do I have to have it removed?"

"Your head?"

"The third kidney."

"No, it seems to be working perfectly. Keep it as a spare."

Every year he suggested I have a physical over at the university hospital downtown, where they'd do MRIs, CAT scans, endoscopies, the works. He was frantic to see what else they'd find, but I always refused. I didn't want to know.

CHAPTER FOUR

When I let Gary in, she handed me several envelopes. "Howdy. Your mail came."

I put the bills on the table in the breakfast nook and dropped the junk into the plastic bin for the recyclables. There were three envelopes left; I deposited them in a kitchen drawer.

Gary said, "Those look like birthday cards. Aren't you going to open them?"

"No. They're from my family. They'll just have signatures and nothing else. Maybe this year a smiley face with something like, 'Glad you're still alive!' Whatever."

She touched my cheek. "Elliot, that's just so sad. They never give you presents?"

"Nope. But I never give them presents on their birthdays either."

"Well, that ain't a family tradition I'm gonna honor. Happy birthday, bud." She reached behind her and produced a small, flat, wrapped gift she'd tucked into the waistband of her slacks.

I kissed her. "Thank you."

She stood beside me with one arm around my shoulders, watching me unwrap the present. We were almost back to normal, the best gift she could ever give me.

Under the paper was a framed color photo of her wearing a charcoal business suit, spike heels, and heavy makeup. She was doing a high kick, her right leg perfectly straight and vertical, her thigh against her chest. Her arms were by her sides, hands balled into fists, and she faced the camera with her upper lip raised in a snarl and her exposed teeth clenched, her tangled blonde hair obscuring one eye.

"Ah decided it was time Ah indulged your kinky desire," she said. Her face and neck were bright red.

"Oh my God, this is incredible. It's exactly what I wanted. Thank you." I kissed her again. "Who took it?"

"Margaret. But don't worry: I said it was for me, as an ego stroke. Prove to myself I still had it." She nuzzled my neck. "Um, the two weeks are up, you know."

Her voice vibrated down my spinal column and into my chest. "They are indeed," I said thickly.

She kept her face against my neck, shielding herself. "I've missed being with you."

"I've missed being with you too."

"Since I've been coming to your place, I've gotten funny ideas, Elliot," she murmured.

"What funny ideas?"

"You've got a beautiful backyard, with the porch and the cactus garden, and that wonderful six-foot-tall board fence."

I couldn't believe what I just heard. In the past year, I'd learned that Gary was passionate but restrained, and two weeks ago she despised me. Now, she raised her head and gazed into my eyes with only a slight jitteriness.

"Is this going where I think it is?" I asked, my stomach fluttering.

She whispered in my ear, "I ain't *never* been nekkid outside. I wanna know how the sun feels on my skin." Her breath gave me hot gooseflesh all over. We always went to bed with the lights out; I'd never seen her unclothed.

"Are you okay?" she asked. "You're shaking."

"I'm fine." I wiped my eyes. "Doctor told me I might be a little emotional for a while. Common after effect. Called emotional lability."

"Aw, sugar." She put her arms around my neck and held me tightly for a moment, the full length of her against me, her cheek fused to mine. "All better?"

"Yes."

"Good. I'm going out back. Give me a couple minutes, then you come out. In your natural state. Not a stitch. Is that okay?" Her chest heaved as though she'd run miles to be with me.

"You bet." I kissed her again, and she hurried into the living room, heading for the back door. I took off my shirt, jeans, underwear, shoes, and socks and stared at the microwave clock. It was very strange to be naked in my kitchen. I expected my parents to burst in at any second. My two-week abstinence, my sense of rebirth, and the restoration of my relationship with Gary produced an astonishing...*capacity*. I felt that I could bore through steel plate.

When two minutes had passed, I went through the living room and opened the back door. I didn't know if "in your natural state" meant no glasses, but I refused to embark on this adventure blind. Outside, birds sang and a dog barked down the street. A light breeze blew across my bare skin, an inconceivably pleasant sensation.

I closed the back door, and Gary emerged from behind the cactus garden, walking on the flagstone path. She was totally nude; she'd even removed her watch. Her nipples had stiffened to the size of my thumbs. She raised her arms and combed her hair with her fingers. It took me a second to recognize what I saw in her smile: abandon. She was wanton. I had to be dreaming.

"Look how pretty you are naked," I said.

She laughed. "So are you. We're like Adam and Eve, ain't we?"

I held out my hand, and she came to me. We kissed in the sunlight, our hands roaming each other's bodies, our hips grinding together. She pulled back and pointed to the armchairs by the redwood table, under the porch eaves. "Sit," she ordered. I sat.

She stood in front of me, grasped the sides of my head, and drew me down toward her. Another wonder; she'd always been uncomfortable when I did that, so much so that I'd stopped asking. At first I thought it was another present for me, given out of obligation, but soon she was panting, "Faster! Faster! There! Right there! That's it! Yes!" Her pelvis *cavorted*. Something had changed.

Just as she seemed about to explode, she lifted my head away and pushed me back in the chair. Then she sat on my lap, facing me. Using one hand to position me, she lowered herself slowly, eyes shut, lower lip clamped between her teeth. She put my hands on her breasts and groaned. It was over quickly. I worried that she'd scream, but instead she clasped me in an urgent bear hug, thrust her face into the side of my neck, and made a series of gasping sighs until her hips stopped bucking. We sat locked together, forehead to forehead, our sweat mingling and our breathing slowly returning to normal.

Finally, she straightened. Her eyes glistened as she gave me her widest, best smile, the absolute rarity that devastated me every time I saw it.

"Lordy, Elliot. If that's what happens at nudist colonies, man, sign us *up*."

"Actually, it happens a lot to couples when one person survives a life-threatening—"

"Shh!" She covered my mouth. "Not now. We're in the Garden of Eden." She slowly climbed off, knelt in front of me, and smiled. "Happy birthday, Elliot. I love you." When she lowered her head in a final surprise, her hair fanned out across my lap.

*　*　*

After a short nap in my bed, we went on the walk I'd taken only three times before my heart attack. I'd told Gary to bring along clothes and shoes for at least a mile-long hike; she dressed in a baggy gray sweatsuit, baseball cap, sneakers, and dark glasses. She despised skirts, shorts, and jeans. Her work and going-out clothes consisted of roomy pantsuits or slacks and blouses, while at home she wore oversized T-shirts and either cargo pants or activewear with elastic waistbands.

I put on my walking ensemble and we set out. The five-mile route began at the end of my street, where we'd turn left and go straight for three blocks. Then we'd turn right onto the sidewalk next to a four-lane road. It was a long stretch from there, straight as a ruler for about a mile and a half. After the first four hundred yards, the sidewalk doubled in width and climbed a steep hill to an elevation of about twenty feet. From there it bordered the western edge of a golf course surrounded by two high fences. The inner barrier was chain link topped with razor wire, while the outer wall consisted of brick pillars and black wrought-iron bars shaped like spears. Between the sidewalk and the golf course was a dirt horse trail protected by a low wooden railing. A full-fledged equestrian center was located near the heart of the golf course, hidden somewhere in the heavy growth of trees.

Ornamental plum, white ash, and eucalyptus lined the footpath along the golf course. They were planted so close together that they formed a continuous archway, like an enchanted tunnel. That was the best part of the walk. Flying golf balls posed a danger, but they were offset by all the women riding horses on the dirt trail. I sometimes saw a line of them trotting along single file, in knee-high black jackboots, T-shirts, and skintight jeans or jodhpurs, bouncing up and down in their saddles, the upward motion ending in a languid forward thrust of the hips that didn't seem related to controlling the horses. But they all did it. Apparently only slender, busty, extraordinarily attractive women in their late teens or early twenties were allowed to join the equestrian center.

In several places the concrete sidewalk dipped down nearly to street level before it climbed back up to a commanding height. Joggers and walkers seemed to prefer the dirt horse trail, probably to avoid the steep hills. I often saw runners who were much fatter than I was; they were probably all Pima Indians with pristine cardiovascular systems.

The equestrian center was accessed through an enormous metal gate set into the outer fence of the golf course. Across the road from this entrance was the high school. It disgorged hordes of students every afternoon, dozens of whom jaywalked across the four lanes of traffic, adding to the flood of pedestrians on the concrete path and horse trail. A mile and a half down the road, the sidewalk turned right at a busy intersection and went straight along the northern edge of the golf course. It was still sheltered by the trees and had plenty of street lamps for walking after dusk. That section of the route continued for half a mile, until it made another right turn.

For the final half mile, the sidewalk climbed a hill that had what looked like a forty-five-degree angle. A client of Soledad Marketing owned the luxurious hotel at the top of the hill, the centerpiece of a sprawling resort complex that also included three restaurants, twenty-odd conference rooms, two golf courses, the equestrian center, swimming pools, and tennis courts. Most of the patrons were from the neighboring city. They were young and vigorous and had gobs of discretionary income. Where I lived, almost everybody was retired except for the single mothers, the gangbangers, and me.

I stayed in the hotel for one night when I had my house fumigated for termites. Though I was charged two hundred dollars, the room had a sort of yeasty smell that made me afraid to touch anything; the bed was so hard, it gave me a backache; and the pornographic film I bought by pressing a button on the TV remote didn't show any genitals, just bare flanks and breasts. The experience as a whole was a letdown.

If I walked from my house up to the hotel and back, it would be just over five miles. It was a beautiful route, almost like promenading around a British estate. There was a lot to see, a lot to occupy my mind. The scenery made me forget that I walked only to save my life. Assuming I kept a constant speed of three miles per hour and didn't continually fall down or break into mad sprints, it'd take about ninety minutes.

* * *

Gary and I didn't hold hands as we trudged along the sidewalk; we'd trained ourselves to conceal our relationship. Besides, neither of us liked public displays of affection. To me, they were smug, while I think Gary felt they were undignified and made her appear clingy and weak.

By the time we reached the gate to the equestrian center, I was soaked with sweat. Across the street, on the sidewalk beside the high school, the quadriplegic Okie medicine man peered over at us and waved. I waved back.

"Who's that?" Gary asked.

"His name is Trey. I met him the same day I had my heart attack."

She grimaced. "What a horrible day that was."

"Yes." It was a perfect segue. I couldn't have planned it better. My heart briefly went arrhythmic, as if warning me. "Actually, I wanted to talk to you about that day."

"Oh?" She looked ahead, suddenly expressionless behind her dark glasses.

I wiped my nose, fairly certain I'd just made the worst decision of my life. Her smell was still on my fingers and in my mustache. David forever jabbered about "mustache rides." Today was the first time Gary initiated one. Now, she seemed about as likely as David to ever ask me for another. But I had to go through with it.

"This is going to be hard," I said. "It's something that we have to talk about, as much as you don't want to. I was wrong to go behind your back and spy on you, but I only did it because I was worried. I still am. I think…" I stopped, trying to figure out how to phrase it. There was only one way. "I think you need help. I only say that because I love you more than anything in the world."

She didn't reply. I couldn't breathe. Her face was smooth as plastic.

"I told you we weren't ever going to talk about that again," she finally said. "It took a lot for me to forgive you. I never had anyone betray me that way. I can't believe you're bringing it up."

"I'm only doing it because I love you."

"Huh. Kind of a funny way of *lovin'* someone, don'cha think? Spyin' on her. Goin' behind her back. Attackin' her again after she tells you not to. If that's love, Elliot, I surely *don't* wanna see what you'd do if you *hated* me."

"Gary, please. I know you're very upset and hurt and…afraid, but you don't have to be."

We'd reached the dirt horse path. She stopped and stared across the street at the high school, her hands on her hips.

"Oh, I ain't *afraid*," she said. "Believe me, fear is *not* what I'm feelin' at this particular moment."

"We were just in the Garden of Eden. Don't you remember saying that? I'm the same man."

She sniffed. "There was a man in the Garden of Eden, and there was also a snake. A sneaky, lying snake with an agenda." And she gave me a look so utterly devoid of feeling that I became nauseated. I was in danger of throwing up at her feet.

"I don't have an agenda," I stammered.

"No? You've brought this up three times now. You say you're worried about me, but that's not what this is about. You know what it's really about? Control. That's what it's about. I never knew you were such a controlling person, Elliot."

I shook my head. "I can't even control myself. Why would I want the added responsibility of controlling someone else too?"

"That's *exactly* why. Because you can't control yourself. You can't face that fact, so you project it onto someone else. You make *me* the one with the problem, which relieves you of the responsibility of addressing your own issues."

"What do you mean I can't face it? I just *told* you I can't control myself. I admitted it straight out. I tell you all the time that I'm compulsive and impulsive and neurotic. I'm a mess."

"You say the words, but you don't accept them emotionally." Arms folded, she was still as a statue. "Controlling people are totally insecure, and that makes them completely untrustworthy. You wouldn't believe what I went through to trust you again, and now we're right back where we were. I can't do it again. Fool me once, shame on you. Fool me twice, shame on me for bein' just about the *dumbest* thing on two legs."

This couldn't be happening. "Wait. Just wait. Today was different. We had some kind of breakthrough and connected like never before. That means you *do* trust me. I don't want to control you. Your independence is one of the millions of reasons I love you. I know this is upsetting and frightening, but you *have* to know deep down that I don't have some nefarious purpose. You're the best thing that ever happened to me. Why would I risk losing you, unless I was truly worried about you?"

"People do messed-up things when they're messed up, Elliot. All I know is you don't see that you hurt me, and you're still pushin' ahead with your agenda, even though I told you not to. Whatever breakthrough you think we had was an illusion. This whole thing is phony. It never existed. I'm going home."

She walked off, arms still folded.

I fell into step beside her. Panic flapped like a trapped bird in my chest. "Look, can we just talk about this?" I asked.

"Nothing to talk about."

"Well, I think there is. I don't think this is a reason to throw everything away, especially after today."

No response.

I wondered what she'd do if I grabbed her and forced her to listen. Probably kick out my teeth. Thirty years of dance had left her strong and agile enough to wipe the floor with me.

To my utter disbelief, I saw Trey had parked his wheelchair in the middle of the sidewalk up ahead. He'd crossed the street to talk to me again. As Gary and I approached, he waved.

"Hey! How's it going, Elliot?" he called. "I've been looking for you, man. Where you been?"

Gary had become something pitiless and implacable, like a harvesting combine. I thought she'd march right past Trey, but she stopped and stared over his head.

"Hi, Trey," I said. "Nice to see you again."

He eyed Gary. "So who's your friend, man?"

"Oh. This is Gary Pruett. We, uh, work together. Gary, this is Trey Gillespie."

Trey cocked his head, blinking several times. "Gary? Like the man's name?"

I had no idea how I kept from bellowing at him to leave us alone.

"That's right," Gary said. "G-A-R-Y." Her voice sounded computer generated.

"Man, that's…different. Nice to meet you."

"Likewise."

Trey peered up at her. When she said no more, the corners of his mouth briefly went down in a facial shrug.

"Where you been, man?" he asked me. "I haven't seen you in weeks. I was worried you'd stopped coming out here after I talked to you."

"Well…no, that wasn't it. Actually, it's kind of funny. Two hours after I met you, I had a heart attack."

His eyes widened. "You had a *heart attack?* For *real?* Holy shit! Are you okay?"

"Yes, I'm fine. It was a mild heart attack. I had it at Gary's condo." I looked at her. "She gave me aspirin as it was happening, and my doctor said she saved my life."

She slowly turned to me. Nothing changed in her face.

"I'm really lucky," I said to her.

Trey glanced from me to Gary. "Yeah, it *sounds* like it," he said, obviously reading my thoughts again. I sent him a message: *I don't want to talk to you. Go away.*

"Well, I'm glad you're okay," he went on. "A fuckin' *heart attack.* That's unbelievable. You look great, though. I thought you'd decided not to walk out here anymore after I butted in on you. I felt bad. See, I scare people off. They don't wanna talk to the cripple because I depress them. I can't tell you how many times I talk to people once and never see them again."

"Well, you didn't get the chance to scare me off, because I immediately had a heart attack," I said. "I can show you my hospital bills if you want."

"He really had a heart attack," Gary said in a monotone.

Trey raised his hands. "Hey, I'm not saying you're afraid to talk to cripples. I'm just telling you that's how lots of folks are. They think I'm contagious."

"Not me," I said. I tried to block off my thoughts with images of brick walls.

"Cool." He looked at Gary again. "So, Gary. What do you do at your company?"

"I'm a copywriter."

"Do you work in the creative department of the frequency marketing division, like Elliot?"

"That's right. We're on the same team." She thawed slightly, her natural Southern politeness overriding her rage at me.

"Let's see: You write the words for club programs, coupons, sweepstakes, mail-in rebates, escalating rebate offers, membership programs, uh, time-release programs, points, stamps, scratch-off games, collect-and-win games, gift cards, and punch cards," Trey said.

She gave him a small smile. "Right. How'd you know?"

"Elliot told me."

"Two weeks ago," I said. "What are you, a tape recorder?" I glanced at Gary. "He's some kind of sorcerer, I think."

He chuckled. "No, I just listen when people talk to me."

"Well, that makes you in a class by yourself," Gary said. She shouldn't have bothered with the innuendo; I'm sure Trey already knew how much she hated me. I had to suppress a gust of unhinged laughter as I remembered a joke David told me.

What do you call an Italian suppository?

Innuendo!

"I *am* in a class by myself," Trey said. "Like I told Elliot, I like learning about new things. So how do you like working for a marketing corporation?"

Gary put her hands in the pockets of her sweat jacket. "I like it. It's very immediate, what we do. We can go out and see our work everywhere. And it's a challenge too, trying to keep everything fresh. A lot of it is boilerplate, but sometimes you really get to hone your creative chops, especially on sweepstakes. In the end it's trivial, like so much is, but I like doing it."

Trey smiled. "Man, I could listen to you talk all day. Where are you from?"

"Wilmington, North Carolina."

"What brought you all the way out to the West Coast?"

Shrug. "Wanted a change of scenery, I guess." She went chilly again, folding her arms and gazing toward the horizon.

He instantly picked up on it. "Well, I've kept you guys long enough," he said. "I'll walk with you back to the intersection."

He spun and led us toward the crosswalk, his chair humming like a golf cart. "So you sure you're gonna be all right, Elliot?" he asked over his shoulder.

"The doctors said I would."

"Well, you look better than you did the day we met. You were all pale and sweaty. Shit, man, you're too young to have heart problems. You gotta take care of yourself, okay?"

"Okay," I muttered. *Cast a spell on Gary,* I begged him. *Make her realize I'll die without her.*

At the intersection he said, "It was nice meeting you, Gary. I'm glad you saved Elliot's life. And Elliot, if you wanna stop and talk to me on your walks, you know where to find me. I'm out by the school every day, on the other side of the street."

"Sure, I'll do that," I said, a total lie. "See you later."

"Nice meeting you," Gary said as we left. Fifty yards down the sidewalk, I looked back. Trey was still on our side of the street, watching us. He gave me a wave, and I returned it.

* * *

Gary and I didn't speak all the way back to my house. When I unlocked the front door, she went to the bedroom to gather her things. I waited beside my toy cabinets.

She emerged, making a beeline toward the door as if I didn't exist.

"Can't we talk about this?" I asked before she could trample me.

"There's nothing to talk about." She still had her dark glasses on. I spread my arms to block her exit; she stopped.

"I think there is," I said.

"There isn't. There never was. Whatever I was doing for the past year was a waste of time. You showed me that today. I deluded myself, but that's nothing new. Are you gonna get out of my way?"

"Not yet. You saved my life. How can you walk out of it just like that?"

"I saved your life because it was the right thing to do. Was I supposed to stand there and watch you die, just because you went behind my back the way you did? No. I'm not that kind of person. But I'm not going to *share* your life. You want someone you can dominate. Well, sorry. Find someone else."

"*I don't want to dominate you!*" I wished she'd take off her dark glasses so I could see her eyes. They were her most striking feature, the color of an overcast sky. "This can't be happening. Two hours ago you were naked in my garden. You never did anything like that before."

"And I never will again."

She'd stand there for as long as it took. No screaming, no throwing things, no flurry of girl-slaps, and absolutely no tears. She didn't cry. In the two years I'd known her, she'd never come close, not when we watched the sappy tear-jerkers that always choked me up and not even when she talked about her dead father.

"Please don't leave me," I said, my voice cracking.

No reaction.

I stepped aside, and she walked out the door. Her car sat behind mine in the driveway; she got in and started the engine. I waited for her to beat the steering wheel with both hands, throw open the door and vault out, her face crumpling as she hurled herself at me, forgiving me, and hugging me so hard, my torso imploded.

While I waited, she backed out and drove away.

CHAPTER FIVE

"And I'm sure I speak for everyone when I say welcome back, Elliot. We're all grateful that you're here and you're going to be all right."

Dennis Yu, the art director of the creative department, chaired the Friday team meeting as usual. All eight of us were present. It felt as though I hadn't seen my colleagues in years. Everyone was the same except for Margaret, who now sported two thin crimson streaks in her black hair, one in front of each ear, to go with the bands of blonde.

Our producer Mitch Collins seemed nervous, probably because he was even fatter than I was. If *I* could have a heart attack, there was no telling what he was in for. He was subdued, laughing only every ten seconds instead of every five. Richard Klein was our marketing specialist and at forty-four the oldest member of the team. DuShawn Addams was our freelance photographer, and Essi Vig our freelance illustrator. Like Mitch and Richard, they were acquaintances. Julian, our traffic controller, came closest to being a friend, while Margaret was my nemesis.

The wild card was Gary. I had no idea how we'd pull off our new relationship. After she left my house, she didn't answer her phone or respond to any of my messages. In the conference room, she greeted me politely, a writing partner relieved that a fruitful, cordial working relationship was back to normal. We shook hands, and I numbly sat beside her at the oaken table. Dennis's voice gently ebbed and flowed in the background, like the ocean setting on the white-noise machine I bought to help me sleep.

"Before we get down to business, would you like to say anything, Elliot?" I heard him ask.

I surveyed the room. "Well, I'm glad to be back, and everything's fine. Thanks for your cards and e-mails. If I'd known you'd be so nice to me, I would've had my heart attack sooner."

A titter from Mitch; uneasy silence from the rest.

Dennis smoothly intervened. "As your boss I'm officially putting the kibosh on any more heart attacks for the foreseeable future. Now, let me tell you what I heard back."

The client was a local public-television station. It was offering subscribers a credit card that entered them in a sweepstakes every time they used it. The grand prize was a luxury sedan with which the winner could "Break Away!" The phrase came to me while I flossed my teeth the night before my heart attack.

First through sixth prizes were; a trip to Paris, a South American expedition, a Scandinavian excursion, a Hong Kong junket, a cruise to Alaska, and a vacation in Florida. If the subscriber didn't win any of these, he or she was still eligible for a week in either Ocho Rios, Toronto, Telluride, Las Vegas, Palm Desert, Palm Springs, Baja, or Washington, DC. For everybody else, there were magazine subscriptions, T-shirts, porcelain figurines, food processors, juicers, binoculars, gift certificates for restaurants, free movie tickets, and free admission to museums. It was a typical campaign, the kind we'd done dozens of times.

"To quote the young vice president," Dennis said, "'the copy sucks and the graphics blow.' That's his entire e-mail."

"I blame Elliot," Margaret said. "And how can something suck *and* blow at the same time?"

"You can answer that better than anybody," I said.

Richard, Julian, and DuShawn laughed. Margaret flapped her tongue at me. It was very long, and she'd once shown me how she could make it ripple like a belly dancer's abs.

"I really missed the warm, comfortable threat of a harassment suit hanging over my head," Dennis said. He spread out Margaret's roughs of the envelope, flyers, and brochures, which she'd done during my two weeks off. "All righty, let's take a look. First, they said the copy's just too hostile. Here, on the entry form: 'Yes! I want this card so I will be eligible to win amazing prizes!' Or this: 'Enjoy a sophisticated dream vacation in upscale Baja Mexico.' Or this: 'A charming and beguiling resort in the heart of the Las Vegas Strip.' And the food processor will let you 'attain a whole new level of kitchen enlightenment'? Just an FYI, they said we should fire whoever wrote that."

Julian guffawed.

"I was just about to have a heart attack," I said. "My mood was…churlish."

"Change it all," Dennis continued, "and change every 'fabulous' to 'great.' Fabulous is homo. Their word, not mine. Now the graphics. They say the graphics are too cheesy."

"They're not cheesy! They're retro!" Margaret shouted.

"They want deeper colors and twinkly starbursts around the title, like on fifties appliance ads. Have you seen those?"

"Jesus, Dennis, I'm not eighty years old."

"Then do some research. Okay, the orange and aqua border's fine, but they want their name bigger, about forty point. And their slogan should be in small caps. Now, the people, the jet planes, the palm trees, and the Eiffel Tower on the back: They're all clip art, aren't they?"

"Yes," Essi said. "All the line art is. Would that be, like, part of the cheesiness factor?"

"Yeah. They've seen them too many times, they said. They want original art. How long will that take?"

"Monday morning?"

"Perfect. Okay, the brochure. The title captions all have to be script, right slanted, demi-bold, all with exclamation marks, not periods."

"Not too cheesy," Margaret muttered, typing on her laptop.

Dennis smiled. "They want another band of orange, aqua, yellow, and pink on the bottom of the entry form. Also, the callout under the sticker on the flyer is too far away. Move it closer. Put more starbursts around the 'Break Away!' here, and change the 'two' in 'two-door' to the number *2,* Gary or Elliot. Don't ask me why, but they don't like numbers written out."

"Got it," Gary said.

"Good. DuShawn? They want the car shinier, the road blurrier, and the driver gone. He's a Caucasian male."

"Horrible," DuShawn said. "I'll darken the windshield."

"All right. That should be it. Overall, we're going for less hostility and cheese. Julian? What's coming up?"

"The casino VIP card and then *Slimeballs III.*"

"Okay. Keep 'em on your radar. Anything? Anybody? Okay, let's get to work. And welcome back, Elliot."

* * *

Dennis left, followed by Gary. I wanted to go after her, but the others hemmed me in to say how good it was to see me again. Gary's footsteps receded down the hall.

"Did they tell you why it happened?" Mitch asked.

"A combination of stress, lack of exercise, and being overweight." *And decades of swallowed rage, according to my idiot doctor.* "I have to lose forty pounds."

DuShawn frowned. "Forty *pounds?* No way. That's crazy. You're not forty pounds overweight, are you?"

"Well...yes. You just can't tell because it's in a uniform layer."

Mitch patted his enormous paunch. "I wish I could say that."

"Then you'd be five inches thicker in all your dimensions," Richard said. He and Mitch laughed. The difference between Mitch and me was that he'd chosen the classic fatty role. If someone expressed an opinion, he'd giggle, "I hear ya!" When asked for a pencil, he'd chortle, "What's a little pencil-sharing among friends?" He actually screamed with laughter. His volume in a sealed room was agonizing. He made up his own acronyms too. If someone got a chocolate bar from the vending machine, it was YNT: Yummy-Noise Time, *mmm-mmm-mmm*. He always looked on the bright side, he never put anybody down, and he loved to be kidded about his "tummy."

"Are you gonna, like, change your diet?" Essi asked me.

"Completely. Low fat, low salt, low carb, and tons of vegetables. I've eaten my last double cheeseburger."

"Awesome. Good for you."

I went to my cubicle, which was adjacent to Gary's. Dennis had put us beside each other to facilitate communication on the days our team worked at the office to beat insane deadlines. After Friday meetings Gary and I always coordinated in the break room, but I saw that her handbag and jacket were gone from her desk. She wasn't in the break room either. I poured myself a cup of coffee and joined the rest of my team at one of the tables. They were well into what Gary called the Friday Rumpus.

"Look," Margaret said, "we have five percent of the world's population, but we're responsible for half of the world's military spending."

"So what?" Julian said. "The US is paying for the defense of just about every free country in the world."

"Who asked us to?"

"Every free country in the world."

"But it's not our responsibility. I want my tax dollars going to schools and health care, not bombs and guns."

"How do you use schools and health care to stop people who want to kill you?"

"Well, they wanna kill us because we keep fucking with them."

"And sometimes people announce in plain language that their goal is to take over the world, and the only choices they offer you are to submit or die."

"How the fuck are they gonna take over the world? That's never gonna happen. We've got ICBMs and stealth bombers and nuclear submarines and Navy SEALs."

"It's not the fact that they'll be successful in taking over the world; it's the damage they can do in trying."

"We've been at war since I was, like, fourteen years old," Essi said. "It's just a way for the military-industrial complex to make money. Perpetual war, like, sells weapons and creates jobs. It's all about lobbyists and, like, cronies getting no-bid contracts and politicians getting, like, military pork for their states."

"That's how all government works," Richard said, "You only care about it when it's the military. What about all the lobbying, cronyism, no-bid contracts, and taxpayer money going to alternative-energy companies that declare bankruptcy, and then some guy walks away with a trunk full of cash because he's friends with the president?"

"Well, that's wrong too," Margaret said. "But it's not the same as starting wars based on lies and slaughtering millions of innocent people just so you can make money and steal oil."

Richard groaned. "Margaret, I was already thirty-two when this started. You were eleven. I've read everything I could about it, and nobody told any lies. Millions of innocent people haven't been slaughtered. We didn't even get any oil from anybody. I'm so *tired* of everything being reduced to the same five slogans that people just repeat over and over. You're smarter than that!"

"Where's the evidence that she's smarter than that?" Julian asked.

Margaret laughed. "Fuck you, asshole! I'm as smart as anyone in this room! You're just pissed because I don't agree with you."

"No, what pisses me off is when you denigrate the motives of people who disagree with *you*. In your mind I couldn't *possibly* have valid reasons for thinking the way I do."

Essi sighed. "I'm sure you, like, think your reasons are valid, but I just don't get why you can't see that all we're trying to do is, like, install puppet governments that'll let us set up military bases so we can, like, project our power."

"I notice you apply the term 'puppet' only to brown and black people," Richard said. "You never call them puppet governments when they're run by white people. Why is that?"

Essi didn't answer.

"I don't know of any white puppet governments, except for the British," DuShawn said.

"*Charming!*" Julian shouted. "What a wonderful thing to say in the presence of a British citizen. Do you people ever think before you speak?"

"Just calling them as I see them," DuShawn said. "And what the fuck do you mean by 'you people'?"

Julian curled his lip. "Oh, get stuffed. Let's talk about those puppet governments, shall we? Before the elections, people are warned that they'll be murdered if they vote. So on election day, they say the prayers of those about to die and go vote. Meanwhile, most pampered, safe Americans don't even *bother* to vote. I'm sorry, but you make me ill."

Margaret stood. "Sweet. What bug got up *your* ass this morning?"

Julian rose and leaned over to look behind her. "I say, do we really want to talk about what people in this office get up their arses, Margaret? I mean, *do* we?"

She gave him what I thought of as her lizard smile, which she executed by turning up only the very outermost corners of her mouth. It was something to see, a potent reminder of the lengthy tongue coiled behind the dark-red lips.

As the room cleared, I'm certain that some of us mulled Julian's question. I myself was clueless about Margaret's propensities. The whole team, however, was well aware that she was callipygian, an adjective that Julian taught me, and that I as a wordsmith should've known.

* * *

We'd hired Margaret in her senior year at Berkeley. She was the youngest graphic designer in the creative department, the replacement for my teammate Jeff, who'd decided to give his garage band one last shot before he turned forty. The first team meeting with Margaret on board went very smoothly. She was bright and funny, and everything she said in her husky near-baritone had an ironic overlay. In the break room, someone brought up the rumor that Soledad planned to open an office in China. Margaret waited for the rest of us to put in our two cents before she made her contribution.

"China looks like a rooster."

In the ensuing silence, she sketched the outline of China on a piece of paper and said, "All it needs is two chicken legs coming down out of Guangxi Province, like this. It's already got a bill and a comb poking into Russia, and it's got wattles over North Korea, and Xinjiang Province and Tibet are the tail feathers. See? It's facing the east and sticking out its neck—Inner Mongolia—and crowing at the rising sun."

With a few swipes of a pencil, China indeed became a rooster. Margaret added closed wings and an eye squeezed shut with effort and wrote, "Cock-a-doodle-doo!" in a word balloon coming out of the beak. Julian burst out laughing, and Essi said, "That's, like, totally brilliant!" DuShawn picked up the drawing and made chicken noises.

"This is why we keep marijuana illegal," Richard said, but he smiled. Even Gary seemed amused. Margaret dropped her China rooster in the trash.

I wondered how many people in the country could draw the outline of China or name even one province. Everybody on my team would forever after see China as a crowing rooster, and in doing so, we'd instantly think of Margaret. Within an hour of meeting her, she'd stamped herself indelibly on our collective consciousness. I marveled over that; had she planned it? Her appearance was memorable enough—skinny jeans and either T-shirts or tank tops that revealed muscular shoulders, a flat stomach, and that amazing bottom. And brains and a sense of humor too. She made quite a splash.

For three weeks Margaret and I exchanged words only in meetings and the break room. Our contact was strictly professional until the morning she came into my cubicle and sat on my desk. She also sat on my left hand, trapping it between cold hardness below and heavy, blazing-hot springiness above. My hand became super acute; it charted and transmitted the contours and texture of the flesh that weighed it down. Margaret raised her arms and stretched, her fingers interlocked above her head, the hem of her tank top rising past her belly button as she grinned down at me like a blissful cat. A big, warm-bottomed, nipply, blissful cat with a pierced nose.

"Whatcha workin' on?" she asked.

I wiggled my fingers.

"Ooh!" She pursed her lips, eyes wide, then she arched her back and slowly lifted her left buttock. I slid my hand out from under her. She quizzed me about my gift-card copy, responding to my mumbled answers with mock-serious nods. Her heat lingered on the back of my hand like a scald.

When I said, "The next time you want a prostate examination, see a doctor," I discovered she had a tinkling, musical laugh completely at odds with her raggedy voice. My acknowledgement of her ass was a barometer. She hopped off my desk and ambled out.

The following Friday I had a sandwich at Amir's, the lunch counter next door to the office. Margaret plopped down across from me at my table.

"Hi, Elliot!" she piped. "How ya doin'?"

"Fine," I said.

"Fine!" she mimicked, making it shrill like a cockatoo's voice. She tore into a vegetable pita and described a rock-climbing trip she'd taken to Utah, where the mountains looked like colossal piles of pastrami, all reddish pink with black specks and a brown rind.

"Holy motherfuckin' cocksucker *shit,* man," she said, "it was beautiful."

"Do you kiss your mother with that mouth?" I asked.

"No, I go down on her with this mouth." She wrinkled her nose and gave me a sassy, pursed, little smile as she patted my forearm.

Thus was her custom. She belittled my copy, imitated my laugh, pinched my cheek, mimicked me, greeted me loudly thirty times a day, commented on my meals, ruffled my hair, and drew pictures of me in my cubicle or in the break room with a black cloud over my head pouring rain on me. It was a mystery why she hated me, but she did.

I often thought of renting an old movie and asking Margaret to watch it with me. There were several films with scenes in which two men met and had some kind of conflict that resulted in a fistfight. As soon as one knocked down the other, it was over. The winner hauled the loser to his feet and brushed him off, and the loser felt his jaw and said something like, "That's quite a right cross you got, kid. Where'd you learn to box like that? Harvard? No kidding! I went to Yale! Put 'er there!" And they were best buddies for life.

They had a system in those days, and it worked. Everybody knew the rules: You had to knock a man to the ground only once, then you helped him up and accepted his friendship. The issue was resolved.

* * *

My first day back at work left me exhausted. I went straight home and wrote copy for two hours before phoning Gary. She was out. I left a short message asking her to please call me, took a nap, and went on my walk.

The quarter mile of sidewalk where the cars came too close was a barren stretch I thought of as No Man's Land, where terrible things might happen to someone caught out in the open. As I traversed it, I saw Trey sitting in his usual place in front of the high school, his head back and his eyes closed. After a mile I turned around. At the first intersection, I impulsively crossed the street over to his side. It wouldn't hurt to show him I wasn't afraid of him. I wasn't like everybody else.

The sidewalk where he sat doubled as a concrete median strip. It separated the main thoroughfare from a short, dead-end frontage road truncated by the high school parking lot. Sometimes Trey sat on the sidewalk; sometimes he sat in the middle of the dead-end street. It was only about fifty feet long and never saw any traffic.

I approached from behind. Since he still had his eyes shut, I scraped my shoes on the pavement to let him know I was there.

He turned his chair around. "Hey! Elliot! Glad you could make it, man. How are you?" He seemed genuinely pleased to see me.

"Pretty good. How about you?"

"Aw, nothing ever changes with me. I've been the same for almost twenty-three years. You know, I still can't get over the fact that you had a fuckin' heart attack. You're really okay?"

"As far as I know."

He sipped water. "That's good to hear. So hey, tell me about that Gary chick. She's your girlfriend, huh? Yow. You dog. She's one hot momma. I saw you guys have a big fight that day. How'd it turn out? You kiss and make up?"

I was about to tell him I didn't want to talk about it, but when I opened my mouth, I heard myself say, "She dumped me right after we left you."

"She *dumped* you? That same *day?*" He was stunned. "This is too fuckin' much, man. I meet you, and you have a heart attack. I meet you again, and your girlfriend dumps you. I'm some kind of bad-luck charm for you. I've had so much bad luck myself, it's starting to rub off on people."

"No, that's not it," I said. "I cause all my own problems."

"Oh yeah? Me, I never got dumped. I was always the dumper, not the dumpee. So why'd she dump you? Did you fuck up? You weren't cheating on her, were you? No offense, but a guy like you shouldn't ever take a chick like that for granted."

"You know what?" I sat on the curb. "I have a feeling I'm going to tell you all about it, but not today. If I talk about it now, I'm going to start crying like a little girl, and you wouldn't like that."

"Nope. I wouldn't. I can't feel sorry for you because at least you had a hot woman up until a few days ago. I haven't been with anybody since I was disabled. I barely remember what it's like. My dick still works, but my head's the only part of me you can touch where it doesn't hurt."

"I'm sorry," I said, wondering why I'd come over to see him.

"You're not gonna do anything stupid, are you?" he asked. "Like off yourself over her?"

"No, of course not."

"Good. Because killing yourself is a lot harder than you think. I've already tried three times."

I groaned; it was completely involuntary.

That seemed to satisfy him. "The first time, I hoarded my painkillers for a couple months. I said good-bye to my dog; I was all crying, 'Good-bye, Yvonne'; and I went out at night with my pills and my bottle of water and thought they'd find me in the morning, but I had to come back after nothing happened. It just wasn't enough pills. The second time I took a hundred and six Valiums, and it didn't do anything except make my legs stop hurting. I came home in time for dinner, not even sleepy at all, and my legs felt great for a week. 'Hey, Ma, what's for dinner? Man, do my legs feel *good!*'"

I laughed. His comedic timing was perfect, and who'd name a dog Yvonne? It was genius.

With a prankster's merry grin, he said, "So then I took rat poison."

Though seated, I almost lost my balance. "Oh my God."

"Yeah, well, I figured *that'd* work. And man, I just got sick. I got the runs and started puking. I would've let myself drown in it, but I couldn't even manage that because I can't lie back. And it didn't kill me! I was like, 'Shit, how'd I develop a tolerance to *rat poison?*' My mom came and found me and called an ambulance, so I lived. I've just got bad luck. If a car came through here right now and hit us, you'd be out like a light, and I'd just get jacked up worse. You'd be gone before you even knew what hit you, and I'd have broken legs, or I'd break my neck *again* and end up on a respirator."

After a sip of water, he continued. "This country, man, with its bleeding-heartedness…it's pathetic. Why can't I get a shot in the arm and go to sleep with dignity? Fuckin' murderers are treated better than people like me. Scumbags who raped and strangled little kids get more consideration. If I coulda done it, I woulda been dead ten years ago. I coulda spared my mom and me the last twelve years."

All I could say was, "I'm sorry."

He glanced around, wheeled toward me, and whispered, "But like I told you before, I figured out how to get outta this. These people in my neighborhood have a big swimming pool, and every Wednesday night, before garbage day, they leave the gate to the backyard open when they put the cans out. I've been scoping it out for a year now. One of these Wednesday nights, I'm gonna drive into their pool."

"Jesus!" That settled it: I'd never talk to him again.

"Jesus, *shit*. If there's a Jesus up there, I'm gonna make him tell me why I had to go through all this. I never did anything to deserve this. I just had a wasted fuckin' life, and I know people say if you kill yourself, you're going to hell, but where do they think I am now? Do they think I'm scared of *hell?* Shit. It can't be any worse than this."

We didn't speak for a while. He seemed tired. I was ready to collapse.

"When it gets cold, I can't take it," he said. "I don't come out here unless it's hot. So I'll do it in the fall. I'd like to wait until I'm sure I won't be missing one of those hot spells like we always have. I'd be pissed if I killed myself, and then there was, like, two weeks where it was ninety-five degrees!" He laughed and sipped water.

"Have you told anybody else about this?" I asked.

"Shit no! I stopped talking about suicide with my friends and family a long time ago. I wanted them to think I don't want to do it anymore. I've uh, uh, uh, *lulled* them—that's the word—into putting their guard down. Nobody knows about this."

Except for me. I knew what he was going to do, and I knew where, how, and roughly when he was going to do it. With that information I could call the police and foil his plan. Legally, I was obligated to.

"Why are you telling me this?" I asked. "It's really an awful lot for me to deal with."

"Man, I'm sorry. I know this is heavy shit, but I had to tell someone. I *had* to. I had to hear myself talk about it to another human being. I mean, I can't leave a note because I can't write, and I can't say good-bye to anyone, or they'll stop me. But I didn't want to just disappear without…without somebody to—whatever you'd call it, I don't know—bear witness or something, you know? I already feel like my whole life was a total waste, so I guess I just want someone to understand the…well, it sounds so lame, but the meaningfulness of what I'm going to do."

"Okay," I said. "I understand."

I stood and brushed off the seat of my shorts.

"Elliot, don't mention this to anyone, all right? I mean it. Not a peep. If anyone finds out, I'm fucked. This is my last chance."

"I won't tell anybody."

He chuckled. "Man, I *know* I'll never see you again *now.*"

I was sick of his cocky ESP and prognostications. "Yeah, well, I wouldn't bet on that," I said much more emphatically than I'd intended. He recoiled with pretend shock, smiling.

At home I treated my legs to a long massage with the pulsing showerhead I bought two days earlier. I wasn't hungry, but I forced myself to heat up a can of low-salt turkey chili, into which I added a double handful of mixed vegetables. Before I went to bed, I left another message on Gary's machine and sent another e-mail.

CHAPTER SIX

As I walked toward the refrigerator, the floor in my kitchen gave out. I fell through the linoleum, the sharp edges slashing my face. My house was built in the branches of a giant tree, miles above the lush green canopy of the Amazon. I plunged downward for what seemed like hours, finally piercing the gray, rain-swollen clouds and crashing through vines and branches into a cacophony of birds and monkeys screeching in outrage as I dropped past. The spinning forest floor rushed toward me, and I jolted awake in my bed, drenched in sweat. According to my clock, it was 5:22 a.m.

Every night of the past week had brought a different falling dream. I fell from mountains, cathedrals, airplanes, trapeze platforms, scaffolding, and smokestacks. The one constant was that I never hit the ground. I'd had worse nightmares, but there was something particularly unbearable about the sound of air rushing past my ears and the sensation of weightlessness.

I made a cup of coffee and went out on the back porch with my laptop. The sun was just coming up, making the dew on my cactus and aloe sparkle like diamonds. Hummingbirds flitted and twittered.

My e-mail inbox had a message from Gary with the subject line "Re: Important message." It was probably about our new project, the sci-fi movie *Slimeballs III,* second sequel to the smash hit *Slimeballs.* Dozens of companies had hired us to link their products with it. We were doing a sweepstakes, rebates, and gift certificates that would bring in sellers of toys, software, computers, cell phones, consumer electronics, and office products. After the team meeting the previous Friday, Gary had again taken off without talking to me, skipping the private conference we should've had to coordinate who'd write what. She'd sent her message at 3:43 a.m., not the best time in the world for her to be awake and alone.

I corrected myself: It was a baseless assumption that she was alone. Her performance on my birthday showed she'd made gigantic strides in the arena of...collaboration. She could've been e-mailing me while she got a mustache ride in someone's moonlit garden. Or while she got two mustache rides simultaneously. Why not? Los Angeles had no shortage of either secluded yards or mustaches.

On the other hand, maybe it was an apology. That might explain the ungodly hour it was sent. A weeping, four-in-the-morning appeal for forgiveness and an invitation to race over and besiege her lanky body.

After a gulp of coffee, I opened her message.

> *Elliot:*
> *Please stop calling and sending personal e-mails. You and I have a working relationship, nothing more. It's time for you to accept that. For the sake of our jobs, please don't contact me unless it's about a project. Things will never go back to how they were before. This is the last time I will ever mention this subject. Don't force me to raise it with our supervisors.*
> *G.*

Hurling a mug of coffee at a cement floor wasn't as cathartic as I'd hoped. The coffee slopped out in midair, forming a brown arc like a coyote's tail and landing in a diffuse splatter at my feet. Though the mug exploded dramatically, the ceramic shrapnel bothered me so much, I had to immediately sweep it up.

I lay on the sofa in the living room and listened to most of a jazz CD. When I went back to my laptop, I had to suppress an impulse to smash it like the coffee mug, because she still hadn't contacted me about the project. She was forcing *me* to make the move. I sat down and composed an e-mail. On the subject line I wrote "Re: *Slimeballs III* question."

> *Gary:*
> *We didn't coordinate after Friday's meeting. If you want, I'll do the p-o-p and you can do the reebs and certs.*
> *Let me know.*
> *E.*

Her answer came in a few seconds.

> *Fine. Let's coordinate by e-mail from now on.*

I wrote a response.

> *I agree. I'm sick of looking at your face. It's a relief to have you out of my life. The worst part of our pitiful relationship was the sex. It was unbelievably boring. I had to fantasize about Margaret just to get it up with you. You were all proud of yourself for coming on to me like you were some kind of hot piece of ass, but you blew your wad doing that. In the end you're just another repressed Southern Baptist. Think about how pathetic you are, for a lapsed Catholic to be saying that to you. And you did it to yourself! You can't even blame your parents for how stunted you are. Anyway, it was a drag, and I'm glad it's over. Ciao.*

I deleted it, experiencing a nanosecond of gut-wrenching techno-horror when I thought I may have accidentally clicked the Send icon instead.

My assignment was therefore to write the copy for the sweeps point-of-purchase items, the coupons and vouchers that customers picked up at the cash registers of retail outlets. They offered a chance to win the grand prize of an all-expense-paid trip for two to New York, where the winners would stay in the presidential suite of a five-star hotel, go to the premiere, and meet the two stars. Those who didn't win the grand prize could still get a desktop computer or a deluxe four-disc DVD set of the first two movies.

Gary would take the rebates and gift certificates. Customers who bought a computer, software, or a cell phone and then mailed in their proof of purchase would get money back and also have their names entered into a drawing for tickets to the Los Angeles premiere. No presidential suite, no meet-and-greet with the stars, but a limo ride and a sumptuous dinner with plenty of cocktails.

I deleted her e-mail, something I'd never done before. Without really thinking about it, I then deleted the folder titled "Gary." Two years of personal and professional messages evaporated into the ether where they belonged.

* * *

By early afternoon I'd reached the staring stage, sitting motionless in front of the screen as the minutes ticked by. I put my laptop to sleep and changed into my walking outfit. It was actually more like a costume or disguise. The enormous white shoes were ridiculous, with ribbed soles an inch thick and as wide as tank treads to distribute my weight. I had to get them because after only twenty minutes in my old high-top sneakers, every step I took went slamming up through my shins and knees, all the way to the top of my head. It felt as if the cement were lunging up at me, pounding my feet flat.

I had two identical pairs of dark-blue nylon shorts that went down to my knees. They were much too big and baggy, but I couldn't find anything else that fit my waist, and besides, big and baggy was the only style available. I now understood how all those middle-aged men felt forty years earlier, when they were forced into pimp bellbottoms, lapels out to their shoulders, and neckties as wide as bibs, ludicrous apparel they had to wear because nobody made normal clothes anymore. The nylon shorts felt sleazy against my thighs, like cheap motel curtains blowing in a hot breeze. There was no way I was going to wear cotton, though. Cotton was absorbent.

One of my high school classmates was a bearded, red-eyed giant named Lem. He perspired constantly, even sitting in the library, but in PE class he was a monsoon. He left droplets all over the wooden floor of the gym, thousands of slippery little dots that made you hydroplane. PE started with a short basketball game to warm us up—the Shirts versus the Skins. Every day for four years, Lem and I—the two fattest kids in the class—were Skins. We stood as still as possible out on the court, trying to keep our breasts from jiggling while our thin, athletic teammates screamed at us because we wouldn't dash back and forth. I didn't care how much people screamed; I wasn't putting on any more of a show than I had to. Lem probably felt the same way, and he may also have thought that by not moving, he'd keep his body temperature down. He was wrong. When he bent over to pick up the ball during one game, his cotton shorts stretched tight across his rear, and someone on the sidelines yelled, "Jesus, look at that! He's sweating in his *crack!*"

I never spoke to Lem. If I had, he would've beaten me to death. I'm absolutely sure of it.

A dark-blue hooded sweat jacket went over my white T-shirt, and a black baseball cap worn the right way shielded my face from the afternoon sun. I also used SPF forty-five sunblock that was like cream cheese. It made me worry about my complexion; I worried more about my father going in every few months to have another melanoma sliced off. Since sun damage was cumulative, it probably didn't matter. As a child I was often burned so badly that the skin on my cheeks and forehead peeled off in sheets. A gentle tug, and I'd have a filmy little scrap to play with. I still remembered that soft, painless, tearing sensation. Some kind of ointment was rubbed on, but only after I was already cooked.

The final pieces of my walking outfit were my contacts and a pair of round, wire-rimmed sunglasses as dark as welding goggles. They were antiques, originally issued to men of the British 7th Armoured Division, the Desert Rats who fought the Germans and Italians in North Africa during World War Two. I wore them because they made me look utterly crazy.

* * *

Out on the street, I walked past the house on the corner two blocks to the west. I didn't know if the residents were actual hillbillies or just fans of the lifestyle, but they'd put together a thoroughly authentic replica of an Appalachian shotgun shack. Most of the white paint had fallen off the warped wooden siding, the asphalt shingles were curly and ruffled, and the brick chimney had a breathtaking daredevil tilt. The front yard was bare dirt except in the spring, when it was a knee-deep meadow of clover. Two junked pickups sat on flat tires in the driveway, half hiding the mattresses leaning against the garage, and the shadows looming across the blinds at night revealed there was no electricity. They used lanterns instead.

The backyard was parallel to the sidewalk and had a board fence about five and a half feet high. As I walked past, I glanced over it, right into the wide, brown eyes of a dark-haired teenage girl holding a trombone to her lips. Since I wasn't expecting to see anybody, especially not an attractive teenage trombonist, I gasped. Her reaction was much more radical: She tucked her chin into her neck, dropped her arms, and let the trombone smack against her thighs. It was as if her power had been cut. I forced myself into a trot to get away from her. She'd given me a head-to-toe chill, wilting like that.

Trey was in his spot beside the high school parking lot. We exchanged waves and I went slightly over a mile. On my way back, I crossed the street.

"Hey, man," he said. "How's it going?"

"Not great." I sat on the curb in front of his chair. "Gary sent my formal screw-you e-mail today," I said. "She told me to never call her again or send a personal message."

"That sucks. But you were expecting it."

"Yup."

"My last girlfriend stuck with me for a year after I got paralyzed. She thought I'd pull off a miracle. You know, one of my fingers would start wiggling, and I'd yell, 'Nurse! Get in here!' and everybody would hug and cry. So when a year had gone by and I was still in bed, she cruised. I don't blame her."

I didn't say anything.

"Shit," he said. "Could you readjust my goddamn foot? I just realized it's out of whack."

I stood and nervously examined Trey's immaculate white shoes. Before I met him, I thought all quadriplegics were numb from the neck down. In the past week, I'd learned that Trey drank water all day because his damaged spinal cord prevented his sweat glands from working. But instead of being numb, he was hypersensitive. Any touch was agony. Sitting, lying, a woman's caress—they all produced the same violent stabs of pain. Nothing could stop the pain. Constant muscle spasms made him feel as though his limbs were being torn off.

"Watch this," he said once, and bit his right pinkie. His left arm flapped in hideous imitation of a chicken's wing. "Nobody can explain why that happens. I have these pressure points all over my body, and if I knock them against something or if somebody touches them, I spasm, and it hurts like shit. Press the side of my stomach with your fingers. Right here, above my girdle."

I did, and his legs trembled violently. He had several hidden connections that he'd discovered one by one, the hard way, over the past two decades.

"Okay," he said. "I need you to move my right foot forward until the sole of the shoe is perfectly flat on the footrest. Be real careful, now."

I knelt and grasped his heel with my right hand. "Ready?"

"Yeah."

Slowly I lifted his heel.

"Ow! Fuck! Careful, Fatso!"

I gently moved his foot forward an inch and set it flat on the rest. "How's that?"

"Fine. Sorry to make you do that, but if my foot fell off the rest when I was driving around, it would've hurt like hell. Thanks." He sipped water. "Okay, you're pissed. What about?"

I sat on the curb. "Don't call me Fatso. You can make fun of me for whatever else you want, but not my weight."

He appraised me. "I'm sorry, man. I say all sorts of shit when I'm in pain. It's like when a woman's in labor and she's screaming, 'Fuck you! I hate you!' to her husband. I didn't mean it."

"Yeah, well, when I was growing up, my brother and sister called me Fatty. They got it from a chant they learned at school:

> *Fatty, fatty, two by four*
> *Can't get through the bathroom door*
> *So he does it on the floor*
> *Licks it up and does some more.*

"They used it as a derangement spell—repeat three times and step back. Every day, several times a day. They'd get our maid Claudia to join in, even though she couldn't speak English:

> *Feti, feti, tuba faw*
> *Kanga trrruda batam daw*
> *Soee dazit tanda flaw*
> *Leeksee tappan dasa maw.*

"They only stopped after I broke my legs. I ended up semi-crippled, but my siblings didn't call me Fatty, Pork, Piggy, Chubster, or Ba-voom anymore, so it was worth it."

"I'm sorry, man," Trey said. "I really didn't mean it. Why'd your brother and sister pick on you?"

"My sister used to tell me there was a slip-up in the maternity ward when I was born. Somewhere out there was a bunch of fatties with a skinny kid who was the real Elliot. I was an impostor."

It was nice to see *him* at a loss for once.

"I was thinking about those pictures you showed me," I said.

In the backpack hanging between the handles of his chair, he kept a small album full of photos of himself in high school, when he was a wiry, deeply tanned kid with huge hands, shoulder-length blond curls, and a reckless smile.

"What about them?" he asked.

"Well, you're one of the cool guys."

"Uh-huh. And who're the cool guys?"

"The guys who gave me wedgies and funny nicknames. Within the first ten seconds of my first day in the seventh grade, some guy in a black Led Zeppelin T-shirt yelled, 'Hey, you! Potato Head! How'd you fit that head through the front door?' The whole school heard it, I guess, because I was Potato Head for a month and then someone shortened it to Tater, and that's what they called me for the next six years."

Trey sipped water and peered across the street.

I stood up to pace the sidewalk. "The cool guys always had the best girls. In the seventh grade, one of the cool-guy girls was named Melanie. She was a beautiful, blue-eyed brunette who wanted me dead the instant she first saw me. I avoided her most of the time, but during one lunch period, she sat at my table in the cafeteria and publicly shredded me for fifteen minutes straight. The only thing I remember she said was, 'You sit in the library looking at encyclo*pedias.*'"

"Did you?" Trey asked.

"Absolutely! The illustrations were magnificent, especially in the section about the human body. It had these transparent celluloid inserts with pictures of a man you could dissect just by turning the pages. You could strip away his muscles and organs layer by layer until he was just a skeleton."

"I remember those. I had to use them once for a biology report."

"So as I tried to explain why I liked reading encyclopedias, Melanie stuck out her tongue and went, *'Blih-thih-thih-thih-thih-thih-thihhhhhhhhh,'* the perfect sound for a hideous, semi-human outcast. Then she gave the cutest little impish smile to all the kids who'd fallen out of their chairs and were thrashing around on the floor. I never sat in the library and read encyclopedias again, but that was stupid. Nobody congratulated me or asked to be my friend. It actually got a lot worse, because now they knew they could control me. They started going after my clothes, my hair, my weight, and especially my head, as if I'd made it oversized as some kind of lame fashion statement. 'Hey, Tater! Why's your head so big? From all that reading, huh? Hey, I'm *talking* to you, Pizza Face! Reading makes your head big and gives you zits, huh?'"

Trey released a long sigh. "I shoulda known you were one of the kids everybody picked on. Ugly story, man."

"Did you make fun of people like me?"

"Yeah. It's not something I'm proud of. I was an asshole. But I'm being punished for it now, that's for sure. Shit, it still really bothers you, doesn't it? Would it help if I apologized?"

"Why? You didn't do anything to me."

We watched the traffic for a while.

"I used to imagine splitting the cool guys with broadswords or boiling them in cauldrons of oil or putting them into some kind of air-pressure room and crunching them into little balls," I said. "I made it through school by fantasizing about murder."

Trey laughed. "Well, twenty-five years later you meet one of us, and all I wanna do is die. You can get your revenge now. Go buy a gun. I'll wait."

"Don't tempt me. I was just starting to like you, before you called me Fatso."

"You shouldn't get attached anyway. I'm not gonna be here that much longer."

* * *

My long shower revived me. I decided I'd drive to Santa Monica and drop in at La Cachette, my favorite bar and grill. It was a relatively small place that catered to Belgian expatriates. The menu was great: chicken with asparagus, meatballs on rice, steak and Liège salad, or Belgian fries in a paper cone with a big dollop of that thick not-mayonnaise sauce. To wash it down, I'd choose a Trappist beer or a golden ale. The music was by bands I'd never heard of, but they all had a dreamy, drum-heavy, techno-house, world-beat flavor, with lush synthesizers and murmuring vocals in French and other languages, maybe Urdu and Esperanto. It put me into a nice trance.

I'd gotten to know the owner, a Belgian named Charles. He was one of those wiry, longhaired European men who dressed in black and had deep facial creases that he somehow made look insanely stylish.

"'Allo, Elliot," he said when he saw me. "I'd like you to meet someone. She's visiting from Brussels."

He introduced me to a woman sitting at the bar, a tousled blonde in her mid-thirties wearing tight, faded jeans, a butter-colored tank top, and a leather jacket. I couldn't understand her name.

"I'm sorry," I said as I shook her hand. "How do you pronounce your name again?"

"SEE-che." She wrote it out on a napkin: SYTJE. "It means 'Cynthia.' You can call me Cynthia if you want."

I liked Sytje better. Tall and long limbed, she was an art dealer and a Fleming. Charles had told me that in Belgium, Flemings are rubes, while the Francophone Walloons are the chic ones. They were out of their minds. Sytje was fantastic. Her slightly nasal, almost-German accent was a perfect match for her angular face. She made me think of windswept polders, guildsmen at the barricades, torchlight reflected on wet cobblestone. We had dinner at a corner table and talked about painters.

"You know, I'm having such a wonderful time in America," she said. "I wish I could stay longer."

"What do you like about it here?" I asked.

"Oh, the people. Definitely. Americans are so friendly and welcoming. Look at you, for instance. How many other men would sit here and listen to me talk about my job for two hours?"

"Every man on the face of the planet?"

She laughed. "Well, thank you, but I'm not so optimistic. It's time for me to ask *you* some questions. This is the one I always ask people when I'm getting past the small-talk time and I want to know them. What's the most important thing about life for you?"

"Wow. Let's see. I guess for me, the most important thing is to not hurt people who don't deserve it. Do you know the Wicca religion?"

"Witches, yeah. People tell me I look like a witch." She turned to display her profile. Her nose was horrifically long by Los Angeles standards, and it had a slight bump in it. "You think so?" She peered at me from the corner of her eye.

"Actually," I said, "I think you belong in an Alma-Tadema painting. There's something totally pre-Raphaelite about you."

She laughed and made a shooing gesture. "Alma-Tadema's women are so beautiful! They're round and feminine, and none of them have this big, eh, what you call it, carrot." She tweaked the end of her nose. "Like a snowman, yeah?"

"No! I picture you wearing a garland of flowers and flowing robes, lounging around ancient ruins."

"Really? That's quite a strange way to see me, but I like it. What were you going to say about Wicca?"

"Well, their credo is, 'Do what you will, but harm none.' I pretty much agree with the 'Do what you will' part. I'd amend 'harm none' to 'harm only those who are asking for it.' Lots of people need to be harmed."

"That sounds a little bloodthirsty." She sipped her beer and combed her hair with her fingers.

"Aren't there people in the world you think need to be harmed?" I asked.

"Oh, sure. Lots. But I don't want to talk about that right now."

"Me neither. So what's the most important thing about life for you?"

"Love, of course." Her brown eyes glittered.

"What kind of love?"

"All kinds. Every kind. Parents and children, brothers and sisters, friends, couples. Pets. It's the only thing that makes life worth living, don't you think?"

"I do. Here's to love." I raised my glass.

"Here's to love." We clinked rims. After she drank, she said, "Now, the big question of the night, Elliot. Do you have a wife or girlfriend?"

"No. I did until last week. A girlfriend. But we just broke up."

"I'm very sorry."

"Thanks. How about you? Husband or boyfriend?"

"No. Single girl, here in America by myself. Going back to Brussels tomorrow. This is my last night here." She smiled and touched my hand.

I gripped her fingers. They were long, slender, and very strong. Her nails were as short as a man's.

"You know, Elliot, my hotel is only three blocks away," she said calmly. She sat with one bare foot hooked on the edge of her seat, her bent leg pulled up against her chest. I could've encircled her thigh with my hands. She was like an elegant wading bird. The men in her life would've been rangy Europeans like Charles.

"I wish I weren't so fat," I blurted.

Sytje had a slow, rich smile. "Well, you're not fat," she purred, stroking my forearm, "but I love fat men anyway."

* * *

I was perfectly fine to drive. When I got home, I took the beer coaster from my pocket. Sytje had written her address, phone number, and e-mail on it.

"If you ever come to Brussels, give me a call," she'd said as she handed it to me. "We can go to the museums."

"I will," I said. "You know, I…boy. I wish the timing were better."

She smiled. "I understand. Really. It's only been a week for you. A year is a long time to be with someone. You can't automatically switch off your feelings for her."

"You're an amazing person. I hope we meet again."

"I do too."

She leaned across the table to kiss me on the mouth, one hand on the back of my head.

When she sat back, I said, "You're the first European woman I've kissed."

"Oh, yeah? What do you think?"

"I *really* hope we meet again."

"Well, don't lose that beer coaster, then, okay?"

I put it in a manila folder, wrote "SYTJE" on the tab, and tucked it away in the back of the lowest drawer in my filing cabinet, behind magazine and newspaper clippings that were at least five years old.

CHAPTER SEVEN

Signaling a bold change in direction for Soledad, we took on our first video-game manufacturer. The new client was adamant about the tone of the promotion and marketing of their first-person shooter *Suicide Ditch*.

"Up your ass and out your nose," Dennis told us at the first meeting. "It has to kick ass, knock you on your ass, put your ass out of joint, and one other ass I forgot. Okay? It's all about the ass."

That sort of copy was easier for Gary than me. Our teammates couldn't understand. "How can she write such wacky things?" they'd ask over and over.

"I don't know!" I'd answer. "It's weird!"

They were fooled by her pantsuits. "Go ahead and sniff." Gary's copy. "It's car meat." Gary's again. "Are you swallowed up or down?" Gary's.

At first I was fooled by her pantsuits too. Then I thought she might have an inner freak she'd let out under the right circumstances. I eventually concluded that her freakiness was only theoretical, but on our last day together, she was as unfettered as I'd ever wished. And now, months after the one time she gave of herself completely, she still wouldn't even look at me unless absolutely necessary. I no longer expected that at any minute I'd wake up beside her and tell her about the ridiculous nightmare I'd had, a dream that expressed all my childish abandonment issues.

We continued to work well together, if only through e-mail. By the second *Suicide Ditch* meeting, we'd jointly come up with the tagline, "Don't be shocked; just be amazed." It'd appear on all the marketing material. Margaret showed us her coupon rough, which had our tag dripping with red-and-green sludge.

"Everything's going to look like it's covered in blood and alien splooge," she said. "That's the visual concept."

"Nice," Richard said.

Essi sighed. "I hate these, like, shoot-the-shit-out-of-'em games. Doesn't anybody make, like, exploring games or adventure games that have, like, educational or social values or are just, like, benign? Just...*decent?*"

"Nah," DuShawn said. "Folks want blood and alien splooge."

"These games are for people who like to have fun, not for Elliot," Margaret said.

"So how many euphemisms for semen do you know?" I asked her.

"Let's see." She silently counted on her fingers. "Nine. Not as many as you know, I'll bet."

I laughed, along with everyone except for Gary.

"No euphemisms for me," I said. "I speak my mind."

She gave me her lizard smile. "You speak your mind a lot about semen, Elliot?"

"Not in front of your boss, children," Dennis said. "What I don't hear can't be used against me in a court of law."

After the meeting I went to the break room for coffee. I poured myself a cup; when I turned around, Gary was in the doorway, waiting. I sat at a table with the paper. She went to the coffeemaker, filled her mug, and sat at another table with her own paper, all without laying eyes on me.

Julian came in. "So, Elliot. Busy tonight?" He dropped into a chair.

"Not in the least. Got a suggestion?"

"Debauchery, mate. Lechery. Drunken madness ending with an expedition into the dreaded Velcro triangle. Are you up for it, so to speak?"

"Absolutely. Have you been to La Cachette in Santa Monica?"

"Heard about it. Frequented by the babes, is it?"

"Wall-to-wall babes," I said. "I recently met this incredible Belgian woman there. Her name is Sytje." I glanced at Gary; she sipped coffee and read as if she were alone in the room. "Gorgeous blonde woman," I went on. "Six feet tall. An art dealer."

"A towering art dealer named Sytje," Julian said. "How exotic. What's the upshot? Something naughty?"

"Tell you later," I said.

He winked, laying a finger on the side of his nose. "Got it. Eight o'clock at La Cachette, then?"

"Eight it is."

Across the room, Gary sedately turned a page of her paper.

* * *

I spent most of the day writing copy on my back porch. When Gary and I e-mailed about *Suicide Ditch,* our exchanges rarely exceeded four words. I knocked off at three and changed into my walking outfit.

As I approached the shotgun shack on the corner, I heard a trombone playing in the backyard. It had to be the teenage hillbilly who'd had a seizure when I looked at her. She had no breath control and flatted every note. The sound was so pitiful and brave that I peeked over the fence. She saw me and swooned again, arms dangling and head down as if she'd been hanged. I decided that from then on, I'd walk on the other side of the street.

My legs felt stronger than usual. I was able to go a mile and a half before turning back. During my conversation with Trey, I told him it was weird to finally acquire a level of physical fitness.

"I still haven't accepted that I totally lost my physique," he said. "One thing I really miss about being able-bodied is the ability to physically exhaust myself. I always slept better after I ran or lifted weights or played basketball. I'm still an athlete at heart."

"I don't know what it's like to lose my physique, because I never had one. I work with lots of athletes, though."

"Yeah? What kind of stuff do they do?"

"One guy, Julian, is a rugby player. He plays with all his British friends every weekend, and he's a gym rat too. Gary's a dancer. She still takes classes and works out every day. Another guy, DuShawn, is a baseball player. Margaret, our graphic designer, practices a Brazilian martial art called capoeira."

"Never heard of that. Is she in good shape?"

"She's got the best body in the universe."

"Really? Bring her out here, man. I'd like to see that."

I laughed. "Well, she doesn't like me very much. I don't think I could get her to come out."

"Why doesn't she like you?"

"I don't know. Probably because she thinks I'm the unhappiest person she's ever met. That's what she said, anyway."

"Ha! Now you *gotta* bring her out here. Introduce her to me. She doesn't know what real unhappiness is." He gazed into the distance and shook his head. "So she actually said that to you? Man. That's pretty shitty."

"Well, that's Margaret. She toned it down after my heart attack, but it's building up again."

"Bring her here. I'll straighten her out. Hey, you doing anything tonight?"

"Yes. I'm going out with Julian."

"The rugby player. Look, let's you and me go out to dinner one of these nights. You'll have to cut up my food and feed me, but—Whoa, you should see your face, man."

I put on my sunglasses. "Sure. Let's have dinner sometime."

* * *

After a shower I took a power nap. There was no telling what my night out would bring. Actually, I knew it would bring nothing for me, but it would almost certainly be very productive for Julian. He'd come to us three years earlier, one of fifty Londoners who joined our office after Soledad was bought by the Brits. I looked forward to their arrival because I was an unabashed Anglophile, a Brit groupie. The British could do no wrong in my book. If it weren't for their soccer hooligans and spanking fetish, they'd be the perfect civilization.

Initially, we were intimidated by Julian's size and almost-shaved head. My colleagues found him even scarier than I did, because he'd say things like, "Oi, 'oo scarpered wif me biro?" They thought he was playing with us, making fun of the provincials, but I'd found out from Dennis that Julian had never spoken to an American before he came to Los Angeles. He used the only words he knew. I'd therefore explain that he'd simply asked who'd run off with his pen.

At some point Margaret astonished me by saying, "'The English and the Americans are two peoples divided by a common language.' George Bernard Shaw."

Soon Julian and I began going out for drinks. Some nights we'd stand or sit and talk until the last call. Other nights he'd scan the room like a tennis spectator, back and forth, inevitably making eye contact with someone, a different someone every time, but always with very large breasts and lips like on a flathead catfish. And when she and Julian connected, he'd say, "Cheerio, Elliot" and bail on me. He'd be gone in a flash, and I'd go home or catch a late movie.

On a few occasions, there was a near-scuffle when a drunk noticed Julian's accent and impugned his manhood. Julian would defuse the situation with incomprehensible Cockney jabber, a bizarre non sequitur ending in "guvnuh." Delivered with a maniacal grin, it unsettled almost all belligerent idiots into backing away. Only once did such an encounter lead to violence: The drunk drew back his arm, but before he could follow through, Julian's fist rammed like a piston into his solar plexus. The guy went down with a horrible, wheezing death rattle, the wind knocked out of him. Julian and I escaped before the bouncers knew what'd happened.

"Christ, I haven't hit anybody since I was fifteen," he said in the parking lot. "Do you think I hurt him?"

"I hope so."

"Me too." And we screamed with laughter.

When Julian wasn't hooking up in front of me, he was talking about his office conquests. In record time he'd become a sort of shared commodity, like a tube of lipstick. One night he told me about a copywriter on another team in our department.

"Do you know her, that tall blonde with the pantsuits?"

"I know who she is," I said, "but I don't know her."

"Well, she's a cold bitch, mate. Like ice. I'm told that she's a fundie."

"What's a fundie?"

"Fundamentalist Christian. Do you know if that's true?"

"I have no idea. I've only said hello to her a few times."

"Well, count yourself lucky. Cold, lonely bitch. I'm not even sure she's a woman. Who ever heard of a woman called Gary? She's probably hiding a cock inside her pantsuits."

So she'd turned him down. As far as I knew, that made her unique. "Did you say her name's *Gary?*" I asked.

"Yeah. How twisted is that? I'll bet she's a sex change. Walks like a man. Good Lord, I've been imagining what a *man's* arse looks like under those trousers. I need a drink."

One of those who didn't refuse him was Aubree, my closest friend at work. She was the traffic controller on Gary's team. A short, freckled redhead, she was all hips and chest. She was also smart, funny, and sarcastic. I was her best pal and confessor. She'd hug me with a sigh, asking, "Why can't I find a guy like you?" It wasn't a serious question. If she'd genuinely wanted a guy like me, she knew where to find one.

The morning after her first night with Julian, she called me. "I know it's too soon," she whispered, "but I think I love him. I think he could be the one." I congratulated her, woman to woman.

Julian phoned that afternoon, and we arranged to meet at a bar in West Hollywood. After a couple of beers, he told me all about it.

"We were swapping spit on the sofa, and she put my hand down her pants to feed the pony. Quite nice, frothing up a storm. Put it in past the knuckles. She was going absolutely mad, licking my face and cheering me on. 'Gaaad, that feeels reeel gooood! Harrrder! Faaaster! Jeeezis!'"

That was what Britons called the Septic Tank accent. Septic Tank was Cockney rhyming slang for "Yank." To sound like a Septic Tank—or Seppo—Brits talked through their noses, stretched out their vowels, and made their *R*'s sound like an accelerating car.

"Frightening, really," Julian went on. "Loud as a fire engine. The only way to suppress her was with the old joystick. Round One ends in the living room, no fear about staining the sofa—she swallows. Hauled me to the bedroom, chucked me on the bed. I had the strangest thought when she took off her clothes: With her freckles and ginger hair, she looked like a gnome, this tiny, squat *thing*. I imagined we were in a glen and I'd caught her, and she had to grant me three wishes before I let her go."

Brits also love to do the hundreds of dialects they have in their kingdom; Julian grabbed an imaginary wrist and switched between a corroded growl and a piping falsetto.

"'Ere! Oi've got yer!"

"O please, kind sir, won't you have mercy?"

"Nahr! Yer moine!"

"For wishes three, please set me free."

"Ahr, keep torkin', keep torkin'."

He went back to his regular voice. "I had to bite the insides of my cheeks to keep from laughing, but her tits are brilliant, well worth putting up with the screaming, weeping, and nattering. Nipples as big as strawberries, great arse—on the far side of large, but only just—and a lovely minge. Creamy, highly delicious. Meaty flaps *but* extremely tight. Oh, and freshly shaved. You know, I think she did it just for me. Yes, I'm sure she did. You said she hadn't been bonked in over a year, eh? Long time to be alone with just your fingers for company. Well, I'm going back tonight. My gnome away from home. Must remember to bring my earplugs."

I saw Aubree at the office a week later, but she wouldn't talk to me. She walked right by without saying a word. I didn't know what to do about it, so I did nothing. The next week she was gone. I came to work, and she'd been replaced by Scott. She didn't leave me a note, send an e-mail, or call. I learned that she'd found a position with one of our competitors.

When I told Julian, he'd said, "Who's Aubree?"

* * *

We made our way through the crowd at La Cachette. Everyone around us fell silent, awed by Julian's height, cornflower-blue eyes, and cleft chin. I introduced him to Charles, and we ordered golden ales.

"Sytje asked me all about you," Charles said as he handed me my glass. "She hopes to see you again."

"I hope to see her again too."

"So Sytje is real, then," Julian said.

I stared at him. "Of course she's real. Did you think I made her up?"

"Well, mate, you just don't seem that interested in the old vertical smile."

"The old vertical smile?"

"You know, the bikini burger. The toothless gibbon."

"I have no clue what you're talking about."

He rolled his eyes. "*Poontang,* as you-all say over here. Cooter."

"Because I don't talk to you about poontang, it means I'm not interested? Why am I supposed to talk about it with you?"

"Because that's what men do."

I sipped my ale. "Well, I guess I'm not a man, then."

"Good. I love talking with women about bonking. So listen, dearie, I'm going to finally pull Margaret. My decades of experience tell me she's very close to cracking. Ah, that's an appropriate word when speaking of Margaret, isn't it?"

"Which word?"

"Crack. I *do* appreciate it when she squats or bends over."

So did I. On her first day at Soledad, she came into the break room, dropped her pen, and stooped to pick it up. Gary winked at me and muttered, "Ah see London, Ah see France…"

I never told Gary that Margaret brought to mind a ditty I learned in kindergarten:

I see your heinie.
It's black and shiny.
It makes me giggle
To see it wiggle.
You'd better hide it
Before I bite it.
Ouch!

Margaret's heinie was probably not black, but I imagined that it was shiny. Smooth and shiny, like butterscotch pudding. I wouldn't have minded biting it, if she weren't talking. Or if she gave it to me to take home.

"It's funny," I said. "I was discussing Margaret earlier this afternoon. A guy I know wants to meet her."

Julian sipped his ale. "As long as he understands that I'm going to have my way with her. And I suppose you won't want to hear the gory details, since you're not a man."

"Well, it's not going to happen, anyway."

"Oh, really? And why not?"

"You two don't even like each other," I said. "You'd have to drug her."

He laughed. "You really are priceless, aren't you? Don't you know that the best sex is hate sex?"

"Hate sex? I have enough trouble with people I love. I can't even *begin* to comprehend sex with people I hate."

"Same as any other sex. In-and-out, up-and-down, back-and-forth, finished."

"I'm talking emotionally."

He looked disgusted. "What's emotion got to do with sex? Especially sex with Margaret? Christ, do you think *she* cares one iota about anyone she bonks? Houseflies care more about their mates."

"Wow. It really *is* hate sex for you, isn't it?"

"No." He shrugged. "I don't hate Margaret. There isn't enough there to hate. To me she's just a lovely arse. Changing the subject, my brother was deployed yesterday."

His brother Harold was an infantry corporal in the British army.

"Are you nervous?" I asked.

"Naturally. But I wish I were going with him. I wish I'd joined the army instead of the VSO."

"The VSO?"

"Voluntary Service Overseas. It's like the Peace Corps."

I almost dropped my beer. "You have hate sex with wild women, *and* you were in the Peace Corps. Makes perfect sense."

"It does, actually. At the time it was the most satisfying thing I'd ever done. You go to a village, and these guys come to you with an idea. You give them twenty bucks; they go off, and by the end of the day, they've set up a business. They're going to be fine. All they needed was that little push. It's incredible. You're saving people's *lives,* mate. How can that compare to anything else?"

"Why didn't you keep on doing it?"

"Because it's just too big a problem. For every person you save, ten die. You only make a difference in a micro sense. Whole nations, entire continents, are rotten, hopeless. It's systemic failure. You can't change millennia of culturally inculcated corruption and fatalism. I used to think you could, but the more you give them, the more dependent they get, and, uh, um…"

He trailed off, looking over my shoulder. I turned; a blonde woman with enormous breasts and fat lips smiled in our direction. Julian stood.

"Crikey, look at *those.* Cheerio, Elliot."

* * *

On my way home, I pictured Julian as a gently smiling aid worker living in a mud hut, handing out blankets, plowing fields with water buffalos, and strumming an acoustic guitar, his head tilted in compassion. Then he evaporated as I contemplated Trey's invitation to dinner and the memory it triggered of an episode I'd sequestered somewhere for over a quarter century.

When I was eleven, I wanted to go to summer camp. My parents were dismissive.

"You'd hate it," Dad promised. "You'd have a terrible time, like you always do. It'd just be a big waste of money."

"You didn't say that when David and Emily went," I protested.

"Because we knew they wouldn't complain about it for a solid year after they got back. They'd actually appreciate it."

"It's just that we don't think you'd be happy there, dear," Mom said. "Camp is for children who enjoy being with other children."

"How can I learn to enjoy being with other children," I asked, "if you don't give me the chance?"

These would be new kids, not my classmates. They'd welcome me with open arms, take me canoeing, and teach me how to swim.

I pestered my parents until they gave in. The camp was on Lake Piru in the Los Angeles National Forest. We stayed in dusty wooden bunkhouses, where we were assigned to beds and counted off by twos. This was "the buddy system," the counselors said. Each of us had to know where his buddy was at all times. My new buddy was already on his bed when we were brought in. His head and shoulders were enormous, as big as an adult's, but his hips and legs were tiny, as if he were a balloon-boy somebody had squeezed too hard on the bottom.

Our bunk boss Mr. Croteau grabbed one of the boy's massive shoulders and squealed, "This is *Sam!* Sam, this is *Elliot!* You fellas get along now, okay?" He hurried to the other end of the bunkhouse.

"Hi," I said.

Sam swung his legs over the side of his bed so he could face me. His body jerked as he moved, his shoes knocking together as if he were applauding me with his feet. A kind of slow-motion groaning came out of his mouth; it sounded like a put-on, the sort of retarded voice everybody did for fun. His words were accompanied by saliva running over his chin. When he stood and got a tissue from the box on his locker, I saw that even with his wooden cane, he could barely walk. His movements were totally awry, as though unseen cables yanked him all over the place. I wondered what he was doing at camp. Sports and crafts were out of the question.

We were told to report to the cookhouse for dinner. Mr. Croteau stepped in front of me as I tried to leave.

"Slow down, pal. Your buddy can't walk as fast as everyone else. We don't want him to be left all by himself, do we?"

We didn't. While Mr. Croteau went ahead with our bunkmates, I hung back and escorted Sam through the woods. He gawked at the trees and forgot to watch where he was going; I had to catch his arm when he tripped over roots. By the time we arrived at the cookhouse, the other kids had already been served and were halfway through the meal. A counselor took us to our seats in the corner.

Sam picked up his knife and fork and tried to cut his meat. Peas and carrots flew everywhere. I was afraid that if I offered to help, he'd scream, "*I can do it!*" But he was making a mess and wouldn't be able to eat a thing unless somebody intervened, so I said, "Here, let me." I took his utensils and sliced his roast beef into small pieces that he could scoop up with his spoon.

He became easier to understand as the meal progressed. His tremors were caused by cerebral palsy, for which he took the drug phenobarbital.

"You should see me when I'm not on it," he said.

I couldn't imagine. Without the drug he must not have been able to do anything except lie there and flail.

We were the last to leave the cookhouse. I walked Sam to the introductory slide show about the camp—we missed the first ten minutes—and then escorted him back to the bunkhouse. He punched his way into his pajamas and headed for the bathroom. I fell back on my bed, nearly passing out from relief that he hadn't asked me to help him *in there*. The thought of what I'd have to see and do if he asked had terrified me for hours.

The next morning Mr. Croteau sidled up as I washed my face at the sink.

"Look, pal," he murmured, his arm around my shoulders. "We got a little problem. You didn't keep an eye on your buddy last night. This is a dangerous place for a guy like him." He skidded his foot along the wet tile floor. "See? How would you feel if he slipped and cracked his skull? Why don't you just take a couple of minutes to make sure he's okay?"

Sam and I therefore became inseparable. Wherever he went, I went, including into the showers. We were tacitly released from the camp agenda of swimming, hiking, playing baseball, running sack races, and making things with leather and wood. Instead, we sat in the grass or took walks in the woods. We were free and easy the entire summer.

Sam spoke so slowly that everybody tuned him out after three seconds. They didn't grasp that he was actually very concise, a master of the one-word sentence. He loved onomatopoeia because it made things easier and faster.

"My parents sent me here to show me I could do anything," he said. "Yeah, right. Swimming? *Glub.* Baseball? *Bonk.* Crafts? *Poink! Ow!* I just wish they wouldn't lie to me. They're afraid if they tell me the truth, I'll die. 'What?' *Clunk.*"

He'd been reading newspapers since he was six, and he made the world clearer for me. By the end of the summer, I knew all about the Vietnam War, inflation, OPEC, and the three branches of the federal government.

I said good-bye to Sam the morning we were bused home. He cried and promised to write. We exchanged letters about eight times before it petered out. I never saw him again.

My parents asked if I wanted to go to camp the next summer.

"I think I'd rather stay home," I said.

Dad nodded. "I told you you'd hate it. Flushed all that money right down the crapper, just like I said we would."

"Well, it was a learning experience," Mom said.

It was indeed. All summer I was covered in Sam's drool. Since he couldn't really brush his teeth or wash himself, he had horrible breath and stank. When he got excited, he brayed like a donkey. He blanketed me in food and always wanted to wrestle in the grass. Counselors and campers watched from a distance, whispering and shaking their heads.

Although I was mostly invisible at camp, people did pay attention to me while Sam was treated at the infirmary for scrapes or bruises. I sat outside, and passing kids asked me where my spaz boyfriend was. They groaned, waved their arms, twisted their mouths, drooled. The counselors who saw this chuckled and told them to knock it off.

After six weeks of serving food, cutting up food, wiping up food, taking showers that made me feel filthy, and ignoring the snickers, grins, smells, and rivers of saliva, I despised Sam. I couldn't wait to get rid of him. He'd ruined everything.

CHAPTER EIGHT

For three days Trey asked if I'd spoken to Margaret. I finally called her Tuesday morning.

"I don't get it," she said. "Explain it again."

"I've mentioned you to a friend of mine. His name is Trey. He's paralyzed and in a wheelchair. Now he wants to meet you."

"Why?"

"Part of it has to do with capoeira. He likes to learn about new things. His quadriplegia and chronic pain keep him from doing anything physical, so all he has left is his mind. If you did this for me, I'd be really grateful."

There was a long pause. "Okay. What the fuck."

"That's the spirit. Be here at about four, all right?"

"Okay."

"And wear walking shoes. Good-bye."

A few minutes later, the phone rang.

"Hi, sweetie," Mom said.

"Hi, sweetie," Dad said on the extension.

"Hello, parents. How are things?"

"We're just checking up on you," Mom said. "We haven't heard anything for a while, so we were wondering how everything's going."

"Fine, I think. I'm walking, working, trying to shed the poundage. No real updates."

Except that my girlfriend dumped me. You remember her. David said she had a curvy ass, perky tits, and a juicy camel toe. We had jungle sex in my back garden, then she split because I treated her the way you treated me when I was small. This fat apple didn't fall very far from the tree.

"So have you dropped any weight?" Dad asked.

"I don't know. I don't have a scale."

"Then how the hell will you know if you've lost weight or not?"

"I'll go over to your place so you can weigh me. You can keep a record, and if I don't lose a pound a week, you can devise the proper punishment."

"Pleasure talking to you, son," Dad said and hung up.

"Elliot," Mom said, "I wish you wouldn't...well...I wish we could all just get along."

"I'm sorry, Mom. It's really not a good time."

"Is there anything you want to...talk about?"

With you? Not a chance.

"Thanks for the offer," I said. "I'm just working a few things out. I'll let you know if I need anything."

"All right. Be well. Good-bye."

*   *   *

The next time the phone rang, it was Emily. I knew she'd call; she and Mom always tag-teamed me.

"I just wanted to see how you were," she said. "And I, uh, won't give you any unsolicited advice this time."

"I'm fine. Working, trying to lose weight. Busy today, can't really talk. How're Nelson and the kids?"

"Great. Terri's suddenly making sense. She went from 'baba' to 'My bottle, please' in one day. She and Alex really liked seeing you. Maybe, um...

105

maybe we can make it more of a regular thing. I mean, they grow up so fast. You don't want to miss out. I mean…you know."

"Sure. Yeah. Let's do that."

Silence fell like a steel curtain.

"I'm…kind of in the middle of something," I said.

"Okay. So everything's fine, then?"

"Yup. I just have this project I have to get back to, pretty much right now, and don't want to be rude, but—"

"Yeah, okay, I'll let you go. Take care. 'Bye."

My palm left a sheen of sweat on the receiver.

* * *

At four on the dot, I heard a car door slam. I went out on my front porch and closed the door, locking it behind me. Margaret ambled up my driveway. She wore round sunglasses with mirrored lenses, sneakers, skinny jeans, and a black tank top. A rolled-up blue-and-yellow parasol dangled from her left hand.

"Aren't you gonna invite me in?" she asked.

"No. This is about Trey, not me. I'm very particular about who I let inside my home."

"Sweet. I come all the way out here to do you a favor, and I'm not good enough to be allowed inside your house?"

"It has nothing to do with you. My house is…I'm…Look, can we please just go introduce you to Trey?"

"Whatever." She fell into step beside me on the sidewalk, popping open her parasol.

"Don't you wear sunblock?" I asked.

"Yeah, but I use a parasol too. I'm not gonna end up a wrinkled old bag like my mother." She shuddered histrionically.

We walked in silence for several minutes. It was very strange to have her with me. A passing car honked; I looked and saw three young men leering at us. Not for the first time, I was struck by Margaret's astonishing beauty. Her profile could've served as a blueprint for plastic surgeons.

"So you always lock your doors, huh," she said.

"Of course."

"'Of course.' Well, I don't lock mine."

"Oh my *God*. Why in the world not?"

She snorted. "People attract trouble with their negative attitudes. I don't expect bad things to happen to me, so they don't. Yeah, you think that's all Zen and idealistic, but it works. You can't be afraid and inhibited."

Leaving her door unlocked at night in Studio City took a certain amount of conviction, but it wasn't the same as doing it in my neighborhood. If she tried it there, the roving patrols of gangsters would sniff her out in eight seconds flat.

"So if a plane is hijacked and flown into a building, it happened because the passengers all had negative attitudes?" I asked.

"No, but if they were a lot more confident and positive, who's to say the hijackers wouldn't have picked another plane? Or maybe not even hijacked a plane at all. Anyway, I don't think anything happens by accident. Who's to say that on some level, those people didn't want it to happen?"

"For what possible reason would you want to be on a plane that was going to be flown into a building?"

"Look, I don't have all the answers. I'm just saying that it's easy to point the finger at the people who hijacked the planes and not see if there's any responsibility somewhere else. Besides, that's not the worst thing that ever happened. A lot more people died in all the bombing attacks we launched before and after, so we need to get off our moral superiority trip."

"I hate our moral superiority trip," I said. "It sucks, man."

"If you don't like my opinions, too bad. I don't get my morals from the mainstream."

"That's great. Congratulations."

"It *is* great. You should try it sometime, instead of letting the power structure lead you around by the nose."

"No, I prefer to let the power structure lead me around by the nose. I oppose thinking for myself."

"*Fuck!*" She glared at me, mirrored lenses flashing. "You never take me seriously. You always have some smart-ass answer."

"Do *you* take yourself seriously?"

"Shit yeah! I'm the most important person in my life. I'm the only one who'll ever really know me, and I'm the only one I'm guaranteed to be spending my whole life with. *Of course* I take myself seriously. I have to. Don't you take yourself seriously?"

"I don't take myself any way at all. I'm not interested in me."

"Dude, that's *so* not good!"

"Dude, why is that?"

"You *have* to care about yourself, Elliot. If you don't, you can't expect anybody else to."

"Who says I expect anybody else to?"

She threw up her free hand. "More fuckin' games. I try to talk to you, and you shit all over me. Well, you can eat me, pal. Fuck you."

That was the end of the conversation. We crossed the street at the first big intersection and headed toward the high school. Trey was in his spot, sunning himself with his eyes closed.

"Is that him?" Margaret asked.

"Yup. Be nice, okay?"

"Don't tell me how to act."

"Okay, fine. Be however you want." When we were about twenty feet away, I called, "Good afternoon, sir."

Trey opened his eyes. His shock was quite gratifying.

"Hey, man!" he shouted. "Is this the infamous Margaret Alvarez?"

"It sure is," Margaret said as she took off her sunglasses. "Is this the infamous Trey Gillespie?"

"It sure is. Man, listen to you! What a voice you got."

We stopped beside him. He held out his hand. Margaret started to shake it, but he hissed, "Easy!"

She snatched back her hand, wincing. "Oh fuck, I'm sorry."

"Hey, don't worry about it." He smiled at me. "You said she was the hottest woman in the universe, and you weren't bullshitting me."

From the corner of my eye, I saw Margaret gape in my direction. "Well, I'm going to leave you two alone," I quickly said. "I'll be back in about forty minutes or so. Have fun."

"Take your time," Trey said.

Margaret was still befuddled. "Uh, yeah. Blow."

* * *

I returned a little after five. Margaret sat on the curb, sheltered under her parasol, laughing with Trey.

"Did you learn all about capoeira?" I asked him.

"Mostly, I learned about how much Margaret admires you."

"Hey!" she shouted. "What the *fuck,* man!"

He chuckled. "Just trying to smooth things out between you two. Deep down you both like each other, so you gotta stop with this fighting shit, okay?"

Margaret and I said nothing.

Trey shook his head at us. "Well, Margaret's gotta go, so be a gentleman and walk her back to her car, Elliot."

"He doesn't have to do that," Margaret said. "I can take care of myself."

"Oh, I know. You got that Brazilian kung fu. But I'd feel better if you let him."

She shrugged. "Okay. Dude, I had a great time. I hope some of you rubs off on Elliot."

"Hey, don't give my boy shit anymore, huh?"

"Oh, all right. Take it easy." She held out her hand, and he gingerly touched her knuckles.

"I'll be back in a minute," I said to him. "We still haven't had our daily blather."

"I'll be here."

When Margaret and I had gone about thirty feet, Trey called, "Margaret! C'mere a second!"

We went back. "What's up?" she asked.

He smiled. "Nothing. I just wanted to watch you walk away from me again."

She laughed, slipped her sunglasses onto her forehead, leaned down, and kissed him on the mouth without touching him anywhere else. There was clearly tongue involved, on both sides.

"Damn, girl," he said when she straightened. His smile was pained. "Get outta here."

"See ya."

We left again. Margaret didn't say anything until I asked what they'd talked about.

"Capoeira. My job. Rock climbing. The world. He's a total hottie. I can't believe he's your friend."

"Every stud has to have a fat, ugly sidekick."

"*I didn't fuckin' say you're fat and ugly!*" she shouted.

"Whatever. Some feminist you are, getting off on men watching your... your walk."

"Feminists can't like it when hot men appreciate them?" She gripped one of her buttocks and jiggled it. "My ass isn't gonna be in this shape forever, so someday when it's hanging down on the floor, I'll remember the compliments I got."

"You're a class act, Margaret."

"Fuck you."

"Good comeback."

"Eat me."

* * *

"*Damn,* Margaret's hot," Trey said. "I haven't been Frenched by a woman in twenty-three years."

"You know what? I'm pretty much Margareted out. We had a fight on the way here and another fight on the way back. I'd kind of like to spend the rest of the day not thinking or talking about her, if you don't mind."

"Sure, no problem." He drank water. "Tell me about Gary instead."

"Gary? What about her?"

"How'd you guys get together? You said you were gonna tell me someday. So tell me."

"Well, we'd said hello a few times in the break room or the lobby, but I didn't know anything about her except her weird name. After I'd been at Soledad a couple years, we got a new art director, who fired some people and rearranged the rest. He made Gary the other copywriter on my team and moved her into the cubicle next to mine."

* * *

When Dennis introduced us, she'd gripped my hand firmly and said, "Gary Pruett. Nice to meet you," in an incongruous drawl.

"Elliot Finnell. Nice to meet you, Gary."

Something flickered in her smooth face and disappeared. After our first team meeting, she and I went to the break room to coordinate. I'd never conversed with a Southerner. She made everybody else sound strident and coarse.

Though she was amiable, every third or fourth time I saw her, she struggled to make it through the day. She'd try to hide the enormous effort it took to answer questions or maintain a train of thought. Her accent would deepen into a patois, and she'd talk to my forehead or chin. I never asked if she was all right; we spoke only about our work.

She was truly dazzling. Her skin was a strange, pale gold, almost the same color as her hair, and her eyes were almost as clear as water. I couldn't tell if they were blue or gray. In our break-room conferences, I missed much of what she said because I'd been studying her eyes.

When we were in the office together, trying to beat a deadline, I'd go on sham errands so I could pass her cubicle and see her sitting straight as a post in front of her computer, tapping a pen on her desk. Back in my cubbyhole, I'd hear it, feeble and hopeless, like somebody trapped under rubble. I wondered if her golden skin would be warm or cool to the touch, if she'd be heavy lying on top of me.

These were trivial, fleeting fancies that didn't get in the way. They were no different than wondering what it would be like to have billions of dollars or the power of invisibility.

One Friday morning before the meeting, I found that a coworker had used the wastebasket in my cubicle to dispose of a putrid, half-eaten sandwich. I picked up the wastebasket to take it to the break-room garbage cans, and when I turned around, there was Gary in the hallway with her hands on her hips and an ear-to-ear smile exploding out at me like a supernova. Her teeth were white and straight as a dream, and her eyes were half closed and glistening as if she'd been laughing for hours. I barely recognized her.

"What's so funny?" I'd asked, my heart suddenly racing.

"*You.* You been talkin' to yourself about how much your wastebasket stinks."

"I have?"

"Yes you have! You talk to yourself a lot. 'Oh my *Gawd,* what *now?* Someone was *eatin'* this? Is that even *possible?* '"

I covered my mouth. "Oh my God."

"See? It's really funny. *You're* really funny."

She went off to the conference room. I found it nearly impossible to sit still during the meeting. She was right next to me, only inches away. That smile—I felt its warmth in the pit of my stomach for the rest of the day. There was something else in it, a perplexing relief. I felt relieved too. And afraid.

After we coordinated in the break room, she said, "Are you going straight home, or are you gonna stick around?"

"I was planning on going home, but I can stick around."

"Well, I was thinking that maybe we could work here in our cubicles and then go have lunch downstairs."

I'd seen how she never lost her composure despite system crashes, crackpot deadlines, inexorable morons, anything, so I tried to copy her. "Yeah, sure." But her invitation made me feel as though I were floating.

We went to Amir's next door and had salads. Sitting across the table from her, I remembered what Julian told me about watching women eat.

"Christ, when they open their mouths and put the food in and start chewing and they're going *mlyemm, mlyemm, mlyemm,* they look like goats. I can't take it! I never eat with women. Never."

I loved watching women eat. My favorite part was when they picked bits out of their salads or sandwiches and ate them with their fingers. I loved women with big appetites. Gary's appetite wasn't especially big, but it was healthy, and she had long, muscular hands with short nails devoid of polish. After every Friday meeting, we worked in the office and had lunch together. On our fourth such outing, she told me about her late father.

"It was Daddy's idea to name me Gary. I'm sure he came up with it after smokin' a bowl or two. It's the sort of thing that sounds better when you're high, and Daddy always was. By the way, I'm completely aware that you never said anything about my name. Thank you. My whole life, you're the only person I ever met who had no reaction. You don't know how much that means to me."

How could ice-colored eyes be so warm?

"Well, you've only had to talk about your name fifteen billion times," I said.

"Sixteen billion times."

"I *am* sort of curious what it's like."

She shrugged. "Everyone assumes I'm trying to get attention, or they think I'm a transsexual."

I didn't tell her that Julian suspected her of harboring a penis. There was indeed a masculine air to her body language, in the vigor of her walk and the way she used her large hands. I realized that if she were a tranny, I could adjust.

"Maybe you could go by your middle name," I suggested.

"Nope."

"Uh-oh. What's your middle name?"

"Macha."

"Maha?"

"Macha, with a guttural *ch*, like in Arabic. M-A-C-H-A. It's the name of a pagan goddess worshipped in ancient Ireland. The Great Queen of Phantoms, whose voice summons men to their deaths and who haunts battlefields to collect men's blood to use in her magic. She's also known as Mother Death."

My jaw dangled; she picked at her pita, smiling.

"That is absolutely…" I said.

"Disturbing? Macabre?"

"*Fantastic.* I'm stunned. Your dad's idea again?"

"No, that was Momma's. To honor her Irish heritage. My parents worked real hard to make sure that no one in Wilmington, North Carolina—or anywhere else, for that matter—ever considered them mediocre in any way."

"Have you thought about changing your name?"

"Well, now, that might hurt my momma's *feelings*. She might think I *resented* her and Daddy."

"Ah."

"In high school I flirted with changing my name to Gretchen or Sissy. When I was seventeen, I insisted on being one of the Belles at the Azalea Festival. Ever heard of it?"

"No. Azalea, as in the flower?"

"Yup. They've got a big tour of ten different gardens, and the Azalea Belles are the hostesses who guide you. They wear hoopskirted antebellum dresses with ruffled bloomers underneath, and they carry cute little parasols. Boy, we fought and fought, Momma and Daddy and me, but they finally let someone sponsor me, and I went. I used my own money to buy my dress, which was coral, and I had my hair done in these little hangin' sausages like Scarlett O'Hara. Got pictures of it and everything."

"Did you wear a corset?" I asked without thinking.

The corners of her mouth twitched. "Yes."

I don't know where I got the audacity to say, "I'd *really* like to see those pictures."

"Naw, they're old as dirt now," she said, obviously pleased. "I ain't seventeen anymore."

"So why didn't your parents want you to go?" I asked.

"Because it scared them. I rebelled by goin' back to my roots. In Momma and Daddy's book, that meant I was gonna end up in the Klan. Anything that celebrated the Old South was racist, misogynist, and above all theocratic. I was a...monu*mental* disappointment to my parents."

I ached to console her, defend her, heal her.

She finished her pita. "When I was growin' up, my parents had tons of friends who were just as non-mediocre as they were. This one guy, Heinz, has a theory that all cancer is caused by mushroom spores. He brings it up every conversation. All he has to do is wait until you mention dust, air, or water."

"Dust, air, or water?"

"Yeah. Try to have a conversation about anything without mentioning dust, air, or water. You cain't. So when he hears one of the magic words, he dumps whatever you were talking about and tells you that mushroom spores make up eighty percent of all dust, which means the air's always full of them, which means they're in all the reservoirs, leaching their cancer out into the water. We're all gettin' cancer, and he's the only one who knows it's completely preventable. Sometimes he starts screamin'."

She jabbed her finger in my face, raising her eyebrows, giving herself a gruesome overbite, and maiming her speech with a snakelike sibilance.

"*Dey are all arrround us! Ve eat, drrrink, und brrreathe zem twenty-four hourss a day! Our skin iss coated mit zem! Dey are even in our eyelashessss!*" Then he takes out this little magnifying glass and wants you to examine his eyelashes. Have you ever looked at somebody's eyeball with a magnifying glass? It's *nauseatin'.*"

I had no defenses against her.

* * *

The sun had set. Trey and I had been talking for hours.

"So what was she like in the sack?" he asked.

I didn't reply.

"Damn, Elliot, c'mon. You can't even see my face. Don't be embarrassed. Just tell me. I'm not gonna laugh or whatever."

"I don't like talking about things like that," I said.

"I'm not asking how her pussy tasted."

"For God's sake, Trey!"

"I just wanna know if she can work that bodacious body."

"No. She can't. She was great the last time we were together, but that usually happens in relationships after somebody almost dies. Except for that one day, she always held back."

"Then why'd you stay with her?"

I was grateful for the dusk. "Because I loved her. And because I'm as uptight and afraid as she is. And because of Vonda."

"Who's Vonda?"

*　*　*

Vonda was my name for the other woman from North Carolina who lived in that condo. She started showing up at the office after the Friday meetings. I'd be at my desk when I'd hear *psst* and look up, and Vonda would be watching me over the partition. I'd recognize her by the glistening of her eyes.

"What?" I'd ask as a foolish grin stretched my face.

"Git back to work," she'd whisper and sink down out of sight.

Or if we had five seconds alone in the copy room, Vonda would execute a fluid high kick, snarling as she snapped her leg vertical and whipped it back, reverting to Gary just as somebody else walked in. It gave me a jolt every time.

One night at her condo, I spotted a straw cowboy hat on top of the bookshelf next to the TV. A green bandanna was wrapped around the crown, and the front and rear edges of the brim curled downward. It looked old and musty, like a dried leaf.

"Have you actually worn that thing?" I asked.

"Absolutely. Why do you ask?"

"Because it's not possible."

She smiled, shrugged, and said nothing more about it.

The next time I went over, she opened the door wearing the cowboy hat. She also had on a pink baby tank top that left her belly exposed, a denim miniskirt with a leather belt and a big oval buckle in silver, tan cowboy boots, heavy mascara, and blood-red lipstick. I almost screamed.

"Whatcha think?" she asked. She backed out of the foyer and stood in the living room with her thumbs hooked into her belt and her hips cocked. One corner of her mouth curved up and the other curved down. Her blonde hair framed her made-up face like spun gold. "C'*mon,* man. Tell Momma."

And she began dancing, her thumbs still hooked in her belt and her boots clonking, stomping, turning out, going pigeon-toed, and flying up, the way Bavarians did their Oktoberfest slapping, hoedown thing, but she also undulated front to back and side to side, a snaky, sometimes spread-kneed movement that had nothing to do with beer festivals or do-si-dos, and as she executed all those complicated maneuvers, she watched me with her raccoon eyes, her mouth half up and half down.

"I think I'm going to pass out," I croaked.

She ended with a flourish of stomps. "Go wash your face. I'm takin' you out to teach you how to line dance."

"Oh my God."

We drove to a club in Westwood, a dark room where lines of men and women in hats, boots, jeans, and miniskirts slid back and forth, left to right, as the fiddles sawed and the guitars twanged. Vonda taught me how to hook my thumbs into my belt and slide across the floor in my black sneakers that didn't clonk. I was the only one there without boots or a hat and who couldn't dance, but it didn't matter. No one paid attention except when Vonda did her slow undulation and provoked a flurry of whistles and yeehaws that didn't bother me at all.

Gary tried hard, but she hated for me to see her naked and was offended by her own scent. I always prayed that one night Vonda would visit me in bed, blessing me with her joy and fearlessness. She never did. Vonda met me in my garden once, and then she and Gary left me forever.

* * *

"You've really bummed me out," Trey said in the darkness.

"I'm sorry."

"Are you gonna tell me why Gary and Vonda dumped you?"

I stood. "Not yet."

"Okay. Walk me home, man."

CHAPTER NINE

On Saturday I went to my first house party in years. It was DuShawn's Halloween bash, held at his bungalow in West Hollywood. Essi, Julian, and Margaret showed up too. Gary skipped it, of course, along with Mitch and Richard, the married members of our team. DuShawn, his wife Sonya, Julian, and I were the oldest people there; everybody else was under thirty. Some may even have been in their teens, although it was hard for me to tell. Young people had started looking a lot older than they were—not more mature or grown-up, just ravaged.

DuShawn gave me a quick tour that ended in his study, where he kept his library of books, videos, and DVDs on true crime, accidents, autopsies, medical curiosities, and executions. He had thousands of titles, covering every conceivable injury, affliction, abnormality, and death. The centerpiece of the collection was a series of very expensive books put out by a man who cut up cadavers with power saws, posed the parts, and took photos of them. I asked DuShawn why he liked these subjects.

"Because I've seen enough beauty," he said.

He left to perform his hosting duties, and I went outside to escape the deafening, anonymous club music that bored through my head without leaving a trace. On the back porch, Julian was loudly engaged in conversation with a young man wearing tiny horn-rims and a daub of beard the size of a postage stamp, like a Hitler mustache but on the *lower* lip.

"We have to figure out why they hate us so much," Hitler Beard shouted.

"They've already *told* us why they hate us," Julian said. "It's because we don't mind when our women have sex with whomever they want."

"Aw, that's fuckin' bullshit, man. That's just some wing-nut talking point."

"But putting all the blame on *us* isn't a talking point. Not at all."

"Look, there's always a reason why somebody acts out."

Julian bellowed with laughter. "'Acts out'? Murdering thousands is now 'acting out'? So what do you suggest we do with them? Give them a *time*-out?"

"Well, if you're so hot to do something, how come you don't join the army?"

"If you think the people we're fighting are so justified, why don't *you* join *them?*"

"*You didn't answer my fuckin' question, man!*" Hitler Beard yelled.

"I'm thirty-three years old, you twerp. The cutoff age for the British army is thirty-two." He saw me. "Elliot! What a relief. The only non-wanker here." He waved at the kid. "Now fuck off, sonny."

"Yeah, well, fuck you too, asshole." He stormed into the house.

Julian rubbed his bristly scalp. "As soon as these prats find out I'm British, all they want to talk about is war. I'm sick of it. I tell them that unless they've experienced combat themselves, they have no right to talk about how horrible war is, and then I call them chicken doves. Usually shuts 'em right up, except for that pygmy. They all assume that since I'm European, I'm a eunuch. Did you know that in Europe, there's a social movement for men to piss sitting down?"

"You're kidding."

"Nope. Pissing while standing is too aggressive. It's an outmoded gesture of male dominance. Men should sit while they piss in order to show their respect for and solidarity with women. In Germany they call it the *Sitzpinkler* movement."

"I can't really see Frederick the Great as a *Sitzpinkler.*"

Julian took a gulp from his plastic beer cup. "Personally, I want to start the *Stehenscheisser* movement, to show my respect for and solidarity with horses. Fucking Europeans. They give us a thousand years of genocide all over the world and then turn into spineless nancy-boys who won't lift a finger to defend themselves. They're only good for one thing, and that's sex. Ever seen Hungarian porn?"

"Yes."

"Then you know what I mean. If Europeans want to talk to me about being a sex object or giving all your money to the government, I'll listen. About everything else they need to shut the fuck up. Except for food. I'll listen if a European wants to talk about food. And beer. Okay, so I'll listen if a European wants to talk about being a sex object, giving all your money to the government, food, and beer. But that's it. Cheerio, Elliot."

He headed toward a gaggle of young women gathered in the far corner of the yard. I went inside and wandered into DuShawn's study, which overflowed with guests reading the books on death, accidents, disease, and crime. DuShawn suddenly grabbed my arm and steered me toward a pale young woman with orangish hair and the same kind of horn-rimmed glasses worn by Julian's pygmy. She looked up from her book as DuShawn did the introductions.

"Elliot, Cicely. Cicely, Elliot. Cicely works in a homeless shelter. Elliot is a copywriter. Have fun, good luck, good-bye."

Cicely was about twenty-three. "So how do you know DuShawn?" she asked.

"I work with him. How about you?"

"We met at a protest a couple months ago. Can you believe all the shit that's going on? War, injustice, the corporate culture, banksters running everything and stealing us blind, the rich not paying taxes. This country sucks."

"That's why everybody wants to move here."

She was incredulous, as if I'd loudly broken wind. "No they don't."

"You're right. They don't. What're you reading?"

It was a coffee-table book titled *Snuffed: Sixty Years of Crime Scene Photos.*

"Nice," I said.

Her face lit up. "Oh, have you seen it?"

"I was kidding. I avoid stuff like that."

"I don't. I like to know what's going on in the underbelly of society."

"Really? Why?"

"It freaks me out." She smiled. "It's addictive. Some of the people I work with are convicted murderers. I've really gotten into their stories."

"Well, I don't want to know about the underbelly of society."

"I think we all have a responsibility to know."

"Not me. I shut my eyes to as much of society as I can."

"Elliot, that's no attitude! You can't hide from reality."

"Sure I can. I do it all the time."

She held up the book. "Tell you what: Let's sit down and look through it. You won't be as upset as you think. There's a kind of, I don't know, a kind of beauty to it, in a way. Because of the honesty of it."

"Murder is beautiful and honest?"

"I know it sounds weird, but I'm just talking about how it's the ultimate expression of your feelings toward someone. There's no bullshit, no equivocation." She sat on the sofa, patted the cushion next to her. "Let me show you what I mean. It's fascinating, because there aren't any limits. Everybody's afraid to live a life without limits, but not the people who did this."

"True. But I like limits, so I'll give it a pass."

"You sure? Some of this stuff is amazing. You go, 'Holy *shit,* who knew you could do that to someone!'" She flipped through several pages. "*Eww.* Like this one. Check it out." She angled the book toward me.

"No thanks," I said, looking away.

In an act I could not possibly have foreseen, she sprang off the sofa and jammed the book in my face. On the left page, a woman chopped into hams and steaks lay on a metal examining table. On the right was a large pile of oatmeal beside a road. I caught the phrase "stick of dynamite" in the caption as I turned my head. Cicely pivoted with me, gripping the book with both hands as though it were a steering wheel, keeping it in front of my nose.

"Wacky *stuff!*" she gushed. "Wacky, wacky *stuff!*"

I tried to walk around her; she backpedaled, bobbed, and feinted, like a boxer.

"Look at this one!" she shouted. The photo appeared to show an infant impaled on a barbecue fork. Before I could stop myself, I shoved her hard with both hands. She skidded across the hardwood floor with a hurt, thunderstruck expression.

"*Get away from me,*" I yelled. I was nauseated and my hands tingled. Another heart attack seemed imminent. I didn't want to have it in that room, in the company of a degenerate lout and surrounded by DuShawn's beloved sewage.

As I moved into the hall, someone snatched at my sleeve. I was about to throw a punch when I saw it was Margaret.

"Dude, what's the matter?" she asked. "You look awful."

"I *am* awful. I have to go."

She tried to hold on. I kept walking, pulling my sleeve out of her grip.

"Great," she called. "So you're not gonna talk to me again? Bastard. Prick."

I looked back. Julian loomed behind her. He bent down to slip his arms around her middle. She didn't react. He winked at me, his chin resting on her shoulder.

"Can't you just stay and talk?" she asked. Her voice had a plaintive note I'd never heard before.

"No," I said as I left.

* * *

I should've told her and Julian about my dream of the night before. It was a break from the nightmares, the endless falling from buildings, trees, flagpoles, airplanes.

Margaret and I were in my corner office at the top of a skyscraper. The floor-to-ceiling windows gave us a magnificent view of the city, complementing my mahogany paneling and black-leather, chrome-and-glass furniture. I wore dark-gray Armani trousers, handmade Italian shoes, a dove-gray shirt with a white collar, and a wine silk tie with matching suspenders. My hair was slicked back with something as light as meringue. I paced my plush carpet while Margaret sat in front of my stupendous desk, taking dictation on a pad as I held forth on transitioned value-adds in our resource-constrained operational space. She was in a black miniskirt and a white, long-sleeved blouse with the top three buttons undone.

I was about to ask if she'd sleep with me when she said, "I'd like to do this in the nude, sir, if that's all right with you."

"Please go ahead, Ms. Alvarez," I said.

She wriggled out of her clothes to reveal a gigantic pink slit that went from her groin to her sternum. Her labia were like the folded-back mouth of a sleeping bag; her clitoris protruded from its hood like a third breast. I knelt at her feet, and she spread her legs and pushed her pelvis toward me.

She was hollow and powder blue inside, with a cluster of five or six fuzzy red balls like cat toys hanging from a bright yellow hank of yarn up where her heart should've been. I inserted my arms and glided my palms over her wetness. My sleeves were instantly soaked. She smiled down at me, her hands gripping my shoulders. I sucked on her grapefruit of a clitoris, being careful to not bite, and she groaned and yanked on my elbows, lodging my arms deeper inside her. They slipped into twin grooves and locked, my wrists held firmly by contracting rings of muscle.

Margaret shuddered and squealed, and a gush of warm fluid drenched my face. It was incomprehensibly delicious—spicy, musky, and sweet. She held her lips apart with her hands, rose on the balls of her feet, and lowered herself, engulfing my head in her hot, wet blueness. I snapped awake and tried for the rest of the night to get back to sleep and find that office again, but it was no good.

When Margaret grabbed me at the party, I could still smell her and taste her flavor of lobster and cinnamon. She made me want to yank off her jeans right there in the hallway and bury my face in her fragrant, mouthwatering flesh.

* * *

Another sleepless night. Unable to write, I watched TV for most of Sunday and then took my walk. Trey waited at the top of the hill on my side of the street, just past No Man's Land. He wore a turtleneck sweater and jeans, his blond crew cut standing tall. Something in his expression chilled me. The unfamiliar clothes and elevated view of his intricate wheelchair made him enormous and phantasmagoric, like a haunted castle. He seemed extra-sunlit and somehow separated from the background, as if he were outlined in black. I approached him with the most profound foreboding of my life.

"*They fuckin' moved!*" he shouted when I was still several yards away. "*My fuckin' neighbors moved! They sold the house to their daughter and went to Barstow! Now I can't get to the fuckin' pool!*"

I was clairvoyant; I heard his next line in my head—a kind of pre-echo— before he actually said it: "You gotta help me, Elliot."

"Okay, wait a second," I said. "Let's slow down. What happened? Your neighbors moved?"

"They sold the house to their goddamn daughter and moved to Barstow. I missed my chance."

"The daughter isn't moving in?"

"No! She's not coming down from Fresno for another year, and she's not gonna rent it. It's gonna stay empty. I'm screwed. I was gonna do it next week because it's getting too cold for me to sit out here, and then my mom told me this morning that there was a fuckin' moving truck in front of their house. By the time I got out there to see for myself, they were gone! In one afternoon! Nobody's there to leave the gate open at night, so you gotta do it for me, Elliot."

"Are you sure nobody's going to be moving in?"

"*You're not listening to me!*"

"I *am* listening to you because you're yelling at the top of your lungs!"

He closed his eyes and put back his head, breathing deeply through his nose. I sat on the wooden rail fence beside the horse path. After about half a minute, he opened his eyes.

"Okay. I'm sorry about yelling. I'm not dealing with this very well. I apologize."

"All right."

"Okay, now listen to me: I'm up shit creek here. The daughter's paying my other neighbor's kid to mow the lawn and clean the pool, but it's gonna be at least a year before she moves down, and she's not gonna rent to anybody because she's afraid they'll trash the house. It's gonna be vacant for a year or more, and I can't wait that long. I can't. I need you to open that gate for me."

"If the kid is mowing the lawn and trimming the trees and hedges, he's going to have clippings," I said. "He's going to have to put out the green trash can like before."

"No he's not. I know this kid. He's an expert lawn mower. That's what he does for his money. He's got a mulching mower that chops the grass clippings up real fine so you can leave it on the lawn as fertilizer. There's nothing to get rid of. He calls it 'grasscycling.' And he's not going to be trimming any trees or hedges because it's almost winter. There's nothing to trim. Not until fuckin' spring, and I'm not doing another winter here. I'm *not*, okay? I can't. It's not an option."

"But they just moved today. You can't be sure about the lawn. You won't know until Wednesday night."

"Look, I asked around and everybody told me the house is gonna be vacant for at least a year and Craig's mowing the lawn. It's exactly how I'm telling you. I don't have to wait for Wednesday night because I know how it's gonna be. Craig's family never puts out the green can. Never. The only time that gate's gonna be opened is when Craig goes in to mow the lawn or clean the pool, and he's gonna be in there the whole time. I can't drive into the pool right in front of him. I lost my chance to do it alone at night, so you gotta help me. That's all there is to it. I can't open that gate by myself. You gotta help me."

"What kind of gate is it?"

"It's one of those chain-link things, with a latch shaped like a horseshoe. It doesn't have a lock or anything; it just swings down on the fence post. If I could get close to it, I could lift it up, even with my fucked-up hands. But I can't get my chair close enough. I can't lean forward, and I can't back up to it and reach around over my shoulder because my arms go into spasms. I can't get them high enough."

"But you've tried to open the latch?"

"That's what I've been saying!"

"Calm down. Yelling at me isn't going to help."

"Okay. I'm sorry. It's just that I lost my chance. This was my last chance. I had it planned down to the last little detail, and then those *fuckers*—No, that's not cool. It's not their fault. They didn't know they were supposed to stay there until I'd drowned myself in their pool. But they're depriving me of my suicide! I am such an unlucky son of a bitch, it's not even funny. Look, I can't sit here anymore. Let's go on your walk."

* * *

We passed through the ornamental plum, white ash, and eucalyptus. Joggers and power walkers moved out of our way as if we brandished weapons. I realized that Trey *was* a weapon. He destroyed connection. Blew it to smithereens, usually before it could threaten anybody by taking place. Yet our connection had survived both our strategies. I wondered if we'd been ensnared in some unfathomably cruel master plan.

"So are you going to help me?" he asked.

I wished I could live on the golf course. Nothing would be better than spending my days on grassy hummocks ornamented with flags snapping in the breeze like at a jousting tournament in Camelot.

"Isn't there somebody in your circle who can help?" I asked.

"My 'circle'? What is this, *The Great Gatsby*? I don't have a circle; I have buddies, and none of my buddies'll help me because they say they love me too much. I'm just too nice. If I'd been a total asshole after my accident, I'd be dead by now. I haven't asked anyone in my 'circle' for five years."

"Well, what if *I* love you too much now?"

He glowered. "Fuck you, you fat piece of shit. You goddamn, pompous, boring *copywriter*. You wimpy, no-girlfriend, scared, spineless, angry pussy-boy. There. How was that? Do you hate me enough to help me die now?"

"How can I hate somebody who's only telling the truth?"

"See? I don't know what it is about me. I never met anybody who didn't like me, and now I'm paying for it. What did I do to *deserve this?*"

His yelling was more like loud wheezing because of his barely functional diaphragm; it startled the two coltish teenage girls coming toward us. They veered off on either side. I stared straight ahead as I walked. Dried leaves blew across the sidewalk with a ghostly scampering sound that made the back of my neck prickle. Suddenly, I was very sleepy.

"You haven't answered me," Trey said. "Are you going to help me or not?"

"I can't," I said. "I'm sorry. It's too much to ask."

He seemed to sag, even though he was strapped upright in his chair.

"It's something you have to ask a family member or a really close friend," I said. "I can't. I'm sorry. It's too much and it's too ugly. I can't open a gate and watch you drive into a swimming pool, and your chair comes down on top of you and pins you to the bottom, maybe upside down. No. I'm sorry."

"Who asked you to watch? Walk away."

"I can't do that either. You want me to go, 'Allow me' and open the gate, and then I'm supposed to walk home knowing you're going to drown yourself like a rat in a sack. I can't."

I expected him to start shouting again, but he wheeled closer and spoke in a soft, reasonable voice.

"Listen, Elliot. You'd be setting me free. I can't go on like this. I don't have a life. I'm in total pain, all the time, twenty-four hours a day. I never have a minute's peace. Never. I can only sleep for an hour or two at a time, and then

I get a muscle spasm, and it hurts so much, I wake up. I haven't slept in almost twenty-three years. I'm beyond exhausted; I'm already dead. Please. I'm begging you."

On the greens behind him, a golfer flexed his club over his head and twisted to stretch his back and shoulder muscles. He sang contentedly to himself in a quiet tenor.

"I can't just ask somebody walking by if he'll open the gate," Trey continued, "because then he's gonna read in the paper the next day that he helped some poor cripple drown himself. Whoever opens the gate has to know what he's doing and why. It has to be an informed choice. You're the only person who can do it."

"But I *can't* do it," I said, watching the singing golfer. "I just told you."

"You *can* do it. You *can*. It's nothing. You're just opening a gate. You have no responsibility for what happens after that. It wouldn't be your fault. And anyway, it's what I want. You'd be helping me. You'd be setting me free."

I lost sight of the golfer. "Look, if you're committed to…to drowning yourself, this golf course has lots of ponds. Why do you have to involve someone else?"

"You're not thinking. You gotta be a member to get in there. You think they're gonna let a quadriplegic sign up? Am I supposed to swing the club with my mouth? And anyway, those ponds aren't deep enough around the edges. If I tried to drive in, my chair'd bog down in the mud, and I'd just sit there like an idiot."

"I just can't believe you've tried everything to deal with your pain," I said. "Why?"

"Because…"

"Because I'm not a quitter?"

"Well, yes."

He stopped in the middle of the sidewalk. "Elliot, listen to me: I *am* a quitter. I quit a long time ago. I thought you of all people would understand that. It's not my job to hang around and be an inspiration for people. It's not up to me to make people go, 'By golly, I can *do* it!' and traipse off to have a beautiful, fulfilling life. You know why? Because I'm still *here* after they go. I'm still here with my pain and my legs and arms that don't work. When Margaret kissed me, part of me wanted to kill her. I'm *angry*. I'm *bitter*. I look around at everybody holding hands and getting laid and playing basketball, and I hate 'em."

Every few seconds, someone jogged or walked past. Many were as physically flawless as Margaret.

"I don't believe it's your responsibility to live as an inspiration to others," I said. "I never said that."

He sipped water, studying the passersby. "When I watch the news and see some twisted-up guy in a wheelchair and he's going, 'Glehhhh,' he makes me wanna puke. He's got some bleeding-heart bitch interpreting for him, and she says, 'Oh, he has *such* a *positive, happy* spirit!' Well, how do we know that? You can't understand a word he says. Maybe he's trying to say, 'Fuck you, you ugly cunt! Get the fuck away from me!' Those bitches never look like Margaret, never. You know, she kissed me, but she'd never go to bed with me."

I climbed up to sit on the fence. "Actually, Margaret told me you're a hottie, and she liked it when you looked at her butt."

It seemed to make him sadder. "Yeah, well, that's as far as it'd ever go with her. And I'm not blaming her. I'm a wreck. The point is, I used to be with hot chicks like Margaret. Don't you understand how much I hate being disabled?"

"Yes. I do. This was the first conversation we had, remember?"

"It's the only conversation I *ever* have. It's all I ever think about. I'm not supposed to be here. This wasn't supposed to be my life. I'm not one of those fucking cripples that only get fat, ugly, do-gooder, busybody bitches who treat them like pets. So are you gonna help me?"

An overweight middle-aged couple bore down on us in a vigorous power walk. The man wore elastic bandages on his knees, and the woman carried hand weights. They puffed and blew like rhinoceroses. I waited until they'd thudded past.

"I can't, Trey. I'm sorry. I really am. I can't do it. I can't help someone commit suicide."

"Why not?"

"It's, it's against what I believe in. I didn't realize it until you asked. I can't. I'm really sorry."

"You're not religious, Elliot. What do you mean it's against what you believe in?"

"I don't know. Maybe it *is* residual Catholicism. I can't do it. I'm sorry."

"Look, I'm one of those cool guys who had it all and made your life miserable. If you off me, maybe you'll finally—"

"*I don't want to off anyone!*" I shouted. After I regained my composure, I said, "Turning you into the sacrificial cool guy isn't going to let me finally do anything. It'll just put the capper on my loserdom. I'll be no different from every angry, ugly, smelly, weird, inadequate guy who goes on a shooting rampage."

Trey sighed through slack lips, a dispirited nickering.

"Are you pissed at me now?" I asked. "I'm sort of pissed at you."

"No, I'm just really shook up. I don't know what I'm gonna do."

"I'm sorry. It's just too much. I'd go insane afterward. I'd never be able to sleep again."

"Yeah, I guess you wouldn't. I guess you wouldn't. Look, you finish your walk, and I'll go back to my spot."

"Do you want me to stop by on the way back?" I asked.

"Sure. I don't know what we'll talk about."

"How about literature?" I winced when he glared. "Well, *I* don't know. You mentioned *The Great Gatsby*."

"Yeah, and you almost shit yourself. You still think I'm this ignorant, white-trash Okie. After all we've been through, you still stereotype me."

"I'm shallow. I can't give up my preconceptions. By the way, did you ever own a Camaro?"

"Nope. I had a low-rider Beetle. But I did have a mullet once, so you're only partially wrong. All right, I'm going. I gotta try and chill. Later."

CHAPTER TEN

Margaret wore her sunglasses at the Friday meeting. She didn't speak, other than to acknowledge Dennis's suggestions. Despite her shades we could all see that her left eye was swollen shut. The purple bulge was plainly visible from the side, and a yellow-and-green stain had spread over her cheekbone.

Nobody said a word about it. I watched how she related to Julian; she didn't seem afraid of him or angry. The only emotion she projected was embarrassment. She sat with a hand over her mouth as though trying to hunch down into herself and disappear, and she was out the door the second Dennis released us. Gary followed; I peeked into the hall to watch them walk off. Before they turned the corner, Gary put her arm around Margaret's shoulders.

I went to the break room for a cup of coffee. Julian came in, unwrapping a nutrition bar. He sat at a table and glanced at me.

"No, I didn't do it," he said.

"Is that the truth?" I asked.

"Of course. I don't hit women. Besides, I have no reason to give Margaret a black eye. She came through for me to a degree that, shall we say, far exceeded my expectations. Margaret is very deep, and I'm not talking about her intellectual prowess. Her prowess lies in what she can...*accommodate*." He smacked his lips. "And it doesn't matter which, um, ingress. *Very* accommodating, Margaret is. To a fault."

I suddenly wanted to throw my coffee in his face.

"And when she blasts off, it's like you're tickling a bear." He made a guttural noise, a sort of growling laugh. "Never heard anything like it."

"Who do you think gave her the black eye?" I asked, confused about why I was so angry at him.

"Ah. Not interested in Margaret's portals or noises, I see. Right. Well, I have no idea who did it. Maybe she ran into a door."

"Jesus, Julian. Aren't you concerned?"

"If she wants to involve me in whatever's happening, she will. She hasn't, so I'm minding my own business. I suggest you do too, old boy."

"Advice noted," I said. I went out in the hall just as Gary passed, heading for the elevator.

"Can I talk to you a second?" I asked.

She stopped, extra imperturbable that morning. "Yes?"

"Um…" It was the first time in months that we'd spoken outside of the conference room. I couldn't remember when we last stood face to face. "I just wanted to ask if you knew what happened to Margaret, how she got that black eye."

A pause as she decided whether or not to answer me. "Even if I knew," she finally said, "I wouldn't tell you. It's none of your business."

"Yeah, that's what Julian said too, but as you know, I'm an incorrigible snoop. Can you tell me where she is? Is *that* something I'm allowed to know?"

I may as well have been taunting a wax sculpture. "Downstairs in front of the building. Waiting for the march."

"What march?"

"The protest march."

"Thank you."

Rather than ride with her in the elevator, I took the stairs. Through the lobby windows, I saw Margaret standing on the sidewalk with Essi. I walked out and joined them. It was a beautiful day, sunny but with a refreshing breeze.

"Hey," I said. "What's happening?"

Staring past me, Margaret said, "Just waiting for the march."

"Me too." I paused. "So is everything okay?'"

She nodded silently.

On both sides of the street, groups of people had gathered, some with signs. I read, "Don't Let Banks Control Us," "Stop the War Now," "The Corrupt Fear Us," "Not in My Name," "This Is What Democracy Looks Like," "Slaughtergate," "Smash the Jewish State," "Time to Rise Up," and "War Feeds the Rich." Directly across from the office stood a handful of middle-aged men in T-shirts, shorts, and baseball caps. They held signs that said, "Get a Job," "Take a Bath," "Shut Up, Useful Idiots," and "Legalize Capitalism."

Next door was Amir's, the lunch counter where our team always ate. The owner was a Syrian immigrant in his late forties. He stood in front of his business, displaying a big piece of foam-core board with the hand-lettered legend "God Bless America" in red, white, and blue. Amir's twenty-two-year-old son Michael was a marine on his third tour overseas.

"Hey Amir!" I called.

He waved, smiling.

Essi had something in her hand. I looked closely and realized that it was a stack of yellow-ribbon car magnets, with "Support Our Troops" written on them in black.

"Are you handing those out?" I asked.

"No. I took them off cars along the street. I'm surprised there're still so many of them. It's, like, *my* statement of support for the troops. I'm trying to stop people from encouraging them to, like, kill or die in illegal wars of conquest. My circle of compassion includes soldiers too. You probably think that's, like, a meaningless gesture."

"Not at all," I said. "It's a very significant gesture."

From down the street came a rumbling, shuffling, tweedling cacophony, the sound of shield-slapping Zulu warriors who'd met up with a Chinese opera and a Salvation Army band. The march approached, a rolling wall of people of all ages and races festooned with signs, banners, red flags, black flags, rainbow flags, Cuban flags, Canadian flags, flags from Middle Eastern countries, and American-flag lookalikes with peace signs, swastikas, or skulls instead of stars. The marchers were flanked by police on motorcycles and bicycles, as well as men and women in fluorescent green vests and caps.

"Who are the people with the green vests and hats?" I yelled at Margaret.

"Free-speech lawyers!" she screamed. "They're here to protect everybody's rights. Woooo!" She pumped her fist.

The march churned past, a slow avalanche of color. Drummers pounded, flautists blew, and chanting demonstrators waved signs that read, "No War for Israel," "Ashamed to be American," "Jesus Is Not for Corporate Greed," and "If We Don't End War, War Will End Us." A very large banner that spanned the width of the street said, "A Better World Is Possible." Looming overhead were enormous papier-mâché effigies of the president, vice president, and secretary of state, demonic figures that seemed to caper with glee.

A few feet away, Amir shouted and waved his "God Bless America" poster. Several marchers shouted back, giving him stiff-armed salutes. A young man leaped out of the crowd to grab at Amir's sign. As I took a step forward, three police officers slammed the attacker to the pavement and handcuffed him. Several of the free-speech lawyers yelled at the cops.

Someone beside me shouted, "*Booyah!* Eat concrete, fucker!"

It was Julian. He held a large American flag on a staff. I recognized it as the one Dennis kept in his office. Margaret and Essi turned away with identical scowls. Julian pushed past me and planted his feet on the curb.

"*God bless America!*" he screamed, causing a section of the parade to instantly grind to a halt in front of us. Seen from the air, the solid phalanx of people marching twenty-five or thirty abreast would've been pinched and torn asunder where Julian and I stood. Our presence cut off the flow.

We were confronted by an ocean of faces, twisted and gnarled and clenched. Fists were shaken. More Nazi salutes were conferred. Two-fingered peace signs were jabbed at us. Middle fingers were displayed. Index fingers were wagged. Voices were raised in earsplitting exposition.

"Give war a chance!" Julian shouted, waving his flag.

A black-clad man with a shaved head and dark glasses yelled, "Why aren't *you* over there with a gun, pussy?"

"Because my gun-pussy's got chlamydia!" Julian yelled back.

A copper-skinned woman with a beaded headband shouted, "How can you support killing women and children?"

"If I don't, who will?" Julian shouted back,

A fat man with a long, white beard and a multicolored, tie-dyed T-shirt roared, "Fuck you, warmonger!"

"Where's my fucking train set, Santa?" Julian roared back.

Another scuffle broke out in front of Amir's. The police carted away what looked like a Greek Orthodox bishop, leaving Amir still standing. More cops surrounded him, collapsible batons in hand. The noise was unbelievable, a churning, crashing, and clattering overlaid by a continual screaming like jet engines. Much of the din was people endlessly shouting, "Shame! Shame! Shame! Shame!" Ten police officers lined up in front of Julian and me, half of them facing the crowd, half facing us.

A heavy, gray-haired woman in pink yelled, "You fuckin' douche-bag cowards, hiding behind the cops! Why don't you come out here? Whatsa matter, scared?" Half a dozen enormous wens sprouted from her cheeks and forehead.

"*Face* nipples?" Julian shouted. "Don't think that'll catch on, luv!"

The woman bellowed like an enraged steer. A policeman gave her a powerful shove; she moved on, trumpeting back over her shoulder.

"Good *Lord,* now I know where the term 'ugly American' comes from!" Julian yelled at me. "U-S-A! U-S-A! U-S-A!"

The free-speech lawyers in their green vests and caps shouted at us. One tried to break past the police, but two officers launched him back into the throng so effectively that I glimpsed the soles of his sandals.

"You will hear my statement!" a woman screamed at me. "This is my statement, and you will hear it!"

"Why are you standing up for corporations?" a man howled. "You're just shitheads!"

A small boy carrying a sign that said, "Wake Me Up from This American Nightmare" gave me the finger, shook his rear, stuck out his tongue, and ran back to his mother.

Marchers left the parade route and came up on the sidewalk, encircling us.

"Liars! Liars!" an elderly man sang.

"I'll pray for you," a bearded man yelled. "I forgive you!"

"Don't you know that they're lying to you?" a ponytailed man keened. "Think about it! They don't care about you!"

An attractive, young, strawberry-blonde woman in a blue sweatshirt that read "Bastard" stopped in front of us. Her sign said, "War Against AmeriKKKa Is the *Real* War on Terror."

She smiled; I smiled back. Her right hand came up in a peace sign and began stabbing at me.

"*Murderers!*" she shrieked. "*Murderers! Murderers!*" Her eyes were like painted wood.

I kept smiling, even though it felt as though icepicks were being jabbed into my ears.

"Oh my *God!*" Julian yelled. "Put a sock in it, for Christ's sake! You'll shatter the windows!"

"*Murderers! Murderers! Mur—*" A police officer pushed her. She almost fell, her chant skipping slightly. "*—derers! Murderers! Murderers!*"

"Good-bye, fetid coloratura!" Julian shouted as she moved away. "When was the last time you washed that saucy bottom?"

The police tied a yellow "Do Not Cross" tape to a couple of parking meters and looped it around a big municipal trash can, separating Julian, Margaret, Essi, and me from the crowd. More cops closed around us with their hands on their gun butts, holsters unbuckled.

"Sweet!" Margaret screamed at me. "Now everybody's gonna think I'm one of you! Thanks a lot!" But she grinned broadly, her thumbs hooked into the front pockets of her jeans.

A chubby, middle-aged man holding a video camera stopped in front of us, beckoning with his free hand. "C'mon! C'mon out here! C'mon past the cops, ya pussies!"

Julian blew him a kiss, complete with a loud *mwah*. The cameraman roared and made strange swimming motions until a police officer shoved him away.

A woman wearing a pink feather boa yelled at Julian, "It's *our* flag too!"

"Then *wave* one, you silly bitch!" he shouted. "Who's stopping you? Here, take mine!" He thrust Dennis's Stars and Stripes at her. She recoiled, the way movie vampires shrank from crucifixes.

And then the march was past. The police officers took down the yellow caution tape around us.

"My first protest march," I said to no one in particular.

Margaret was subdued again. She barely glanced at me. Essi tossed her stack of yellow-ribbon magnets into the nearby trash can, and she and Margaret went back inside our building.

Julian rolled up Dennis's flag. "Let's get some coffee at Amir's," he said. "Maybe he'll put vodka in it."

* * *

Amir stood on a chair, taping his poster to the wall above the cash register.

"Julian! Elliot!" he yelped. "Holy smokes! Did you ever see anything like that in your life?"

"Every day, right before I flush the toilet," Julian said.

Amir blanched. "That's just repulsive."

"I know. Which is why I flush it away."

Amir's poster was in terrible shape. Three of the corners were folded over from people trying to tear it out of his hands, and it was spattered with red paint and partially dried raw eggs. One edge was ragged, as if somebody had gnawed on it.

Amir stepped down off his chair. "Have a seat, fellas. Would you like some coffee?"

"Yes please," I said. "Have you heard from Michael?"

Julian and I sat while Amir poured us coffee. "Yes," he said. "His regiment is moving east. He didn't say, but I know it's another offensive."

"My brother just got deployed," Julian said. "He's not going to see as much combat as the marines, but I'm still jumpy."

Amir sat with us. He'd aged dramatically in the past two years. "Well," he said, "the only advice I can give you is to not watch the news. Michael sends me lots of e-mails and videos with the real story. Maybe your brother can do that too."

"I'll ask him."

We drank our coffee in glorious silence.

* * *

At home I coordinated with Gary by e-mail. When we were done, I realized that for the first time, I hadn't visualized her face as we wrote. She was now just words on a screen. It didn't seem real. I had the urge to write her about the sheer strangeness of no longer having her in my life.

Since I'd read in a medical journal that afternoon naps were good for heart patients, I stretched out on my sofa for an hour and then had a long, groggy session with my laptop before taking my walk. When I was in the middle of No Man's Land, a Honda whipped by no more than seven feet away. It was filled with boys and girls piled all over each other, peering in my direction and laughing excitedly. A tattooed, hairless kid stood in the front passenger seat, halfway out the window.

"*Fuck yoooooo!*" he screamed and bit his lip as he made a throwing motion. Something clanked against the wrought-iron fence a few inches in front of me, at the level of my head. As the vehicle receded, I willed it to flip over and eject everybody onto the asphalt so I could run up and laugh in their abraded-away faces. Nothing happened. Whatever was thrown at me had disappeared into the tall grass on the other side of the fence. It sounded like a hammer or wrench.

At the sidewalk bordering the golf course, I climbed the wooden railing, making for the dirt horse trail. Just as I swung one leg over the top, a car horn blasted right behind me. It triggered an adrenaline rush that nearly sent me airborne. I figured the lip-biter and his friends were back, this time with assault rifles. I turned, and there was David in his red Mercedes, parked in the small lot beside the entrance to the golf course.

"Hey!" he called as he stepped out. "I dropped by your place and got no answer, so I figured you might be on your walk. How's it going?"

It was the first time in my life I was glad to see my brother. I could've kissed him.

"I'm okay," I said, still sitting on the fence. "Nothing new to report. Walking, working, trying to drop the weight."

He approached in his suit and leather-soled shoes. "Maybe I'll go with you."

"Well, it's kind of a trek, and I do it pretty fast. You'll get blisters from your shoes."

David looked around. "Jesus, what kind of trees are those?"

"Eucalyptus." At that time of the year, they'd shed their papery bark and turned smooth and pinkish-tan as if they were covered with skin.

"They look just like naked women," David said.

I'd noticed the same thing when I first started taking my walk. Most eucalyptus had a trunk that split into two boughs like a *Y*, and those boughs usually had a small mound of dark, stringy bark at their junctions. Now I knew why that part of a tree was called a crotch. We seemed to be surrounded by hundreds of naked women standing on their heads with their legs spread, the sort of yoga class I dreamed about in high school.

"Look at those things!" David drooled. "It's like they have *pussies!*"

I hated the eucalyptus. They were mirages, hard as stone to the touch.

"So do you want me to come with you?" David asked.

"This may sound harsh, but I really need to be alone when I come out here," I said. "It's the only time I have for myself, away from my phone and computer and e-mails and texts."

He shrugged. "I understand. I just thought I'd see how you were doing. Haven't heard from you."

"I'm fine. How're Andrea and the kids?"

"Kids are great. Andrea's…She's…If it weren't for the kids, I think she'd probably…oh, whatever. Everybody's got their…something. Okay, I'll leave you alone. Let me know if you need anything. Toodles."

He headed back to his car, and I jumped off the fence and hurried away.

*　*　*

"Who was that guy I saw you talking to?" Trey asked.

"My brother. He wanted to go on my walk with me, but I said no."

"Why?"

"Not in the mood."

He smiled. "You really hate your family, don't you?"

"No! Of course not. It's just that they think I'm a complete screw-up and a failure. It really upsets me. All they do is criticize me."

"Yeah, you're one pissed-off dude. But so am I, so it's okay."

We watched the traffic. "Now I feel guilty about saying no to my brother," I said, "and that's making me angry because he just badgers and ridicules me. Why should I feel guilty about not wanting him around? He's tormented me our whole lives."

"Hey," Trey said, "I just realized I can use your anger. I just gotta keep after you until I piss you off so much, you push me in the pool yourself."

"My doctor said my rage is going to kill *me,* not you."

"As long as you help me before you croak, that's fine."

We always ended up talking about death. Ghouls, that's what we were.

"Aren't you even the tiniest bit afraid of dying?" I asked.

"Nope. We're all just flank steak walking around. When you die, you just tune out and smell real bad for a while, and that's it." He winked as he sipped water.

I told him about the kid in the car throwing whatever it was at me. "It sounded hard, like metal. He could easily have killed me."

Trey sighed. "It's the curse. I'm bad luck for both of us. That means you're gonna die and I'm gonna live."

I shivered and stood; pacing helped. "The thing I can't deal with about death is you're either extinguished or you have to hang around forever. Both possibilities terrify me. What am I going to do for eternity? Won't I get bored? After trillions and trillions of years, won't there be nothing left to do or even think about? God, I *hate* talking about this. It makes me feel like I'm going crazy."

"Look," he said, "there's no heaven and there's no hell. There's only this shit pile we call earth, and when your time is up, you're gone and you don't even know it. So you have to help me leave. You'd be doing me the best favor anybody did for me my whole miserable life, and you'll be getting rid of the curse."

When we talked, passing cars honked every five minutes. In response he'd point his clenched hand and go, "'Ayyyyyy!" like a sleazy Vegas lounge singer. Two hours divided by five minutes equaled twenty-four carloads, at least thirty-odd people for just the time that I sat with him. He obviously had hundreds of acquaintances, but not one of them was willing to open the gate for him? I was his only hope?

"I had a textbook in first grade," I said. "In one story a kid fell through the ice on a frozen lake. The illustration showed him with one leg pointing down and the other up almost over his head. His fingers were splayed like claws, and his eyes and mouth were shut tight. The underside of the ice was pale green, and the water was green that faded into dark blue. That picture made me feel the cold water going up my nose, down my throat, and into my lungs."

"*Shit,* Elliot!" he burst out. "You're saying you're not gonna help me because of some *picture* you saw in first grade? That's the dumbest thing I ever heard!"

"I saw a picture of some nonexistent kid drowning, and it's haunted me all my life. How do you suppose I'd deal with actually helping a close friend drown himself?"

He started to say something but changed his mind. We watched the cars go by.

"So the only guy who can help me," he mumbled, "isn't going to because he saw a picture of a drowning kid in a first-grade textbook thirty years ago. What're the odds of that happening? How unlucky can a person be in one lifetime?"

"Well, maybe it isn't healthy to think about odds. Maybe it's better for your peace of mind to try and accept reality."

"That's easy for you to say. You're not here in this chair."

"You wouldn't want to trade places with me," I said.

"How can you say that? You don't know."

"Yes I do."

"Aw, what a load of *crap!*" he shouted. "You gotta stop with this stupid self-pity, because it's getting pretty boring to hear. You think you're such a loser that you'd rather be me paralyzed than be you able-bodied? Don't make me laugh."

"Laughter's good for the soul."

"I just told you: We don't have souls. And what you said about accepting reality? Well, I *don't.* I never have. You know that in almost twenty-three years, I've never *once* had a dream of me in this chair? I'm always walking and running in my dreams. This isn't my reality. This isn't how it was supposed to be."

"But why make yourself even more unhappy thinking about how things were supposed to be?" I asked.

"Because I can't give up on that guy who was supposed to have a life that meant something. I can't just say, 'Oh well. He didn't get that life. Too bad.' *That* would be suicide. If I go into that pool because I refuse to accept this guy with his stick legs and big potbelly and his twenty-four-hour-a-day pain, then I won't kill *me,* I'll kill *him.* I'll be freeing *me.*"

I sat in silence, thinking that I could've been listening to David talk about vaginas.

Trey looked me over. "Well, I've planted the seed. I can see it in your eyes. Hey, you wanna hear my idea for the war effort?"

"Not even remotely."

"No, this is great. Check it out: We need to form our own suicide battalions."

"Of course we do."

"Well, nobody's expecting it, are they? Recruit guys like me, give us explosive vests, and send us in. Pack my chair with thirty pounds of TNT, point me toward the people who need to be blown up, and *boom!* Or send us over as fake human shields. They'll put us in all the important military targets, and we can blow 'em up ourselves. I bet we could sign up at least ten million people. All those emos, drunks, and divorcees? The army could have a new slogan, like, 'If you're gonna kill yourself anyway, do it for your country.' Whatta ya think?"

"Since you brought the subject up, what does the instructor at a suicide-bomber training camp say to the students?" I asked.

"What?"

"'Watch closely. I'm only going to show you this once.'"

He chuffed. "Not bad."

"Do you have any friends with relatives in the military?" I asked.

"Yeah. Lots."

"Here, give them these." I pulled Essi's stolen yellow-ribbon magnets from my sweat-jacket pocket.

"Cool. Where'd you get them?"

"Found them in a trash can."

"Figures. Put them in the bag on the back of my chair. I'll hand them out tomorrow."

I tucked them away. "Well, I'm exhausted. Are you heading out?"

"Nah," he said, "I'm gonna sit here for a while. I like walking home in the dark. Take it easy. And cheer up. I know you don't wanna talk about this anymore, but it's really not an awful thing. I'm gonna make you see that."

"The daily suicide pep talk. Wonderful. See you tomorrow."

As I left him, I thought about what he'd said, that he'd never once dreamed of himself in his chair. He also "walked" home, "made" sandwiches, and "cut" his meat. It was frightening, the iron willpower it took to maintain that for almost twenty-three years.

CHAPTER ELEVEN

Every couple of months, I came across a shorn-off concrete lamppost in No Man's Land, lying either on the sidewalk or in the gutter where the cleanup crew left it. Sometimes there were black skid marks in the street, but in most cases the driver hadn't even touched the brake pedal. I could tell by the piles of shattered safety glass, bent strips of aluminum trim, and shards of red and amber plastic scattered across the fresh oil and coolant stains at the base of the broken cement stump. According to the newspaper, these car-to-post encounters generally took place at three in the morning. I therefore figured I could play the odds.

One afternoon, smack in the middle of No Man's Land with my back toward the oncoming traffic, I heard screeching tires. The sound was nothing unusual in my neighborhood; the streets teemed with absent-minded vagrants, children, bicyclists, dogs, and cats. Cars blew stop signs and red lights, drifted out of their lanes, slalomed around each other, darted from parking lots and blind alleys.

This particular screeching was very close, however, as though the car hurtled right at me, so I turned and saw a car hurtling right at me, up on the sidewalk, enlarging with meteoric speed. The headlights and grill gave it a wide-eyed, clench-toothed face.

I spun away, thinking, "Brain," which made me grab the back of my head with both hands. Frogmen did that when they jumped out of helicopters. I also tried a spread-eagled cheerleader leap, apparently believing that the car would torpedo under me. Instead, it hit me in the small of the back. Though the actual blow didn't hurt, there was a loud *wham!* so perfectly articulated, it sounded spoken, and my feet were suddenly out in front of me at eye level. Around them everything broke up into streaks of white, green, and yellow. It confused me because I'd been there before. Time ceased to exist. At the heart of all that movement and color, part of me drifted along in a cocoon of peace and silence, vaguely curious about what would happen next.

It took forever to land. My heels met the concrete first, then my buttocks, my shoulders, and finally my laced-together fingers, still protecting my brain. There was a series of painless, scraping jolts as I rebounded a few times, slid, and came to a complete stop. Flat on my back, I heard apocalyptic hip-hop: thundering drums, jagged synthesizer stabs, sampled guitar power chords, and a high-pitched wind instrument such as an Andean panpipe, over which a man shouted what sounded like, *"Groan! Misshape the maiden! I say groan! Misshape the maiden!"*

The music made my head vibrate on the sidewalk. I realized I had to take stock and make decisions. With my feet flying away like that, I'd probably been torn in half. I didn't want to look, but it was necessary to know if my intestines had plopped out onto the pavement. When I was ready, I sat up and found my waist still intact; my bowels weren't exposed. The damage seemed limited to bloody abrasions on the backs of my fingers and a hot numbness in the seat of my pants.

Behind me, another screech of tires. Overjoyed at the lack of visible intestines, I'd forgotten all about the car. I rolled onto my stomach and watched as the vehicle careened backward off the sidewalk in a billow of rubber smoke. Since I'd never been able to tell one brand of automobile from another, all I knew was that it was large, black, old, and American. Through the smoke I caught sight of the two occupants, young men with mustaches and reversed baseball caps. They gazed at me blankly, the car's wheels spinning, and out of the open windows came that hip-hop beat and the voice shouting, *"Groan! Misshape the maiden! I say groan! Misshape the maiden!"* The tires got traction, and the car fishtailed down the street before it occurred to me to note the license-plate number. I stood; the road was empty for a few seconds, then streams of cars poured in from both directions. I'd been hit while inside stoplight gaps in traffic.

The skid marks on the road and sidewalk seemed to indicate that the driver hadn't hit me deliberately. On the other hand, he may have put on the brakes only to keep his car from being demolished. He may have mistaken me for somebody else, an acquaintance who needed to be only slightly run over. Or maybe it was just a spur-of-the-moment impulse, like stopping for a fast-food taco.

If it was an accident, he'd managed to hit the only pedestrian in sight. Billion-to-one shots like that happened all the time. I'd once read about an angry and heartsick man who finally gave up and withdrew from the world, only to meet his long-lost childhood sweetheart at an ashram in Nepal. And they lived happily ever after. The driver of the car probably lit a cigarette and dropped the dashboard lighter. He and the passenger both dove for it and bopped their heads together, sending the vehicle out of control and up on the sidewalk to smack into me instead of the bus stop sign, the fire hydrant, or the telephone pole.

My fingers dripped blood, and my rear was on fire, so I went home without finishing my walk or talking to Trey. The upshot to being hit by a car was a few abrasions, nothing more. I took a long hot shower, bandaged my fingers, and had several beers with my dinner of leftover beef Pad Thai. By the time I went to bed, my lower back had developed a not-unpleasant muscular ache, the kind I got after a day of heavy physical labor in my garden. The beer and pain-suppressing endorphins eased me into a deep sleep.

* * *

I awoke the next morning feeling fine. As I sat up, an iron bar smashed across my lower spine, making me scream. I fell back and caught my breath.

After a few seconds, I tried to sit up again; the iron bar struck harder. I'd never felt such an *internal* pain, a reminder that I was just bones and meat, no different than a butchered chicken. Something ground and scraped inside me, between my kidneys. Sharp edges rubbed together. My spinal cord hadn't been severed, because I could still move my legs, but it took almost a full minute of very slow, very careful movements to turn myself over onto my belly. I then rotated ninety degrees and pushed my legs over the edge of the bed.

When my feet touched the floor, I raised myself on my arms and tried to stand; all I could manage was a panting semi-squat. A more upright stance brought massive jolts of pain and the most disgusting bodily sensation I've ever experienced, the feeling that my pelvis was unfastened somehow, greased up and precarious, about to slide like a desk drawer right out of my body. Sweat poured off of me in rivers.

The only way I could walk was to tip both shoulders to the right and push my hips forward, canting them upward to the left at the same time. In this posture, I could proceed inch by inch, my left heel raised and my right foot flat on the floor, my right arm out to the side in a downward-pointing *L* shape, and my left arm out to the side in an upward-pointing *L* shape. I felt like a swastika or Christmas tree, but if I deviated from this form in the slightest, I was knocked to the floor by the pain, and it'd take five minutes to get up again.

Sitting was agony. Lying was agony. Trying to stand was agony. Crawling was agony. Using the bathroom was physical and spiritual suffering beyond my endurance. By the afternoon I'd developed shooting pains down the backs of both legs, thin little electric zips like wires shorting out under the skin. I phoned Dr. Larkin from my bed.

"Call an ambulance," he ordered. "Right now."

"I don't think that's necessary," I said.

"Why did you call if you're not going to listen to me?" he roared.

"I don't know!" I shrieked and hung up. I switched off the telephone ringer before I passed out.

* * *

In the dream Dr. Larkin stood at the foot of my bed, saying his prayers. I watched him mumble and hiss, his white hair shining in the gloom, until it dawned on me that I wasn't asleep; he was actually there in my bedroom. *He was inside my house.*

"Get out," I whispered.

"Ah, he's awake," Larkin said. He'd addressed someone; I looked around and saw David lurking off to the side. That was how Larkin had gotten in. David had a key to my house, and he was listed in my medical file as the person to notify in case of an emergency. Larkin had called David, and my traitorous brother had let him in.

"Give me back my key," I said as I tried to sit up. The iron bar smashed me; I screamed.

"Don't move!" Larkin bellowed.

David jumped and backed away. He'd never met my doctor, and Larkin really punched it that time. The air in my bedroom rang as if a grenade had gone off. I laughed and screamed again.

"It's possible you've fractured a vertebra or two," Larkin said. "If you don't lie still, you could end up paralyzed. You won't be laughing then."

"I'm not paralyzed," I said when the pain stopped. "I can move my feet. Look."

Larkin shrugged. "You could still have a fracture. Movement could cause further injury, including paralysis. I strongly urge you to let me call an ambulance. They'll have a neck collar and a backboard, which is what you need. Don't be stupid."

"Come on, Elliot," David said. "This is ridiculous. You're really hurt. Do what he says." *So I can get the hell out of here,* he meant.

"All right! Call the damn ambulance, then."

Without a trace of acknowledgment, Larkin picked up the phone.

"Since when did you start caring about me, anyway?" I asked.

"Self-pity slows the healing process," he said as he pressed the keys. "Try not to indulge in it."

* * *

My third ambulance ride and the intense pain vividly brought to mind not my heart attack but the afternoon I broke my legs.

Our next-door neighbors, the Dickinsons, had a tree house that seemed to be about a hundred feet off the ground, like something out of a Tarzan movie. I thought it was incredibly irresponsible to let us children use it. Somebody was bound to fall out, because instead of being a regular box, it had only three walls. Mr. Dickinson had built it with an open front to keep us from getting too comfortable inside. He'd gone crazy the time he caught his daughter LuAnn and Billy Hanlon playing doctor behind the garage. I could understand; when David explained what they'd been doing, I was shocked, flabbergasted, and jealous.

There were two ways of accessing the tree house: a knotted rope tied to one of the ceiling beams and draped out the open front, or a ladder made of narrow boards nailed to the trunk, leading to the trapdoor cut in the floor. David and Emily could scamper up either. At the top, they'd make fun of me for being too afraid to join them.

On a Saturday afternoon, I tried to climb the rope one more time because Emily said I was too fat and chicken to do it, and David chanted, "Fatty, fatty, two by four." I jumped as high as I could and grabbed on, and suddenly I ascended, dragging myself up the rope, hand over hand, using both feet to push off against the knots. Higher and higher I went, my sweaty hands slipping, but I didn't look down and I didn't listen to the noise LuAnn and Mikey Dickinson made, cheering or jeering—I couldn't tell which, but it was high-pitched and excited. I hauled myself over the edge of the floor and into the tree house, stood, and lost my balance.

I fell forward into a blur of streaky colors. The wind rushed past my ears. My stomach was in my throat, and I was weightless, treading air, until I smashed into flat hardness. The impact was tremendous, a resonant thud like the single beat of a bass drum. I was now at the foot of the tree, looking up at Emily and David, who peered over the edge of the tree-house floor with their eyes like ping-pong balls.

Something shrieked, peal after peal, a bird set on fire, so I tried to get up to see if I could help it. I didn't feel any pain until that point, but then it was as if my legs were violently and instantly inflated with compressed air full of hot sand and razor blades. I collapsed and struggled into a sitting position. My legs were all wiggly and *S*-shaped, with new joints here and there. I realized that the birdcalls came from me.

David and Emily appeared at my side. "His legs are broken," Emily said. "Go get Mom!"

"*My legs aren't broken!*" I screamed.

David ran off. Emily knelt beside me to hold my hand, sobbing as if her own legs were broken. I wanted her to stop. She embarrassed me. Mom came with a blanket, and soon afterward an ambulance backed into the Dickinsons' yard. The two attendants unloaded equipment and a bright white-and-chrome wheeled bed that was too clean and shiny, like a giant syringe. When they touched me, the compressed air, hot sand, and razor blades returned. I wailed and pummeled them.

After that it was a jumble of lights and enormous blasts of pain, until I woke up in a hospital bed with my legs encased in metal splints, one of them held up by a system of cables, pulleys, and weights. Mom and Dad were there.

Dad explained what happened. "You've banged up your legs pretty badly, Elliot. You broke your right knee and shattered your right tibia and fibula, the long bones in your lower leg. You also broke both ankles and your left femur, the thighbone. On top of all that, you severely sprained or tore the tendons and ligaments in your ankles and your knee. The doctors set all the breaks and put on these splints, and they think almost everything'll heal fine. The only real problem is your femur. It's broken at a forty-five-degree angle."

He pulled out his little notebook and drew a segment of pipe with an oblique dotted line through it. "The doctors say it's very hard to set. The broken ends of the bone can slip out of place with the slightest movement. So you're going to have to be in traction for at least two months, and then you'll have to be in a body cast for probably another two months."

A metal pin had been inserted all the way through my thigh, like a thermometer poked into a roast. The weights attached to the pin would keep me still so that my leg would heal the right way. Since a sheet would interfere with all the rigging, a washcloth was draped over my crotch. I wore only that and a T-shirt for two months.

Mom came every day, tutoring me to keep me up to par academically. When my thighbone had knitted sufficiently, I was put in a body cast from ankle to chest, with a big hole at the groin that went down between my legs and up past my tailbone. This was for the bedpan. I was sent home to spend another two months in bed, except for the times Mom loaded me into an old metal wagon and pulled me around outside so I could get some fresh air.

For four months I led a life of total immobility and dependency, calling for help when I needed to go to the bathroom. One night I overheard my parents discussing their fear that I might be holding it in because I hated the bedpan so much. The doctor had warned them that if I did so, I'd increase my risk of bladder infections and intestinal trouble, serious complications. The problem wasn't the bedpan. It was my mother turning me on my side and wiping me as if I were a baby. I wouldn't let Dad do it; when Mom wasn't around, I did hold it in. The longest retention was three hours, which I counted off on my bedside clock.

The two months in the cast were followed by two months of daily physical therapy at the hospital and at home. All told, it was six months before I could walk the way I had before. I could sprint for short distances, and like an old man, I learned to forecast the weather by subtle changes in my joint pain. Years later I found out that Mom and Dad were convinced that since so many of the breaks happened on the bones' growth plates, I'd end up with stunted legs. My legs grew out to a normal length, however, and my house became a tease-free zone, a haven where nobody ever called me Fatty again.

* * *

This time I didn't have to stay in the hospital. The diagnosis was a herniated disk, severe muscle strain, and neuralgia, for which I was prescribed two weeks of bed rest, painkillers, and muscle relaxants. Mom and Dad brought me home and helped me into bed. David and Emily came along too. They all crowded into my bedroom, asking what they could do.

"You can leave," I said. "I can manage on my own."

"Like hell," Dad said.

Emily shook her head at the ceiling. "Elliot, you can't even walk. How are you going to feed or wash yourself?"

"I can walk, just slowly and weirdly. The kitchen isn't that far, and I can order pizza. As for washing myself, well, it's just me here alone. I'll stink for a while. So what?"

"Lovely," Mom said. "Look, I'm your mother. I've washed you more times than I can remember. Let me help you."

"It's not like she hasn't seen your wiener before, bro," David said. "You're in no shape to refuse."

"You're wrong. I do refuse. Thanks for the offer, but I don't need any help. The painkillers and muscle relaxants are already making a difference. I want you all to go home, please."

"You're not being reasonable," Dad said. "If we leave you here alone and something happens to you, how do you think that's gonna make us feel?"

"Nothing's going to happen."

"You don't know that. What if there's a fire or somebody breaks in?"

"Then I'll call nine-one-one. If you're here hovering over me, interrogating me every two seconds about what I need, it's just going to irritate me. I can take care of myself. I appreciate the fact that you all came out, really. It's just…" I stopped.

"It's just what?" Mom asked.

"I need my privacy. I know you think this sounds insane, but you're invading my space here. I need to be by myself. You'll help me more by leaving."

All four of them sighed at exactly the same time, like a tiny Greek chorus.

"We're invading your space by trying to help?" Dad demanded. "What the hell kind of bullshit is that? Invading your space. We're your family, goddammit. You're hurt."

David said, "We come all the way out here—"

I interrupted. "Yes, and I'm just not grateful enough for your sacrifice, am I?"

Mom let out a soft groan. "No one's asking you to be grateful, Elliot. We just don't know why you're being so truculent."

"Oh, *I'm* being truculent. Who's saying that what I want is bullshit? Who's reminding me about how far you had to come? Who's implying I'm too stupid to know what I can and can't manage? But *I'm* the truculent one. Okay."

Dad beheld the others. "See? I told you this would happen. I told you it would turn into another goddamn pissing match for no reason at all. I give up. You're a grown man, Elliot. Do it your way."

"Ah yes, do it my own pigheaded, unreasonable, truculent, childish way, and when it all falls apart, as it surely will, won't that be a delicious comeuppance for such a clown as me? Boy, I can't wait!"

"I don't have to listen to this," Dad said to Mom. "I try to help and it just gets thrown back in my face. I'll wait on the front porch."

He stalked out. Mom briefly closed her eyes. "Elliot, I know you're in pain, but there has to come a point when you rein yourself in."

"Okay, Mom. Reining in…*now!*" I imitated the sound of car brakes. "There. I'm rational once more, and it's a relief. Whew." I wiped my forehead. "But I still want you all to go. It's my house and my body. I'd like to do something different with my latest health crisis and not involve you."

"Why don't you want to involve us?" Emily asked.

"Because you're making me feel worse."

She raised her hands in surrender. "All right. Okay. I get it. You're not going to join us for Christmas dinner again, are you?"

"That's right. I got hit by a car so I could skip Christmas dinner again. You figured out my diabolical plan. Curse you!"

Mom touched Emily's shoulder. "Sweetie, let's just go. Elliot doesn't want us here. He'll let us know if he needs help. Good-bye, Elliot. I hope you feel better soon."

They left. David nodded, impressed at a job well done.

"Thanks for coming all the way out here," I said. "Get my wallet off the dresser there. I'll pay for your gas."

He departed, smirking.

* * *

I walked to the end of the I-beam and looked down. The street was thousands of feet below, the pedestrians like ants. I took off my hard hat, flung it away, and stepped into space. As I dropped past a window, someone shouted, *"Fatty!"* in my ear. The pavement rushed up to greet me, and I jerked awake in my bed. Two hours had passed. I carefully reached for the phone. Dennis was away from his desk, so I left a message on his machine.

"Hi, Dennis. It's Elliot. I'm sorry to tell you that I was hit by a car this afternoon on my walk. I've got a herniated disk, and I have to spend the next two weeks in bed. This won't have any effect on the Forsyth project. I can write fine in bed. I'll e-mail the rest of the team as soon as I hang up. Unfortunately, I won't be able to attend the Christmas party. Please say hi to everybody for me. Sorry about this, Dennis. First I have a heart attack, and then I get run over. What next? Don't even speculate. It'll involve something—or someone—with teeth, I'm sure. I'll talk to you later. Good-bye."

My laptop was in the breakfast nook on the other side of the house, and my cell phone was on the table beside it. Neither my family nor I had thought about that. I rolled onto my stomach, clawed myself into a position perpendicular to the edge of the bed, and pushed with my arms until my feet touched the floor. In my swastika stance, I inched my way to the breakfast nook. It took half an hour. The act of sitting caused two flares of agony, the first as I began the descent and the second when my buttocks met the seat cushion.

I sent an e-mail to Gary, with copies to everyone else on the team. Then I picked up the phone and called Trey. His mother Jenny answered.

"I'm so glad to finally meet you, Elliot," she said. "Trey talks about you all the time. Every day he tells me about the conversation you boys had. I'd like to invite you to supper. We'd be proud to have you." Her voice resembled a slow, finger-picked banjo; Trey's accent was more subdued. Like Gary, he really drawled when angry. I had no idea if happiness also changed his inflection, since I'd never seen him happy.

"Well, Jenny, I'm calling to tell Trey that I was run over by a car today, and it gave me a herniated disk. I won't be able to take my walk for two weeks."

"Lord, Elliot! Trey's out waiting for you. I'll make sure to go tell him. How on earth did it happen?"

"Someone came up on the sidewalk and mowed me down. It was probably an accident."

"Don't you believe it. Did you get his plate number?"

"No. It happened too fast. But tell Trey I'm going to be all right, and I'll see him as soon as I can. Um, it really hurts to sit, Jenny, so I have to go. Sorry to be so abrupt."

"No, that's quite all right. You take care, now, Elliot, hear? I'll tell Trey you called."

I hung up and tried to stand. It was impossible. The slightest movement sent huge stabs of pain into my lower spine. Inside me, something had shifted into a new position, creating a completely different form of immobilizing torment. I chuckled; I'd have to call someone in my family to save me.

Tom Jones sang "Burning Down the House" from my cell phone. Margaret had sent a text.

wtf? r u ok? m

I typed my reply.

i r ok. c u n 2 wks. e

An e-mail dinged into my box. It was from Margaret.

Did you just call me a cunt?

I laughed out loud, which hurt so much, I almost fell off the chair. It hurt even to type my answer.

That's what I get for trying to communicate in your gibberish. I said, "See you in two weeks," not "See you next Tuesday." I can't write anymore. Good-bye.

I put my laptop to sleep, gathering strength for the next call. My parents were the logical choice. As I reached for the phone, I heard the front door open. Sitting there utterly defenseless, I marveled at Dad's prescience. With my luck it was a home invader who was also a rapist and an arsonist. The floorboards creaked under the carpeting; all I could do was wait.

Gary stepped into the breakfast nook. She inclined her chin at me and said, "Hey." No smile but no ice either. A calm, agreeable work face instead of a wax mask.

"Is that really you?" I asked.

"Yup. David called and told me what happened. He said you couldn't walk, so I let myself in. He left his key in the mailbox. Sorry if I scared you. I'd like to help." She patted the large canvas bag hanging from her shoulder. "I brought some extra clothes. I can stay a few days, if you need me to."

I burst into tears.

CHAPTER TWELVE

"I can't stand up," I wept. "It hurts too much."

She put her bag on the floor. "Okay. Relax. Here." She handed me some tissues. "Let's figure out how to get you from here to the bedroom."

I blew my nose, wiped my eyes. "I'm sorry. If I put my arm around your shoulders and you bear my weight, I think I'll be able to walk pretty normally."

"All right. Let's try that."

Before she approached, she pushed aside the throw rug in front of the sink so I wouldn't slip. It would never have occurred to me to think of that. Her consideration made me choke up again. She knelt beside me.

"Okay. Put your arm around my shoulder."

I did, and she slowly, gently stood. There was an initial flash of pain above my tailbone, but it dissipated as soon as I was upright. We moved through the kitchen and down the hall. I was acutely aware of how her body felt against mine, how she smelled. She held me around the waist and gripped the wrist of the arm I draped across her powerful shoulders. Her hips softly bumped against mine; the sides of our heads brushed. I looked down; my erection protruded through the fly of my boxers. She must've seen it too. I tucked it back inside.

She carefully sat me on the edge of my bed, lifted my legs as I pivoted, and supported me as I lay back.

"Oh my God, that feels so good," I said. "Thanks so much."

"Do you have to go to the bathroom?"

"No. I'm fine."

"When was the last time you ate?" She stood with her hands on her hips like an army drill instructor.

"Last night, I think."

"Okay. I'll go make something. Would you like a drink?"

"Yes please. Some ice water would be fine. Thanks, and I'm sorry about this."

"Forget it. I'll be back in a second."

* * *

She slept on the sofa in my living room. We quickly established a routine: In the morning she'd help me into the bathroom, leave me so I could use the toilet, and come back to scrub my back in the shower. Once she'd dressed me, we'd have breakfast in the nook, then we'd go to the living room and write copy until lunch. She'd fix us something light, usually sandwiches or salads. After we ate, she'd half carry me to my bedroom so I could take a nap. We'd write more copy in the afternoon, have dinner, and watch TV until it was time to sleep.

We spoke mostly about work. When we watched TV on opposite sides of the sofa, she'd comment on an actor, a plot, or a news item, and I'd respond in the same vein.

From my bed I could look out the window and see the lamp in the living room. She stayed up as late as I did, or maybe she slept with the light on.

I couldn't quite believe she was with me again, under my roof, walking my floors in her bare feet, yawning sleepily in the mornings, running her fingers through her tousled hair, touching me, eating with me, talking to me, looking me in the eye, even smiling on occasion.

Like my wife.

* * *

Margaret called the third day. "Dude, why'd someone wanna run you over?"

"Dude, good question," I said. "I need to figure out what made the people in that car angry enough to do such a desperate thing. This is an opportunity for me to examine my walk-taking policies."

"Yeah, well, you can make fun of me all you want, but people don't get run over for no reason."

"Look, I'll save us a whole conversation and concede that it was my fault. I'm to blame in any situation, from now on and forever, because of my negative attitude."

"Kiss my ass, Elliot."

"I can't do that. I don't know where it's been."

Neither of us spoke for a while.

"So are you done cheering me up?" I asked.

"Eat me."

"No thanks. I had a Margaret sandwich for lunch. Buh-bye."

*   *   *

By the fourth day, my back felt good enough for me to walk unsupported, so I went out on the front porch. Gary stayed in the breakfast nook with her laptop. The pain still at bay, I stepped onto my front lawn to catch a few minutes of sun. A red Mercedes rolled down the street and pulled into my driveway behind Gary's Saab. David climbed out, wearing an elegant gray suit.

"Greetings," he said. "How're you feeling?"

"Much better. What're you doing here?"

He shrugged with far too much indifference. "Just...wanted to know how you were. Can't stay. Gotta get right home."

"Well, you should've just called."

"I *could've* called, yeah." He rocked up and down on his toes, his eyes bright.

"But then you wouldn't have been able to see Gary," I said.

His grin was that of a crafty five-year-old. He stepped closer and whispered, "Is she here?"

I sighed. "Yes. Come on. Let's go inside."

He was so excited that he almost sprinted. I led him into the breakfast nook. We caught Gary in the act of stretching, her hands interlocked over her head and her arms bent in a strange dancer's contortion. She looked up, pleasant and alert.

"Gary, David wanted to say hi," I said.

She offered him a polite smile. "Hello, David. Nice to see you again."

He shook her hand. "We have to stop meeting like this, Gary."

She cocked her head. "Meeting like this?"

"We only see each other during Elliot's latest disaster. It's gotta stop!" He made a ghastly, simpering *ish-shish-shish-shish-shish* sound.

"But my disasters bring people together," I said.

Gary continued to smile like a bank teller. She disengaged her hand, and the three of us gazed at each other.

"So what're you working on?" David asked.

"A baby food sweepstakes. When you buy a jar of baby food, a game piece is automatically dispensed at the checkout, giving you a chance to win a life-insurance policy for your child."

His whole demeanor changed. "Life-insurance policies for babies? *Eww.* That's pretty cold, isn't it?"

"I couldn't say. People do buy them, though."

"That's too much like tempting fate for me. I'm superstitious that way. I have life insurance for me and my wife, of course, but for the kids? I just couldn't. It'd be like I wanted to profit from their deaths."

Another silence. David and I had never discussed how he felt about being a father.

"Well," I said, "you can't stay, and Gary has to get back to work. The deadline's coming up."

"Nice to see you again, David," Gary said.

"You too. Maybe you and Elliot can come over some time. Meet my family." His upper lip was beaded with sweat.

I grabbed his arm. "Sure! We'll do that." I frog-marched him out. In the driveway he came unglued.

"Holy *shit,* bro! How can you stand having her spend the night? God, I'd go outta my *mind!* You're just friends? What, are you gay or something? Are you dead from the waist down?"

"I think you should ask her out," I said. "I'm sure she'd say yes."

His reply died as he gazed up the street. "Oh. My. *God.*"

The teenage hillbilly trombone player from two blocks over rode toward us on a ten-speed bike, her sensible crash helmet canceled out by her tank top and bralessness. Her breasts bounced, quivered, and shimmied as if strapped to a paint mixer.

"Uh-oh, here comes *trouble,*" David slobbered, his eyeballs about to fall out of their sockets. The hillbilly zipped past in the tail-up posture assumed by riders of ten-speeds. Her rippling buttocks were mostly bared by her tiny denim cutoffs, the bike seat pushing them up, out, and apart.

David panted, clutching his chest.

"Wait," I said. "You were lusting after Gary a second ago."

"Yeah? So? I can walk and chew gum at the same time. Bring Gary over, huh? She'd make a great sister-in-law." He winked. "See ya."

*   *   *

The next afternoon Gary said, "I need to talk to you, Elliot. Let me go take a shower first, okay? I feel grimy."

"Okay. I'll be on the back porch."

She was noticeably tentative. It *had* to be what I'd begged for every night, month after month. In my euphoria I thought I heard someone call my name. Then the doorbell rang. My back had recovered enough that I could walk almost normally; I made it to the front door and peeked through the sidelight. My neighbor Carlos Garza stood on the porch. Behind him, Trey sat in the driveway. Carlos saw the slight movement of the curtain and waved. With no other option, I opened the door.

"Hi, Elliot," Carlos said. "I heard your friend Trey yelling for you, so I came out to see what was going on."

Trey said, "Hey, man. I probably shoulda called, but I figured what the hell and just came over."

What did I ever do to you? Why are you haunting me?

"That's okay," I said.

Carlos examined my porch. "I can help Trey get his chair up the step there and over the door sill, but what about when he wants to go? You shouldn't be lifting anything right now. You want to give me a call?"

"I can do it," Gary said from behind me, toweling her wet hair. She wore a baggy T-shirt and sweatpants. Her shoulders looked massively wide, her biceps like tennis balls.

Carlos smiled. "Wow. I guess you can."

After I made the introductions, Trey backed his chair up against the single step of my porch. Carlos leaned him back and with Gary's help heaved him onto the porch. The doorsill was much easier; Trey bumped over it by himself.

"Thanks a lot, man," he said to Carlos.

"No problem, buddy. You guys call me if you need a hand."

"I really appreciate it, Carlos," I said.

He left, and I directed Trey through the kitchen into the living room, where there was more space. "Nice toy collection," he said. "What kind of copy would you write about me if I was a toy?"

"Uh, let's see...'QuadriVenger, Lord of Infinite Rage. Contains small, sharp parts and viciousness. Danger of choking and stabbing. Not for children of any age.'"

He laughed. Gary seemed uncomfortable. She sat on the sofa in the living room, I took the armchair, and Trey positioned himself between us.

"So how've you been?" he asked her.

"Pretty good. Busy. How about you?"

"Oh, I never change. Elliot can tell you that. Poor guy. He has a heart attack and then gets hit by a car. He's had nothing but bad luck ever since he met me."

My toes clenched as I waited for him to remind her she'd dumped me too.

"Personally, I don't believe in good or bad luck," Gary said. "I think things happen randomly. I don't believe the world is governed by a force that singles people out just to inflict harm on them."

"I can see how people who'd never had bad things happen to them would want to believe that," Trey said.

"Well, you can't tell if bad things have happened to people, unless they talk about it or you see evidence of it."

He sipped water from his plastic tube. "Yeah, that's true. I didn't think of that."Margaret was right: Trey was a hottie. I tried not to be jealous of how easy his life should've been.

"So what brings you to Elliot's neck of the woods?" he asked.

"I'm just here to give him a hand, until his back heals."

He turned to me with a triumphant look. "*Really.*"

"I couldn't have managed without her," I said.

The doorbell rang.

Gary rose. "I'll get it." She went into the kitchen.

"You think this is the beginning of a whatchamacallit, a reconciliation?" Trey hissed.

"I don't know. I hope so. She said she wants to talk to me about something."

"Well, play it cool, man. Don't crowd her."

Heavy footsteps came toward us. "Um, there's someone here to see you, Elliot," Gary called.

Dr. Larkin thrust himself into the room and clomped across to my chair.

"Stand up," he commanded. "Strip down to your shorts. Let me see your back."

* * *

While I got dressed, Larkin explained that the tops of my feet felt wet all the time because of sciatica. Maybe it would go away, maybe it wouldn't. I needed to build up my muscles by lifting weights. Larkin himself was a weight lifter.

I hated letting Trey see me in my underwear. Gary had stayed in the breakfast nook during my examination.

"Are you feeling depressed these days?" Larkin asked me.

"No more than usual. When did you start making house calls?"

"I don't. I knew you couldn't make it to my office, so I stopped by on my way to the hospital. I'm glad to see your girlfriend is here. Did you ever thank her for saving your life?"

"Yes. I did." *And I think she's about to do it again as soon as you all leave.*

"*I'm* pretty depressed," Trey said.

Larkin shifted in his chair to face him. "Because of your quadriplegia."

"Damn straight. I've got severe chronic pain that can't be treated. I've tried every drug, every therapy, acupuncture, hypnosis, everything. It's so bad that all I think about is killing myself to get away from it."

"If someone tells me he's suicidal, I'm required by law to report him to the police, who will place him under psychiatric observation for seventy-two hours." He sat on the sofa.

Trey made a face. "Well, I wasn't serious. I'm not at all suicidal. I *love* being alive, in fact. Whoopee!"

"He really does love life," I said.

"I'm sure," Larkin said. He turned to Trey. "Tell me how you sustained your injury."

"Fell off a stool while I was hanging curtains. Hit my head on the dining-room table and broke my neck."

"How old were you?"

"Eighteen."

"And how old are you now?"

"Almost forty-one."

"Speaking theoretically now, if there were a man who became a quadriplegic at the age of eighteen, and later in life he expressed a desire to die, do you think he would have attempted suicide?"

Trey squinted. "Probably three times."

"I see. As a quadriplegic, he must have had help."

"If he did, he wouldn't say."

Larkin sniffed sharply. "Nine years ago my wife Sarah and I decided to visit Israel for the first time. I was afraid to go, but she'd had her heart set on it since she was a little girl. She wanted to see Yad Vashem, the Holocaust memorial in Jerusalem. After we decided to go, our son Jake said he and his family wanted to come with us. I tried to talk him out of it, but he said if it was safe enough for Sarah and me, it would be safe enough for him and his family. So we all went, and it was fine. We spent three days in Jerusalem, three in Tel Aviv, and a weekend on a kibbutz. There were police and soldiers everywhere, but they made us feel safe. I stopped worrying."

He perched on the edge of the sofa as if waiting for the right moment to pounce on me. I clutched the arms of my chair.

"Two days before we were supposed to leave," he continued, "we took the bus out to the beach. We got on and everybody found a seat except for Jake. After a couple of stops, Jake suddenly began grappling with the man next to him. The man was holding his fist over his head, and Jake was clawing at it. I could see a wire going into his sleeve. Jake screamed, 'He's got a bomb!' and everybody started yelling and yanking the stop cord. The driver stopped and opened the doors. Jake screamed, 'Get the kids out of here! Get them out!' and Sarah shoved us toward the door. Jake was bent double with the man on top of him like they were playing piggyback. The man's feet were off the floor, and he was kicking and yelling, '*Allahu akbar! Allahu akbar!*' and Jake was holding his hand down between his knees."

Larkin's enormous hands were between his own knees, clenched in a strangler's grip.

"A policeman came through the door and pushed the kids and Monica and me out onto the sidewalk. Jake screamed, 'Shoot him! Shoot him!' More officers hustled us around the corner of a building, and there was a crash that sounded exactly like a giant cabinet full of glassware falling over. I handed the kids to Monica and went to look. The bus had been turned inside out. I identified myself as a doctor, and the police let me through. The bomber's vest was packed with ball bearings, rat poison, and human feces. The ball bearings ripped the victims open, the rat poison prevented the wounds from coagulating, and the feces caused infection. Jake and Sarah were both on the bus when the bomb detonated, so there was nothing for us to bury. Unlike me, Sarah refused to leave our son. I'm certain that she dove in and boxed the bomber's ears or kicked his testicles. Five people died instead of forty or fifty, so it could have been much worse."

Larkin looked from me to Trey and back again.

"My point," he finally said, "is that my pain was almost unendurable. As a doctor I could have killed myself in several ways. I spent months at home, wondering whether it was worth it to continue, feeling as I did, and then I realized I have an obligation to continue because I'm not a solitary man. I have family, friends, and patients who need me. I'd do more harm than good by killing myself, and my profession demands that above all, I must do no harm."

"Your pain went away, though," Trey said.

"No it didn't." Larkin smiled for the first time since I'd known him. "I feel it today in exactly the same intensity as I did nine years ago. What allows me to live with it is the gratitude I have for the years my wife and son gave me, and gratitude that I didn't lose my grandchildren and daughter-in-law too."

"I'm very sorry that happened to you and your family," I said.

"Thank you." He stood and spoke to Trey. "You may not have exhausted all the potential avenues of pain management. If you'd like, I could examine you and make recommendations."

"Well, I don't know."

"All right. Here's my card. Call me if you make a decision." He put it in Trey's backpack. "Mr. Finell, now that you can walk again, you need to start physical therapy. Call this number and make an appointment." He wrote on another card and handed it to me. "Gentlemen." With a nod at each of us, he departed.

Trey puffed out his cheeks. "Shit, that was close. I don't know why the fuck I told him. Do you think he'll call the cops?"

"No. He let you make a retraction, and then he only spoke in theoretical terms."

"Well, I'm sorry about his family, but his pain doesn't compare to mine."

"You don't think the pain of having your wife and son murdered could be as bad as physical pain?"

He barked his angry laugh. "Are you fuckin' nuts? You have no idea what I'm feeling."

"I know. And you have no idea what he's feeling."

"Well, but—" He closed his mouth.

The doorbell rang.

I groaned. "It's like Union Station here today."

Footsteps through my kitchen again. Gary emerged first. "Guess who's here?"

Julian came through the door. "Ah, so you're up and about," he said. "Smashing. Bully. Tickety-boo."

"Please tell me Margaret's not with you," I said.

"Margaret's not with me."

"Thank God. Have a seat."

He and Gary sat on the sofa.

"Margaret's not with you?" Trey asked. "Damn."

"Don't believe I know you," Julian said. "Julian Buckley. I work with Elliot. How do you know Margaret?"

"Trey Gillespie. Elliot's conversation partner, I guess. He mentioned her and that Brazilian martial-arts thing she does, so I asked him to bring her out here. I wanted to meet her."

"Did you now? And what did you think of her?"

"Well." Trey closed one eye and tilted his head. "Before I answer that, what sort of relationship do you have with Margaret, if you don't mind me asking?"

"Ah, smart fellow. Don't lead with your chin. Margaret is my coworker, nothing more."

Beside him, Gary blinked several times.

"Well, I'm kind of shy about discussing women in front of a woman," Trey said.

Gary rolled her eyes. "Boy talk. Fine." She went back into the breakfast nook.

Trey wheeled closer to Julian. "That's better. I only talked to Margaret once, but she's the hottest chick I ever met in my life. Great body, funny, smart, interesting. She's got it all. And I *never* seen such a perfect ass."

"But you only met her once, old boy," Julian said. "With repeated exposure one becomes inured to her charms, including that perfect arse."

"You're an English guy, aren't you?" Trey asked.

"We prefer the term British, actually."

"Man, I love how you guys talk. I remember you now. Elliot told me you're a rugby player."

"Correct. And judging by your shoulders, you must be a football player, meaning the pigskin variety, with downs and cheerleaders and all that, not the *real* football, which you colonials have besmirched with the name 'soccer.'"

"The *real* football? You mean that game where all they do is flounce from one end of the field to the other and never score any points, and when one pansy brushes against another, they both fall down and cry? You mean *that* football?"

"Oh please! At least they don't armor themselves from head to toe to protect their delicate little forms. And they don't squat and hoist their bums in the air and invite some other bloke to run his hands all over them."

Trey sipped water, grinning. "Football is what *real* men play. Real men aren't afraid to let other real men touch their butts, because they're secure in their sexuality. Soccer is what fairies play, and rugby is what apes play."

"Apes? *Apes?* How *dare* you, sir!"

"I've seen rugby players, with their cauliflower ears and flat noses. They're too dumb to wear protective gear. They get in that scrum and bash their skulls together like cavemen."

Julian nodded. "They're so dumb, they never get injured, unlike your arse-fondling American footballers, who all have artificial knees after just one season."

"Hey, Elliot," Trey said. "You wouldn't happen to have a couple of beers, would you?"

I tried to shake off the day's second sense of exclusion. "I would. Julian, they're in the fridge. I can't have one because of the painkillers, but you guys go ahead."

"Right." Julian took two bottles of beer from the refrigerator and sat in the armchair next to Trey. "So tell me, old boy," he said as he twisted off the caps, "what in God's name is the point of all the arse patting in American football?" Without being asked, he held the bottle to Trey's mouth and tipped it, allowing him to drink.

"Leave it to a limey to obsess about that," Trey said as Julian drank from his own bottle.

* * *

Gary and Julian lowered Trey's wheelchair down the single step of the front porch.

"Christ, your machine must weigh five hundred pounds," Julian grunted.

"Do all rugby players whine so much?" Trey asked. "I don't hear Gary complaining, and she's a ballerina."

"Ballerinas suck it up," Gary said. "Like marines."

They carefully settled Trey's chair on the cement. Julian dusted his hands. "Well, old boy, I hope someday you'll give up your pitiful delusion that American football is actually a sport."

"And I hope you don't end up with one of those rugby jack-o'-lantern heads, with knocked-out teeth, a caved-in nose, and big ol' lumpy flap-ears."

"Good Lord, that *would* be a waste. Cheerio, mate. Nice to have met you." He held out his hand, fingers curled.

Trey touched his knuckles against Julian's. "Take it easy, man."

After Julian drove away, Trey said, "Cool guy."

"He's the kind of person you'd rather hang out with, isn't he?" I asked.

"When I was able-bodied, yeah." He smiled. "We just have a lot in common. You and I wouldn't have gotten along if I weren't in this chair, but so what? You're the one who told me it's better for your peace of mind to accept reality, so don't worry about it. Nice to see you again, Gary."

"You too, Trey."

"You're gonna have to come to my place now, Elliot. Give me a call sometime."

"All right. See you later."

He wheeled down the driveway, turned left, and drove up the sidewalk. Gary and I went inside. I collected the empty beer bottles from the living room, and when I returned to the kitchen, I found Gary waiting with her bag on her shoulder.

"Where are you going?" I asked.

"Home. You're okay now, so I'm leaving."

"But you said you wanted to talk to me, before everybody came over."

"It was nothing." She avoided eye contact. "I have to go."

"Please don't leave. Look, can't you...Just give me another chance. Please."

She shook her head. "We can never go back to how we were before. I'm sorry."

This time she seemed sad when she walked out of my life.

CHAPTER THIRTEEN

The woman who answered the door was a sixtyish female version of Trey. That lean, stubborn face originated in a Scottish hamlet, but to me it brought to mind only the plains of Oklahoma. The sun, wind, and grit were all there, probably on a cellular level. Trey and his mother ought to have been in black and white.

"Hi, Elliot," she said. "I'm Jenny. You look just like I imagined. Come on inside. Trey just got out of bed. He's out back with the dog. You wait here and I'll go get him."

She led me to the living room and went off through the kitchen, leaving me to inspect the framed photos covering the walls. They showed that Trey was a very happy baby, boy, and teenager who fully enjoyed the able-bodied stage of his life. The disabled man in the images never smiled, even when posing with a birthday cake or beautiful young women. As I listened to the approaching hum of his chair, I noted there was very little furniture. Trey had lots of room to maneuver and almost nothing to knock over.

"Hey! You're here!" he said. "How do like my crib?"

He looked terrible. With his ashen skin and the dark circles under his eyes, he appeared to be the same age as his mother.

"It's quite the crib," I said.

"C'mon, let's go to my bedroom. Want you to see all my neat cripple stuff."

I followed him down a short hall. Jenny stayed in the kitchen; I wanted her to come stand next to Trey so I could see who had the darker circles. His room was as Spartan as the rest of the house. It was dominated by a high bed with a miniature electric crane next to it for lifting him into and out of his chair. There were also a recliner chair, ten or eleven overflowing bookshelves, and a large-screen TV in a black entertainment center opposite the bed. The walls were bare, like in an institution or a monk's cell.

"Nice," I said. "Quite a library."

He gestured toward a huge glass door set into the wall. "Go look at the shower."

I opened the door. The entire bathroom was one enormous shower stall, a tiled enclosure the size of a cedar closet. A manual wheelchair sat under the showerhead.

"I shower three times a week," he said. "That's all I can stand. It hurts to have the water hit me, but it hurts more to have someone rub my skin with a washcloth, so I can't take a tub bath. I've never been in a Jacuzzi, but I bet that'd hurt the most. All those jets. The worst part of my shower routine is when my mom and my nurse exfoliate my feet. Since I can't walk, I don't wear off the outer layers of dead skin, so they have to scrub it off. I was watching a show about one of the wars, and they said that in the prisons over there, they tied people up and beat their feet with wooden clubs. That's what exfoliation feels like. Having my feet beaten with a wooden club. So what do you think?"

"I think you're in a lot of pain, all the time," I said.

"You got it. I was wondering how *you* liked being in a lot of pain, all the time."

"Well, as I'm sure you already know, I didn't like it."

"How's the physical therapy going? Does it help?"

"Yes. It's mostly assisted stretching exercises. Things are getting back to normal."

He smiled, but it was closer to a sneer. "'Back to normal.' I wish I could say that about me."

"I wish you could too. I really do."

* * *

The TV was on in the living room. Jenny lay in the reclining chair. She was asleep when we came in but woke with a jerk.

"You boys going out now?" she asked groggily.

"Yeah," Trey said. "Gonna twist Elliot's arm until he does what I want."

My stomach dropped.

"Now, Elliot, don't you let him push you around," Jenny said. "He thinks he can always get his own way, and he's mighty put out when he doesn't. He's been that way since he was a boy. Got it from his father, God rest his soul."

That was another aspect of Trey's house I'd noticed: no pictures of his late father. I wondered if he'd been cast out, or if—like me—he'd just hated to be photographed.

"Elliot's gonna give in eventually," Trey said. "I can feel it. He's close."

Jenny covered a yawn with her hand. "Stand your ground, Elliot. By the way, how's your back doing?"

"Much better, thanks."

"I told one of my friends what happened to you, and she said it was probably a gang initiation. I don't know what the world's coming to. You watch out, now. You're the one person Trey can talk to on his level. Every day he tells me what you two talked about, and it's like the radio serials they had when I was a girl. I look forward to each installment. You've done wonders for my boy."

"Cut it out, Ma," Trey said. "You're embarrassing him."

"Well, I don't mean to. I'm just grateful, Elliot."

I instantly developed a headache. "It's all Trey," I said. "He's one of the smartest people I know."

Trey laughed. "Sure. Let's get going before we all drown in the bullshit."

"Compliment my son and he'll bite your head off," Jenny said.

"I'm the same way," I said. "It was nice to finally meet you, Jenny."

"The pleasure was all mine."

Outside, Trey said, "Let's go past the high school. I wanna show you something."

Along the way I said, "I don't appreciate you dropping hints to your mother that you're trying to convince me to help you commit suicide. It's not funny."

"I'm sorry. I don't know what's wrong with me lately. I can't control what I'm saying. I won't do it again."

"Thank you."

He'd never looked worse, gray and shriveled, his eyes overly shiny as if they'd been lacquered.

"Hey, how about dinner?" he asked. "You wanna go to that steak house in Pasadena?"

"I'd love to sometime, but not right now. I've got a project that I have to finish, and my back still hurts. Maybe in a couple of weeks?"

"Sure. Whenever you want."

We passed the high school.

"What did you want to show me?" I asked.

"It's just this thing I figured out yesterday. I'll show you in a minute."

The sidewalk gradually rose until we were almost twenty feet above the school parking lot and courtyards. Trey stopped beside a long flight of concrete stairs with a metal handrail. He motioned toward a scattering of magazine-paper scraps on the cement. Each was about the size of a half-dollar. They were torn-up photos—shots of arms and legs, hands, mouths, closed eyes, noses, backs, curly and straight hair, breasts and buttocks, unidentifiable expanses of skin, and veined shafts tucked into glistening folds and puckers. The scraps surrounded a black plastic bag, an empty vodka bottle, over a dozen cigarette butts, and three beef jerky wrappers. A chocolate cupcake was stuck to the near-est lamppost, about six feet off the ground. It'd been slammed there hard, the cream filling mooshed out in a star shape that glued the flattened pastry tight.

"You're looking at somebody's social life," Trey said. "This was his night out on the town. I bet if you brought one of those black lights that the crime scene investigators use, you'd find glowing splashes of come every-where."

I shuddered. "Is this what you wanted to show me?"

"It's part of it. I wanted you to see that I don't even have what this guy has. I can't jack off. I can't look at porn because someone would have to turn the pages or work the mouse for me. Who? My mom? Some trusted buddy? I'm a bigger loser than this guy, who gets drunk, whacks off in public next to a high school, and then tears up his mag and has a tantrum with the cupcake he bought as a little treat for himself."

"Look, I...there's nothing I can say or do to make you feel better. All I can say is that I'm so sorry."

"But Elliot, there *is* something you can do."

"No." I sat on the cement and leaned back against the metal railing. "I can't. You can't ask me again."

He moved his chair toward me. "Last night I saw a show about Eskimos. When an Eskimo gets too old to hunt and he's just a useless burden on the rest of the tribe, he gets in a canoe and paddles out to the horizon and disappears. They say he's chasing the last whale. That's what they call it. I think it's great, letting someone go out with dignity. I'm useless, I'm a burden to everyone, and I want you to help me chase the last whale. That's all."

"*I can't do it.* I'm sorry. You have to stop asking me."

"Okay." He nodded. "I won't ask you again."

"Thank you. I'm really sorry. If there were any other way—"

"Nah, just forget about it. It's all right. But I did wanna ask you something else. You said a long time ago that you'd tell me why Gary broke up with you. Well, why don't you tell me now? I'd really like to know."

"All right. It's not the happiest story in the world, but here goes."

* * *

Without having to discuss it, Gary and I had kept our situation from our colleagues. We were like spies in enemy territory. I took clean clothes to her condo so that we wouldn't give ourselves away. Part of me wished I could brag to everybody, especially about her smile. I was the only person who ever saw it, and I seemed to be the only reason for it. I put a lot into making it happen, such as sending her letters. It was silly; I was right there with her when she pulled them from her mailbox, then we'd sit on the sofa as she read them. It was like watching my boss Mr. Lipmann go over one of my performance reviews, except that the creative director didn't crawl onto my lap and put me in a gentle headlock afterward.

"The day we met, I knew we'd get together," she told me one afternoon.

"Oh my God. Really?"

"Yup. This little voice said, 'There he is.' That's never happened before." I didn't say anything.

"Well, thanks for listening, hon," she'd said, patting my cheek.

"Wait. Wait. I'm sorry. I just have a hard time talking about this."

"Why is that?"

"I don't know. Too much good news, maybe. I'm not used to it. After we met, I thought you didn't know I was alive."

"Well, I did. I just wasn't sure what you'd do if I approached you."

"You didn't think I was totally negative, the way everybody else does?" I asked.

"No. I knew that underneath it all, you were a nice man. Besides, you may have noticed that I'm not the most positive person on the planet myself."

I'd noticed. She regularly had nightmares that made her thrash and moan, "Please!" The best way to ease her out of them was to softly call her name without touching her. Bathed in sweat, she'd go to the kitchen for a beer or a cup of herbal tea. When she finally came back to bed, she'd wrap her arms and legs around me and burrow her face into my neck. That was how she coped: She'd have to be alone for a while, then she'd be the one to reestablish physical contact. The few times I asked her, she said she didn't remember what she saw in her dreams.

Her moodiness was another issue. For no reason I could discern, she'd fall silent, staring into space and sighing. Sometimes it lasted an hour, sometimes a day. I was used to it from having worked with her. When the dark cloud formed, I watched TV, read, or wrote copy. She'd signal it was over by giving me a tired, sheepish look, laying her head on my shoulder or pulling me down to lie next to her on the sofa. For the only time in my life, my touch had the power to heal.

She also manifested a sexual shyness that was unexpected, given the forthright way she initiated our relationship and requested that we be tested for STDs. Her knowledge and breadth of experience seemed limited, particularly for someone her age. It was almost impossible to persuade her to try new things. She genuinely liked sex as long as it was gentle, quiet, and plain vanilla.

I attributed her reserve to her background in the Southern Baptist tradition. She attended church every Sunday, while I waited in her condo. We briefly discussed religion in the beginning, during our lunching phase. All she said was she was much less devout than she used to be. The only other time she mentioned it was the night we watched a news story that included footage of a dark, hulking, turboprop aircraft unleashing gouts of flame from its side. The reporter said this was a gunship armed with cannons that fired one hundred shells per second. Then there was video taken on the ground after one of these things had attacked a convoy.

"Are those *men?*" Gary asked about what looked like piles of black rags.

"They used to be," I said.

She went the bookshelf to retrieve a Bible. "Momma and Daddy didn't like me going to Sunday school with the neighbors," she said as she thumbed through it, "but they didn't stop me. They were afraid that if they pushed too hard, I'd start speakin' in tongues and handlin' snakes." She muted the TV with the remote. "Here, listen to this."

And ye shall hear of wars and rumors of wars; see that ye be not troubled: for all these things must come to pass, but the end is not yet.

For nation shall rise against nation, and kingdom against kingdom: and there shall be famines, and pestilences, and earthquakes, in divers places.

All these are the beginnings of sorrows.

Then they shall deliver you up to be afflicted, and shall kill you; and ye shall be hated of all nations for my name's sake.

And then shall many be offended, and shall betray one another, and shall hate one another.

And many false prophets shall rise, and shall deceive many.

And because iniquity shall abound, the love of many shall wax cold.

But he that shall endure unto the end, the same shall be saved.

Although she spoke softly, her accent and cadence gave the words a fervor I associated with tent revivalists.

"I've got the shivers," I said when she finished. "What's that mean to you?"

"Don't give up."

She'd done the impossible. "Could you read it again, please?"

And so she did, while the muted TV showed the piles of black rags that were once men of deep religious convictions.

* * *

I easily accepted Gary's mood swings and lack of erotic adventurousness. Plain-vanilla sex with her was better than any other sex I'd had, and there were other benefits too. At her condo we sat on her balcony during the full moon and peered through her telescope, talking about selenography, tides, madness, menstruation, Galileo, Jules Verne, and Claude Debussy. Both our fathers had explained that the moon had oceans and seas, lakes, bays, and marshes. She knew them all.

The Ocean of Storms. The Sea of Rains. The Sea of Clouds. The Sea of Vapors. The Sea of Moisture. The Sea of Cold. The Sea of Nectar. The Sea of Serenity. The Sea of Tranquility. The Sea of Fertility. The Sea of Ingenuity. The Sea of Crises. The Moscow Sea. The Eastern Sea. The Southern Sea. The

Lake of Dreams. The Seething Bay. The Bay of Dew. The Bay of Rainbows. The Marsh of Sleep. The Marsh of Decay.

"When I was little," she said, "Daddy promised that someday we'd go up and sail them, just him and me. I used to look for the descent stage of the Apollo 11 Lunar Module. I'd be out on the deck of our house every full moon with my little twenty-dollar rinky-dink scope, thinkin' I could find that thing squattin' up there like a big ol' spider."

I did exactly the same when I was a kid.

She was also the only person I knew who could make fun of me in a way that I enjoyed. One morning she told me she'd prefer to do the driving. I asked why.

"Well, I'm a tad worried about your blood pressure, bud."

"Really? Why?"

She whipped her head around, glared, and creased her brow. "Oh my God, *look* at that!" she yelped. "Perfect! Unbelievable! Did you *see* that? What's *wrong* with people? What is *wrong* with them, I *ask* you?"

Then she grabbed me in one of her crushing hugs, because I'd told her about Fatty, Tater, and one other name, Peeaigee, coined by Emily after Mom said I was eating like a P-I-G. Gary shouldn't have worried how I'd react. It never occurred to me to be angry with her. She was only satirizing. Besides, from the millions of toned Los Angelinos, she'd chosen me.

"Fer Gawd's sake," she'd say, stomping around like a ridiculous, windup toy soldier, swinging her arms and scowling. "Cain't nobody do nothin' right? Gawdawmighty! Whut's the world comin' to? Am Ah the only sane person left? Nyah!"

I was in her car when I said the most idiotic thing of my life. We were driving back to her place after dinner and a movie in Santa Monica; we had the jazz station on the radio and were talking about how much fun it would be to play piano solos.

"Do you think you're a bitter person?" she abruptly asked. "I mean, with your legs and your family and childhood and all. Do you think it's made you bitter about life?" It wasn't an accusation, just a question. Sometimes she audited me, out of the blue. It was quite flattering.

"Being bitter means you still care," I said. "If you don't give a damn anymore, you can't be bitter."

She didn't sigh or backhand me across the face or kick me into unconsciousness. Instead, she hunched over the wheel and gave me a crazed, somehow conspiratorial smile. I wish I'd had my camera. I've never seen such an expression before or since. It made me laugh until my sides ached.

*   *   *

Although almost everything about her surprised me, I wasn't particularly surprised when I found an empty aluminum-foil cake pan in the garbage can under her kitchen sink. It was nothing, just an empty foil cake pan, the kind that frozen cheesecakes come in. But she never ate cheesecake. She was paranoid about her weight. She complained constantly about how fat she was. It was funny because she didn't care about my weight at all. She didn't even see it. The only time weight was discussed was when she clutched at her thighs or rear and growled, "Ah am *such* a *sow!* No, don't look at me! Look somewhere else."

I'd been waiting for something like an empty cheesecake pan. Gary's handbag was always full of breath mints and sugarless gum. She brushed her teeth six times a day. I found eleven tubes of toothpaste, eight boxes of floss, and five bottles of mouthwash in her bathroom cabinet, tucked behind the towels. And she often woke me up at three or four in the morning when she slipped into bed smelling minty fresh.

So I became a real spy. I started living my own secret life within our secret life. When I was certain she was asleep, I went through her trash with a penlight. Every now and then, I found things: folded chip sacks. Crushed cookie boxes. Flattened ice-cream cartons. More aluminum cheesecake pans. Greasy doughnut sacks. Candy wrappers. Cardboard frosting cans. Cardboard cashew cans. Cardboard peanut cans. And it wasn't just snack food: frozen lasagna pans—the family-sized portions. Styrofoam platters, plastic wrap, and gummed labels from steaks, roasts, chops, and maxi-packs of chicken drumsticks. Chinese and Thai takeout containers clean enough to have been scrubbed.

I spied on her for two months. By carefully arranging my stays and inspecting her trash, I calculated rates of consumption. One night I'd find nothing out of the ordinary in her garbage can. Before I went home the next morning, I'd tell her I'd come over that evening after nine. I'd show up at the appointed hour, and we'd have a late dinner. After she fell asleep, I'd rummage through her garbage can and see that sometime during the day, she'd devoured five pounds of deli roast beef, five pounds of Swiss cheese, a jar of mayonnaise, and four baguettes. Or three pounds of pasta with a one-pound, ten-ounce jar of Alfredo sauce on it. I estimated that she ate at least five times as much as I did.

She seemed quite healthy, strong enough to wrestle me to the floor whenever she felt like it. But I worried about her teeth, her flawless white teeth, and I'd read about electrolyte imbalances and potassium deficiencies. Mostly, I pictured her completely alone, kneeling in a prison cell lined with tile. But the second time I brought it up, I didn't have my heart attack to protect me from her wrath.

*   *   *

"That's really sad," Trey said. "You were just trying to help her."

"Yeah, by taking inventory of what she ate and confronting her with it. Just like my parents did to me. And she reacted the same way I did."

"When she stayed with you after you were hit by the car, was she still doing it?"

I hadn't thought of that. "You know, I was so happy she was there, I completely forgot why she broke up with me. She spent all her time with me and never went out, and I know she didn't bring a hidden stash of food, so I don't think so."

"Maybe she's getting help," he said.

"Maybe. I don't care anymore."

"Don't lie to me. You care. She's a great person, and you guys make a nice couple. Maybe someday things'll work out."

"They won't. I know that now."

"Give it time, man." He sipped water and gazed at the traffic. "It's not your fault. You gotta remember that. You did what you thought was right."

He was oddly serene, as if mildly sedated.

"What's on your mind, Trey?" I asked.

"Hmm?"

"What's up? You're acting weird."

"Am I? Sorry." He seemed to snap out of it. "Listen, man. It's time for me to show you what I brought you out to see. Wait right here." He drove his chair over to the top of the concrete stairway, stopped, and peered down. "Like I said, it's not your fault. Tell Mom I love her, and I'm sorry. There was nothing else I could do."

"What are you talking about?"

Without looking back, he drove his chair forward, down the flight of stairs.

"*Trey!*" I screamed. I sprang to my feet and lurched forward, expecting to see him tumbling head over heels, the sharp concrete edges of the steps hacking chunks out of his body.

Instead, he was still upright. As he clattered toward the parking lot, his wheels bounced off the edges of the stairs like a flat stone skipping across the surface of a lake. His head and shoulders juddered violently, and his arms flapped as if they were made of rubber. He didn't make a sound.

At the bottom he jolted to a stop with such force that his body flailed like a crash-test dummy against the waist strap holding him erect.

"Aw, goddammit," he screamed. "God*dammit.* Fuck!"

The heavy motor and batteries in his chair made his center of gravity so low that he hadn't flipped over.

"You bastard," I shouted as I started down the stairs, and suddenly I was nine again, up in the tree house, holding on to the rope I'd just climbed. Emily rushed at me, her contorted face expanding into a satanic billboard, shrieking, "Look who's here! Fatty-Fatty-Fatty!" It wasn't a memory; I re-experienced it. Emily had two red plastic barrettes in her hair, and she wore a tie-dyed purple-and-white T-shirt and blue shorts. A tiny scratch marred the left side of her forehead, about an inch above her eyebrow, and there was a smudge of dirt on her right cheek, shaped like a map of Italy.

At her screech I turned and jumped. I didn't fall.

Trey let out a wordless roar. I groped down the remaining steps to stand beside him.

"You bastard," I heard myself say. "Are you out of your fucking mind?" The words sounded very far away, drowned out by the echo of Emily's shrill, murderous joy.

Trey laughed. "Can you believe it? Can you fuckin' believe what just happened? A professional stuntman couldn't do what I just did."

"You son of a bitch. You brought me out here to watch you kill yourself?"

Look who's here! Fatty-Fatty-Fatty!

"If you paid someone to try what I just did, he'd die. I mean, in a normal world, he'd die. There's no doubt."

"Trey, you bastard!"

Fatty-Fatty-Fatty!

"Man, I *knew* I was unlucky, but *this* takes the cake." He shook his head and shrugged helplessly. "I just—This is a conspiracy. There's aliens involved or something. That's all there is to it."

I walked away from him, my skull splitting again. If my brain dropped out at my feet, I'd stomp it to jelly.

"You just witnessed a miracle, man," Trey giggled. "I mean a genuine, old-timey, Jesus-loves-you miracle."

"*How could you do that?*" I shouted.

"How could I do that? I'm desperate. Did you think I was kidding?"

"I have to go. I have to get out of here. Does your fucking chair still work?"

He pushed the joystick; his chair moved forward with a smooth hum. "Yeah. Works fine! I need to write the manufacturer. They could use me in their ads. Imagine the repeat-business programs they could come up with!" He laughed.

I suddenly vomited on the asphalt, but it didn't clear my head of Trey juddering down the steps, my sister squalling like a demon in my face, and my leap into a swirling blur that rose up and shattered my legs.

CHAPTER FOURTEEN

My launch from the tree house replayed endlessly, interspersed with Emily's distorted face and Trey rag-dolling down the flight of stairs. All three images tumbled over each other like clothes in a dryer. Nothing could banish them—not long cold or hot showers, not massive amounts of beer, not TV, not music, and certainly not sleep. When I lay down and closed my eyes, Emily screeched, I jumped, and Trey drove down the steps. Unconsciousness was the solution, but I had no idea how to achieve it without heroin or some form of autoasphyxiation.

I didn't take my walk the next day because I didn't want to see Trey. My every thought was devoted to self-destruction in all its forms, whether my botched attempt, Trey's four botched attempts, or the detonations of those who murdered thousands in the name of God the merciful and compassionate.

Wandering through my house, I lifted various objects, examined them, put them back. In one of the living-room bookshelves, I found *A Manual of Prayers for the Use of the Catholic Laity,* which I hadn't read in decades. According to the title page, it was prepared and enjoined by order of the Third Plenary Council of Baltimore. I opened it at random and read Psalm 142, one of the Seven Penitential Psalms.

Hear me speedily, O Lord: my spirit hath fainted away.
Turn not away Thy face from me, lest I be like unto them that go
down into the pit.

"Fuck you," I said to the book. If anyone should be penitent, it was Gary, for driving me away because I tried to save her. It was Trey, Margaret, Emily, David, my parents, the camp counselors who saddled me with palsied Sam, the cool guys who christened me Tater, the PE coach who told me to get rid of my titties before some man tried to fuck me, and the subhuman who blew up Dr. Larkin's family. Actually, everyone in the world *except* for me should be penitent. I wasn't afraid of heavenly faces turning away and making me like unto them that go down unto the pit. Where did the Third Plenary Council of Baltimore think I'd been since the day I was born?

And it was only nine in the morning.

* * *

After he ended the Friday meeting, Dennis asked me to stay behind a minute.

"Elliot," he said, "as creative people we have to be careful that we don't play the same riff over and over. The challenge is to stay fresh. All of us have our riffs. Mine is tiny heads. I want to give everybody a tiny head. I don't know why; it just really appeals to me to see people with heads no bigger than lemons. When I have to draw people with normally proportioned heads, it makes me sick. They look like monsters."

"So what's my riff?" I asked.

"Past participles with adverbial modifiers. You're starting almost all your sentences with them."

"'Exquisitely handcrafted, the herald angel comes with a marble pedestal and brass trumpet.'"

He touched the end of his nose. "Bingo. Sometimes you start sentences with two past participles with adverbial modifiers in a row."

"'Exquisitely handcrafted, beautifully animated, the herald angel, et cetera.'"

"That's it. Do you think you could maybe limit yourself to one or two past participles with adverbial modifiers per project?"

"No problem."

"Good. I only let myself do one or two lemon heads a year now, and always in crowd scenes. We all have to make sacrifices." He stood, paused. "Um, is everything all right, Elliot? You don't look so hot."

"I'm fine, boss. Really. In the pink."

"Well, if you have a problem, I hope you'll let me know. Not just as a boss, but as someone who's concerned."

"I will."

I followed him out. Gary stood in the hallway, clutching her laptop to her chest. She looked like a nervous schoolgirl waiting for the bus. I tried to walk past, but she said, "Elliot, can I talk to you for a second?"

"You know what?" I stopped. "No. You can't. Don't sit by me in the meetings anymore. Don't look at me or talk to me. Anything you have to say, send it by e-mail. Don't ever speak to me again."

The color drained from her face as if her throat had been cut, a reaction I welcomed with savage jubilation. She'd worked so hard to make me feel about her the way she felt about me, but now she didn't like it. How tragic. I turned and went into the break room.

"Ah, Elliot," Julian said. "Scott requests the pleasure of our company at his house at eight tomorrow night."

Scott was the traffic controller of another team. He was also a chef who could whip up anything in no time flat. We loved him because he was so good-natured and had an overpowering urge to feed us.

"Grilled chicken, scalloped potatoes, and broccoli with cheddar cheese is the menu," Julian said.

"Who's going?" I asked.

"He's invited everyone on both teams. Interested?"

"Sure. See you there."

*   *   *

On Saturday afternoon I decided to take my walk. I couldn't stay inside my house another second. Two blocks over, the teenage hillbilly trombone player squatted on the curb in front of her shotgun shack, her legs spread and her jaw slack. I locked my eyes on her puffy crotch, since she displayed it to the world. She snapped her thighs closed and looked away. I laughed.

Trey wasn't in his spot, which was fine with me. I hoped he cowered at home, wracked with guilt over what he'd done. Thanks to him some circuit in my brain was stuck in the "on" position, engulfing me in a stream-of-consciousness death-barrage. When I looked at the clouds, I saw avalanches. The trees were gallows. Cars could explode in mushroom clouds at any second.

A large orange tomcat lay on his side in the gutter. I knew he was a tom from his enormous testicles. He looked completely natural and relaxed, as though he were taking a nap, except that his head was tucked into his armpit. At first I thought he'd been decapitated, maybe after a group of men in masks filmed themselves reading a pious, bombastic rationalization over him.

As I came around a bend in the path, I saw a lower body about fifty feet ahead: two motionless legs and a waist wearing black pants, poised in the middle of the sidewalk, the legs of a suicide bomber left standing after he triggered his belt. It gave me a shock like a fist to the chest. I stopped and stared, thinking about how in 1947 a woman named Elizabeth Short had been cut in two and left in an empty lot in Leimert Park. They called her the Black Dahlia, and her murderer was never caught. He could still be out there, spry and undiminished from all the advances in gerontology. But then the lower body unfolded into a full body—it was a woman touching her toes.

The embankments next to the horse trail had been planted with seedlings, each marked with a tiny white vinyl flag on a wire. I hadn't seen such flags used that way before; usually they designated human remains at airplane crashes. The embankments seemed covered with fragmented corpses.

I never flew if I could avoid it. Flying was just another way to meet a violent end. When I was three years old, our neighbor Mrs. Glass knocked on our front door one night. She was my favorite person because she was nice and funny and brought plates of chilled brownies covered in foil. But that night she looked like a stranger pretending to be my friend Mrs. Glass. After she said hello to me, she and my parents stood in the living room, murmuring with their heads close together.

"They're all *dead?*" Dad boomed. "Christ!"

I knew the word "dead," which was what the flies lying on the windowsill were, so I thought my parents and Mrs. Glass were talking about flies. I snuck in behind the armchair and listened. They were saying something about an airplane and dead people. To be dead, you had to "die." I knew that word too. We'd gone on an airplane once; it smelled bad inside, like detergent, meat, and the cigarettes Mom and her friends smoked out on the porch. I wasn't supposed to talk to adults unless they talked to me first, but when Mrs. Glass started to leave, I stood and asked her what happened.

"Elliot, this is grown-up talk," Dad warned.

"Glenn, I think we should explain to him what he's heard," Mrs. Glass said, "so he won't be afraid."

I couldn't process the fact that someone scolded my father, even in such a soft voice. Before I could run away, Mrs. Glass knelt in front me. "Well, Ellie, there's been an accident. Something went wrong with an airplane, and it crashed."

"Did people die?"

"Yes. Everyone on the plane died."

"Did you die?" I asked.

It was agony to perfectly recall life before specific hateful knowledge, to remember being unable to comprehend what'd now taken over my existence. I fully expected Mrs. Glass to tell me that yes, she'd died in the crash. Instead, she put her hands on my shoulders.

"No lovey, I didn't die. I wasn't on the plane."

Her touch was comforting. It was the only thing I understood that night.

* * *

When I was six, I finally grasped what Mrs. Glass and my parents had discussed. It happened while my family and I watched the news during dinner one evening, as we always did. A man with a floppy head and big maroon stains on his camouflaged clothing was dragged over to a helicopter.

"What happened to that guy?" I asked.

"He's dead," Dad said. "A Grenadian or Cuban shot him. He was killed."

I suddenly realized that the floppy-headed man would never walk, run, breathe, think, or feel again. He'd never eat birthday cake again. That's what "dead" was. He couldn't do anything anymore, forever, and that would happen to me someday. It made me hot and dizzy, the way I felt when I went to the doctor.

For months, I dreamed of "Grenadians"—men segmented like pineapples—and cigar-smoking Cubans under my bed. To keep them at bay, I slept with a lamp on, a practice I resumed after Trey drove down the steps. But the lamp failed to ward off the question that kept me awake: Why had my family and I never discussed the fact that I tried to kill myself? Mom and Dad certainly knew I jumped. Emily, David, and the Dickinson kids saw me do it. The children had to have been interrogated at length by both sets of parents.

Maybe my family had erased it, the way I had. Or maybe they figured my leap had nothing to do with them and was just one of many loser options I'd exercised throughout my life.

* * *

Everybody from both teams showed up for Scott's dinner party. Gary was the lone absentee. I stayed in the kitchen, watching Scott prepare the food. He talked while I drank and listened. As he went to work on the scalloped potatoes, he said, "You know, I invited Gary, but she told me she had other plans. I wanted to ask you about her."

"Why ask me?" I gulped my greyhound.

"Because you're her writing partner. You know her pretty well, don't you?"

I looked up from the potatoes. Margaret stood behind Scott; she seemed to be holding her breath. I hated her.

"Margaret knows her better than I do," I said. "Ask her." I motioned with my drink.

Scott glanced over his shoulder. "Do you know her pretty well, Margaret?"

"Yeah. What do you want to know?" She eyed me.

"I heard she's a fundamentalist Christian. Is that true?"

"She's a Southern Baptist, if that's what you mean."

He raised his eyebrows. "Interesting. She's a mystery stuffed into an enigma and wrapped in a tortilla. However that goes. Is she dating anyone?"

Margaret looked away from me. "No. She's single."

Scott lined a casserole dish with a layer of sliced potatoes. "So do you think she's hot, Elliot?"

"I don't know," I said.

"What do you mean you don't know? It's a straightforward question, man. Do you think she's attractive?"

"Well, what makes you think I'm attracted to women?"

He and Margaret stared.

"Oh," Scott said. "I, uh, didn't know."

"Didn't know what?"

"Well, I didn't know you're gay."

"What makes you think I'm gay?" I asked.

Scott silently appealed to Margaret. She gave him the tiniest of shrugs. He turned back to me.

"Um, Elliot? Is something wrong? I'm just trying to find out about Gary, because I always thought she was really hot. She's such a loner, though, I never had the chance. If you don't want to talk about this, fine."

"Gosh, why would I not want to talk about it? Ask away, Scott. I'll tell you everything I know."

"No, that's okay. Let's talk about something else."

"Suit yourself." I drained my greyhound and helped myself to a beer from the refrigerator.

Margaret walked out of the kitchen. As I watched her swinging bottom, I was again hit with a vivid memory that led directly to a realization. My own mind now assaulted me whenever it could, like a clown with an endless supply of whipped-cream pies.

* * *

"So what do you think about her?" Gary asked. We were at Amir's, having our seventh lunch together.

"Her who?" I asked.

"Her *who?* Margaret Alvarez, who. Who do you think?"

"Oh, so if you say, 'What do you think about her?' I'm automatically supposed to know who you mean, because *of course* I'm thinking about Margaret Alvarez? Isn't it possible that I could be thinking about some other her?"

"Yeah, but you're thinkin' about Margaret."

"Am not."

"Are too. We all are. She's stirring things up. She's got way too much self-confidence for someone only twenty-two and right out of college. I think people are jealous. I am, a little. I remember how I was when I was her age. I wouldn't have been able to walk into a huge marketing corporation and be totally at ease. And her clothes! I used to have nightmares about being naked in public. I'll bet Margaret's never had one of those dreams in her life. Seems like everybody's either for her or against her. Nobody's neutral."

"*I'm* neutral."

"Oh yeah? I was right there on the other side of the partition when she went into your cubicle and sat on your hand. You didn't know I knew she did that, didja?" She poked my arm.

"No." I smiled; her teasing was a benediction that helped me through the day. "How'd you know? Did you look?"

"No, she told me, of course. She's a reg'lar little chatterbox. And I got to say, when she had your hand pinned under her butt, your voice didn't sound very neutral, wobblin' all over with this opera-singer vibrato in it."

I laughed. "I never had a woman put my hand up her rear end. I'm not one of Margaret's fans, but I don't dislike her. She doesn't mean anything to me one way or the other."

Gary regarded me for a moment before slowly rubbing her palms together. "I believe she could grind corn into flour when she walks. And I'm not thrilled about how she sits on the edge of my desk and puts one leg in that lotus position and leans forward on her forearms so I can look down her tank top. And she needs a towel or a blanket over the back of her chair when she sits at her computer. You can see her dang tailbone."

"She does that half-lotus-desk thing with you too?"

"All the time."

"Do you think she's hitting on you?" I asked.

Gary used to twinkle, back when she could stand me.

"No, Elliot. She ain't hittin' on me. She does it to you and Mitch and Julian and Essi. She cain't be hittin' on everybody in the whole office. She's only been here a month."

"Maybe she's trying to turn us all against each other."

"So we'll fight over her?"

"Maybe. But you can have her."

She snorted. "Well, *I* don't want her! And I can't figure out where she fits the metal lip on the edge of the desk when she sits in her half lotus. I've tried sitting on the edge of my desk the way she does, and it hurts. Maybe she has a special notch or groove that lets her sorta click into place."

"A channel," I said.

"A *channel!*"

We called Margaret "Channel" behind her back for a while, which Gary soon amended to Cha-NELL.

A week after that lunch, Gary invited me to a movie. In our seats, while the ads still ran, she smiled and took my hand. A few minutes into the film, she laid her head on my shoulder. When I said good night at her door, she stepped into my arms and kissed me for the first time. She showed no hesitation or anxiety at all.

My realization two years later was that our conversation at Amir's had been an audition. Without knowing it, I'd sealed my fate.

*   *   *

Scott's dining room was a clattering roar, getting louder and hotter by the second. Essi talked about her newly pierced clitoral hood, DuShawn complained about the economy, and Mike from Scott's team did an impression of the president. Margaret asked me if I was all right.

"Hey, I'm fine," I said. "Don't worry about me."

She'd obviously told everybody about Gary and me. They all talked about other things so I wouldn't leave. I was the guest of honor. They were having a blast, reveling in the exquisite hideousness of Elliot the Lovesick Hippo. Good for them.

I lifted my glass to Margaret and asked, "Can you imagine how utterly revolting it is to be the object of my affection?"

The room was instantly silent as a tomb. Throats were cleared and utensils were carefully put down. Margaret looked as if she might throw up.

Julian reached across the table to grasp my wrist. "Steady, mate. Time to stop with the boozing."

I yanked away my hand, spilling my drink. "I just wanna put the icing on the big, fat, slapstick cake Margaret baked for you, okay? I'm gonna tell you all something really funny."

"No thanks, mate. We're not interested."

"Aw, sure you are. Listen. Gary and I used to play word games, on account of us both being writers. We liked to channelenge, uh, *challenge,* each other's minds. One of her games was to think of things that're as bad to say as they are to hear. Got that? I came up with, 'You're just like all the others.' She came up with, 'You're my only friend.'"

Margaret turned away, holding her crumpled napkin to the side of her face. Julian grabbed my forearm. "Let's go take a walk, Elliot. Just you and me. Get some fresh air. You're pissed out of your skull, old boy."

I grinned at him. "She turned you down, *old boy,* and then she hit on me. That still burns you, doesn't it? The only woman in the whole office who said no to your giant British dick. None of you can understand why she chose a fat loser over a studly British stud. Well, you were right. She made the wrong decision, and then she corrected it, so go ahead and laugh. I don't give a shit."

"Elliot, for Christ's sake! Let's go outside!"

"No! I have to tell you what I came up with. Absolute genius. Left it on her voice mail. Wish I coulda seen her face, 'cause I *know* she knew she'd never beat this."

Julian rose and walked around the table. "Let's stand now, Elliot. Time to say good night."

"*Just wait a second!*" I shouted.

He stopped and sighed. I glanced around the room. Like Margaret, everybody looked ill.

"Here it is," I said. "My masterwork. The prizewinning thing that's as bad to say as it is to hear: 'But I *love* you!' See? I've achieved immortality." I stood. "And now, it's time for me to say good night." I pulled my car keys from my pocket. "Thanks for inviting me, Scott. Had a *wonderful* time."

"You are *not* driving," Julian said.

"Of course I'm driving! Can't you see I'm in no shape to walk?" My voice sounded incredibly loud and harsh, as if coming from a public-address system. "*That's a joke, people!*" I roared. "*What's wrong with you? Are you all crazy?*"

The room tilted; Julian caught me, slung my arm around his shoulder, and half carried me down a hallway.

"Let's step outside and settle this once and for all," I said into his ear.

He shook his head. "It's already settled, mate. You win."

Margaret's raspy voice said, "You need to crash, Elliot. You're totally out of it."

My head was as heavy as a sack of wet sand. I ponderously turned it and saw Margaret on my other side, supporting me.

"You too," I said. "Let's go. Outside. I'm gonna kick your magnicefent—*magnificent*—ass. Break my foot off in it."

"Some other time."

They maneuvered me to a sofa. "Let's put him on his stomach so if he pukes he won't choke on it," Margaret said.

"Mind your own business," I said as I fell forward into whirling blackness. In what seemed like the same instant, my shoulder was shaken and shaken and shaken. I opened my eyes. Scott stood over me.

"Good morning," he said cheerfully. "Would you like some coffee?"

I followed him into the kitchen. My nose filled with the smell of freshly brewed French roast.

Scott smiled. "Hey, how about a three-cheese omelet fried in real butter, some bacon, and homemade hash browns with sour cream?"

A freight train prepared to thunder up from my stomach. "Don't say another word. Just the coffee." I sat at the table, holding my head.

"Sure." He poured me a cup and sat down across from me. "So, Elliot. Boy. How do you feel?"

I sipped my coffee. "Like I'm decomposing."

"You know, I have to say, none of us had any idea."

"Any idea about what?"

"You don't remember what you said?" he asked.

"No. And I don't want to know. I'm sure it was horrifying for everyone, so let's just skip it, okay?"

"Well, but I think we should talk about it."

I put down my cup. "Scott, I can't deal with this sort of thing. I'm a very private person. Whatever I said was caused by beer and greyhounds and self-pity and all the plaque accumulated in my brain. Please change the subject."

He nodded. "All right. I have to say this, though. Margaret never said a thing about you and Gary. Nobody, and I mean *nobody,* in that room ever gossiped about it. We didn't know, and anyway, we all like you. Nobody would ever make fun of you for any reason whatsoever."

I held my head again. "Please. We have to stop talking about this."

"Okay."

* * *

The drive home was wave after wave of nausea warmly sloshing through me as sunlight reflected off windshields and speared my eyeballs. I collapsed into bed and slept until four in the afternoon. When I awoke, I forced myself to drink two full glasses of water, eat an apple, and go for my walk. I'd learned in college that hydration, fruit, and exercise sped my recovery from mammoth hangovers.

On the sidewalk beside the four-lane road, a man walked ahead of me, carrying a plastic grocery bag lumpy with items. Every few feet he turned to look back. I walked faster than he did; as I approached, he began making an odd gesture—a dart-throwing motion—at me with his free hand. I could've paused and waited for him to move on, but I sped up almost to a jog. He stopped and tried to cross the street; there were too many cars. I narrowed the gap between us.

The closer I got, the more agitated he became, and the more agitated he became, the better I felt. I wanted him to become *much* more agitated, to jerk his head around, fling his arms, shake, sweat, and suffer. If he accosted me, I'd tear off his head with my bare hands and shove it down his neck stump. One word to me—just one—and he'd die. He endured it until I was about thirty feet away, then he ran howling out into the middle of the road. Cars veered, honked, and skidded. Somehow he crossed all four lanes in one piece. Safe on the other side, he put down his bag and raised the middle fingers of both hands. I ignored him, though I celebrated inside.

At the top of the hill past No Man's Land, I saw that Trey was still gone.

CHAPTER FIFTEEN

After four days I was sure Trey had found someone else to open the gate for him, maybe the person who'd provided the Valium and rat poison for his previous exploits. He hadn't told me who it was, and I refused to ask. I couldn't determine how I felt that he'd honored my request to not say good-bye. Instead of calling his mother, I checked the local paper every morning. I figured a quadriplegic in a swimming pool would be pretty newsworthy.

I kept the TV on while I wrote copy, and I listened to jazz on my cell phone when I took my walks. Against my will I studied Trey's empty spot; at home again I wrote, catnapped, woke, ate, and drank beer or wine, always with the TV blaring to blot out the tree house, Scott's party, and the bare patch of asphalt where Trey once sat.

At 3:30 Wednesday morning, massively drunk and afraid of the night, I punched in the area code and first six digits of Gary's number but hung up before I completed it. Every time I tried to sleep, strange neural flashes shot through my head, making my legs kick. I'd become a disgusting science experiment, like Galvani's skinned, dancing frogs. My chest hurt and my racing heart threatened to explode. So I lay on the sofa, watched TV, and drank.

On Thursday afternoon Trey was in his spot. For a second I thought I was asleep and dreaming him, or maybe it was his ghost. I jaywalked across the street in a stew of relief, anger, and dread.

He looked much older, yellowish and waxy, as though he'd spent years underground. Hunched over, his right hand on his chin, he resembled *The Thinker*, except for the tears streaming down his face.

"Are you all right?" I asked.

"No," he whispered.

"What's the matter? Where've you been?"

"In the hospital. I have a bladder infection."

I sat on the curb.

He wiped his nose with the back of his hand. "I woke up in the middle of the night with a hundred-three-degree fever. Mom called the ambulance, and they took me to the hospital and put me in a room with a dead guy. At least I think he was dead. He didn't move or say anything all night. There was nothing Mom could do, so I made her go home. They moved me to another room with some lady with a broken leg, and she was crying and praying in Spanish because she was in so much pain. They don't like to give you painkillers anymore, did you know that?"

"No. Why not?"

"Because of the war on drugs. They don't want you to get hooked. So then they forgot about me. I couldn't press the call button, and they couldn't hear me when I yelled for water or when my piss bag was full. Or maybe they didn't think it was worth it to walk down the hall. They brought me food, but they didn't stay and feed me. I had to lie there and stare at it. Mom came that second night and gave me water and fed me, but I still had the fever. She went out and kicked some ass. I heard her screaming up and down the hall, 'You gitcher fat *bee*-hinds in there and hep mah son, or you gonna have a buzz-saw to deal with!' So these pissed-off nurses moved me to another room, but it took them three days to bring the fever down, and every time Mom left, they stopped checking on me. I was burning up, but when they gave me ice water in one of those glasses with the lids and the bendy straws, they left it on the tray in front of me, right in front of my nose, and of course I couldn't reach it."

He sighed, sipped the water from his bottle.

"They also put a humungous catheter up my dick, and it ripped up the lining of my urethra, so it felt like my dick had a knife in it, all the way up to my bladder, but it was easy for them to put it in and pull it out because I can't fight, so they didn't have to hold me down. I can thrash my arms a little, like this, but that's all. Got back home a couple days ago. Still getting over the infection. Can't sleep. Can't watch TV. Can't think. Mom's lost another ten years off her life. So that's what I've been doing. How about you, Elliot? What've you been up to?"

"Look," I said, "why don't you go to Holland?"

"Holland, huh? Gum."

I went to his backpack, pulled out a piece of gum, unwrapped it, and held it in front of his mouth. He nabbed it with his teeth and chewed slowly, squinting at me.

"You want me to go to Holland because assisted suicide is legal there, right?" he asked.

"Yes. I've heard that they'll...help people there, no questions asked. Or very few questions asked."

"They'll kill me, you mean."

"Okay, *yes*. They'll kill you. If your family agrees, I'll go with you. We'll take the plane, get drunk all the way over, go out and smoke hash from one end of Amsterdam to the other, pick up some sweet little Dutch whores in the red-light district, and then we'll go to the hospice. I'll pay for the plane tickets."

He shook his head. "No. We can't. My family would never agree. They're totally against me dying. And anyway, I can't travel. I'm too sick. I've never been in an airplane, you know that? Twenty-first century, and I've never flown. You can't be my knight in shining armor, Elliot. You can't make my death all comfy. The only thing you can do is open that gate."

I sat on the curb. "Something happened when you drove your chair down the stairs. It made me remember something I'd...well, something I'd repressed, I suppose."

"Oh yeah?" He couldn't have cared less. "What?"

"I didn't fall out of the tree house when I broke my legs. I jumped. I tried to kill myself."

He seemed to awaken slightly. "You tried…why?"

"Because of what we talked about before, everybody attacking me all the time, especially my brother and sister. It just hurt too much to go on living."

He nodded slowly. "That means you understand exactly what I'm feeling."

"Yes."

"So you're going to help me." Hope dawned in his face.

"No." I took off my sunglasses. "I'm sorry. I really am. Remembering what I did made me even more opposed to helping you kill yourself. I can't."

"*Why not?*"

"I can't go behind your family's back. They love you. My family never even liked me, but what I did totally screwed them up anyway. They're afraid of me, angry at me, and I've been angry at them for almost thirty years. We don't have any relationship at all now, except for fighting. As bad as things were before, they got worse. And I didn't even die; I just hurt my legs. If you actually kill yourself, it's going to destroy your family. I can't be a part of that. You're asking too much. It's not right."

He nodded. "Okay. I'll accept that."

"I'm sorry. I really am."

"Me too. Listen, don't stop and talk with me anymore."

I didn't think I'd heard him correctly. "What do you mean?"

"I mean don't stop and talk with me anymore. Leave me alone from now on. I don't want you to hang around with me anymore. I got enough loser friends who won't help me. I don't need another one."

"Are you serious?"

He wouldn't look at me. "Get out of here. Fuck off."

I stood. He used his joystick to turn his chair away from me. After a few seconds, I crossed the street to continue my walk. On my way back, he was gone. I came home, showered, put a CD in the player, and wrote copy. When I was done, I turned on the TV and opened the first beer.

* * *

It was a clear night with a full moon. At one o'clock I took my telescope out into the backyard. It was hopeless; my carefully constructed retreat was wrecked. The cactus and aloe were mummified corpses, and the moon was a gleaming skull. Each of the flagstones was a memorial plaque.

I went back inside, paced for a while, and sat at the table in the breakfast nook. After a moment I picked up the phone and dialed.

"Hello?" I'd woken her. She was afraid, as everyone is when the telephone rings in the small hours.

"Mom, it's Elliot," I said, trying not to slur. "I…uh…I…did you just call me?"

"Elliot? Did we—No, we didn't call. We were asleep."

"What's going on?" I heard Dad groan in the background.

I improvised. "I just got a hang-up call, and I was worried it was you and Dad. It had a…a crashing sound in it, like someone dropped the phone. I was afraid something happened to you, like a home invasion or an accident."

"No, we're fine, sweetie. We're fine."

"That's good. That's great. Both of you? Dad's all right too?"

"He's fine. Would you like to speak to him?"

"Um, sure. Okay. Yes."

"Elliot got a strange hang-up call and he was worried about us," Mom said. "Tell him we're fine."

There was a fumbling, and Dad came on.

"Elliot? We're fine. We were asleep."

"I know. Sorry I woke you, Dad. Just got this weird call. Hang-up call. Sounded like the phone got dropped. Nobody said anything. Afraid something happened to you and Mom."

"No, we're great." A pause. "How about you? Are you okay?"

"Yeah, I'm fine. Had some beer is all."

"I kind of thought so. Are you…"

He didn't finish.

"Am I what?" I asked. "Go ahead, Dad. Ask away."

"Are you doing well, Elliot? I mean, healthwise and your job and, and everything else in your life?"

Well, I'm afraid of the dark. I hate everything. I'm crazy. I was dumped by the only woman I ever loved, after I did to her what you did to me. Emily made me try and kill myself. You and Mom let her and David torture me. They called me Fatty and Pork and Peeaigee. Everyone at school made fun of me, and you never protected me. My best friend—correct that, former *best friend—wants me to help him die. My life is utterly without meaning or value.*

"I'm all right," I said. "Back's doing okay, heart's doing okay, losing weight. No complaints about work. So how's everybody else? Heard from David and Emily lately?"

"Yeah, they're great. Your mother and I had lunch at Emily and Nelson's the other day, and David and Andrea dropped by on Sunday with the kids. We had a nice time. Everybody's happy and thriving, thank God. Knock on wood."

"Good. Good. Glad to hear it. And you and Mom are doing okay?"

"Elliot, we're fine. Really. Tell you what: Why don't you come on over to-morrow for lunch? I'll show you the plans for the extension we're gonna build for your mother's studio. It's got a skylight and everything."

"It's gorgeous!" Mom called. "Come on over, sweetie."

"Thanks, but I can't right now," I said. "Got a dooming ledline, uh, looming deadline. But soon, okay? Real soon."

"Sure, son." He'd already lost interest. "We'll be here. You get some sleep now. Turn the phone's ringer off."

"I'll do that. Say good night to Mom for me. And I'm sorry I woke you. I was just...in a bad place. Just upset."

"It's no problem. It's nice you checked in on us. Good night, Elliot."

I had another beer, then four more. Too drunk to drive or even walk, I couldn't go look for Trey's pool. Cartoon swimming pools had large rubber plugs in the bottoms that could be pulled, allowing the water to rapidly drain out with a loud slurping noise. Sometimes, the plugs were pulled after some-one dove off a high platform. The water drained out while the hapless diver was in midair; when he landed in the empty pool, he left a hole shaped like his body in the cement. Flat as a pancake, he climbed out and shook himself until he reinflated. Then he was fine.

If I drained the pool, Trey would drive in anyway. In fact, he might prefer an empty pool because it meant an eight-foot drop headfirst onto cement, the wheelchair landing like an anvil on him. He wouldn't be flat as a pancake, though. He'd be a sack of pulverized bone, leaking from the nose, mouth, and eyes, his teeth broken off and scattered across the concrete.

"But *I'm* the loser," I muttered as I staggered to the kitchen for another beer.

* * *

Friday morning I rose from the living-room couch and showered. According to my watch, I hadn't slept in seventy-five hours. I drank three cups of coffee in front of the TV and left my house at 7:50 a.m., which I'd calculated would allow me to arrive at work right as the meeting began. Driving my usual route was a strange experience; the view through my windshield appeared two-dimensional, the screen of a flight simulator. I pulled over once along the way to wait six minutes because I was ahead of schedule.

I parked in the basement garage, took the elevator up to the office, hurried to the men's room, and sat in a stall. As far as I could tell, nobody had seen me. At one minute after nine, I went to the conference room. Everybody was there, the table adorned with laptops, notebooks, pads, and cell phones. Margaret and Essi huddled together in conversation, and Julian sat quietly with his arms folded. Gary scribbled on a pad, while Richard and DuShawn shared a newspaper. I sat next to Dennis, in the chair closest to the door.

He frowned at me. "Good morning, Elliot. Are you all right? You look terrible." His voice sounded hollow, with a slight echo, as if it came from a cave.

"I just didn't get much sleep last night," I said. "I'm fine." My voice sounded as though I were in a cave too. Everybody except for Gary watched me. They were all far away, on the four sides of a conference table that seemed fifty or sixty yards wide. All the straight lines in the walls—the vertical corners and horizontal joints at the ceiling—were curved; the room seemed to be blowing up like a balloon.

"Are you sure?" Dennis asked.

"Am I sure?" I thought about it. "Yes. I'm sure."

"Well…okay." He swiveled back to face the rest of the team. "Let's get started, people. The client wants this to be called the 'Win Buckets of Loot' game."

There were a few sighs and groans.

"Aha," Dennis said. "I see I'm going to have to incentivize some of you. Well, according to the client's value proposition, this new margarine is trans-fat free. Customers therefore not only get a chance to win buckets of loot, but they can also lower their bad cholesterol. We can all be proud that we're a part of that."

Margaret muttered, "Fat-assed fuckwits."

"And now that we're all on the same page," Dennis went on, "here's what we'll be doing."

I didn't pay attention. Instead, I tried to imagine what would happen if I announced to the room that Gary and I would now spare them the effort of trying to picture us together. We'd get up on the table and strip; I'd lie on my back, and she'd ride me like a cowgirl until she produced the soft, breathy, discreet moan that signaled her orgasm.

"Would you like that?" I asked.

Dennis stopped talking. Everybody looked at me, even Gary, though she quickly glanced away.

"What was that, Elliot?" Dennis asked.

"Nothing," I said. "I'm really tired. I'm sorry."

A measureless amount of time after that, I heard Dennis ask, "Anything? Anybody? Okay, let's get to work."

* * *

I was first out the door. At some point I'd have to ask Julian what the meeting was about, but all I wanted to do was get home, lie down, and turn on the TV. Gary caught up with me before I reached the elevator.

"Elliot, please," she whispered. "I have to talk to you."

"Go away."

"Please." She looked as bad as I felt. Someone must have told her about my performance at Scott's party.

"It hurts to beg, doesn't it?" I asked. "Get out of here."

"No." She made strong eye contact. I'd almost forgotten the unique, light blue-gray of her irises. "No, dammit. We have to talk, and I'm not going to stop bugging you until you agree."

Before I could reply, Julian appeared. "I'm sorry, Gary, luv, but I really must speak with Elliot. It's very urgent."

"Well, I have to go home," I said to both of them. "Talk to me later."

Julian shook his head. "Nope." He grabbed my upper arm and pulled me down the hall. "Let's go to the break room. I have to show you something."

I was too nauseated to resist. Gary followed us.

In the break room, Julian placed his laptop on the table. "Sit. You have to see this."

"What is it?" I mumbled as I took a seat.

"Video my brother took. Combat video. Watch."

He pressed a key on his laptop, opening a window. It showed a dusty alleyway with sand-colored buildings on either side. Harold had mounted the camera on his helmet. A line of soldiers in tan uniforms and full battle gear, weapons at the ready, knelt along the wall on the right.

A deep voice shouted, "*Doan fink so, fooka,*" and gunfire immediately began. The rattle of automatic weapons filled the break room; the scene in the laptop careened dizzyingly as Harold ran. Several explosions sounded. Every soldier screamed unintelligible commands, warnings, or observations.

"Watch this," Julian said. He sat beside me.

The alley abruptly stopped spinning. Several yards ahead, a man popped out of a doorway. His head was wrapped in a black scarf, and he carried an assault rifle. As he raised it, the barrel of another rifle came into view at the bottom of the screen. There was a series of odd, huffing crashes, like someone pounding on a padded door; the man in the black scarf sprawled backward, dropping his weapon. Almost instantly, he sat up and scrabbled for it on his knees. More door-pounding, and the man collapsed face-first into the dirt. He lay still, looking grotesquely broken, as though he'd fallen from a high building.

"And that's what we call a good terrorist," Julian said with a smile. The image of the dead man faded to black.

My arms broke out in gooseflesh. "That's incredible," I said. "It looks exactly like a video game, like *Suicide Ditch.*"

"Sweet," Margaret said from behind me. "Snuff films. How's this different from the videos of people having their heads chopped off?"

Julian laughed. "Well, let's see. In one case the person is kidnapped, tied up, and murdered for political-religious reasons. In the other case, the arsehole there died because he tried to shoot my brother, who was helping build a school, but Harold was faster on the draw. If he hadn't tried to kill my brother, he'd still be alive. Fuck him."

"*He was defending his country,*" Margaret shouted. I turned to look at her. A vein stood out in her forehead, and her eyes had a raging, furnace-like glow.

"Dear, this is a private conversation," Julian said. "I told you before the meeting that I'm not talking about this with you. Bugger off. Go screech like a fishwife somewhere else."

"Yeah, well, it's really awesome to see you guys congratulate each other over your killer brother's shooting. It's people like you two who make the world the fucked-up place it is. I hope you're proud."

Julian slapped the table, making his laptop jump. "*Who the* fuck *do you think you are?*" he bellowed. "You'd better shut the fuck up right now if you know what's good for you!"

Margaret grinned. "Blowing holes in some peasant makes you feel a lot safer, huh? Boy, when I see all those dead brown people, *I* feel safer, that's for sure. Good job, guys! Yay for the army!"

Julian scrambled to his feet, knocking over his chair. Margaret turned to me.

"What kind of bombs do we drop on women and children, Elliot?" she snarled. "The ones with all the little bombs that come out. Clusterfucks? Isn't that what they're called?"

"Right," Julian said. "That's it. I have to go, or I won't be responsible for my actions." He closed his laptop.

"What, are you gonna kill me? Shoot me like your killer brother shot that guy?"

"*Don't bloody tempt me!*" Julian shouted.

"*Come on, big man!*" Margaret bawled. Her voice was like the rusty cry of some primordial beast, some gargantuan bird of prey. "Kill me! Let's see you do it!" She whipped around to confront me. "What about you? You wanna kill me?" She snapped her fingers an inch from my nose. "Hey! I'm *talking* to you!"

It happened again; the room vanished, and I was nine, falling away from my sister, the wind rushing past my ears. I stood and screamed, "*SHUT UP!*" into Margaret's contorted, purple face. She cringed, her hands flying up to shield herself.

"You…harpy," I said in the silence. "You toxic moron. All you do is spew poison. I don't want to know you anymore. Fuck you."

Dennis stood in the doorway, the rest of the team crowded behind him. Everybody was pale with shock. I walked over to them, my legs on the verge of giving out.

I said to Dennis, "I'm sorry, but I quit."

His mouth fell open. "Now, hold on, Elliot. You don't have to do that. There's no question that people have let their emotions get the best of them"— he shot a furious glance at Margaret and Julian—"but that's something we can address. No more political discussions at the office, is that clear? And if you think that's infringing on your right to free speech, take me to court. After today's little display, any jury in the country would side with me."

Nobody spoke.

Dennis touched my shoulder. "We'll work it out, Elliot."

"I'm sorry," I said. "I quit. I'm giving my two-week notice, and now I'm taking my sick leave. Good-bye." I tried to squeeze past him. He moved to block my way.

"Elliot, you can't leave us like that. If you were actually going to quit, you'd have to give us time to find a replacement. You can't just walk out the door."

"Dennis, I'm sorry. I can't stay here another second. I have to leave, *or I'm going to lose my mind!*" I lowered my voice. "Look, if I stay, I won't be able to get anything done anyway. I'm through. I can't work anymore. I'm spent."

"Wait. Take your sick leave. Take two weeks off and cool down. Things'll be much better after that, I promise."

I looked at Margaret. She still held her hands up in loose fists, her eyes and mouth wide open. Gary stood beside her with the saddest, most pained expression I'd ever seen.

"I'm sorry, Dennis," I said. "I can't stand this anymore."

They all followed me to my cubicle. I opened my desk drawer and took out my stapler, three notebooks, some pens, my grammar guide, my dictionary, and my thesaurus. There was a plastic bag from a bookstore in the drawer; I put my things in it. Faces peeked in on me from the hall.

"You can't quit," Margaret said.

I didn't respond.

She made a scornful, panicked, almost-sneezing sound. "Gary, tell him he can't quit. Talk him out of this bullshit."

Gary said nothing.

"I can't write you a reference if you do this, Elliot," Dennis said.

"I know. I'm not asking for a reference. I'm really sorry, Dennis."

"Mate, I know that was a truly *disgusting* scene just now, but this isn't smart," Julian said. "Really, you should stop and give it a second thought."

"I've given it second and third and fourth thoughts," I said. "I have to go. But it's been a real pleasure working with you, Julian. I really enjoyed it. Good luck." I stepped into the hall with my hand out. Julian reluctantly shook it.

"Truly bad idea," he grumbled. "Don't do this."

"I'm sorry," I said. I turned to Gary. "It's been a pleasure working with you too." She gazed at my hand for a moment before taking it. Her grip was soft and moist. She seemed utterly lost.

"You're acting like a little boy," Margaret said. "This isn't what adults do. Adults don't run off when they're upset."

I shook hands with DuShawn, Essi, Richard, Mitch, and Dennis.

"I think you're, like, making a big mistake," Essi said.

"Just wish me luck," I replied.

She gave me an exasperated grunt. "Good luck."

"Don't do it, Elliot," Dennis said. "I'm asking you."

"I'm sorry, Dennis."

As I started down the hall toward the elevator, Margaret clutched at my sleeve. I pulled away. She swooped in front of me and grabbed my shoulders. Wild-eyed, frantic, desperate—it was a new look for her. I liked it.

"You're not really going to do this," she said. "You can't. Please." She was so close, I could smell her breath. It was tangy and spicy-sweet, exactly like the taste of her all-encompassing, sheltering, powder blue vagina in my dream.

I didn't answer. She released me with an angry hiss, clasping her hands on the top of her head like a prisoner of war. I walked around her, rode the elevator to the lobby, and emerged into the sunshine.

CHAPTER SIXTEEN

I lay on the couch in my living room and watched TV for up to twenty hours at a stretch. Dennis left two messages on my machine, the first asking me to please come back, the second saying how disappointed he was in me. Margaret also left messages almost every day. They evolved over time.

Hi, Elliot. It's Margaret. Listen, we have to talk. Please give me a call at home or work or on my cell. Check your e-mail too. Please. Thanks.

Elliot? It's Margaret. I know you're really pissed at me, but we still have to talk, okay? So give me a call. You can't blow me off this way. It's not going to solve anything. Call me. Good-bye.

Elliot, please pick up the phone. I know you're there. We have to talk about this. I'm not going to give up. Call me. Act like a grown-up.

Pick up the phone, Elliot! Pick it up now! This is bullshit, man! Pick up the fuckin' phone!

Her e-mails and texts also traveled an arc from tentative through impatient to furious. I deleted them all. She was right that ignoring her solved nothing. I couldn't get her screaming purple face out of my mind. Every time I thought of her, I felt myself dropping through empty air. Quitting my job also solved nothing. I still couldn't sleep, eat, or concentrate. The only difference it made was that I now had an antsy, suffocating sense of dereliction. I'd experienced it before, when I broke my legs and spent four months in bed.

It was hard to keep track of how old I was. One of the cable channels was programmed entirely with ancient tapes of the daytime game shows I'd watched while my legs healed. Hearing the theme music again made me think that at any minute Mom would come in and serve me a mug of tomato soup and a bologna sandwich on white bread with mayonnaise, mustard, and iceberg lettuce. Then she'd get the bedpan and a damp washcloth.

I forced myself to take my walks. Sometimes I saw Trey sitting in his spot. He was there less often because of the cooler weather. One afternoon he'd be on my side of the street again, chatting up another potential gate opener and smirking at me like a defiant ex-girlfriend. It was inevitable because to him I was just a mechanism. As so often happened, the mechanism failed and had to be replaced.

Though my days were consummately empty, I didn't look for another job. I couldn't stomach the idea of updating my résumé and perusing the want ads. The world had changed since the only time I did that, right out of college. I worked at a transcribing company for four years before I had a chance meeting at a bar that led to freelance copywriting for toy companies. Another freelancer got me the interview at Soledad. I was terrible at creating my own opportunities.

Watching old game shows, I thought about researching only one occupation. I'd discovered it when I was in elementary school, the time my family went to Long Beach Harbor to pick up the Mercedes that Dad bought on one of his trips to Germany and had shipped over here. It had a special transmission that wasn't for sale in the States. At Dad's request, we were taken down to the dock, where a giant freighter slowly berthed itself.

"This tub came all the way across the Atlantic and through the Panama Canal," Dad said. "Boy, would I like to take that voyage again." In the early sixties, he was a boatswain's mate on the aircraft carrier the USS *Valley Forge*. It made calls at ports in the Mediterranean, the Red Sea, the Indian Ocean, the Atlantic, and the Pacific.

The bow of the freighter opened up like the mouth of a whale, and a line of cars drove down a long tongue-like ramp and sped across the parking lot toward the gate.

David was excited. "Why are they driving so fast?"

"That's their job," Dad said. "They're driving those cars to dealerships or private buyers. They have to get there in a hurry."

"Why don't they just put them on those big trailers?" Emily asked.

"Because the cars are all going to different places. It's faster and cheaper to do it individually. Those drivers pick up cars all over the country and drive them wherever they need to go. They spend their whole lives in cars."

I could easily do that. Spend my life staring at the changing landscape, listening to the radio and CDs, eating nothing but burgers, picking up hitch-hiking trollops, sleeping in motels, living out of a suitcase, keeping on the move. The drivers I saw that day looked totally centered, with their sunglasses and baseball caps, their competent hands gripping the steering wheels as they roared past.

* * *

Margaret screeched at me like a Hollywood pterodactyl, and I jumped out of the tree house. I landed in a dusty alleyway, where a man with a black scarf wrapped around his head aimed a rifle at me. He was also Gary, holding a bottle of aspirin.

"I need to talk to you, Elliot," she whispered.

"*Get out of here,*" I shouted.

She opened fire with her aspirin; I looked down and saw a line of bloody holes across my chest. They didn't hurt at all. While I stared at them, Trey rolled up in his wheelchair, the electric motor humming.

"Fuck off," he said. "You don't even have the decency to die."

I toppled forward. Someone knelt and turned me over: It was Emily, trying not to laugh.

"Peeaigee, you're not fooling anyone," she said.

Suddenly, I was lying on the floor of a murky, empty room. An open door showed a line of people shuffling past in a darkened hallway. I couldn't see their faces.

"Get up," a voice said. A young man leaned into view. He had a thin teenager's neck and a wispy black mustache and beard. I knew his name was Fayez Samir Hamad.

"Are you an angel?" I asked as I rose.

"Yes. I killed Dr. Larkin's family. Let's go."

"Where?"

"To hell." He pointed to the line of people trudging past the door. "Come on."

"*I'm going to hell because I'm fat?*" I wailed.

His laugh was light and untroubled. "Oh, you're not fat anymore. You're like me. Look." He opened his long coat and showed me the explosives strapped around his trim waist.

I awoke on the sofa. Outside my windows the world was shades of bluish gray. The clock on the DVD player read 5:49, but I didn't know if it was morning or dusk. I turned on the TV; it was 5:49 a.m. on a Saturday. After a shower, two cups of coffee, and a bowl of cereal, I felt slightly less insane.

At ten I called Emily. She was surprised, almost shocked.

"Elliot? How *are* you? Is everything okay?"

"Fine, everything's fine. Listen, can I come over and play with the kids?"

Silence. It was the first time I'd asked to do that. I'd been to her house only on the kids' birthdays or other family occasions.

"Well, sure," she finally said. "Of course. They'd love to see you. We'd all love to see you."

"I just felt like seeing them. And you."

"Well heck, come over for lunch. Let's have hotdogs."

"Great. I'll see you in about an hour?"

"Perfect. See you then." She sounded so happy.

That'd make it even better.

* * *

Emily and Nelson lived in an eighty-year-old, shingled two-story in West Covina. They were pleased and wary. We didn't hug when they let me in; I shook hands with Nelson and simply greeted Emily. I realized that I'd never once hugged my sister.

"How're things in the copywriting business?" Nelson asked.

"Busy. The usual."

"What're you working on? Anything interesting?"

"A collect-and-win game. Margarine. Kind of boring."

"Well, it pays the bills, though."

"That it does," I said.

Emily tucked her hair behind her ears, folded her arms, and shifted her weight from foot to foot. I took great pleasure in her apparent second thoughts about having me over. She told Alex, Terri, and me to go play in the backyard, where Nelson had erected a fort-slide-swing-set conglomeration equipped with low-power telescopes, a rope ladder, and a flag. The kids climbed and swung. As always, they wanted to know things.

"Why can't statues move?" Alex asked.

"Because they're not alive," I said. *Just like me.*

"Why do people plant trees?" Terri asked. She'd just turned three and was talking up a storm.

"They do it for shade or fruit, or because they think trees are pretty." *And they're great for jumping out of.*

217

I saw Emily in the kitchen window; the nanosecond we made eye contact, her head flicked in another direction.

"How come you're not married?" Alex asked.

"I haven't found the right person yet." *I thought I had, but she dumped me because I'm a debacle, thanks to your mother.*

"Who's the right person?"

Nobody. "Well, I don't know."

I caught Emily watching me again. She seemed to be afraid that I'd hurt her children. A blast of white-hot rage shot through me.

The kids and I played catch with plastic coffee-can lids. They soared like miniature flying saucers. We invented a game resembling horseshoes; the goal was to see who could get their lids closest to the base of the avocado tree. Terri threw a lid that landed under the bushes, so I got down on my hands and knees to root around for it. The kids squatted beside me to watch. As I rummaged, I heard Emily approach.

"Lunch is ready, everybody," she said. "Let's go inside and wash our hands." I retrieved the lid and stood up.

"Why do your legs make crunchy noises?" Terri asked.

"Terri!" Emily barked. "That's not the sort of question you ask somebody!" Her gaze flitted on and off my face.

Look who's here! Fatty-Fatty-Fatty!

I wanted to say, "Answer the question, Emily. Why do my legs make crunchy noises?"

My heart thundered; I was dizzy and out of breath. Emily stared at the ground.

You know, I realized. *You've known all along.* She glanced up and confirmed it. My hatred of her was total.

To keep from punching her, I said to Terri, "I fell out of a tree house when I was nine years old and broke my leg bones and damaged the tendons. They never really healed the right way, so now they crunch when I move."

"Why'd you fall out of the tree house?" Alex asked.

Emily turned her face to the sky, her eyes closed. She looked like Trey sunning himself.

I let her squirm for a couple of beats before I said, "I lost my balance. If I'd known what would happen to me, I never would've gone up there."

"Do your legs hurt?" Terri asked.

"All the time."

Emily clutched her forehead. "Let's go in the house, everybody. Come on. Move." She was flushed and seemed close to tears.

* * *

We sat at the dining-room table. The all-beef kosher hotdogs smelled wonderful, but I wasn't hungry. I was consumed by how my loving, selfless sister—the perfect wife and mother who'd given up her law career to raise her children—had destroyed me for the sheer pleasure of it and then hid from what she'd done.

Fatty. Peeaigee. Pork. Piggy. Lardo. Chubster. Fatbutt. Ba-voom. Names that cut like a blade. And no apologies, no remorse, no acknowledgment. No taking of responsibility. Now she had the gall to scold her children in front of me? For asking why my legs made *crunchy* noises?

You see, children, my legs crunch because your mother and your Uncle David made my life so horrible that I tried to kill myself to get away from them. I'm partially crippled, and now, after decades of pain and countless missed opportunities, the recovered memory of what I did is wreaking all sorts of brand-new havoc. The moral of the story is don't be a weakling, kids. Kill the other person, not yourself.

Emily set a platter of hotdogs on the table. Red and guilty, she incarnated the best word of all human languages: *Backpfeifengesicht,* German for "a face badly in need of a fist." I focused on her as Nelson got napkins from the sideboard. The adults thus distracted, Terri grabbed a wiener, bit off about a third of it, and promptly choked. Her eyes bulged, she made a clicking sound, and her hands scrabbled helplessly on the tabletop. My rage turned to terror.

"*She's choking! She's choking!*" I yelled and jumped to my feet. Nelson lunged forward with a wordless bellow. Alex screamed. It was an instantaneous pandemonium of shouts, knocked-over chairs, and dropped utensils.

While Nelson and I lost our heads, Emily calmly slipped her arms around Terri's chest, put her fist just below her sternum, and jerked her up and back. The chunk of hotdog popped out and landed on my plate, unchewed and pristine. Terri took in a huge gulp of air, following it with a beautiful howl. She whimpered in Emily's embrace for no more than twenty seconds, after which she was fine. White as chalk, Nelson methodically sliced her next hot dog into at least eighty pieces. Emily served Alex and me with a mother's briskness, her fear of me gone for the moment.

"Elliot? You okay?" she asked.

"I'm fine," I said, but I wasn't. My hands wouldn't stop trembling. I'd invited myself over so I could figure out the best way to make my sister suffer for what she'd done to me. My always-taxing presence was made even more stressful by the crazy vibes I was giving off and Terri yanking our skeleton out of the closet. I'd short-circuited Emily's parental vigilance as she served one of my favorite foods, a treat she'd prepared just for me. What'd happened was entirely my fault, on every level. Because of me, Terri almost died. My sister's expertise was the only thing that saved her.

You're a very angry person, Dr. Larkin had told me. *It's going to kill you.*

But he hadn't said it'd kill anybody else.

I chatted, laughed, and pretended I'd gotten over our little scare, while my shame grew until I could actually taste it, an effluvium like garlic and vinegar.

* * *

When I got home, I immediately took a long, very hot shower. I scrubbed myself in a frenzy. Every time I closed my eyes, I saw Terri's scrabbling hands. I tried to cast out the image by recalling the look on Emily's face as she dislodged the hotdog from her daughter's throat. It was the same expression Japanese sculptors gave to their renderings of the Buddha, a serene knowingness that came from absolute faith.

I checked my answering machine. Another message from Margaret. Gone was the cocky, hostile young woman who'd tormented me for two years. This Margaret was broken, abject, defeated.

Elliot. I know you hate me and don't want to talk to me ever again, but I had to tell you that Julian quit too. He gave his two weeks' notice yesterday. You know what else he did? He joined the army. The American army. And he asked to be in the infantry so he could be sent overseas. He's gonna go fight in the war if he can. I just...I can't believe all this shit is happening. It's like a bad dream. Look, I have to talk to you. Call me. Please. Don't punish me anymore. Please. 'Bye.

I called Julian at his house.

"Yep, it's true, mate," he said. "Decided I couldn't sit on my arse on the sidelines anymore. In two weeks I'm off to Fort Benning, Georgia, for training. I was going to call you tonight, in fact, and let you know."

"I'm...flabbergasted," I said.

"Look, here's a British term I want you to start using: gobsmacked. Edgier, I think. A good copywriter needs it."

"All right; I'm gobsmacked. When did you make this decision?"

"After you quit. But let's not hash this out over the phone. Meet me at La Cachette at eight, eh? I'll give you all the details."

"Okay."

"So, everything copacetic with Elliot?"

"Couldn't be better."

He did his squawking charwoman voice. "Oo, wha' a whoppa you told."

"No, really. I'm fine. So I'll see you at eight."

"Right. Cheerio, mate."

* * *

He was different. Warmer and…*bouncier,* like someone who'd thrown off a heavy burden. We sat at a window table with our golden ales.

"Here's how it works, old boy," he said. "I've signed up under the 11X, the Infantry Enlistment Option. When I go to Fort Benning to start my training, they'll decide my MOS, or Military Occupational Specialty. I'll be either an 11B or an 11C. That's an infantryman or indirect-fire infantryman. The latter plays with mortars! Can you *imagine?* If I'm an 11B, I do thirteen weeks of Basic Combat Training and Advanced Individual Training. BCT and AIT. If I'm an 11C, I get an *additional* eight weeks of AIT for the mortars. Don't you love these manly acronyms? Make me right giddy, they do. After that, hopefully I'm off to war. So there you have it."

I sipped from my glass. "What was it like to enlist?"

His laugh had changed too. There was actual humor in it. "Amazing. We had the best time. They asked why I wanted to serve, and I told them I got a buzz from social work. We understood each other right off the bat. It's what I've been looking for my whole life. As soon as possible, I'm going to apply for citizenship. *Christ,* I wish I'd done this in my twenties."

"Aren't you even a little nervous?"

He waved away the question. "Not in the least. Look, all I do is make money, play rugby, and get laid. I've never had a meaningful relationship. I don't really have any friends, except for you. Oh, I have loads of pals, but you're the only person I ever really talk to. Remember Scott's party?"

"Oh God. We can't discuss that. Please."

"Wait a sec. Hang on. I just wanted to say that when you were telling us about Gary, I envied you."

I covered my face. "You envied me making a complete, pathetic, drunken jackass out of myself?"

"No, I envied you your pain. I never care when a woman leaves me. Dumping or being dumped never hurts. When Margaret told me she didn't want to be with me, it made no impression at all. She may as well have told me she was off to have a bath. I've never felt much for anybody except my brother and you. The closest I came to caring about my fellow humans was when I was in the VSO, and I burned out on that in just a couple of years."

He raised two fingers to the waitress. She nodded, and he turned back to me. "I don't think you're a jackass at all. If anyone's a jackass, it's me. Your relationship with Gary didn't work out, but at least you loved her. I've never loved anybody."

The waitress brought our next round of ales. She was a beautiful woman in her early twenties, with a gold nose ring and a red Chinese dragon tattooed on her right shoulder. Julian dropped a twenty on her tray. "Keep the change, luv."

She offered him a model-perfect smile. "Wow. Thanks. You must be in a good mood."

"Yup. I just joined the army."

Her smile disintegrated, replaced by seething revulsion. She glanced at the bill he'd given her.

He winked. "If you don't want my money, darling, fine. Hand it back and I'll give it to someone else."

She hesitated a moment longer, spun, and walked off.

"Thought so," Julian called after her.

"Do you get that a lot?" I asked.

"Uh-huh. Several of my British rugby so-called friends aren't speaking to me anymore. But I don't have time for cretins like that. They can go fuck themselves."

"So you're not afraid of something bad happening to you?"

"Something bad already *did* happen to me." He drank, wiped his mouth. "I've spent thirty-three years feeling and doing absolutely nothing. Whatever comes next will happen in the pursuit of something other than quim and cash, and that can only be good."

I didn't say anything.

Charles appeared at our table, businesslike, hands clasped in front of him. "Julian, Tarynn tells me that you 'ave joined the army. Is that true, or were you just kidding 'er?"

"It's the gospel truth, mate. Quit the job, and in two weeks, I'm off to Georgia to be trained."

"Seriously? No joke?"

"No joke."

Charles made one of those lippy, French-type faces and went back behind the bar.

"Watch, he's going to produce a large stick," Julian said. "Going to tell me to clear out or he'll crack my skull."

"Charles couldn't lift a large stick," I said.

The music abruptly stopped and the house lights went on.

Julian grimaced. "Shit. Doesn't look good."

"Ladies and gentlemen," Charles said over the PA. "Can I 'ave your attention, please? I 'ave an announcement to make. Please, could I 'ave quiet?"

The bar fell silent.

"Christ," Julian whispered.

Charles went on. "Thank you. I wanted to announce that one of my customers, Mr. Julian Buckley, a British citizen, 'as just joined the United States Army. He is the tall, very 'andsome man with no beard, sitting there by the window."

A hundred heads swiveled to stare at us. Many of the patrons were Belgian expatriates, but the majority were trendy, young Santa Monicans like Tarynn.

"We're so dead," Julian said. He smiled and waved.

"Please join me," Charles said, "in wishing 'im a safe return 'ome. Julian, take care of yourself, and when you come back, we'll 'ave a table waiting for you. Thank you."

There was a click as the PA system was switched off. Charles began clapping loudly. Others joined in. It spread until almost everyone applauded. Some abstained; a few glowered and folded their arms. Julian stood, bowed, and toasted the crowd. Several raised their glasses in return. The music came on again, and the applause tapered off.

"Well, that was mortifying," Julian said as he sat.

"You loved it," I said.

He grinned. "I did, actually."

A waitress—not Tarynn—brought over a glass of golden ale and set it in front of Julian. "This is from the table over in the corner," she said, pointing.

We looked. Two devastating young women smiled in our direction. One was a pale blonde, the other African-American. Both wore snug tank tops that exposed their tattooed shoulders and deep cleavage. Their generous mouths were decorated with lipstick so dark, it was almost black.

"Crikey," Julian said.

I finished my ale in one gulp and stood. "I leave you to your fate, young man."

He shook his head. "Forget that. We're talking. This is more important than, than..."

"Than two gorgeous young patriots who are so moved by the selflessness of an Englishman volunteering to defend them that there's literally no telling what might happen on this long night of infinite possibility? Talking to me is more important than that?"

"Well, when you put it *that* way."

I clasped his hand. "We'll go out again before you leave."

"We will. Drive safely."

"You too."

"Something tells me I won't be in the driver's seat tonight, mate. That's fine. Must get used to taking orders. Cheerio."

Glass in hand, he marched toward the corner table.

CHAPTER SEVENTEEN

I came up the hill past No Man's Land and saw Trey on my side of the street, where he was the day I met him. The only reason for him to be there was that he was waiting for me. It struck me that one defining characteristic of quadriplegics was their enforced patience. Trey could sit motionless for days, a spectacular accomplishment for someone as body oriented and sensual as he once was. It was good to see him feeling well enough to be outside, but I knew that whenever he crossed the street to intercept me, he had an announcement.

"There you are," he called. "How's it going?"

"As usual. How about you?"

"As usual."

I stopped in front of him. He looked better than the last time I spoke to him. The smudges under his eyes were lighter, and his skin had more color.

"Listen," he said, "I came over to tell you I'm sorry about what I said before. I was angry, but that's no excuse. I didn't mean it, and I'm sorry."

"That's okay. I didn't take it personally."

"Good. Listen, I miss our conversations. If you want, you can stop by to talk on your way back. If you feel like it."

"All right. I will. Thanks."

"I also wanted to tell you that I'm not gonna go into the pool after all."

I waited, but his twenty-three years of patience gave him the upper hand.

"Really," I finally said.

"Yup. I'm gonna go out in front of a truck instead."

For an instant—just a blip in time—I honestly wanted to punch his lights out, to feel my knuckles colliding with his jaw. I hated his guts.

"Hey, that's great," I said. "Congratulations."

"Thanks. I knew you'd approve."

"You're forgetting that I got hit by a car, and all it did was mess up my back. Getting hit by a car isn't a sure thing."

He gave me a pitying look. "I'm not talking cars; I'm talking big-ass trucks. Pickups, rental vans, SUVs. You see how fast they go down this street. The other day I actually saw an eighteen wheeler doing about seventy. That's what I mean."

"If you want to do that, fine. You're not going to blackmail me into helping you."

"*Black*mail?" He was aghast. "Who said anything about blackmail? I'm just telling you what I'm gonna do."

"You're going to let a truck splatter you all over the street where your mother can see. That's neat. Oh, and don't forget the driver. He'll have a precious memory to carry around with him for the rest of his life. You're all heart, Trey."

"I *am* all heart. That's why I've stuck it out as long as I have. I didn't want to hurt people. And now I can't hack it anymore. I'm in hell. That last bladder infection was the worst thing that's ever happened to me, including breaking my neck. You can't even begin to understand how…how…how *ugly* it was, how totally inhuman, so don't lecture me about my selfishness, okay?"

I climbed up the wooden fence beside the horse trail to sit on the top rail. From that vantage Trey was a grotesque amalgam of angular limbs and oversized belly, like a giant insect. At last I saw him as he saw himself.

"I'm not lecturing you," I said. "But I can't take this anymore. I'm at the end of my rope."

He nodded as he sipped water. "I'm sorry. I really am. But I'm at the end of *my* rope too. I'm sorry for what my mom and my friends are going to go through when I go out and get hit by a truck, but I can't live like this anymore. I won't."

"Look, I know you hate to talk about this, but they keep saying there's a real chance that stem-cell research is—"

"You don't understand, Elliot," he interrupted. "All the scars on my arms and legs, and these here on my neck? You know what they're from? Operations to sever ligaments. My arms and legs were contracting and the spasms were getting worse, so they just cut everything. Even if they had a breakthrough with that fuckin' stem-cell bullshit—and I don't believe they will—it wouldn't do me any good."

"Why not?"

"Because then I'd just be in for years of operations to reattach the ligaments, and then years of physical therapy and pain, and at the end, I'd be able to shuffle around with a walker if I was lucky. I'd never run or surf or play football. I'd be this fifty-year-old guy who'd never had a job and couldn't do anything except make a couple circuits around the room on his walker and bitch about how miserable he was."

He stopped to look me in the eye.

"Elliot, you know me better than anybody else in the world. Do you think I could possibly live that kind of life?"

After a few seconds, I said, "No. You couldn't."

He bobbed his head, a knight graciously saluting his vanquished opponent. We watched the traffic for a while. Most of it was enormous sports utility vehicles of a mass and velocity that indeed made them perfect eradicators. For the eradicated, it would be over in a rupturing, splintering, rending, yet totally insensate flicker. The brain would be obliterated before nerve fibers could report a thing.

"There's another point to think about," Trey said.

"You know what? I don't care."

"Well, I do. Even if they have a stem-cell breakthrough in five years, they'll have to test it for another ten years. When it's finally available, it's going to cost a shitload. I'd use up all my insurance and my savings and investments.

After all the operations and physical therapy, I'd be in my sixties, broke, jobless, and just barely able to walk. Maybe."

"But wouldn't it be worth it to end the pain?"

"What if it didn't? They told me they could end the pain with medication, morphine pumps, electrical therapy. None of it worked. Biofeedback, hypnotism, acupuncture, acupressure—I tried everything, and I'm still in pain. All I want now is to be free. I just want to *go*. Can't you understand that?"

"Look." I unzipped my sweat jacket to let out the heat. "You're depressed. Did you ever try therapy?"

He sighed. "What's therapy going to do? Make me see the bright side? There *is* no bright side. It's all dark. You can't accept that because you think we're the same, and that's why you won't help me. You're afraid if you help me, it'll mean your own life sucks so bad, *you* should kill yourself too."

"I...that's not true," I said.

"It is. And you're wrong. We're not the same. You can change almost everything in your life; I can't. Your darkness is self-imposed; mine isn't. You're a great guy, Elliot, but you're in love with your own unhappiness. I hate being unhappy."

There was a clopping on my right. I turned my burning face toward the sound and saw a horse ambling toward us. The rider was a stunning woman in her early twenties, a Thai, Cambodian, or Vietnamese with very full lips.

"Your story and mine are totally different," Trey muttered. "I'm asking you to help me be free, not punish people who hurt me."

"Hey, guys," the woman said.

"That's a beautiful horse," Trey said. "What's his name?"

"Janine."

"*Janine!* Does he know he's got a chick's name?"

She laughed. "*She* knows her name, smarty. She comes when I call her."

"Girlfriend, who wouldn't?"

She laughed again and tossed her hair as she rode off.

"This is so unfair," I said to Trey. "You want me to do something that's going to haunt me the rest of my life."

"I know," he said. "I'm sorry. But you're literally my only hope. I swear to you I'll go out in front of a truck if you don't help me."

"Bastard. Son of a bitch. All right."

"All right what?"

"I'll open the fucking gate."

He grunted as he spun his chair away from me. His shoulders trembled for a moment, then he faced me again, wiping his eyes.

"You're serious, right?" he asked in a husky voice.

"Yes."

"Hot damn. Hot *damn*. You're not kidding around, right?"

"Right."

"Oh my God. When?"

"Whenever you want," I said.

"Tomorrow night. Let's do it tomorrow night. My sister's coming over tonight, so I'd like to see her one last time."

"Great." I jumped off the fence and started walking.

"Wait a second," Trey called. "Hold on."

I halted. "What?"

"You have to take your walk tomorrow as usual. Everything has to be exactly the same as it always is. People have to see you talking to me in my spot across the street."

"Oh, that's right. Because I'm going to be the prime suspect in your illegal assisted suicide. I might spend the rest of my life in jail, but who cares? You don't, so why should I? The most important person in this story is *you*, Trey. What Trey wants, Trey gets, or he'll turn himself into a speed bump."

"You're not going to jail," he said, unfazed. "No one's going to suspect anything if we're smart."

"So what the hell are we going to talk about on your last day on earth? Movies? Sports? All the great times we had together?"

"Whatever. We can just sit there and not talk at all, if that's what you want."

"Let me ask you something." I went back, crouched beside his chair, and removed my sunglasses. "If you knew I'd go to jail, would you ask me to help you anyway?"

He met my gaze with ease. "If I *knew* you'd go to jail? No, of course not. I'd go out in front of a truck. But I've been real careful. You're the only one I told about the pool. If you kept your mouth shut, no one'll ever know you were involved."

I rose. "I haven't told anybody."

"Good. I'm sorry you're gonna feel guilty and be haunted. All I can say is thank you. This is the kindest thing anybody's ever done for me, Elliot. I'm nothing but a giant bolt of pain. You're the only person I ever met who really listens to me and understands what I'm going through. Helping me is the greatest gift you could possibly give."

"Well, I'm only doing it because you're forcing me to. If I had any guts, I'd call your bluff about the truck." I put on my sunglasses. "You're making me do something completely against my will, after I told you how suicide affected my family. It's going to hit your family hard too."

"I know. If there was any other way, I'd take it. I'm sorry, Elliot."

"Sure." I started toward home.

"Hey, aren't you gonna finish your walk?" he asked. "I mean, people might wonder why you didn't."

"Gosh, what a shame." I kept walking.

* * *

Back inside my walls, I did one hundred fifty sit-ups, lifted the weights I'd bought a few weeks back, took a shower, lay on the sofa, turned on the TV, watched eight seconds of news, turned off the TV, stared at the ceiling as dusk fell and the living room darkened.

Trey didn't tell me if he'd decided to go into the pool forward or backward. Forward would allow the chair to fall on him and hopefully knock him out or even kill him before he drowned. Backward would let him see the stars in the sky, he said, but that was absurd. I knew what it was like to open my eyes in a chlorinated pool; he wouldn't be able to see anything unless he wore goggles or a swim mask, which would be a real head scratcher for the homicide investigators. A man in an electric wheelchair at the bottom of a pool, wearing goggles or a swim mask. One for the scrapbooks.

The phone rang. Margaret left another message.

Elliot, if you don't talk to me, I'm gonna come over. I don't care how pissed off you are at me. We need to talk. Pick up the phone. No? Okay, fine. Don't say you weren't warned.

When my living room was completely dark, I got up off the sofa, went into the breakfast nook, picked up the phone, and punched in the numbers. She answered after the second ring.

"Hello?"

"Hi, Gary, it's Elliot. Can we talk?"

The pause was briefer than I expected. "I was hoping you'd call. I really wanted to talk to you. I almost called lots of times, but I figured you didn't want to hear from me."

"Well, I did want to hear from you. I really need to talk to you."

"Elliot, is something wrong?"

"Yes. I'm going to help somebody commit suicide."

"You're...I...I don't know what to say."

"I'm sorry to just throw it out there like that."

"Who is it?" she asked. "It's not someone in your family, is it?"

"No, it's my friend Trey. Remember him? The quadriplegic man in the wheelchair? You met him a couple of times, on my walk and at my house."

"Yes, I remember him. You're going to help him commit suicide?"

"Yes. Can I tell you about it?"

"All right," she said, calm as I needed her to be. "Let me get some coffee going. I'm putting the phone down."

I listened as she got the beans from the cupboard to the right of the stove, ground them up, took a filter from the drawer to the left of the stove, filled the pot from the cooler, poured the water into the coffeemaker, put the pot on the gas ring, and turned the stove dial all the way to the left. If she didn't turn it all the way to the left, it would slip back to low because I sprayed it with a lubricant when it was sticking, and it'd been too slippery ever since.

"Elliot? Okay. Go ahead."

She was probably leaning against the sink with her right foot on top of her left, holding the receiver with her left hand, rubbing her right thigh with her right hand, and frowning. I called it her "phone face." I'd always wanted to take a photo.

"Well, he tried to kill himself four times already. He's in chronic, agonizing pain that can't be alleviated."

* * *

"And if I don't open the gate, he's going to go out in front of a truck," I finished. "That's the story."

She didn't say anything; she'd switched from the kitchen to her bed, where she'd be sitting back against the headboard, her knees drawn up to her chest.

"Again, I apologize," I said. "I've kept this inside for so long, it's the focus of my life. He's been after me for months. I had to talk about it with somebody. I thought about going back to church and confessing it to a priest, but Catholics aren't big supporters of suicide. And I can't talk to my family. But you know, to be honest, none of that's relevant because you were the only one I wanted to talk to about it. I'm sorry I'm still overstepping my bounds."

"You're not overstepping, Elliot," she said. "I'm wondering, though, if you want me to tell you not to do it."

"No. I just needed to talk to you to make sure that it's really happening and not some extended hallucination. I had to make sure it's reality. I can't believe I'm actually going to help somebody drown himself."

"You don't have to do it."

"I know."

"Would he really go out in front of a truck?"

"Yes," I said. "Absolutely. He went down those stairs lickety-split."

"If he did let himself be hit by a truck, it wouldn't be your fault. You know that, don't you?"

"Yes. But if I help him drown himself, it'll only be him and me instead of him and a truck driver and everybody who sees it happen. And his mother won't have to identify a pile of meat and wheelchair parts. He screwed up by introducing me to her. I was almost going to help him before he did that, then I decided not to, and now I'm going to again."

"What changed your mind back to helping him?" she asked.

"Well, besides the way he's blackmailing me, he also convinced me. He has no quality of life at all, and he never will. He's suffering too much."

"Well, I'm really sorry that you're going through this."

"Thanks."

"I never told you," she said, "but I went through it myself."

"You did?"

"Yes. With my father."

It was my turn to be silent. "Would you mind telling me about it?" I eventually asked.

"Well, my parents had an open marriage, and he died of AIDS. He contracted it during one of his 'romps,' as he called them. He'd go off on weekend dalliances with some guy he met in a bar or picked up at a bookstore. He was a very handsome man. He refused to do anything about his disease until it was too late. We brought him home when they told us he only had a month or two to go, and it was just horrible. He was in pain, he weighed about eighty-five pounds, he had sores, he couldn't swallow."

She cleared her throat several times. "I took time off from work because Momma couldn't cope. They always had a lot of problems anyway, and then he went and got AIDS from who knows where or who, so she was scared out of her mind that she was going to get it too, and that made her resent him and then feel guilty, and then she'd get angry at feeling guilty. It was a real death spiral she escaped by drinking."

The comforter rustled as she slipped under it. "Well, Daddy started going in and out of comas and having psychotic episodes, and in between he'd ask us to kill him. 'Please,' he'd beg. 'Just smother me with a pillow. It won't hurt. Please!' He'd cry and beg, and Momma refused to even listen. Daddy would start up, and she'd just walk out of the room. She wouldn't accept that she was losing him. She was always telling me that he was doing better, and maybe he'd recover on his own. So he'd beg me. 'Please, punkin, please. I can't stand this. Help me.' He and Momma are these big supporters of the right to die, but now she craps out on him and he has to ask his Baptist daughter to help him kill himself, even though he knows it goes against everything she believes in. Hold on."

She sighed, cleared her throat, blew her nose. "So I went to his doctor and told him that Daddy was in a *lot* of pain, more than anybody should be forced to endure. The doctor looked at me for a long time and then wrote out a prescription for morphine sulfate. It was so powerful, we had to be careful not to overdo it. More than ten tablets would be *really* dangerous, he said. I went to the drug store and got the tablets and brought them home and told Momma to go out and see a movie. Just a sec, I have to get something to drink. Sorry to keep stopping like this."

"That's all right," I said. "Take your time."

"I'll be right back." She put the phone down. The refrigerator door opened and closed; a bottle hissed. I didn't have any beer in the house, but I'd never wanted one more badly.

"Elliot?" She was back on her bed.

"I'm here."

"So Momma left, and I went in and woke Daddy up and told him I was there to do what he asked. He cried and thanked me. His hands were shakin' too much for him to take the tablets himself, so I had to give them to him. Sixteen of 'em. Fed 'em to him two at a time in applesauce and told him to chew 'em up good 'cause there was a big warning label on the bottle that said chewin' extended-release tablets causes rapid absorption and can be fatal. After the morphine, I gave him a Brass Monkey, his favorite cocktail."

Her voice broke, something I'd never heard happen before.

"Then I got into bed with him and held him until he went to sleep. He kept telling me he loved me and loved Momma, and he was sorry for everything, and I kept telling him to go to sleep, that everything was fine, and he relaxed more and more until he stopped breathing, and that was it! He was gone!"

She was keening now. My hair stood on end.

"I called the doctor, and he came over. When Momma got back, we told her Daddy had just slipped away, and she cried but said at least he was out of his pain. There was no autopsy. I got away with it clean, even though the doctor surely knew. Oh my God, I'm sorry, I gotta stop! Just a minute."

Wrenching sobs in my ear as she covered her face with her hands or her pillow. Macha, the Great Queen of Phantoms. Mother Death, who simply didn't cry.

After several minutes she croaked, "You're the only person I've ever told what I did. It feels good to get it off my chest."

"Well, I'm glad you told me," I managed. "Do you have any regrets?"

"No. I know it was wrong in God's eyes, but I couldn't refuse my daddy. He asked me to end his suffering. He was a sinner and a rotten father, but he only sinned against himself, and he was my father. Maybe God understands."

She broke into a fresh bout of weeping. I waited, trying not to listen too closely.

"Man, I'm knocked out," she gasped. "Woooo. I feel like I just went through about three hours of dance rehearsal. I have to go to the bathroom. Excuse me."

* * *

Running water, splashing, deep sighs, the *flump* of her falling back into bed. "Lord, I had no idea that telling someone would have this effect." She sounded drunk.

"Do you think you'll ever tell your mother?" I asked.

"No. There's no point. It'd just hurt her. She never really dealt with any of this. Besides, I've told you now, so I don't have to tell anybody else. Thank you, Elliot, and—" She made a strange noise, a sort of grinding whine. "Look, there's something else we got to talk about."

"What?"

"I tried to tell you this twice. I chickened out at your house, and then the day I was gonna tell you at work, you ended up quitting. After that I just couldn't work up the gumption. I'm still so ashamed to talk about it."

"Gary, you can tell me anything. Really."

"Okay. I'm addressing that problem I have. The one that you pointed out. The one that..." She fought not to cry again.

The one that made you throw me away like a used tissue.

"What are you doing about it?" No bitterness in my voice. Good.

"Oh, I'm seeing a therapist. It's long overdue. I was so humiliated you caught me, even though I wanted you to, so it would all be out in the open and I could finally stop. I'm so sorry I attacked you. One night I was kneeling in my bathroom, uh, p-p-purging like an animal, and I thought about you trying to help me, and I just decided I'd had enough. If it hadn't been for you, I wouldn't be trying to get better. And I *am* getting better, little by little. So I have to thank you."

"Well. I'm glad. That's...I'm glad." Part of me really *was* glad, the part that didn't wonder why her recovery was supposed to be such great news, since aside from Gary, the only beneficiary was some future mate who wouldn't even be aware of the abyss she'd put herself into and the price I paid to help her climb out.

There was nowhere else for us to go. We wrapped it up.

"Listen, I know it's hard," she said, "especially since Trey wants to do it that way. Are you sure about going through with it?"

"No, but I'm going to anyway. We have no other option that I can see. If I have nightmares for the rest of my life, I just won't sleep. Did you have nightmares about your father?"

"You saw me have them. But they're less frequent now. Usually when I dream about him, he's just Daddy again, not this dying *thing* covered in purple spots. I think the therapy might be helping. Now that I've told someone what I did, maybe the bad dreams'll stop completely."

"I already dream about Trey dying," I said. "I'm sure it's going to get worse after I help him drown himself."

"Is it the drowning that upsets you the most?"

"That, and the fact that he's part of the landscape now, and I hate...ah, forget it."

"What?"

"Nothing."

"Elliot. Please. I've said so much to you tonight."

I hate having to accept that nobody ever stays.

"I hate being a complete horse's ass about so many things. That's all. I can't seem to help it. Thanks for listening, Gary. I really appreciate it. And thanks for telling me about your father. It really puts things in perspective."

"You're not a horse's ass, Elliot. I just wish you hadn't quit. I feel responsible."

"Don't. I shouldn't have done it that way, like some hysterical old diva. Maybe someday I'll grow up. Anyway, take care of yourself, Gary."

"You take care of yourself too, Elliot. Good-bye."

"Good-bye."

After my shower I went out and got a case of beer. Thus fortified, I raided my study for boxes of old photos that I piled on the living-room sofa. With my rotary CD player full of jazz, I went through image after image of my family, snapshots and cabinet photos that went back a century and a half. Mom had lent them to me a couple of years earlier. I hadn't told her why I wanted them, but it was to see if there were any fat ancestors on either side.

I couldn't blame my weight on ancient fatties who'd passed down their gluttonous genes, because there simply weren't any. However, I'd discovered that perusing old photos relaxed me into a state of transcendental broadmindedness and surrender.

The night was a long, black corridor, but my forebears were with me, promising that in a hundred years, nobody would care a whit that once upon a time a gate was opened, and a man dropped gratefully into the waters of oblivion.

CHAPTER EIGHTEEN

The doorbell rang at three in the afternoon; I came to and rolled off the sofa. My guest was probably another mush-mouthed, teenage con man peddling chocolate bars from a plastic tub so he could go on a field trip or attend Harvard. They began showing up in force after an anonymous imbecile on our street bought something from one. I crept to the front door and peeked out from behind the curtain over the left-hand sidelight.

It was Margaret, standing ramrod straight on my porch with her arms folded and her feet together as if she were about to click her heels, the iconic and intensely sexy female stance of grim determination. She saw me.

"I told you I'd do this if you didn't answer the phone." Even muffled by the glass, her voice was terrifying. "Well, here I am. Now open the fucking door and let me in."

If I made a run for my car in the driveway, there was no telling what she'd do. Tackle me, trip me, use her Brazilian martial-art expertise to immobilize me by dislocating my hips.

"Goddammit, Elliot, open the door, or I'll start screaming as loud as I can. I mean it. I'm gonna count to three. One."

She'd blocked my escape.

"Two."

I was trapped.

"Three!"

"Okay, you win!" I threw open the door. "No screaming, please. You'll startle my neighbor Carlos, and he'll come over and beat you up."

She barged into my house, brows knit, folded arms like an armored breast-plate. "Nice. Sounds just like the kind of neighbor you'd have."

"Oh, hey, come on in, Margaret. My house is your house."

"Yeah, okay, whatever." She stopped, stared at my cabinets, shrugged. "Toys. Sure, why not? Where're the light sabers and blowup dolls?"

"Nobody uses blowup dolls anymore," I said. "Today they're poseable silicone. Or you can get just silicone orifices you hold in your hand."

"Woo-hoo!" She bobbed her head from side to side, still shooting daggers.

"What do you want, Margaret? This is a really bad time for me. I have nothing to say to you, and there's nothing you could possibly say that would make any difference to me."

"Oh, yeah? How about 'I'm sorry'? Would that make any difference?" A vein stood out in her forehead, and her eyes sizzled with rage.

"Well, it might make a difference if you didn't say it like you wanted to kill me."

She vibrated and crackled for a moment longer, then she exhaled slowly. Her eyes lost their mad cast.

"Let's go into the living room," I said. "Can I get you something to drink?"

"Do you have any beer?"

"Sure. Follow me."

On our way through the kitchen, I snagged two bottles of beer from the fridge. Margaret took one to the sofa. I sat in the armchair by the fireplace.

"You have a really nice house," she said.

"Thank you." We each drained half our beer in two swallows. She crossed her legs, holding the bottle between her breasts. I waited.

She picked up a photo from the pile beside her, showed it to me. "Who's this?"

"That's my mother in 1964."

"She's hot. How about this?"

"My father. Same year."

"He's hot too." She put down the photos. "I'm sorry I was so pissed when I came in. I also need to apologize for what happened at work. I just lost it. I'm sick of these endless wars and all the killing. It's making me insane. But I can't have it on my conscience that you quit because of me."

"I didn't quit because of you. That was just me being a drama queen. I can't go into the real reasons I quit. I'm sorry I made you think it was your fault. It wasn't."

"Yeah, well, everybody at work hates me now. They all think I'm a total asshole. Dennis says we're not the best team anymore. And we're not. We suck. We just sit there, sucking. Dennis hired some idiot named Ched to replace you. He's this nightmare dork with this stupid *dee-hee-hee-hee* laugh, and he's driving everybody nuts with his fuckin' dorkage."

"I'm sorry."

She sipped from her bottle. "All I can think of is you calling me a harpy. Yeah, I know what the word means. I'm not an idiot. I have a bachelor's degree. I went to college."

"Look, I don't think you're an idiot."

"Yes you do. You called me a toxic moron. You and Julian have always thought I was stupid."

"I can't speak for Julian," I said, "but I don't think you're stupid."

"From the day we met, you thought I was a stupid, ignorant, crude, insensitive shithead."

"No, I thought you were incredibly intelligent. I had no right to call you a moron. I'm sorry."

She breathed heavily. "But why'd you call me that? I have to know."

"Please, Margaret. I don't want to discuss this. I'm having a terrible day, and I don't want to fight with you anymore. I was wrong to call you that, and I'm sorry. Let's drop it."

"*Elliot, goddammit, tell me why you called me a toxic moron!*"

"Fine. I hear snark and hipster bullshit every day, coming from a certain kind of person, and I didn't want you to be that kind of person."

"What kind of person?"

"A void. A drone. A zombie. And I know that's not you, so I shouldn't have said it. I'm sorry."

Hummingbirds twittered their high-pitched machine-gun calls in my garden. I wished I were a hummingbird, with nothing on my tiny mind but nectar and girl hummingbirds.

Margaret was shaken but not ready to stop. "You wouldn't have called me a moron if you didn't think I was. And why would you care if I were a zombie?"

"I called you a moron because I was angry at you for how you treated me for two years, and I wanted to hurt you. I never once thought you were stupid, and I can prove it."

"Oh yeah? How?"

"Just a second."

I went to my study and rummaged through my filing cabinet until I found a sheet of paper. Back in the TV room, I handed it to Margaret. She turned it over in her hands, confused.

"You saved this? Why?"

It was the drawing she'd made on her first day at Soledad, of China as a rooster.

"Because I had a massive crush on you," I said. "I didn't want you to be a zombie because I thought you were one of the funniest, smartest, most unique people I'd ever met."

Her olive skin turned a plum color. She stared at me until I felt the redness in my own face.

"I have absolutely no response to that," she said. "Fuck. I always thought you saw me as just this fuckin' asshole chick you couldn't tolerate for shit."

"Could you do me a favor?" I asked. "In my house, could you please moderate your language?"

"Moderate my language? Why?"

"Because I don't like to hear beautiful young women talk like fifty-year-old, toothless meth whores."

She mouthed *ah* as if everything suddenly made sense. "My father calls me that too," she said. "A whore. A stupid slut. That's his favorite term for me. He says I have the voice and vocabulary of a street whore."

A ball of ice dropped into my stomach as her eyes glistened and spilled over. She wiped her face and examined her fingers in an abstract way, barely interested. Other than a congested sniffle, she made no sound. I slunk into the bathroom for a box of tissues. When I returned, Margaret was out on the back porch. I joined her and handed over the tissues.

"You're not a whore," I said. "I'm sorry. I told you I'm having a bad day. My brain isn't working. I shouldn't have said that. I always say the wrong thing to you."

She blew her nose, sighed. "You have such a beautiful garden. Why are you having a bad day?"

"I can't tell you." I sat down at the redwood table. "Margaret, have you ever tried to commit suicide?"

"*What?*" She peered at me over her tissue. "No. Of course not. Have you?"

"Yes. I'd totally forgotten. I never believed you could block out huge, important memories, but you can. It's crazy. I tried to commit suicide."

Her arms dropped to her sides as if they'd lost all strength. She gawked. "When did you do this?"

"When I was nine. I jumped out of a tree house and tried to land on my head, but I broke my legs instead."

"When you were *nine?* Elliot, why'd you do it?"

"I was tired of being teased. Everybody made fun of me all the time, especially my brother and sister. That day I tried to climb the rope up into the neighbors' tree house because I'd been too afraid to do it and everyone always made fun of me, calling me Fatty and Fatboy and Piggy and Pork and Peeaigee, so I figured if I climbed the rope, it'd stop, but when I got to the top, my sister screamed, 'Fatty-Fatty-Fatty,' so I turned around and jumped."

As I spoke, Margaret's eyes got bigger and bigger.

"I'd had enough, that's all," I said. "I knew I couldn't live the life everyone had decided I'd have, as this universal target. I never did anything to anybody, but people have always assaulted me as far back as I can remember. No one ever showed me the slightest mercy."

Margaret covered her face and howled. I stopped, petrified. She fell into the other chair and stamped her feet like a flamenco dancer for a few seconds.

"Elliot, I'm *sorry*," she moaned from behind her hands. "How was I supposed to know? You never told me a thing about your personal life. I just lash out when I feel threatened. I thought you hated me from the first day we met. I'm really sorry."

"Look, it's not your fault. I shouldn't have said what I said just now. You're right: You had no way of knowing. I'm just...really used to feeling sorry for myself. It's disgusting, and I have to stop. I'm sorry. Please don't feel bad. You have no reason to." I touched her arm.

Keeping one hand over her eyes, she clutched my fingers.

* * *

I took two more beers from the fridge while Margaret went to the bathroom to wash her face. She came out with her hair in a bun, one of her best looks. We drank and watched the hummingbirds flit from aloe to aloe. Tired and makeup free, she was incredibly appealing. I tried not to stare.

She cleared her throat. "Remember when I came to work with the black eye?"

"Yes."

"My father did that. I was over at his house, and he called me a stupid slut, so I called him a fat asshole, and *pow*, he decked me. I saw stars, just like in the cartoons. Nobody said a word. Not my mom or my brothers or sisters, no one."

I wanted to hold her. "I'm really sorry, but at the same time I picture you standing there with no fear, telling him what you think of him, and, well, I'm proud of you."

She smiled. "Really?"

"Really."

"I'm not a slut, you know." She drank from her bottle, keeping her eyes on me. "I've never had an STD. Have you?"

"No."

"I have an HIV test every year. Do you?"

"Well, I had one almost two years ago, before Gary and I got together."

"Have you had one since?"

"No, but I haven't been with anybody else."

"Did you always use condoms?" she asked.

"She was on the pill."

"So am I. But I always use condoms too. I'm the most sexually responsible person I know. I've never had any kind of VD or an abortion. I'm no slut."

"I know you're not," I said. "I never thought you were. I'm sorry I gave you that impression."

She finished her beer, set the bottle on the table, slouched in her chair. "Tell me something, Elliot. You said you had a massive crush on me. Why didn't you do anything about it?"

I laughed and drained my bottle. "Because I'm not delusional."

"Still feeling sorry for yourself, I see."

"You're right. It's force of habit. Scratch that. Let's just say that since you obviously didn't like me, I moved on."

"Dude, you've got this idea that you're down here"—she leaned forward to hold her hand a couple of inches above the cement—"when you're really up here." Her hand rose until it was two feet above her head. The motion pulled her T-shirt high enough to expose the lower edge of her rib cage. "You never know how things are gonna go until you try." She crossed her legs and adopted a teasing expression of challenge.

"A month after I met you, Gary and I got together," I said.

A clownish shrug. "Oh, *well!*"

"Can I ask you a very personal question?"

She made a wry face. "Eww. Okay. What? Is it gross?"

"Did you and Julian go out for very long?"

"Oh *God.*" Now she looked as if she'd bitten into a lemon. "We spent one night together. Big, big, *big* mistake. It was awful."

"I'm sorry to hear that."

"Don't be. Everything's a learning experience. So listen: Is there any chance of you coming back to work?"

I thought of what Gary told me the night before, and how I'd always wondered what'd compelled her to travel across the country and settle in the strangest of all strange lands, about as far from North Carolina as she could possibly go.

"No," I said. "I'm going to be moving soon."

"Dammit, Elliot. We're just starting to not hate each other. Can you tell me why? Does it have to do with why you quit?"

"I just have to get out of here. It has nothing to do with you, though. You can't blame yourself, okay? I'll write and tell you about it someday."

*　*　*

On my front porch, Margaret extended her arms like a toddler wanting to be picked up. Surprised, I hugged her. She turned it into a very tight embrace that made me aware of how muscular and warm her body was. The pressure of her pelvis against mine triggered an erection and an aching desire to let my hands slide down and cup her spectacular buttocks. Her hair smelled like peaches.

"I wish we could do it all over again from the beginning," she murmured against my cheek. She either didn't feel the bulge against her groin, or she didn't care. "It sucks that you're gonna leave right when we figure out we're not total jerks."

"Well, I'm sure I'll be back. My family's here. We'll keep in touch. Who knows what'll happen?"

She released me and walked to her car. After she opened the door, she paused. "Good-bye, Elliot. I'm really sorry things turned out the way they did."

"Don't be sorry. We're not enemies anymore. That's something."

"Yeah, I guess." She drove off with a wave and a honk of her horn.

My sad erection dwindled as she disappeared around the corner. I went inside to change. Everything had to appear normal. I'd take my walk, and on the way back I'd sit and talk with Trey for the benefit of prying eyes. If all went well, nobody would suspect a thing. They'd go to bed and wake up to the news that Trey had been found at the bottom of the pool.

I locked my front door and set off. A few yards down the street, I pulled out my cell phone. It was odd that I remembered the number off the top of my head.

"Hello?"

"Hi, Margaret. It's Elliot. I just wanted to thank you for coming over. It was great to see you."

"It was great to see you too." I could hear the smile in her voice. "I'm glad I came over."

"I'm sorry I blew you off after I quit, and I'm sorry I ever made you feel stupid."

"I'm sorry for all the bullshit, I mean, all the rotten stuff I did or said to you. I wish I could take it all back."

"I wish I could too."

We didn't speak for a while.

"Well, anyway," I said. "That's all I wanted to say. Drive carefully. Maybe we can go out and have dinner or something before I leave."

"I'd like that, Elliot. Call me, okay?"

"I will. Good-bye, Margaret."

"'Bye."

I kept walking, saturating my mind with how she felt and smelled, the sensation of her arms around my neck and her breasts flattened against my chest, her warm groin pushed into mine and her bottom right there below my palms, only inches away.

Tell me something, Elliot. You said you had a massive crush on me. Why didn't you do anything about it?

What if I had? Where would I be if I'd asked her out instead of letting Gary into my life? Would Margaret have introduced me to capoeira, so I would've lost weight and not had to take walks and not had a heart attack? If I'd asked Margaret out, would I have avoided meeting Trey and not had to help him kill himself? Would I never have remembered that I tried to kill myself when I was nine?

Did it ruin my life, the decision to not ask Margaret out?

* * *

I trudged up the hill past No Man's Land, my head down. At the top, I nearly bumped into Trey. He was on my side of the street again.

"What're you doing here?" I asked, readying myself for fresh hideousness.

"Waiting for you," he said. "Wanted to ask if you still had the backbone to go through with what you promised me."

"For God's sake, yes. But not until it gets dark. That was our deal. Go back to your side of the street and leave me alone."

"No."

"*No?*" I wanted to smack him. "Why not?"

He winked. "Because I can open the gate myself."

My knees gave out. I slammed to the pavement cross-legged. "What?"

"Well, after you said you'd help me, I felt really guilty. You really didn't want to, and I mean *really* didn't."

"Well, yeah, but, it's, I—"

"Aaah. Don't worry about it. You were against it, and I didn't want to force you. So last night I went back and tried one more time to open it by myself. I told you I couldn't reach the latch because the side of the house was in the way. Last night I looked real close and thought the wooden siding down near the cement might have a little give in it. So I drove my chair up against the house and floored it, and there was just enough give in front of my footrest that I could move about an inch forward, and that did it. I could lift the latch with my left hand."

At that instant I created a new emotion: joyous grief.

Trey sipped water. "I pushed the gate open and I was in the *yard,* man. I drove around like a maniac, went up to the pool, checked it out. Then I got worried about how to get out and close the gate again, so I went back and slowly pushed the gate with my chair until it swung all the way open and I was out on the driveway, then I turned around and pushed the gate closed, really carefully, and I dropped the latch with my hand. Just to make sure, I went in and out five more times. No problem. I can do it by myself. I don't need your friggin' help."

Was it a blessing that someone had figured out how to kill himself?

"Come on, man!" he shouted. "You're off the hook! Aren't you gonna say something? Like, 'Thanks for getting me off the hook, Trey'?"

"Thanks for getting me off the hook, Trey."

"You're quite welcome. My pleasure." His smile was broad and genuine, an expression I'd seen only in photos of him as a teenager. "I'm free," he crowed. "Be happy for me."

"Okay, I'm happy for you," I said.

"Yeah, you sure look it."

"Well, it's not something I can really celebrate, is it?"

"Sure you can. Kick up your heels. Run in circles. On your feet. Stand tall. Hut-hut-hut."

I stood. "So when, um…"

"You know what? I can do it anytime. Isn't that just the coolest? I can go in and out of the yard whenever I want. There's no timetable. I can actually enjoy life for a change. Do the things I want for a while, and then split."

"Well, but what if something happens? What if there's an earthquake and the foundation shifts and you can't open the gate? God, listen to me. I'm trying to talk you into doing it right away, when I don't want you to do it at all. But I don't want you to lose your chance again. Actually, I don't know what the hell I want or what I'm saying."

He laughed, a mellifluous sound very different from his usual bark. I'd never seen his teeth before. They were as white and straight as Gary's.

"Look," he said. "I refuse to believe that after I finally figure out how to do this without involving anybody, God is gonna cause an earthquake or some other bullshit to screw me over. Everything's gonna be fine."

"But you don't believe in God," I said.

"I know. I'm just trying to be positive. I been thinking, though, that maybe Gary was right and there isn't some force that singles people out to destroy them. Maybe it's all just random, like she said. Who knows? I just have to be careful not to make anybody suspicious. Before I took the rat poison, I said good-bye to my friends, and they went and told Mom, and she and my sister came out and found me before I could kick. So I just won't say good-bye to anybody this time."

"You will to me," I said.

He squinted. "That's what you want?"

"Yes."

"You won't go all smarmy, will you?"

"No."

In the afternoon sun, he had a glow. He looked like every quadriplegic I'd seen on TV and in the movies—well-adjusted and heroic, undaunted by the cards he'd been dealt.

"You were freaked just now," he said, "thinking I might believe in God. Well, check it out: If I hadn't been in this chair, I never would've met you, so something good *did* come out of my accident after all, didn't it?"

"You don't believe that for a second," I said.

"Nah, I don't. Knowing you hasn't made up for the last twenty-three years."

I sighed. "Well, I'm glad I got to be friends with one of the cool guys. Makes it easier to put the past to rest."

"Yeah, because *I'm* being put to rest." He laughed; when I didn't join in, he rolled his eyes. "Aw, come *on*. Lighten up."

"Inside I'm doing cartwheels."

"Look, I know you're bummed, but I have to be totally selfish this one time and make a totally fucked-up decision that's gonna hurt everybody but me. It's not my fault, your fault, or my family's fault. It's not even my dad's fault. He didn't plan for me to break my neck. It just happened. I lived with it as long as I could, and I finally found a way out. End of story."

"I know," I said. "I just wish it wouldn't end this way."

"It will, so get over it already. Hey, wanna hear a joke?"

"Now you're telling *jokes?* Your suicide is making you pretty fun to be around."

"Just listen. Back in prehistoric times, these two mastodons are taking a walk, and they come across a lake. They jump in to cool off, but the lake turns out to be the La Brea Tar Pits. They struggle and struggle, but it just makes them sink faster until they're completely submerged in the tar. They lie there for five hundred thousand years as the glaciers melt and the geography around them slowly changes and erodes and evolves, and then one turns to the other and says, 'You know, I keep thinking it's Thursday.'"

We were one of those intriguing pairs that people saw and briefly pondered—the good-looking, indefatigable quadriplegic and his sidekick the bearded loon. Laughing their heads off as though they didn't have a care in the world.

* * *

When I got home, I e-mailed Gary.

Yesterday we talked about a project that I didn't want to do. I just wanted to let you know that the client has figured out how to do it himself. My services won't be needed. The project has no deadline at this point, but the client will soon decide and let me know when he will complete it.

She immediately wrote back.

I'm very relieved. I have to say I'm sorry that the project will go ahead. I know you don't agree that it's a worthwhile investment, but the decision has been taken out of your hands. Thank you for telling me. God bless you and your client.

CHAPTER NINETEEN

Julian called at eight in the morning, waking me from a dreamless sleep.

"I'm headed to Fort Benning tomorrow, mate," he said, "and I'd like to have a drink with you and Margaret. I don't give a shit if she thinks I'm off to train as a racist baby killer, though on second thought, I'm sure she believes that racist babies deserve to be killed. Whatever her opinion, she can stuff it up that lovely arse of hers. She's got the ability, I assure you."

He paused. I remembered Margaret crying, telling me she wasn't a slut; I pictured her black eye and tried to imagine what she felt when her father's fist smashed into her face.

After a moment Julian said, "As you know, a perk of my new occupation is sudden removal from the planet. Of course, that's actually the human condition, but most of us just don't accept it. The point is, once you're gone, you can't take anything back. I'd like to see if Margaret and I can bury the hatchet, and I want you along, since we helped drive you from the office."

"Sure, I'll come," I said.

"I owe her a chance to clear the air. After all, I was once up to my nuts in her guts."

"Spoken like a true gentleman."

"That I am, old chap. So meet me at La Cachette at twelve hundred hours, as we baby killers say. Cheerio."

* * *

I chose a table with a view of the sidewalk so I could watch the gorgeous passersby. Margaret arrived, administered a tight hug, and sat across from me. I was getting used to touching her.

"Well," she said, "at least he chose a nice place to have this…conference. I've never been here. Nice décor. Weird music. Hot waitresses. So how you doing?"

"I'm okay. How about you?"

"Nervous about this." She smiled when I took her hand. "Are you and I still gonna go out for dinner before you leave?"

"Absolutely," I said.

"Good."

I released her hand because mine had started to sweat.

Charles came over for Margaret's order; I made the introductions.

"I'm in the wrong business," Charles said. "I should 'ave gone into marketing."

"Why's that?" Margaret asked.

"Because obviously that's where the most beautiful women in America work."

Margaret beamed, wrinkling her nose and hunching her shoulders nearly to her ears. "And the best-looking men are European. That's what I always say."

Charles skipped off to fetch Margaret's beer.

"So, you like European men?" I asked.

She blew a long raspberry. "No way. They have personal hygiene issues no amount of ooh-la-la is gonna make you forget." She fanned her fingers at me like a belly dancer. "'Zat eez where zee most bee-*yoo*-tee-fool weemeen een Amereeka work.' Puke-o. Does he think I'm gonna fall for that?"

"He's happily married. He's just flirting."

"Dude, nobody's happily married."

Before I could reply, Julian entered and sat at the head of the table.

"Afternoon, all," he said. "Thanks for coming. How are we this fine day?"

255

"Peachy, soldier boy," Margaret growled.

"Ah. Very clever. However, I'm not yet a soldier boy. It'll be several months before I'm a trained infantryman ready for combat."

She snorted at the window. "You're outta your fuckin' mind."

"Actually, I've never been more *in* my fuckin' mind. I'm hoping we can put aside our differences and have a nice friendly drink before I leave."

Charles served Margaret her beer and took Julian's order.

"If you think I'm gonna congratulate you for joining the fuckin' army, think again," Margaret said. "It's sick."

"Right," Julian said. "This will be my last attempt to speak to you as if you were a rational, intelligent human being. Look at me. Look at me, Margaret."

She faced him, chin jutting.

He put his hands on her shoulders. "We've had our problems, God knows, but do you actually think I'm joining the army to go off and kill women and children?" He gently rocked her back and forth. "Do you?"

Margaret hung her head. "No."

"Of course you don't." He let go. "Now: Do you think the men trying to force brutal, misogynist, theocratic dictatorships on unwilling people ought to be stopped?"

"Yes, but—"

"Wait. You believe they deserve to be negotiated with. I, however, believe they deserve to be fought. But we both agree they should be stopped, correct?"

"Right, but—"

"No buts."

Charles slipped Julian's beer onto the table.

"Look—" Margaret said.

Julian held up his finger. "No, *you* look. What it comes down to is we have the same goal, but we disagree on the methods of achieving it. We'll just have to agree to disagree."

"I can't support war," Margaret said. "Not ever."

"Luv, that's irrelevant to me. I don't care if you can't support war. I don't need your support. I asked you here today as, well, if not a friend, then a close acquaintance. I wanted us to part company on a more positive note than the last time the three of us were together, in case I never see you again."

"Shit." Margaret leaned forward until her forehead touched the table. "Shit, shit, shit. Fuck. Sorry, Elliot."

"I support you, Julian," I said. "A hundred percent."

Margaret looked up at me with a strange, wistful expression.

Julian smiled. "Thank you, Elliot. I appreciate it."

"I'd like to propose a toast to Julian's safe return," I said. "We can all agree on that."

"Count *me* in," Julian said.

"Jesus." Margaret straightened. "Of *course* I want you to return safely. I'm not one of those assholes who want our troops to be—" She stopped and ran her hand through her hair.

"I know you're not," Julian said. He touched her cheek.

She pushed her face into his palm and gripped his wrist. "I just want peace, that's all," she said, close to tears.

"So do I. That's why I joined the army."

They eyed each other until I raised my beer. "To Julian's safe return."

"To Julian's safe return," Margaret echoed.

All three of us clinked glasses.

"Thank you," Julian said after he drank. He put down his beer, spread his great arms, and scooped Margaret and me into a rugby huddle, our heads touching. "We'll meet again, I think," he murmured, "but if not I'd like to thank both of you for everything. You bloody Seppos really made me feel at home."

"Oh, goddammit." Margaret covered her mouth and sobbed once.

"None of that, now. Stiff upper lip. Come on, Mags."

"Fuck you, *Julie An*-drews. Sorry, Elliot."

We sat in our huddle as Charles's happy Europop washed over us.

* * *

Later that afternoon I stopped to talk with Trey. Our conversations had changed; we no longer discussed pain and death. In their place we went over trips we'd taken, attractive women, favorite meals. I'd recently discovered the joys of eggplant hummus and tofu.

Trey scoffed. "Pitiful. Hippie food. The best meal you'll ever have is at that steak house I told you about. After you eat there, you'll throw that tofu junk in the garbage."

"All right. Why don't we go tonight?"

He raised an eyebrow. "I've been trying to get you to go out with me for months. What changed your mind, man? The fact that I'm not gonna be here much longer?"

"No. When I was eleven, I went to summer camp, and the counselors saddled me with a boy who couldn't feed himself because he had cerebral palsy. He and I spent the summer isolated from everybody, and they all made fun of me. I ended up hating that kid and hating myself for it. The idea of feeding you brought back the whole nightmare and the guilt and rage I felt. Your invitation made me relive it all."

Trey sipped water as he watched two high school girls jog past on the other side of the street. "So," he said, "you know what it's like taking care of someone like me. You only did it a few weeks. Think how my mother feels after doing it twenty-three years."

"I was a child. I didn't even know that kid. Your mother's an adult, and you're her son. She loves you."

"Yeah, I know. I know." With a visible effort, he shifted his mood. "Okay. Be at my place at six. I gotta change into my going-out clothes. Hot *damn*, we're gonna have fun tonight."

"Really?"

"No. But it's too late, pal. You already asked me out."

* * *

Trey's old Dodge van had an electric lift on the right side. To operate it, I had to open the sliding door and press a button in the remote control attached to the key ring. This caused a metal platform to emerge and lower to the driveway. Trey backed his chair onto the platform, which I then raised and retracted with the remote. Once inside the van, Trey maneuvered his chair behind the driver's seat, where clamps in the floor held his wheels. I crawled in to set the clamps manually.

"You boys have a good time," Jenny called from the front porch. "And Elliot, you be careful now, hear? No drinking and driving with my baby in the back."

"I'll only have fizzy water tonight," I said.

"And don't let Trey drink too much either. His tolerance is nowhere near what it was. I don't want to be up half the night swabbing out the van."

"All right, Mom," Trey shouted. "I promise I won't puke tonight. Get in, Elliot. Move your ass."

I pulled out of the driveway, heading for the mall. Behind me, Trey monologued.

"You're really worried about feeding me, huh? Well, don't be. I got a system. People been spoon-feeding me for twenty-three years now. You'll be surprised at how smooth it goes. I just say, 'Meat and salad,' and you give me a bite of each. No problem. And giving me beer is easy because I can support the glass with my hands. You just have to steady it. Man, I can see you in the rearview mirror. You look like I'm asking you to give me a sponge bath. You won't even be thinking about it after the first couple of minutes. As long as you don't spill anything on my shirt, I'll be a gentle little lamb. You know, chicks dig guys who take care of their buddies. I'll bet at least one'll come over and hit on you. Hey, listen, if you're freaking about cutting up my food for me and giving me my beer, you'll never make a good private nurse. Feeding is nothing. Sponge baths and catheters—that's where the money is."

"Giving or getting?" I asked.

"You know, it wouldn't surprise me a bit if there's people out there paid to get sponge baths and be catheterized. I shoulda looked into it. Made some extra bucks for my mom."

The staff of the steakhouse was gracious and accommodating. They gave us a table at the front so Trey wouldn't have to weave in and out of customers. He ordered a rib eye, medium rare, with a baked potato and salad, and I had a New York strip, well done, mashed potatoes, and salad.

"What a waste of a good piece of meat," Trey said. "It's gonna be like shoe leather."

"Well, I'm the one eating it, not you."

"Yeah, but I have to watch."

"No you don't. Close your eyes. Since I'm going to be feeding you anyway, you don't have to see anything. In fact, I could blindfold you if you want."

"Then I wouldn't get to see this," he said, pointing with his chin as the ravishing young waitress brought our drinks. She set the beer in front of Trey and served me the carbonated water.

"Thanks, uh, what's your name?" Trey asked her. "I can't make out your tag."

She smiled and moved her long black hair off her chest.

"Cozamalotl," Trey read. "That's one of those Aztec names, huh? It's really pretty. Does it mean anything?"

"Rainbow."

"Wow. I like that. It suits you."

"Thank you." As she walked off, she looked back at him once.

He sighed. "I hate being a cripple. Just hate it."

I lifted his mug of beer by the handle while he supported the base with both hands. He took a large gulp and gasped. "Thanks. God, that's good. Let me get another sip." After the second swallow, he said, "Wipe my upper lip, please. Thanks. Boy, that Cozamalotl's almost as hot as Margaret. You ever had a Mexican girlfriend?"

"No."

"Well shit, you poor bastard, how are you gonna attract the babes when you dress the way you do? You dropped all that weight, but you still have the same baggy clothes. You got those circus-tent T-shirts and big-ass jeans like a rapper. No one can tell how thin you are. Go out and get some duds that fit."

"Yes, master."

The steaks were as good as Trey had promised. He was also right about feeding him. I instantly forgot I did it.

"You know," he said, "if my mom wasn't in the picture, and if you had any balls, we could do like in that stupid movie. After our nice steak dinner, we could go out and get all drunk and drive right off a cliff together, going, 'I love you!' Meat and potato. Thanks." He chewed, swallowed. "Where's the nearest cliff? Pacific Coast Highway?"

I wiped his mouth. "Mount Wilson is just down the street. Nothing but cliffs all the way to the top. It's a cliff superhighway. We could be a fireball in about half an hour, if you want."

"You'd jump out right before I went over the edge, wouldn't you? Meat and salad."

"Affirmative." I gently put the loaded fork in his mouth.

He chewed and swallowed. "Yeah, that's what I figured. The point is to do it together. Hold hands. Make a statement."

"What statement would that be?"

"Change is good. Sip of beer, please."

* * *

Trey safely home, I paced through my house.

Once you're gone, you can't take anything back.

After sitting on the back porch for over an hour, I called David, then Emily, then my parents. I told them all the same thing: "I need to speak to everybody face to face. It's very important. No, it's not bad health news."

We agreed to meet at Mom and Dad's house the next evening. My siblings could bring their spouses and children if they wanted, but the meeting was for the immediate family only. They were resigned, wearily unsurprised at my latest imposition.

Sleep eluded me; I spent the night in sweaty rehearsal of my speech, editing and rephrasing until I lost the sense of it. Dawn was breaking the last time

I went out on my back porch to sit and stare at the cactus as stomach acid percolated up my throat. At seven I lay on my sofa and dozed for several hours. It only made me dizzier and more exhausted.

I ate an apple and some nonfat peach-flavored yogurt, threw up, lifted weights, and took a shower. In the late afternoon, I drove out to the high school to tell Trey my decision.

"Wow," he said. "What'll happen?"

"It'll wreck my family. I mean, it'll kill *their* relationships. I'm already out of the picture, so it won't be a big change for me. But they'll scapegoat each other. Mom and Dad'll blame David and Emily, who'll sever all contact with them, and then my parents won't get to see their grandchildren anymore. It's going to be a huge mess."

"Then why do it?"

"Like you, I can't stand this anymore. I don't want to hurt them, but this is the only way we can get on with our lives. We're all stuck in the past, even if they won't admit it. As bad as it'll be for them, in the long run, it's for the best."

"You sure you're not doing it to punish them?" he asked.

"God, I don't know. I'm already punishing them just by being here. At least this way, they won't have me and my crap hanging over their heads anymore. And what you said is true; some people do choose to be unhappy. My family doesn't have to let this destroy them."

"Okay. Tell me how it goes."

"I will," I said.

Then it was on to Pasadena.

* * *

My parents and siblings weren't happy to see me. David had come alone, but Emily brought Nelson and the kids, who stayed in the living room while the rest of us silently headed for Dad's study. I made a detour to the hall bathroom for a bout of dry heaves.

In the study I sat by the bay window. Mom, David, and Emily chose the couch, and Dad settled in the high-backed, leather swivel chair at his rolltop desk, leaning back with his arms folded and his right ankle resting on his left knee. It was the posture he'd assumed the many times he'd talked to me about my fatness, discussions that took place in that very room almost thirty years earlier.

As I surveyed my family's tense faces, I imagined Trey and me holding hands as we plunged off a cliff, weightless and free, making our statement, exchanging exultant glances and howling in triumph all the way down, until we burst apart on the rocks below.

"Well," I said. "Okay. This isn't going to be pleasant, but it has to be done. I'm sorry for the pain it'll cause."

They shifted uncomfortably and said nothing. The consensus was to hear me out, let me exorcise the asinine bee in my bonnet, and then leave.

I rubbed my sweaty palms on my thighs. "Okay. Okay. When I fell out of the tree house and broke my legs, I did it deliberately. I jumped. I tried to kill myself." My voice cracked. I waited a moment and went on. "It was the wrong choice to make, and it ruined any chance of us having a healthy relationship. I'm sorry I did it."

Silence. Emily trembled visibly. Mom was as still as a photograph. Dad's lips moved as if he repeated my words to try and make sense of them. David was plainly agog.

"I only remembered it recently," I said. "I don't know if you all knew or didn't know or had amnesia about it the way I did. I always thought I'd lost my balance and fallen out. I even had a hazy memory of it happening that way. But then I remembered what really happened. I had to get it out in the open because it's been weighing on all of us."

There. Done. If I looked down, I'd see my heart punch eight or nine inches out of my chest with every beat. Emily covered her face and leaned forward until she was bent double. Mom rubbed Emily's back; she was calm, sitting with her head up, watching me. She didn't seem as bowled over as the others.

"Why'd you do it?" Dad finally asked.

At that defining moment, decades in the making, I fizzled. "Do you really need to know? I'm not being flippant. It's just…It might do more harm than good to go into the reasons."

Let's forget the whole thing. I'll leave now. Good-bye.

"I'd like to know," David said.

"Tell us, Elliot," Mom said.

I tried to stop the shaking in my legs. "All right, but you need to understand that this was the thinking of a child. I did it because ever since I could remember, I was picked on and made fun of, all the time, by everyone, adults and kids, it didn't matter, and I just reached a breaking point. It seemed like the only way to make it stop."

Emily sat up. Her eyes were wet and red. "Oh my God, Elliot, I'm so sorry," she choked. "I'm so sorry. Please forgive me." She lurched off the sofa to kneel in front of me. "This has been eating at me for thirty years. Please forgive me. I'm so sorry. It was all my fault. I was so cruel to you. I, I, I tortured you. Please forgive me, please, please." Weeping, she put her head on my knees.

I shuddered as I stroked her hair. "You were just a kid. You didn't mean for things to get that bad. It's all right."

"No, it's not all right." She looked up, her cheek on my knee. "You broke your legs and never recovered. I did it to you, and then I hated you for making me realize I'm a bad person." Her eyes squeezed shut as she wailed softly, her tears falling onto my jeans.

"You're not a bad person," I said. "You're my sister. Of course I forgive you."

And with that, it ended. It was over. I leaned down and hugged Emily, and she flung her arms around me.

"I'm sorry," she sobbed. "I'm sorry."

Dad blew his nose into his handkerchief. David went to the window and stood with his back to me, his hands in his pockets.

"You did it because we teased you," he said in a hoarse voice. "Picked on you is a better way of putting it. How come you never said anything in all the years after? I've been giving you a hard time your whole life. Why didn't you ever tell me to stop?"

Emily let go and sat at my feet. She swayed, almost nodding off. I awkwardly held her hand.

"I only recently remembered jumping," I said. "Anyway, you give *everybody* a hard time. It's your shtick."

"Oh, great shtick," he mumbled.

Dad scrutinized him. "Did you know Elliot jumped?"

"No. I mean...I don't know." He jerked his shoulders in a listless shrug. "I don't know what I knew. It was so long ago."

"Well, it sounds like you had an inkling. Why'd you keep making fun of him if you thought he tried to kill himself over that shit? I didn't know, but I would've kicked your ass if I had, goddammit."

"I...I don't remember. I'm not sure."

"You knew, Glenn," Mom said. We all stared.

Dad frowned. "No I didn't."

"Yes you did." Mom smiled, her eyes welling. "LuAnn and Mikey Dickinson said Elliot jumped. And I told you too, but we only talked about it that one time. We agreed it couldn't possibly be true."

I'd never seen Dad so utterly dumbstruck. "You *told* me? I don't remember that. I don't remember it at all."

"You and I never talked about it again, and we never mentioned it to Emily and David. That's how we all...disposed of it."

"I never disposed of it," Emily said. "I've thought about it every day since it happened." She went back to the sofa. Mom handed her a box of tissues; they both blew their noses and dried their eyes. David wiped his cheeks with his fingers.

"Well, the rest of us put it out of our minds," Mom said. "Elliot, I guess we convinced ourselves that you were just naturally angry, and we had nothing to do with it. I'm so sorry, honey." She looked around the room. "We need to ask ourselves why you were picked on and why we as your parents ignored it. That dynamic didn't come out of nowhere. Everyone here except for you is responsible."

Dad expelled a giant gust of air. "Jesus Christ, is this a family to be proud of, or what? I've done a bang-up job as a father. All the grief I gave you about your weight really helped too, huh? God almighty."

"Look," I said, "I didn't bring this up to make anybody feel guilty. I just wanted to get it out in the open so it wouldn't be festering inside us anymore. We can try to move forward. Maybe we can eventually get along better."

David cleared his throat. "I need to ask a question. You don't have to answer, Elliot. I'm always breaking your balls about your friend Gary. It's none of my business, but are you two closer than friends?"

He was right; it was neither his nor anybody else's business. The thought of telling them about Gary made me feel like a fat two-year-old caught playing with his own feces. After I left, they'd gossip about how amusingly pathetic it was for me to fantasize that a beautiful grown woman ever had anything to do with me.

I forced myself to say, "Yes. We were together for over a year. It didn't work out, but we're still good friends."

"Great." He threw up his hands. "I'm a complete, across-the-board asshole."

"Well, I never told you the truth about her, so there was no way you could've known. And I never told you I hated to be teased either. I should've done that. What I'd like to do is start over from today. We can't change the past, but maybe we can put it behind us."

"Boy, would I like to do that," Emily said.

"Do you think we can?" Mom asked.

"We can try," I said.

There was a knock on the door. Dad shouted, "*What?*"

Nelson timidly poked his head inside and found Emily. "I'm sorry, hon, but the kids are getting hungry and cranky. Should I feed them something, or should we wait?"

"I think we're done here," I said. "Could I order pizza for everybody? Is that all right?"

"No, I'll spring for it," Dad said. "And don't argue."

"Well, I have to get home," David said. "Maybe we can all do something together another time."

We stood up in an unknown and frightening world. When nobody moved, I shooed them forward with both hands, saying, "Let's go. Food. Dinner."

In the hall David slung a clumsy arm around my neck. "I'm sorry for everything I did," he whispered.

Emily gripped my shoulder from behind. "Me too."

"Please don't think about it anymore, either of you," I said. We entered the living room.

"Who wants pizza?" Nelson asked Alex and Terri.

"I do, I do!" they chorused. Dad patted me on the back as he went to the phone, and Mom touched my cheek before she and Emily disappeared into the kitchen. I sat on the floor with the kids.

Alex examined me. "Do you have a cold, Elliot?"

I rubbed my forearm across my face and smiled. "No, I'm okay. I was sick a while ago, but I'm fine now."

CHAPTER TWENTY

Dennis seemed to have been expecting my call.

"How've you been, Elliot? We've missed you."

"I'm fine. I've missed you too. I'm calling first to apologize for running out on you. It was inexcusable. I'm sorry I did that. The only thing I can say is that I wasn't thinking straight. It was a childish, irresponsible thing to do, and I'm sorry."

There was a pause. "All right. I accept your apology."

"Thank you." I pushed ahead. "The other reason I'm calling is to ask if there's any chance I could have my job back. If you're not interested, I understand. But I can promise you that I would never do anything so stupid again. I'd also agree to a probationary period of however long you want, and I'd take a pay cut too. I really want to come back, and I'll do whatever you need me to do."

This time the pause was longer. "Well, Elliot, you really put us in a bind. We could've lost important clients."

I covered my eyes with my free hand. "You're right. You're right. I'm sorry. Forget I asked. Good-bye."

"Wait! Don't hang up! You ran out on me once before. I won't let you get away with it again. You're going to listen to what I have to say. Is that clear?" He'd never spoken to me so sharply.

"Yes sir. I'm sorry."

"Good. Elliot, you were an asset to the company. You're a highly skilled copywriter. But beyond that, we all liked you. We thought we were your friends. When you quit, we were all hurt and confused. On top of that, your actions also threatened our livelihoods. You left several crucial projects hanging. We felt that you'd betrayed us."

"I did betray you," I mumbled. "There's no question."

"Without Gary, I don't know what we would've done. She practically lived at the office until we found a replacement for you. She single-handedly saved our bacon."

I was no more than an inch tall, the size of a baby rat.

"If we did rehire you," Dennis said, "we'd have to be absolutely sure you'd never walk out like that again. There are procedures. Julian used them. He gave us the proper notice, and we were able to replace him without the company taking a hit. If you need to move on, you have to do it the right way. Would you promise to do that?"

"Yes sir. Of course."

"Just a sec; I need to talk to Joel. I'm going to put you on hold."

A ghastly, flute-heavy instrumental began playing in my ear. Joel Lipmann was our creative director, Dennis's immediate superior. He was a shy, remote figure who stayed out of the day-to-day business of our department. Like a hagfish, he had a mucoid reaction when confronted. Instead of exuding a protective layer of slime, he became phlegmy and had to clear his throat continually.

Waiting, I thought about what I'd done to Gary and how she hadn't shown the slightest resentment the night I called her.

"Elliot? Joel wants to talk to you. I'll transfer you."

There was a click, followed by, "*Era.* Elliot? It's Joel Lipmann. *Era.* How are you?"

"Mr. Lipmann, I'm very sorry that I quit in such an irresponsible way. It was inexcusable. Dennis told me I jeopardized Soledad's relationship with some of its biggest clients. That wasn't my intention, sir. In fact, I wasn't thinking about anybody but myself. I caused a lot of damage, and I'd like to make up for it by coming back and doing the best work of my life. I don't have any right to ask you to rehire me, but if you give me a second chance, I promise you won't regret it."

"*Era.* Well, Elliot, we were always very pleased with your work. *Era.* You're an excellent copywriter. The problem is, *era,* how do we know you won't do that again?"

"Sir, I don't know how personal we want to get here, but I can tell you that several very horrendous issues hanging over me have finally been resolved. I'm not under the same pressure as before, so I won't be making the same bad decisions. After talking to Dennis, I also realize that my actions were incredibly unfair to my team. I would never do that to them again."

"Would you agree, *era,* to a six-month probationary period, during which, *era,* you'd waive your right to legal recourse or even mediation if you were terminated for any reason whatsoever? *Era.* It's a pretty harsh condition, I know."

"I'll do whatever you require, Mr. Lipmann. I just want to come back to work."

"Let me talk to Dennis."

"Thank you, sir."

A nauseating synth-rock anthem had replaced the ghastly flute music.

Dennis came back on the line. "Elliot? I'm scheduling a team meeting for tomorrow morning at nine. You need to apologize to everybody. They're pretty demoralized because of what you did and because they haven't gelled with your replacement. We were thinking of moving him to another team and restarting the interview process. You'd make things easier for us by coming back, but I'm going to leave it up to your team. If they agree to work with you again, we'll rehire you under the terms you and Joel discussed."

I can't do it. Put me on another team. Please.

"I'll apologize," I said. "I'll let them kick me in the shins."

"They might just do that. See you at nine. Good-bye."

* * *

"So you have to take responsibility for your actions and make amends," Trey said. "Big deal. That's what adults do. Man up."

"But I'm not a man."

"Then stay home tomorrow. Get a job as a dog walker."

"I'm afraid of dogs."

"You sicken me, Elliot. You really do. Holy shit."

* * *

Dennis met me at the elevator. "Are you nervous?" he asked on our way to the conference room.

"More ashamed than nervous."

"Well, just apologize and hope for the best."

How about if I go all Twelve Step on them, Dennis? They know me as a ludicrous drunk and melodramatic quitter, but I'm also a jumper, a spy, a hater and worshiper of cool guys, a near-miss niece killer, an almost-facilitator of drownings, and a smug self-exile.

The most surreal aspect of the situation was that the only one I looked forward to seeing was Margaret. It comforted me to know she was in there. Her presence gave me the courage to face Gary again.

"By the way, you look great," Dennis said, opening the door. We stepped inside.

Heads swiveled; the room fell silent. From the doorway I took in everybody. Margaret stood next to her chair, her hands in the back pockets of her skinny jeans. Essi sat beside her, chewing on the end of her pen. Richard and DuShawn played hangman on a sheet of paper. A red-haired woman I didn't know—presumably Julian's replacement—was slumped over the table with her head pillowed on her folded arms. Gary sat at the end of the table typing on her laptop. She'd had her hair cut in a shorter, layered style that framed her face and made her look five years younger. When we made eye contact, her hand flew to her mouth.

"Here he is," Dennis said. "Elliot Finell, version Two Point Oh."

The room exploded. Margaret crouched, slapped the table with both hands, and screamed like a caged ape. Essi shouted, "No way!" Richard and DuShawn shook their heads at each other. The red-haired woman sat up, looking startled. Gary was motionless, her hand over her mouth, eyes glistening.

"Hey there, little boy," Margaret rasped. "Where's your mustache and beard?"

"Down the sink."

"Forget your mustache and beard," DuShawn said. "Where's the rest of *you?*"

"Look at those cheekbones," Essi said. "I knew you were, like, losing weight, but this is insane. What's your secret?"

"Pie and ice cream three times a day."

"Those starvation diets are hell," Richard said.

Gary didn't speak, but she'd recovered and donned her poker face. I tried not to look at her more than anybody else.

Dennis introduced me to the red-haired woman. "Elliot, this is Bonnie, our new traffic controller. Bonnie, Elliot was the other copywriter of the team, as I'm sure you've heard."

I waved. Bonnie said, "So you're Elliot. You don't look much like how everyone described you." She twirled a lock of coppery hair around her finger.

"Hey, don't blame us," Essi said. "He's, like, pulled off some kind of science-fiction transformation. This isn't what he looked like when he dumped us."

It hurt like a slap; I'd almost convinced myself we wouldn't have to talk about it.

"Okay, everybody, settle down," Dennis said. "I called this meeting because Elliot has something to say. Elliot?"

I rubbed my clean-shaven chin. "I'm very sorry I quit that way. It was unfair, irresponsible, and very childish. I put you all in a very tough spot, and it's inexcusable. Nothing can justify my actions. If you give me another chance, I promise I'll never do anything like that again. I don't deserve another chance, but I'd like one. That's pretty much it."

Nobody spoke for a few seconds.

"The one you really screwed was Gary," DuShawn said.

"That's right," Richard said. "She did the job of two copywriters for weeks."

Essi nodded. "There was, like, nothing we could do to help her. It sucked."

I turned to Gary, wishing I could crawl under the table. "I know. I'm really sorry. I completely blew—"

"Please." She held up her hand; it blocked my view of her eyes. "It's all right. I'm not angry."

"We were pissed and hurt and now we're not," Margaret quickly said. "You were fuh...messed up. You're sorry, and you won't do it again, so let's move on."

There was a murmur of assent around the room.

"So I take it Elliot's coming back?" Dennis asked.

"Sure."

"Fine by me."

"Don't see why not."

"Yeah."

"Thank you," I muttered. "I really appreciate it."

"Well, that was quick and painless," Dennis said. "Thank you all for coming. See you on Friday for the real meeting. Elliot, let's go to Joel's office and sign the contract."

* * *

When I emerged, I was a probationary employee flooded with excitement and misgivings. I'd come full circle, back to my first day at Soledad.

In the break room, Margaret sat on the counter next to the coffeemaker, legs crossed, foot swinging. She grinned, her tongue covering the gap between her upper front teeth.

"Dude, that's quite a bodacious bod you were hiding under those quadruple-XL shirts. I approve of your new threads. And thanks for shaving off that scuzzy beard and mustache. I hate facial hair. And yeah, it's because of my adorable father, okay?"

"Then I'm glad I did it. Where'd everybody go?"

"Home. Except for Gary. She's in her cubicle." She hopped off the counter. "So tell me the truth: Is everything okay now? I mean, are you gonna be comfortable working here again?"

"Sure. I'll be fine. Now you tell me the truth: Is everybody really okay with me being back?"

"Sure." She stood on tiptoe and gave me a quick peck on the cheek. "Especially me. We're still going out sometime too."

She executed a funny little prancing step on her way out. I touched my cheek; it felt hot, as if I had a fever.

* * *

The magic of finally being alone with Gary again was blunted by another rush of shame. Because of me she'd had to stay in her cubicle for days. It made me think of her kneeling in her bathroom. I knocked on her doorway; she looked up, calm and pleasant.

"Could I talk with you a second?" I asked.

"Of course." Her new hairstyle was gorgeous.

"Listen, I'm really sorry I left you in the lurch."

"You already apologized. Don't worry about it. You look great, by the way. Congratulations."

I stopped and stared at her smooth face, not believing, but it was true. The night on the phone, the crying, the confession, the fluster when I came into the conference room—they were all gone. There was no trace of them whatsoever.

"I'm not angry, Elliot. Not at all. You were under a lot of stress. I'm glad you're back. I felt awful about the way you left. It's good to see you again." She brushed her hair off her forehead, and I sank down through the floor.

"Well, I'm glad I'm back too," I said. "Friends?" I held out my hand.

"Absolutely." She gripped, squeezed, and released. A cordial nod and she turned back to her laptop.

I left.

* * *

After my walk I sat with Trey. "Your team went easy on you because you're just too sexy now," he said. "You're one fine-ass hunk of male. See, you should've shaved a long time ago. That beard and mustache were what made you look fat. Did you wear your new clothes?"

"I did. And guess what? Margaret kissed me."

"Whoa! On the mouth?"

"No, on the cheek. It was a very sisterly kiss."

"Too bad. She's a great kisser. So how'd Gary react? She throw her arms around you? Beg you to come back to her?"

"No. She accepted my apology, said she was glad they'd rehired me, and shook my hand. We pledged to be friends."

He winced. "That sucks. Think you can do it?"

"I don't have a choice. She can't deal with..."

With someone who knows her. I wish I could tell you about her father, Trey. Then she'd be your goddess too.

"Well," I finished, "she won't ever trust me enough to let me in again. When she was taking care of me after I got hit by the car, she said we could never go back to how we were before. She really meant it."

"And you accept that now?"

"Eventually I will."

"I mean, it's not gonna throw you into a depression or anything, is it?" he asked.

"No. I'll try to be happy with what we once had."

"So you talked to your family, got your job back, buried the hatchet with Gary, and you're not gonna have another heart attack anytime soon. Things are looking pretty good, huh?"

"Pretty good, yes. Finally."

"Great. Because I have something to tell you."

My supposedly healthy heart skipped. "You're going to do it."

"Yup. Tonight." He sipped water, squinting at me.

"Oh my God."

"You told me to tell you."

I clutched my head and rocked on the curb. "But you always wait on the other side of the street when you're going to tell me something. You didn't give me any warning!"

He moved his chair closer. "Now don't freak out, Elliot. Don't lose it. You told me you could handle it."

"I...I...I...I..."

"Just calm down." His voice was low and firm. "Just relax. This isn't something bad. Take it easy."

I stopped rocking.

"Are you okay?" he asked.

Deep, slow breaths. "Yes."

"Good. I'm gonna wait until it gets dark. I told my mom I'm gonna go see a buddy, so she won't start looking for me until about ten or so. That'll give me a few hours in the water. I wanna make sure I can't be revived. That's my biggest fear, that they'll pull me out, and I'll survive with brain damage. So I'm gonna exhale all my air before I go in."

"Oh God."

He smiled, and for the first time I saw something like regret. "Look, Elliot, I wish I could stay and be your pal, but I can't. I put it off until you got your life back together. You're gonna be all right, so it's time for me to go. Hey. *Hey!* You said you wouldn't get all smarmy, so knock it off, goddammit."

I wiped my eyes on the sleeve of my jacket. "Sorry."

"You gotta see it my way. It's the end of my pain, a release from this shitty, ruined life that came from one stupid choice. I'm finally gonna be free, so you should be happy for me."

"I'll try."

The sun was about to set, a flaming orange disc swathed in billows of pink, red, and dark purple. Trey sipped water as he watched. I stared at him, looking for signs of anxiety, but he was utterly at peace.

"You know," he said, "people don't even notice what's beautiful. They're too busy working and running around. I been sitting out here for twenty years, and every single time I watch the sun go down, I'm just blown away at how beautiful it is." He turned his chair around to face me. "I don't want you to go home and sit there all gloomy, thinking about me. Go out and do something fun, some kind of celebration. Will you do that?"

"Yes," I whispered.

"Thanks." He wheeled around to look at the disappearing rim of the sun. "Time for you to go, Elliot."

I rose, wondering what to do next. Trey held out his hand. I touched his knuckles with mine.

"It's been damn good knowing you," he said with a warm smile.

It was impossible to speak, so I nodded.

"Okay. See you later, Elliot. Have a beer for me. I'm gonna stay here until it's time."

I walked away. When I crossed the street, I looked back. Trey waved; I waved. Once out of his line of sight, I broke into a run, sprinting all the way back to my house, even though my knees and ankles shrieked in protest. I rushed inside, gathered up a clean pair of jeans, a T-shirt, boxers, socks. They went into a gym bag, along with a pair of black sneakers. I found my wallet and cell phone and raced out to my car. The sun had set. Darkness was falling.

I started the engine, threw the car in reverse, pulled out of the driveway so quickly I left skid marks, shifted again, and roared down the street, trying to outrun the night.

* * *

Freeway traffic was light. I drove with the radio on an FM classic rock station that played songs I'd heard hundreds of times. A distortion of the space-time continuum kept me from making any progress. My engine purred and street lamps and exit signs flashed past, but I was also stationary. Each song played for an hour. I'd glance at the clock, wait fifteen minutes, check it again, and see that the blue digital numbers hadn't changed. It was obvious that I'd died and gone to hell for not stopping Trey. At any second Fayez Samir Hamad would appear in his bomb belt to guide me. I was about to scream when my headlight beams illuminated the exit sign I sought.

It took years to travel ten blocks. I found a parking space and stepped onto the sidewalk with my gym bag. As I walked, I took out my cell phone. My call was answered after only one ring.

"Hi, it's Elliot," I said. "Listen, I'm sorry to bother you, but I need your help. I really need to talk to you. Is that okay? Well, could I do it in person? Could I come over? Yes. Actually, I'm right outside your house. Yes. Look out the window. Yes, that's me. I know, I'm sorry. Okay. Thanks."

I opened the gate. A cobblestone path led to a one-bedroom bungalow from the twenties, with wooden siding painted purple and the trim done in emerald green. The front door opened.

"Dude, what's up?" Margaret asked. "Come on in."

I entered a cozy den of Persian carpets and wooden folk carvings of winged, bare-breasted women hanging from the ceiling. A giant slipcovered sofa and several stuffed bookshelves dominated the front room. The walls were a deep orangish red, hung with art-festival posters and abstract paintings. There was no television, but a large stereo system squatted in one corner.

Margaret closed the front door. She was puzzled but pleased to see me.

"I'm really sorry," I said. "I'm having a crisis. Do you remember Trey, my friend in the wheelchair?"

"Sure. What's going on?"

"Well, he killed himself tonight."

Her hands flew to her face. "Holy shit! How?"

"He drove his chair into a swimming pool and drowned himself."

"Oh. Oh no. God." She ran to me, head down, and hugged me as hard as Gary ever had. Her strength was phenomenal. "I'm so sorry. What a horrible thing. I'm so sorry."

I dropped my gym bag and held onto her.

"Did you know he was going to do it?" she asked into my chest.

"Yes, but I can't talk about that right now."

"I'm so sorry, Elliot."

I rested my chin on top of her head. "He asked me to go out and have fun tonight, as a celebration of his life. Can we do something?"

"Yeah, sure." She looked up. "What would you like to do?"

"Well, Trey said he wished he could've seen you dance. Let's go dancing."

Her lower lip trembled. "He said he wished he could've seen me dance? He should've asked. He just should've asked."

I took a shower and changed into my clean clothes, and we walked to a reggae club down the street. Before we danced, we ordered two beers.

"To Trey," Margaret said. "May he be at peace."

I blotted my eyes with a napkin. "Amen."

As I knew she would be, Margaret was a spectacular dancer. Her every movement seemed unplanned, as though the music made her body react on its own. Reggae put her into a swaying, serpentine stance, her knees bent and her hips moving in time with the slow, heavy, throbbing bass. She danced with her eyes closed, sometimes holding her arms over her head, sometimes keeping them at her sides or putting them behind her. Her multicolored hair fell over her face; she'd let it stay for a while, then she'd either comb it off with her fingers or whip her head to swing it into place.

The last time I'd danced was more than a year earlier, when Gary took me to the country-western bar. I was horribly out of practice. Looking at Margaret, I'd sometimes catch her watching me through the strands of hair across her face. The packed club was hot and humid. After three or four hours, we were drenched in sweat.

"I think I've had enough," I shouted to her.

She nodded and pointed toward the door. The cool night air made us shiver in our wet clothes. We didn't speak.

In the living room of Margaret's bungalow, I said, "I have to ask another really big favor that you can refuse."

She twisted her hair into a bun. "Go ahead."

"I don't want to go home. Can I spend the night here on the sofa? If you're not comfortable with that, it's okay."

"Of course you can. It's fine."

"Thank you so much. I really appreciate it. I wish I'd brought an extra set of clothes. These are so wet, they're going to ruin your sofa."

"Just a second." She went into her bedroom and emerged with a large terry-cloth bathrobe. "This belonged to a jerk whose name I'll never speak. Go take another shower."

I showered and put on the robe. It was a perfect fit. I had no more clean boxers, so I wrapped the belt tightly around my waist and vowed to move carefully.

While Margaret took a shower, I sat on the sofa and examined her bookshelves. Most of the titles were art tomes, volumes of poetry, and novels by writers I'd never heard of. There were also how-to books on computer graphics, digital photography, and graphic design.

Margaret came out of the bathroom in her own robe, a towel wrapped like a turban around her hair. She leaned back against the door frame, hands tucked behind her.

"Do you have any blankets and pillows for the sofa?" I asked.

She slowly shook her head. "I thought we'd just sleep in my bed. It's a queen size."

Though I understood what she said, it was still incomprehensible. I responded with a confused flare of panic and elation. Obviously, what she meant was that she pitied me, and we'd *sleep* in her bed, separated by two feet of space she wouldn't allow me to cross.

She came to the sofa, sat, examined my face for a moment, and kissed me on the mouth. I tasted toothpaste, mouthwash, and a rich flavor that had to be her own. Her tongue was as smooth as wet rubber.

The kiss broke, and I said, "I didn't come here for this."

Her smile was incredibly gentle. "I know that. You came because you wanted company to help you cope with a horribly traumatic experience, and you chose me. You don't know how flattering it is that you trust me that much. Nobody ever has."

Taking my hand, she led me into her bedroom. The only light came from two large, scented candles on the nightstand beside the bed. We turned back the bedspread, blankets, and sheet, then she approached and untied the belt of my robe. I undid her belt, and she pressed her warm, naked body against mine. Her towel-turban fell off when I kissed her; I stroked her damp hair as her hard-tipped breasts pressed into my chest and her hips moved against mine with the rhythm of a reggae bass line. We slipped off our robes.

"Come on," she whispered. When we were in her fragrant, extravagantly comfortable bed, she began to kiss her way down my body.

"Wait." I asked a question.

Her candlelit eyes gleamed. "Yeah!"

She positioned herself, and I began.

"Oh my *God,* Elliot," she moaned.

CHAPTER TWENTY-ONE

In the morning Margaret presented me with two black T-shirts, a pack of boxer shorts, and several pairs of tube socks she'd bought down the street while I slept. She sneered when I said I needed a toothbrush.

"What, are you worried you're gonna get cooties from mine? How come you're not afraid of this?" And she plastered herself against me to run her long, smooth tongue into my mouth.

We spent the day in bed, rising only to eat and bathe. She was lighthearted, utterly uninhibited, adored being naked, and had no problem telling me what made her shudder and squeal. I knew that the memory of her astonishing, unclothed bottom—the sight and feel of it—would fuel my solitary nights for decades. She was also ferociously eager to please. I'd never dreamed that a woman's body could be so much fun. Her tangy, musky, spicy-sweet smell rubbed off on everything. It was in the sheets and pillows, the furniture, and all over me. I could still smell it even after I soaped and rinsed every square inch of her in the shower.

"I had a dream about you once," I whispered in the darkness of our second night. "You asked if we could sleep together, and when I said yes, you pulled me all the way up inside you."

"That's where you belong," she whispered back. Then she swung a leg over my hips and slid me into her warmth. I spent most of the night there.

The next morning I told her I had to go home for my walk.

"You can take walks around here," she said.

"I have to visit where Trey and I talked. I have to stand there and see for myself that he's gone."

She hugged me tight, cheek to cheek. "I'm so sorry about Trey. Do you want me to go with you?"

I buried my face in her hair. "That'd be great. Thank you so much."

We drove to my place in her car. I changed into my walking outfit, and we set out. We didn't speak. When we reached the high school, we saw that across the street, a shrine had been erected on the spot where Trey sat for twenty years. It was a plywood sheet about three feet tall by two feet wide, mounted upright on two short planks. Diagonal braces made from two-by-fours were nailed to the planks to keep the structure from blowing over. A sloping, pogoda-like roof complete with shingles protected a large color photo glued to the plywood. It showed Trey in his chair, shirtless. Cards, votive candles, and bouquets of flowers were piled around the shrine, while silvery Mylar balloons were anchored to the support braces.

"I didn't really believe he was gone until now," I said. "Let's look at it on the way back. I'd like to keep going."

Margaret grasped my hand and nodded. In the forest of eucalyptus trees, she said, "God, this is beautiful. It's so tranquil. I wish I could come out here and walk with you every day."

"I'd like that."

We made it halfway up the last hill, to the blue-and-red pipe rearing out of the ground like a baby soccer goalpost. According to a sticker on the side, it was a fire main gate valve for the hotel at the summit. I was winded, but Margaret had barely broken a sweat.

"Dude, you're in incredible shape," I gasped.

"Thank you." As she kissed me, a passing car honked.

On the way back, we crossed the street at the first intersection, making our way to the shrine. The photo of Trey had been taken recently. He'd refused to smile for the camera and looked like an angry bird of prey—a wounded eagle. Below the photo was a paper square laminated in plastic.

TREY GILLESPIE
GONE TO THE RIVER

The cards had farewell messages and expressions of love written in every color imaginable. Margaret knelt and leafed through a few, handling them gingerly. Her eyes brimmed over when she looked up.

"This is just so fuh—so sad. I only talked to him that one time, but I'm so upset. How do you feel?"

"Rotten. I have a doctor's appointment tomorrow. Maybe I'll ask him to give me a tranquilizer."

She squeezed me tightly. "You did what you needed to do. You paid your respects. So would you like to stay with me for a few more days? We can take walks out there. I'll show you all my favorite hangs."

"I'd love to. You're really something, Margaret."

Her new, gentle smile reappeared. "Who knew?"

I touched the roof of the shrine as we left.

* * *

"I'm glad you took my advice," Dr. Larkin said. "I wasn't sure if you would. A significant number of males make no lifestyle changes, even after multiple heart attacks."

"One heart attack was enough for me," I said as I stepped onto the scale.

Larkin adjusted the counterweights. "Well. You've lost forty-seven pounds since your last physical. Congratulations." He strangled my arm with the sphygmomanometer and raised his eyebrows. "Low-normal. Very good. You have every right to smile; your physical condition has improved dramatically. Try to keep it up. How's your back these days? Any pain?"

"Some."

"Do more sit-ups. Strengthening your abdominal muscles will relieve much of the pain."

"All right. By the way, I never thanked you for coming out to see me after I got hit by the car. That was very considerate of you."

He grunted, clicked his pen, wrote in my file.

"Do you remember my friend Trey, the quadriplegic man?" I asked. "You met him at my house."

"Yes. He said he wanted to commit suicide. How is he?"

"Well, he went ahead and did it. He drove his wheelchair into a swimming pool."

Larkin stopped writing. "I see. When?"

"Three days ago."

"Was he a close friend?"

"Extremely."

He took off his glasses to study me from under his tangled white eyebrows. "When my wife and son were killed, I was very angry at her. I was angry she'd insisted we go to Israel, and I was angry she hadn't gotten off the bus before the bomber detonated himself. For a long time, I was furious that she'd killed herself, which was how I viewed her death. She chose to die, and as a result I was left alone. My anger was a natural part of the grieving process. I'm not ashamed that I felt such rage. But I'm no longer angry at her. With time I was able put her choice in its proper context. That didn't make it any less painful to accept, but I could at least understand it."

"I'm angry, but not all the time," I said. "Mostly I'm just sad. I'd like to ask you something: If you'd known he was going to drown himself, would you have helped him by prescribing barbiturates?"

"Physician-assisted suicide is illegal in this state."

"I know. But if there were no chance of getting caught?"

"No. As a doctor I couldn't help someone commit suicide simply because he no longer wished to live. If he didn't have a terminal illness, I couldn't consider it. I'd also have to think about his family. Would I hurt them by helping him? It's a very complicated ethical question."

"It sure is," I said.

"At any rate, I'm sorry for your loss. If you'd like to see a counselor, tell Jayda at the front desk. She'll give you the names of several I recommend. Counseling helped me immeasurably, although it's not for everybody." He stood and slapped my file against his palm. "All right, then. You should be very proud of yourself. Barring accident or illness, I'll see you in six months."

* * *

The last quarter mile to the hotel was murder, as steep as a flight of stairs. I always quit halfway up because I thought I'd die of an aneurysm if I kept going. In the news, aneurysms dropped people in their tracks when they were shopping or waiting in line, not climbing hills with a gradient of forty-five degrees. My head, neck, and chest pounded, and my eardrums thudded and clicked in my extra-long canals.

I'd experienced such high pulse rates before, during another impossible endurance trial: the high school Presidential Physical Fitness Test. Of course I never won a patch; I was terrible at everything except the fifty-yard dash. When I ran it, the coach was baffled by my speed. He said the only explanation was that my weight let me build up tremendous momentum, like a bowling ball. Since I was a washout at the other challenges, I never rose above the twenty-fifth percentile, a province I shared with the boy who was only four feet tall, the blond androgyne with the pouty lips, and the walleyed kid who smelled like chili.

People driving past me to the hotel invariably had the same stupefied look of *Christ, my* car *can barely make it.* I tried using my bowling-ball inertia to fling myself up the last few hundred yards, but I could never go farther than the hotel's fire main gate valve. That pipe made me sick. All it had to do was sit there in the bushes. It'd never get fat, have a heart attack, or lose anybody. At the top was a straight section with two spoked submarine-hatch wheels and the names of the manufacturers cast in raised letters. The wheel mounts were made by Zurn/Wilkins, the rest by Clow. As I stood there beside the device, gasping and spitting, it sighed and dribbled water, mocking me.

On this day I tackled the hill with everything I had, aneurysms be damned. Dr. Larkin said I should be proud. That brought to mind an image from the previous evening, of Margaret lying naked on her sofa, smiling and biting her lower lip, beckoning with both hands, knees apart, rock-hard nipples pointed at the ceiling, hips gently undulating. Suddenly, I realized I was past the despicable fire main gate valve.

A ruminative loop began. By meditating on the rumbling chuckle Margaret produced during her orgasms, I was able to go sixty yards more. I recalled Julian's imitation of the sound and the things he'd said that now made me ashamed I'd listened. From there I imagined I was Julian running an obstacle course, carrying eighty pounds of weapons and equipment. With only thirty yards left, I marched to a cadence he'd learned at boot camp and e-mailed me.

A yellow bird with a yellow bill
Was perched upon my windowsill.
I lured him in with a piece of bread
And then I smashed his fuckin' head.
The doctor came to check his head.
He said, "For sure, this bird ain't dead."
Oh me, oh my, I'm such a klutz.
I missed his head and crushed his nuts.
The moral of the story is
To get some head you need some bread.

I silently chanted each line twice. It set the right pace and took my mind off the strip of pavement in front of me, the gray ribbon that didn't seem to get any shorter and looked more like a wall than a sidewalk. Then I found myself swaying and gulping in a parking lot full of late-model sports cars, luxury sedans, and SUVs. I staggered around to the back of the hotel to survey the city.

The smog usually obscured the fact that I lived in a valley, but not that day. The air had been purified by the Santa Ana winds—the Devil Winds—blowing in from the desert, and the mountains were crystal clear. They seemed magnified, as if I were at the foot of the Himalayas. Everything was orange and pink in the sunset, and off in the distance the towers of downtown Los Angeles barely poked above the horizon.

My pulse rate returned to normal in about a minute, proof of my excellent physical fitness. I wasn't surprised that it didn't make me feel much of anything.

When my sweat began to chill, I trudged back down from the hotel. It was even more unpleasant than the trip up, a kind of prolonged forward fall on the very edge of my control. Each step jolted my ankles and knees, no doubt doing more damage. It was ridiculous, the notion that climbing to the top of a hill would somehow be meaningful.

I crossed the street at the first intersection and approached Trey's shrine. It was half hidden by bouquets, cards, and balloons, the candles covering several square feet of sidewalk. I reached into the pocket of my hoodie and pulled out a small sculpture I'd bought at a Christian bookstore, a crystal whale with an etched Jonah sitting cross-legged and serene in its belly.

"Made it to the hotel," I muttered as I slipped the whale between two lit candles. "Sucks. And Margaret says hi. Hope you're okay."

A block from my house, I heard a long, expertly rendered wolf whistle. I glanced around and saw the teenage hillbilly trombone player on the front porch of her shack. She stood with her thumbs in the front pockets of her raggedy cutoffs, her splayed fingers framing her crotch.

In the past few months, she'd become outrageously voluptuous. Her hips had split the seams of her cutoffs, the top two buttons of which were undone to display a band of red panty. The thin, white cotton of her belly shirt showed braless breasts as large and round as honeydew melons, with dark areolae the size of silver dollars. By the arch expression on her freckled face, I gathered she'd overcome her fainting spells. As I approached, she lowered her chin and gazed at me with her mouth slightly open. The angle of her head exposed crescents of white under her dark irises. She looked like a panther about to spring. We were in a total eye lock until I wrenched free.

It was the first time in my life someone had wolf-whistled at me. I wondered what she'd do if I sauntered over, smiled, and buttoned up her shorts. Or pressed her nipples and yelled, "Ding-dong!"

I pulled out my cell phone. "Margaret? It's me. Can I come over?"

"Sure. I was just about to call you. Hurry."

"Thanks. I'll be right there."

"Dude," she breathed, "I hope you're not planning on getting any sleep. If you wanna sleep, you can just stay home."

"Hey, I don't need no stinkin' sleep."

"Good. 'Cause you ain't gonna get none. Now hurry up."

* * *

On Friday morning Margaret and I drove from her place to the office. We went in separate cars because she said she had errands to do later. Following the team meeting, Gary and I met in the break room to coordinate. We sat at one of the tables and divvied up the Waldman catalog. She hated writing copy for clothes, particularly shoes. With me it was towels and sheets. We agreed that I'd be responsible for women's, men's, home furnishings, and housewares. She'd handle windows, rugs, bath, and bedding. I got up to pour myself a coffee.

"Would you like some?" I asked.

"Yes please." She took it black. I brought the cups over and sat down.

"Thank you," she said.

"You're welcome."

We sipped in silence, studying our notes.

"You know, I can't get used to not seeing Julian in here," I said. "I keep thinking he's going to walk in."

She nodded. "I know what you mean. Did you read his last e-mail?"

"Yeah. You'd never know it was him. He's so happy, I don't recognize him."

He'd also sent me a private message.

One of my sources (Margaret) told me that a certain Latina graphic designer has been polishing your knob. After I regained consciousness, I realized the logic of this development. You and she always had a certain tension between you that could've gone either way, into a mad and passionate affair or a mutual journey to the morgue. I'm glad you both chose the former. She'll rock your world, old boy. I'm sure you'll do the same for her. Don't ask her about my anatomy, there's a good chap.

"I'm really worried about him, but like you said, he's found the one thing that makes him happy," Gary said. "I envy him."

"Me too." I wondered what she'd say if I told her that Julian envied my mourning of her.

"Well." She crossed to the sink and washed out her cup. "I think I'll leave. Did you need me for anything else?"

"No, we're all set. See you next week."

"All right. Have a good weekend."

"You too."

*   *   *

In no mood to go home, I stayed at the office to start on the catalog. I chose the jewelry section, since I loved women in dangly earrings. At noon there was a light knock on my cubicle doorway. I swiveled around; it was Margaret.

"Hi," she whispered, eyes glowing.

"Hi." *Save me. Make me whole again. Please.*

She came in and lay across my desk, braced on her forearms and gently swinging her bottom as if to cool it off. I ran my hand over it and marveled yet

again that she let me, even *wanted* me to. She kissed me. "Whatcha workin'
on?"

"This: 'Alight with the flame of a Balinese dawn, these exotic carnelian
earrings fuse sterling silver filigree with intricate sprays of glass seed beads,
dangling three inches from sterling French hoops. Catalog/Web only.'"

"Nice. Makes me wanna get 'em. So how about lunch at Amir's? My
treat."

"Sure."

We ordered vegetarian pita sandwiches. Margaret excused herself to go
to the restroom, and I asked Amir how his marine son Michael was doing. He
was a patient at Walter Reed National Military Medical Center in Bethesda,
Maryland.

"He's been fitted with his prosthesis," Amir said as he put together our pitas. "You know, he told me that when he can walk again, he wants to go back."

"Have you ever heard of Douglas Bader?" I asked.

"No, I don't think so."

"He was a British fighter pilot in World War Two. He had *two* prosthetic
legs. When he was shot down over France, one of his prostheses was damaged,
so after the Germans captured him, they arranged for a British bomber to drop
a replacement leg by parachute. He tried to escape from the German prison
camp so many times that they threatened to take away his legs if he didn't
stop. There's a movie about him called *Reach for the Sky.* Maybe you can get
a copy for Michael."

He seemed to slightly cheer up. "I'll look for it. Thanks, Elliot."

Amir plated the pitas, which I took to a seat by the window. A blonde
woman in her early twenties sat at an adjacent table. She smiled at me. "Hi.
What kind of sandwiches are those?"

I opened Margaret's fruit nectar and set it beside her pita. "Vegetarian."

"Yummy. Are you a vegetarian?"

"No."

"I'm the vegetarian," Margaret said, thumping down across from me.
"He's just humoring me to get in my pants. And guess what? It works!"

The young woman quickly returned to her magazine.

Margaret tweaked my nose. "I can't leave you alone for a second," she cawed. "You're my little stud muffin, ain'cha?"

"Lower your voice," I begged. "For God's sake."

"You got it." She took a bite of her pita. "How do you like all these chicks hitting on you?"

"I hate it."

"Really?" A zany, frowning grin. "Why?"

I had a bite of pita and a sip of fruit nectar. "It's intrusive. I always wondered what it was like to be as good-looking as Julian."

"Oh, *please.* You're much better looking than Julian."

"Are you cra—I mean, thank you. But it's depressing, being hit on all the time. It's never the right kind of woman, and none are interested in *me.* They just want to jump my bones."

"Can you blame 'em?" Margaret asked with her mouth full.

"Yes. Before, if I was with someone, I knew it had to be because of who I was, not how I looked."

She wiped her hands on her napkin. "You wanna know something funny?" She took my hand in both of hers and kissed it. "I really love you."

"Why's that funny? I really love you too." I paused. "Wow. *That was easy.*"

"Yeah, for me too. I know you love me, Elliot. It makes me feel nice and clean. But you're *in* love with someone else."

I tried to withdraw my hand. Margaret smiled and held on.

"Even if I were, it doesn't matter anymore," I mumbled.

"Oh, but it does. All of a sudden, you're red as a tomato." Her fingertips poked into my wrist. "And your heartbeat just jacked up." She laid my hand across her cheek. "The nutty thing is, we could make it work. You're a genuinely nice person, you're funny as hell, and you're incredible in bed. It's the best sex I ever had, period."

I wanted to pound my chest. "It *is* pretty amazing, isn't it?"

She whistled. "*Oh* yeah. But I see how you look at her and how sad you are around her. Shhh. Just listen. I'm not jealous. I love you and I love her. I want you both to be happy."

"I *am* happy. I'm happier than I've been in ages."

"Elliot. Honey. If Gary walked through that door right now and said she wanted you back, who would you choose, her or me?"

Why was she doing this?

"It's not going to happen," I said. "She acts like there was never anything between us."

"She's just protecting herself. You haven't told her you're still in love with her. I'm sure she thinks you aren't. Since we're talking great sex, remember when she came over after your heart attack and you did it in the backyard?"

My scalp tightened. "She *told* you about that?"

"Dude, girls talk. I know everything. In detail."

"Good God." I imagined Gary primly telling Margaret all those details. It was mortifying and tremendously arousing.

"Do you know why she was so into it?" Margaret asked.

"It happens with couples after one person survives a serious illness. They get more intimate."

"That might be part of it, but the main reason is because you discovered her secret."

"She told you about that too?"

"We're like sisters now. When you found out she was sick, you didn't reject her. She was so relieved, she lost all her inhibitions and finally let you get close."

"But she dumped me the same day," I said.

"You broke the spell. For the first time in her life, she allowed herself to be this crazy sexpot, and it was fun and beautiful. After she gave herself to you completely, you brought up her problem again. It cut right to her self-worth issues. She felt like you spit in her face. It took her almost a year to realize that you set her free."

"Trey said I'd set him free too. By killing him."

She kissed my hand again. "You didn't kill Gary; you saved her. Stop feeling bad about how you did it."

"So has she said she wants me back?" I asked.

"No. And she won't. I told her you're with me now."

"Jesus. First Julian, now Gary. Who *haven't* you told?"

"They're the only two. Dude, I'm happy. Sue me."

"How'd she react?"

Margaret shrugged. "You know Gary. She got all polite and composed and said she was glad for us."

"So you have no idea what she wants."

"Right. You'll have to find out yourself."

"Can't I just stay with you?" I almost shouted. "It's so effortless. I'm sick of having to fight for everything. She treats me like I'm just this...It's like we never...She's...Dammit, what about *me?* We've only been talking about her. Why can't I do what's good for *me?*"

"Elliot, I have to say this, okay? Don't take it the wrong way. You're not the man you used to be. There's a spark gone out of you. As happy as you are with me, you were happier with her. And you know what she told me? You were the only guy she'd ever met who thought she was funny. She loved making you laugh, and you loved it too."

"Stop. I can't talk about this anymore."

"Okay. Finish up; I have to get back to work."

* * *

At the office, Margaret paused with me at my cubicle.

"Whatever happens, I love you," she said.

"I love you too."

She put her palm on my chest as if to feel my heartbeat, then she proceeded down the hall, head up and shoulders squared.

I sat at my desk, billions of miles from the catalog. Time passed. I opened my laptop, went to my mail program, and started a new message.

Dear Gary:

More time passed.

I deleted the message and went home.

Changing into my walking outfit, I contemplated what lay ahead: that horrendous final hill, Trey's shrine, women drooling like cannibals, and no Margaret to anchor me throughout the night.

But I made the trip anyway.

CHAPTER TWENTY-TWO

I couldn't have asked for better weather that Saturday. It was unseasonably cool and breezy the afternoon my parents threw me my first birthday party in almost a quarter century. The whole family got together in Pasadena for burgers and hotdogs; I agreed to a cake, but insisted there be no presents. We had to manage our expectations. I didn't want them to invest time and money and then find out they still didn't like me.

We coped by focusing on the kids. They chattered and drew with crayons, while the adults quizzed them about their creations. At some point the doorbell rang.

"I'll get it," I called. I made my way across the toy-strewn floor and opened the front door. Gary stood on the porch in tight, faded jeans and a pale-yellow polo shirt that clung to her torso, outlining her breasts and emphasizing the breadth of her shoulders. Her hands were tucked into her front pockets.

My brain simply cut out. I could only stare.

"Your mother invited me," she said. "Happy birthday." Steady gaze, face smooth and untroubled. She was like the figurehead of a majestic, old schooner.

I recovered. "Hi. Gosh. Why didn't you tell me Friday you were coming?"

"I wasn't sure how you'd feel about it, since this is a pretty important family event. I thought I'd just show up and see if you'd let me stay. I'll leave if you want me to."

Okay. Beat it. Get lost.

"That's crazy," I said. "We're friends. Come in."

I stepped aside and she entered.

"I haven't been to Pasadena in years," she said. "Your parents have a beautiful house."

"They do. This is where I grew up."

"Oh, your mother said no presents, so I didn't bring one."

"Good. We're keeping it casual. No pressure on anybody."

David waited in the hall. "Gary!" he yelled. "Glad you could make it. It's great to see you again."

"Nice to see you too, David."

They shook hands.

"So you knew she was coming?" I asked David.

"We all wanted her to come. We wanted to be with her in a nonemergency situation for once." He grinned. "Just kidding. But not really. Look, we just wanted to see her."

I led her past him into the living room, where the kids sat on the floor with their blocks, cars, stuffed animals, and pads of paper. "Gary, this is Alex and Terri, who belong to Emily, and this is Rudy and Kathleen, who belong to David. Nieces and nephews, this is my friend Gary. We work together at my company."

"Hi," Gary said, waving.

The kids greeted her. "Are you a man?" Alex asked.

Gary chuckled. "No, I'm a woman. I have a man's name, though."

"Why?"

"Well, that's what my momma and daddy named me, so that's the name I have. It's a funny name, but I like it."

"Oh. Do you know how to draw?"

She squatted beside him. "Sure. I love to draw."

"Do you want to draw with me, maybe?"

"She can draw with you after I take her to see Grandma and Grandpa, okay?" I said.

"Okay."

Kathleen touched Gary's knee and pointed to a rectangle of dominoes on the floor. "I built a rocket ship, Gary. If you press the red button, it'll turn into this many things: It'll turn into a horse, a boat, a flower, a casserole, and a trap. It can also turn into a chair. It can turn into one more thing—a door. It's a secret passageway that goes to dead mummies."

"Ooh, I don't like mummies," Gary said. "They scare me. Don't they scare you?"

"No. They can't hurt you because they're dead. You don't have to be afraid of dead things."

Gary glanced up with the pleasantly neutral cast she'd always presented to everybody. Except for me. I reached out to her. "Let's go say hi to Mom and Dad."

She rose without my help. I quenched the flash of rage as we went into the kitchen. It was my birthday, I reminded myself. A joyous occasion.

Mom and Emily rinsed lettuce and tomatoes; my sister-in-law Andrea stirred a pot of baked beans. Dad and Nelson shaped hamburger patties and stacked them on a platter.

"Gary's here," I said.

Mom dried her hands on her apron. "Oh, it's so nice to see you again, Gary. I'm so glad you could come."

"Thank you for inviting me, Mrs. Finell."

"Call me Bev." She held Gary's hand instead of shaking it.

Dad pulled off his meat-flecked latex glove and thrust his hand forward. "Call me Grampa."

Gary went mega-Southern. "Oh, Ah could *nevuh*."

We all laughed, even though I thought it was an amazingly cryptic remark. Gary shook hands with Andrea and Nelson and accepted a bottle of beer from Dad.

"How've you been, Gary?" Mom asked. "The last time I saw you wasn't the best day we've ever had."

"No, it wasn't. But I've been quite well, actually. I think we're all a lot better now than we were back then."

"Well, dear, you certainly look happier. And look at Elliot! Aren't you proud of him?" She slipped an arm around my waist in a brief, only slightly forced hug.

Gary nodded. "Yes, I surely am. Elliot's been through a lot this past year. I'm very proud of how he's overcome it all. There aren't very many people who could've done that without giving in to anger."

You're proud of me, but you won't let me touch you. You're too much work. Not like Margaret.

"Stop it," I said.

An alarming expression, shaky and glistening, came over Mom's face. She silently touched Gary's forearm.

"*I'm* proud," Emily said.

"Come on," I said. "I get angry. I'm not Gandhi."

Gary sipped her beer, not looking at me.

"Nobody's blowing smoke up your ass, for Christ's sake," Dad said. "We're proud of you. Is that something you wanna talk us out of?"

"No sir. I'm sorry."

"All right then." He snapped on his glove and scooped a handful of ground beef from the bowl.

"Can I help with anything, um—" Gary said.

"Glenn."

"Can I help with anything, Glenn?"

"Thanks, but Nelson and I are just about to take the burgers out and grill 'em, so we've got that end covered."

"We're pretty well fixed in here too, I think," Andrea said. "I heard Alex asking if you wanted to draw with him. Maybe you can do that."

We went back into the living room. David sprawled on the sofa; as we entered, he stared at the ceiling and began whistling, pointedly ignoring Gary.

She knelt beside Alex. "So whatcha wanna draw, fella?"

Alex doubled over. "You talk funny," he giggled.

"Ah dew nawt!"

"Yes you do!"

"Well, gimme a piece of paper and a pencil, and I'll draw funny too." She lay on her belly, propped on her elbows, with her legs stretched out behind her. "Come *on,* boah." She snapped her fingers. "Hop to it."

David leaned forward to scrutinize her bottom. When he saw me watching him, he flapped his eyebrows. I had to laugh, even though it made me so sad, I nearly wept.

* * *

Dad and Nelson brought in the burgers. The extra leaves in the dining-room table made room for all of us. Gary sat next to me, and Alex scrambled for the seat beside her. He couldn't take his eyes off her. Neither could David.

When we'd all settled in, Mom said, "Gary? Would you say grace, please?"

We hadn't done that in decades. As children, David, Emily, and I had an unspoken competition to see who could invent the most unnatural, incoher-ent, singsong gibberish: "Blessas alord an kneesai gifs whichera bau tareesee threw thyboun teethrew christar lordie men."

Gary bowed her head. "Well, I'd like to express my thanks for being in-vited here on this birthday, to spend time with these wonderful people, to draw with Alex and Terri and Rudy and Kathleen, to see Bev, Glenn, David, and Emily again, and to meet Andrea and Nelson. Thank you for Elliot's health and recovery, and thank you for this delicious food. Amen."

"Amen," we all said. A moment of silent confusion followed.

Gary saved us. "Those hamburgers smell fantastic."

Mom had that glistening expression again. "Yes. Please serve Gary a ham-burger, David."

He used the spatula to slide a burger onto her plate. "Just one?" he asked.

"I'll start with one, but I just might have another later, if nobody's lookin'."

"We'll all close our eyes," Dad said.

Gary put pickles and a tomato slice on her hamburger and squirted mustard on the top half of her bun. She passed the plastic mustard bottle to Alex, who unloaded a massive dollop all over his hamburger.

"What're you doing?" Nelson asked him. "You hate mustard."

"No I don't," he said.

"Sweetie, you're not going to be able to eat that," Emily said. "You put way too much mustard on it." She reached across with her butter knife to trowel the mass of yellow off the meat. "Oh, Alex. Yuck."

He looked as if he were about to cry.

Gary leaned over and said, "Hey, pardner. I didn't put nowhere *near* enough mustard on mah burger. Yours looks a lot better'n mine, all yeller an' juicy. Wanna trade?"

"Oh, you don't have to do that, Gary," Emily said.

Gary made her eyes bulge. "But I *wawnt* to. I *wawnt* that burger, Alex. *Wawnt* it, *wawnt* it, *wawnt* it!" With each *wawnt,* she softly poked at his side, not making actual contact.

Alex recoiled from her finger and guffawed into his hands. "Okay."

Instead of exchanging hamburgers and leaving him with his giant, yellow glob of humiliation, she switched plates and gave him back the top half of his bun, which he'd managed to avoid squirting. She placed her own mustardy bun top on Alex's troweled-off patty, took a bite, and winked at him. "*Dee-*licious. Thanks, bud."

His face pink, Alex sputtered, "Are you going to marry Elliot?"

There was a collective mini-flinch by all the adults except for Gary and me. She nudged Alex's shoulder with her elbow and said, "If he can draw pictures as good as you, maybe. Otherwise, ain't no way."

"Maybe when I grow up, *I* can marry you."

"Could be. Could be. But I'm gonna be a little old lady by the time you're ready to get married, Alex, so you shouldn't make any promises just yet."

"How old are you?" Rudy asked.

"It's not polite to ask that question, Rudy," Andrea said.

"Why not?"

When Andrea couldn't come up with an immediate response, Gary said, "Well, some grown-ups are afraid of gettin' old. So when you ask them how old they are, they don't like it because it reminds them they aren't kids anymore. But tell you what: If your momma says it's okay, you can ask me and I'll tell you."

"Is it okay, Mommy?" Kathleen asked.

"All right. But only because Gary says she doesn't mind."

"I'm thirty-six," Gary said.

"You sure don't look it," David said. Without missing a beat, smiling at Gary, Andrea whacked him hard on the back of his skull.

"But my wife looks even younger," David added.

* * *

After dinner, Gary helped Mom and Emily do the dishes. The rest of us sat in the living room, watching the kids drawing and playing.

"Gary's really good with children, isn't she?" Andrea asked.

I nodded. "Yes, she is."

"Did you know that?" David asked.

"No. I've never seen her interact with kids before."

"She doesn't have any children of her own?" Dad asked.

"No."

"So it's natural for her," David said. "That's something to keep in mind, isn't it, since you love kids so much?"

I didn't say anything. David punched my shoulder. "You're not dumb enough to let this one get away, I hope," he said.

"It's not up to me."

"Of course it is." I looked at him. "Of course it is," he repeated with genuine irritation, as though he'd lost all patience.

"I'm with David, Elliot," Nelson said.

Gary and Emily came out of the kitchen, in animated conversation. They seemed to have become friends during the time it took for them to do the dishes.

"So, Gary," David said, "we were just talking—"

"Actually," I said, "Gary and I need to go outside and discuss our current project. We won't be long."

"Don't forget. Cake and ice cream," Emily said.

Gary and I went into the backyard to sit on the bench in Mom's pergola, among the potted succulents.

"Did you really want to talk about work?" she asked.

"No. Would you like to hear about Trey's funeral?"

There was no change in her expression. "Yes, I would."

* * *

It was held in the chapel on the cemetery grounds. About two hundred people attended. At the front door was an easel supporting a large piece of foam board covered with photos of Trey at various ages, from smiling baby to grim, wheelchair-bound adult with dark circles under his eyes.

Trey's casket was behind the altar at the rear of the chapel. It was open, but I didn't go up to look at him. I wanted him to remain as I last saw him—calm, happy, and relieved. From my seat in the fifth row, I could see his nose protruding over the edge of the coffin. It was so unreal that I thought it might all have been just a game. When the sham funeral was over, we'd joke with him as he lay in his box, and he'd laugh and tell us what a good time he'd had.

The service was nondenominational and only vaguely religious. People were invited to come to the podium and share reminiscences of Trey. His sister Cindy, an uncle, and several friends went first. When it appeared no one else would speak, I rose, explained who I was, and told the mourners how Trey had taught me about water-skiing. The crowd laughed several times. I forgot my words as soon as they came out of my mouth.

Three feet behind me, Trey lay stretched out in his open casket. I could easily have turned around to see how the funeral home had fixed him up. He'd been in the water for at least twelve hours. Jenny had called the sheriff's department when he didn't come home, and they sent out patrol cars and a helicopter. The chopper spotted Trey in the pool at four in the morning, and because the coroner was particularly busy that night, they hadn't pulled him out until eight.

As I spoke, Jenny and Cindy cried, studying me as though for clues. I imagined Trey pale and bloated at the bottom of the pool, huddled under his chair, his face squashed against the blue-painted cement. Part of me was desperate to see if the mortician had erased the signs of those final moments; I wanted magic and banishment, but it was as if invisible hands gripped my head and kept me facing forward. My voice droned on until I heard it stop.

After I returned to my seat, a weather-beaten man with a thick, black mustache went to the podium carrying a Bible. He looked like a gardener.

"I didn't know Trey," he said, "but for ten years, I drove past him every evening on my way home from work. He was always alone out there, until about a year ago, when Elliot started to sit and talk with him. I wanted to talk with him too, but I never did. I was afraid to impose on him. I worried that Trey—I didn't know his name until I saw in the newspaper that he'd died—I was worried he'd think I pitied him. I was worried he'd think I was patronizing him.

"So when I saw that Trey had died, and I saw how he'd died, I prayed for him. I thought he'd died that way because he didn't have people in his life he could turn to. I felt so guilty that I'd never spoken to him. I decided to come to his funeral to be there for him, the way I should've been there before he died. But you know what? I look around, and I see so many people here, and I listened to the stories you told about him, and I realize that Trey was blessed. He was loved. It comforts me to know he had so many people in his life, and I'm sure it comforted Trey. Without you, he may not have lived as long as he did. You made him want to stay, until he just couldn't anymore.

"I came here to pray for someone I thought was a lost soul. Now I know he wasn't. He had a hard life, but it was a meaningful life because he touched so many of us. He changed us. He changed me just today. When people talk about everything being part of God's plan, it doesn't mean that God caused the accident that put Trey in a wheelchair. Tragedies like that happen, and it's just pure chance. But I do think God uses even the worst moments of our lives to show us how important it is to make those connections that so often we're too afraid to make. I'm honored to have had the chance to speak about Trey. I wish I'd met him. Thank you."

The service concluded a few minutes later. I searched the departing crowd until I found the man with the mustache.

"That was an incredible eulogy you gave," I said as I shook his hand. "You're a terrific speaker."

"Thank you. I wish I'd done what you did and talked to Trey. But I was just too afraid."

"Well, he was the aggressor, not me. He sought me out. If it'd been up to me, I never would've spoken to him either."

He nodded slowly, pursing his lips. "Did he change you?"

"Completely."

"Then you're lucky he came to you."

"Yes. I am."

Jenny walked over. Her eyes were red, and her skin was almost translucent. "Can I have a minute, Elliot?"

"Sure." I said good-bye to the man with the mustache and followed Jenny away from the rest of the mourners. My heart pounded and my hands dripped sweat. Under a tree Jenny looked me straight in the eye and asked exactly what I expected.

"Elliot, did Trey tell you he was going to kill himself?"

I'd wondered what I'd say when the moment came. Now I found out. "Yes, that afternoon he told me he was going to do it as soon as it got dark."

It was as if I'd slapped her. "Why didn't you stop him?"

"What could I do, Jenny? I couldn't physically restrain him. I wouldn't do that to him."

"Then why didn't you tell me?"

"I couldn't. I'm sorry. He begged me not to tell you. It was…I'm sorry, but I had to honor his request."

Jenny gazed at the throng of black-clad people milling around the chapel door. "Don't you know what this has done to our family? My daughter hasn't stopped crying since it happened."

"I'm sorry."

"That ain't good enough!"

"I know, but it's all I have."

She seemed to thrum with rage, the muscles in her jaw rippling. "Well, I don't know how you can live with yourself."

"I don't either. I didn't want Trey to do it, but he put me in a terrible spot. He said he was going to go out in front of a truck if he couldn't find any other way. He even asked me to help him open the gate to the swimming pool."

Her mouth was a thin, trembling line. "Did you?"

"No. I said I would, but then he figured out how to do it by himself so I wouldn't be involved."

"But you *are* involved. You knew what he was going to do."

"Yes, I'm involved. I have to live with that. It was either the pool or a truck. He drove his chair—never mind."

Quick as a striking cobra, she grabbed my sleeve. "What were you gonna say? He drove his chair?"

"It doesn't matter."

"Elliot!" She twisted my sleeve and violently shook my arm. "Tell me! He drove his chair what?"

"He drove his chair down a flight of concrete steps at the high school. He did it in front of me. His chair didn't turn over, so he wasn't hurt. But he promised me he'd go out in front of a truck if I didn't help him. I believed him. I didn't want him to be hit by a truck. I didn't want him to go into a swimming pool either. I loved him. But those were the choices he gave me. If I'd told you about the pool and you'd stopped him, he would've gone out in front of a truck. So I didn't tell you."

Jenny let go. She turned her back and put her hands on her hips, stared at the ground, and sighed deeply several times. I didn't move. Cindy watched from the chapel door, her arms folded. After a few seconds, Jenny faced me again. Her eyes were swollen almost shut.

"What you did was wrong. It was just plain wrong."

"Yes," I said. "It was."

"I don't want you there when we bury Trey. I'm sorry, but I can't look at you right now. God have mercy on you."

She marched off.

* * *

Gary didn't need the pack of tissues I'd brought out with me. Her eyes remained dry.

"Well, hell," she said quietly. "That's just awful."

"Yeah, but I'd be furious too, if it were my child."

"So would I. What a disaster."

"Yes."

"I'm sorry it happened to you. Are you angry at Trey for putting you in that position?"

"Sometimes. But it's ebbing. He was suffering so much that I can't sustain it. I can't blame him."

"Yeah." She gently stroked one of Mom's potted succulents, something with thick, round leaves like mint candies. "I know exactly how you feel. That's how it is with me and Daddy. I hate to say this, but do you think Trey's family will file a lawsuit against you, God forbid?"

"I hope not, but if they do, I'll deal with it. By the way, his friends built a shrine for him where we used to talk. Would you like to see it after we have the cake?"

"Yes, I would. Thank you."

We didn't say anything for a long time, until Gary murmured, "Look at the window."

My family stood there, ten pairs of eyes on us. "Oh God," I said as I waved. Everyone waved back and withdrew, leaving one small head at sill level.

"Is that Alex?" Gary asked.

"I think so. You made quite an impression on him."

"He's a great kid. They're all great. I'm so glad I came. Your family's really special." She went Southern again. "Ah think David's the *mostest special* of *all.* He says whatever he wants, huh?"

"Yeah. He's missing the part of his brain or the gland that produces embarrassment. You know, things are getting better with the family. We sat down and had a long talk."

"Really? Can I ask what about?"

"Didn't Margaret tell you about the time she came to my house?"

She became the figurehead again. "Yes. She said that's when she fell for you. She loved sitting and talking in your backyard, looking at your beautiful cactus garden."

You called it the Garden of Eden. Remember?

"No, not that," I said. "Margaret and I were involved for a while, but it didn't last. What I meant was my family and I talked about what I told her at my house. Didn't she pass it on to you?"

"No. The only thing she said was that you and she were an item, and she was the happiest she'd ever been."

Margaret had kept her big mouth shut. I still misjudged her. And she was the happiest she'd ever been? With *me?*

"Well, I'll tell you about the family conference later," I said. "Not today."

"All right."

My back ached. I got up from the bench and leaned against one of the support beams holding up the roof of the pergola. Gary wandered over to the life-sized wire figures in Mom's garden. They were like pencil sketches in the air, dancing women in long skirts. She ran her hand over one.

"So you and Margaret aren't together anymore?" she asked in a soft voice, picking at the rusted metal with her thumbnail.

"No."

"Do you mind if I ask why not?"

"We decided we're better as friends."

She watched her nail gouge the wire.

"I've got a question for you, if that's okay," I said.

"Sure."

"Are you with anyone?"

"No," she said.

"Do you mind me asking why not?"

"Not interested. Or…capable."

As I approached, she turned away and seemed to shrink.

I put my hand on her shoulder and said, "I miss you so much, I can't stand it."

She whirled and I caught a glimpse of her face; it was flushed and twisted, unrecognizable. I braced myself for a smashing blow to the jaw, but instead I was nearly yanked off my feet. Sinewy arms enfolded me, crushed me as though she wanted to fuse our bodies or pull me inside her. Lips beside my ear, a sobbing whisper.

"Oh my *God*, Elliot. I miss you too."

Then I tried to pull her inside me.

Alex exploded onto the back porch. "Elliot! Gary! Come have cake!"

"Be right in, lovebug!" she called.

We loosened our grip. She drew back slightly, let go with one hand to wipe her streaming eyes, and there it was, right in front of me, the supernova smile I hadn't seen in forever.

ABOUT THE AUTHOR

Thomas Wictor is the author of the *Ghosts* Trilogy:

Ghosts and Ballyhoo: Memoirs of a Failed L.A. Music Journalist.
Chasing the Last Whale.
Hallucinabulia: the Dream diary of an Unintended Solitarian.

Other books by Thomas Wictor:

In Cold Sweat: Interviews with Really Scary Musicians.
German Flamethrower Pioneers of World War I.
Flamethrower Troops of World War I: The Central and Allied Powers.
German Assault Troops of World War I: Organization, Tactics, Weapons, Equipment, Orders of Battle, Uniforms.

He lives in Southern California. For now.

Made in the USA
Lexington, KY
28 August 2018